D1239196

BOOKS BY

FRANK O'CONNOR

More Stories by Frank O'Connor (*1954*)

The Stories of Frank O'Connor (*1952*)

Traveller's Samples (*1951*)

The Common Chord (*1948*)

Crab Apple Jelly (*1944*)

THESE ARE *Borzoi Books*

PUBLISHED IN NEW YORK BY *Alfred A. Knopf*

MORE
STORIES
BY
FRANK
O'CONNOR

MORE
STORIES

BY

FRANK
O'CONNOR

ALFRED A. KNOPF: NEW YORK
1967

L. C. catalog card number: 54-7199

THIS IS A BORZOI BOOK,
PUBLISHED BY ALFRED A. KNOPF, INC.

PUBLISHED 1954
SECOND PRINTING, JULY 1967

CONTENTS

MORE
STORIES
BY
FRANK
O'CONNOR

Frank O'Connor

THE LADY OF THE SAGAS

I

It is a terrible thing to have the name of a saga heroine and have no saga hero. Deirdre Costello, the new teacher at the convent, was a slight girl with reddish-brown hair pulled back from her ears and a long face with clear grey eyes. Having a name like that, she naturally thought of herself in terms of the sagas and imagined Connacht raided and Ulster burned for her.

But whatever our town may have been like in saga times, it is no great shakes today. It seemed to Deirdre to be more like an island; a small island where you couldn't walk a few hundred yards in any direction without glimpsing the sea, only that the sea was some watery view of pearly mountains and neglected fields with a red and blue cart upended beside a stack of turf. The islanders, except when they took a boat (which they kept on referring to as a car) and visited some other island ten or fifteen miles away, were morose and self-centred, and spent their leisure hours not in cattle-raiding and love-making but in drinking and playing cards.

Tommy Dodd was the only man she met who even looked as though he had the makings of a saga hero in him. Tommy was the town's smartest solicitor, a tall, handsome man with a heroic build, a long pale face, dark hair, and an obstinate jaw. He was built more for defence than attack; a brusque man, rude and loud-voiced when it suited him, polite and stiff when it didn't. He was a high official in a Catholic secret society, the members of which wore coloured cowls and robes in the manner of the

Ku Klux Klan, talked in an elaborate jargon with titles like
"Worthy Warden," and had a complicated system of grips and
signs. He was almost obtrusively pious, and went to Mass each
morning before breakfast. His room was filled with mechanical
gadgets which were supposed to develop different parts of him,
and he was quite obtrusively pernickety about food, insisting on
all sorts of unusual things like bran, nuts, and nettles. He became
quite violent if Joan, the landlady's daughter, crossed him in this
fad.

"Take that away, Joan," he would say in a dead voice whenever she happened to bring him the wrong thing.

"Oh, Law!" Joan would exclaim with a laugh. "Aren't you
eating that now?"

"I never eat it. Are there any oranges left?"

"Oranges, oye!" Joan would mutter. "A wonder you don't turn
into a monkey!"

"If you knew anything about the general health of monkeys,
you wouldn't talk about them in that ignorant way," said
Tommy. "I don't know how you eat that stuff at all, Deirdre,"
he would go on anxiously. "You should see what that does to your
insides. I couldn't touch it at all. 'Twould kill me."

As hard as Deirdre tried, this solicitude about what she ate was
as close as she could get to a lover's attention from Tommy. He
seemed more interested in her bowels than any other part of her.
It was the same when they went driving. Tommy had a fine but
blunted intelligence, so that he never seemed to know what
would interest her. It took her quite a while to get him talking
about his job ("Ah, what is it only old rubbish? You wouldn't
care about things like that"), but when he did, he was fascinating.
He knew who everyone was and what everybody was worth.

"How do you get all the information?" she asked. "I suppose
the bank manager is in the Ku Klux Klan as well?"

"Is it Con Doody?" exclaimed Tommy, giving nothing away.
"Ah, Con is too smart for that."

"He'd want to be."

"Begor, he would. And even then he's not as smart as the last
man. Delaney used to have a phone on his desk, and if you asked
him for an overdraft, he'd ring up head office in Dublin and

recommend you. Oh, one of his most valued customers! And you wouldn't know the phone wasn't connected."

"But why would he do that?" she asked in bewilderment.

"Because after hearing all he said about you, you'd blame the bank and not him at all. Oh, begor, Delaney was a first-rate man."

"And did he charge for the calls?" Deirdre asked coldly.

"How would I know?" exclaimed Tommy in astonishment. "Why?"

"Is there anyone in this town that isn't an exploiter?" she asked with burning indignation.

"An exploiter?" echoed Tommy in bewilderment. "How do you make that out?"

"But you're all exploiters, man," cried Deirdre. "Doctors, priests, bank managers, and solicitors; you're out only for what you can get. Don't you ever want to give people anything?"

"I'm sure I'm as charitable as the next," Tommy said in a hurt tone. "Last year I must have given a good slice of my income in charity."

"Ah, who's talking about charity?" she cried impatiently. "You don't even know what I mean. Ye all have the minds of robbers, even you. This isn't a town at all. It's a camp of highway robbers."

"Begor, I wish it was," Tommy said blandly, stepping on the accelerator. "You'd get nice pickings."

II

For a man of such piety his morality struck Deirdre as deplorable. His sentiment was just as bad, and she sometimes wondered if she'd ever get down to the saga hero in him. He was far from being an uneducated man, and he had a lot of books of his own—serious works on history and philosophy which he read right through. The lighter types of literature he borrowed from her, and she made him read Joyce, George Moore, and Hemingway, in the hope that they might fan the spark of passion in him; but if they did, he managed to conceal it well. Instead he embarked on long and obscure arguments about St. Thomas Aquinas, Communism, the sanctity of marriage, and even anatomy. He called this "picking her brains." When he had got all he

wanted, he said he had "got great value out of her." He talked
as though she were another sort of chest-developer.

"But you wouldn't call that girl's conduct natural, would you?"
he asked one night when he was discussing some novel she'd
given him. "You don't imagine Joan here would let a fellow behave like that with her?"

"And who said Joan was natural?" asked Deirdre.

"Begod, I don't know," he said with a laugh. "Maybe she isn't.
But to come back to the girl in the story. Now, she knew the man
was living with somebody else already. Wouldn't that show her
he wasn't reliable?"

"She mightn't want someone reliable," suggested Deirdre.
"Anyway, lots of women would like it."

"Would you say that, Deirdre?" he asked in surprise, sticking
his thumbs in the armholes of his vest. "Why would they like it?"

"Well, at least they'd know where they were with him," said
Deirdre with a laugh.

"Excuse my being personal," he went on, "but as I'm picking
your brains, I'd like to know what you think of it yourself. Would
you like it?"

"That would depend on the man, Tommy," she replied.
"Damn it, the girl was in love with him." Then seeing from the
blank expression on Tommy's handsome face that he didn't even
know what she was getting at, she beat the sofa cushion in exasperation. "Love, Tommy, love!" she cried. "Don't tell me you
never heard of it."

"Oh, begor, I heard of it all right," said Tommy, who was very
difficult to shake when he was on the defensive. "I was through it
all before you were out of long clothes. I'm past it now though."

"Why? How old are you?"

"Thirty-five," he said with finality.

"But, my God, man, that's only the prime of life!"

"You feel the years beginning to tell on you all the same," said
Tommy gravely. "What I'd like now is to settle down."

"Settle down?" Deirdre repeated in disappointment (as if anybody ever heard of a saga hero settling down!). "What do you
want to settle down for?"

"I want a home of my own, of course," said Tommy. "You

don't think I'm going to go on living in lodgings for the rest of my life, where I can't get a bit of decent food or anything?"

"And have you a girl?"

"I have not. Not yet."

"Ah, Tommy, you're putting the cart before the horse," she said mockingly. "You should get the girl first."

"I believe 'tis customary," said Tommy without permitting himself to get ruffled.

"But, Tommy," she burst out, "you don't want to make a home for a girl till there's nothing else left for you to do with her. She'd hate it. Surely you understand that?" But it struck her that he didn't; not entirely, at any rate; and if she wanted to reach down to the passion in him, she would have to begin in a key without sharps or flats. "Anyway," she added, "you'll find plenty to jump at you."

"I dare say," replied Tommy complacently. "I mightn't want to jump at them though."

"Now, who is there you couldn't get if you wanted to?" she asked cajolingly. "A fine, upstanding man like yourself!"

"Can't you guess?" he asked, causing her to groan within. This wasn't even C major; it was more like puff-puffs.

"Do I know her?"

"What would you say to the doctor?" asked Tommy.

"Dr. O'Brien?" said Deirdre with a sinking of the heart. She knew now she wasn't in for courting, but confidences, and if there was one thing more than another that destroyed her self-respect, it was confidences. It was revealed to her at that precise moment that the nuns and herself would have to part company. It was bad enough in the mornings, having to hitch down her dress behind to cover her chest without having to endure fellows talking to her about the charms of other women. "I suppose she has bags of tin?" she added.

"Fifteen thousand," replied Tommy complacently.

"You'd overlook a lot for that," said Deirdre.

"Begor, you would," said Tommy thoughtfully. "But isn't she very good-looking, Deirdre? I'd say she had great distinction."

"Another five thousand would make her a beauty," said Deirdre. "Honest to God, I used to think I knew what Irish towns were like, but I was only fooling myself. They're nothing but calculation and greed and cunning."

"Oh, come, Deirdre!" said Tommy gravely. "Aren't you taking things to the fair?"

"No," groaned Deirdre. "That's where ye take them."

III

She was so disgusted that next day she told it all to Joan. It wasn't that she particularly cared for Joan, who, in her opinion, was the sort of Irishwoman who make Irishmen what they are, but she had no one else to discuss it with. Joan was a big, platter-faced Child of Mary who scouted round men like some member of a primitive tribe observing the behaviour of the first pale-faces.

"Mother of our Divine Redeemer!" she cried dramatically. "The box of chocolates!"

"What box of chocolates?"

"He have them for days hidden inside a clean shirt. Maybe he thought we wouldn't find them! Would you ever be equal to men? And what did he want telling you about her for?"

"I suppose he wanted someone to talk to," said Deirdre.

"He did, I hear!" retorted Joan ironically. "I suppose he thought you might put in a good word for him."

"But how could I when I don't even know the girl?"

"Maybe you might know someone that do," Joan suggested shrewdly. "Or maybe your father might have influence."

"Ah, it's not that at all," Deirdre said impatiently. "The man is soft on her, and he wants someone to talk to. Sure, 'tis only human nature."

"The divil a much nature that fellow have unless it suited his book," said Joan derisively. "He wouldn't tell you the time of day unless he wanted to borrow a match from you."

This all-pervading cynicism about love didn't agree with Deirdre at all. The country had obviously gone to hell since saga times. She wrote to a friend in Dublin, asking her to find her a job; after that she felt considerably better.

A few nights later Tommy invited her to the pictures. Afterwards, as they came down Main Street in the moonlight, he looked so imposing with his great build and long, handsome Viking head that she took his arm. She stopped him at the bridge. The abbey tower soared over its cluster of ragged gables with its fantastic battlements like cockades in the moonlight, and the water, tumbling over the weir, was so hatched with shadow that it seemed still, like seaweed left after the tide. There was a great sense of space and joy and contemplativeness inside her, as if a bit of the night had gone astray and nested in her.

"God, Tommy, isn't it lovely?" she whispered.

"Tell me," he asked, as though he were picking her brains again, "what do you see particularly beautiful about that?"

"Ah, stop your old cathecism and try and feel something, man!" she said impatiently.

"I don't know why you say that," Tommy said in a hurt tone as he rested on the parapet of the bridge. "As a matter of fact, I feel things very deeply. As a kid, I was so unhappy at home that I had a row with my father and ran away to sea."

"Did you?" she asked in surprise. "How long were you at sea?"

"A fortnight," said Tommy.

"You didn't stop long enough, Tommy," she said as she sat up on the bridge. "Tommy," she added coaxingly, "did you ever go to bed with a girl?"

He flashed her a quick look of mistrust.

"Why?" he asked suspiciously. "Did someone tell you?"

"Nobody told me anything. I only asked. Did you?"

"Oh, begor, I did," said Tommy with a nod of his head.

"I never did anything like that," she said regretfully. "At least, I did, once, but the fellow said he respected me too much."

"Begor, I hope so," Tommy said in some alarm. "You're too young to be going in for that sort of thing, Deirdre."

"Ah, I don't know," Deirdre said, shaking her head regretfully. "People think they have time enough, and then, before they know where they are, their lives are wasted and they have nothing to show for them. For God's sake, look at the people of this town, Tommy! You'd think it was something they could put in the bank. Was this some girl you picked up?"

"No," replied Tommy, getting more and more guarded. "A girl in a house I was lodging in in Dublin."

"Was she nice?"

"I thought so anyway," said Tommy gallantly.

"But were you in love with her?"

"Oh, begor, I was in love with her all right," he said with a laugh.

"Ah, but I mean really, madly, hopelessly in love," persisted Deirdre, exasperated by his temperate tone.

"I was mad enough."

"And why didn't you marry her?"

"I wasn't in a position to marry her. My family wasn't well off and I couldn't afford it."

"Ah," Deirdre said angrily, as much to the night as to Tommy, "I have no patience with that sort of talk. Ye wouldn't starve."

"I wouldn't be too sure of that."

"And if ye did, what matter?"

"What matter if we starved?" he asked incredulously.

"What matter if ye lived? God, if I loved a man, I'd marry him on tuppence ha'penny. You're all terrified out of your wits of life, as if it was going to bite you."

"Now, that's exactly what it would do," said Tommy.

"Ah, what signifies a bite or two?" Deirdre asked laughingly, throwing off her irritation. "Anyway," she added reasonably, "you could marry her now."

"Is it Elsie?" said Tommy in surprise. "She's probably married herself by now."

"Well, can't you go and see, man?" said Deirdre. "Even if she is, she won't eat you. Anyway, wouldn't she be better for you than your old doctor and her fifteen thousand? God Almighty, Tommy, that's not life!"

"That's the question, of course," Tommy said sternly. "What is life?"

"I don't know, but I'm going to try and find out."

"I read a good many books, and I can't say I ever learned much about it," said Tommy. "How would you find out?"

"By living it."

"That was tried."

"It's a novelty round these parts. I'm hoping to go to a job in Dublin after Christmas. Did I tell you?"

"You did not," Tommy said in consternation. "What do you want going to Dublin for? Aren't you all right here?"

"My views are too large for a place this size," Deirdre replied with a laugh.

And after Tommy had drunk his cocoa in the sitting-room, Deirdre went to drink tea with Joan in the kitchen. The two girls had the room to themselves.

"Well," asked Joan, "had you a great clatther with Mr. Dodd?"

"Oh, great!" said Deirdre, thinking how disappointed Joan would be if she knew how little clatthering they did.

"Maybe ye might make a match of it yet?" Joan said hopefully.

"I wouldn't say so," said Deirdre. "I fancy Tommy doesn't care much about me, except to be talking to."

"That fellow never cared about anyone," said Joan. "Only himself and his monkey nuts."

But Deirdre couldn't feel critical of him just then. She felt that the memory of his abortive romance would be linked in her mind with the bit of the night that had gone astray and nested in her; that she'd always have a soft spot in her heart for the town and its people because of that glimpse into their frustrated and lonely lives.

"Ah, Tommy is romantic enough when he gets the chance," she said. "You never heard about the girl he was living with in Dublin?"

"Living with in Dublin?" Joan said incredulously. "Tommy Dodd? You're not serious! Who was it?"

"Some girl he was in digs with. A university student, I suppose."

"And he was living with her?"

"Oh, not openly, of course," Deirdre said with regret. She could have wished Tommy some experience less furtive, but she knew it was impossible.

"Jesus!" Joan exclaimed. "I'd never trust a man again."

IV

A week passed and one wet afternoon Deirdre came in from school and Joan gave her dinner in the parlour. It was cold there and there was no fire. In the street she saw a father and son

coming together at the other side of the road, each of them sucking a ripe tomato. They scarcely looked human.

"Mr. Dodd didn't say when he was going to give the doctor the
chocolates?" asked Joan, turning as she reached the door.

"He never mentioned them," said Deirdre. "Why? Are they
there still?"

"The divil a stir out of them," said Joan. "He's laying his traps
well, but he might get a poacher's welcome."

"How's that?"

"I heard the doctor was saying she'd fling them in his face if he
as much as opened his mouth to her," Joan said in blood-curdling
tones.

"But how does she know about them?" Deirdre asked in alarm.

"I suppose he told someone," said Joan with a guilty air. "You
don't think you were the only one he talked to about her, do
you?"

That was precisely what Deirdre did think, and it gave her a
nasty shock to know that his words had been passed on. She had
only just begun to realize that in a town like ours every remark
starts a long and successful career as a public event.

"She needn't be so cocksure," she grumbled with her mouth
full. "He's a better man than she's likely to get, even with her
fifteen thousand."

"Is it fifteen thousand she have?" Joan asked in an awe-stricken
whisper, and Deirdre realized that she'd done it again. To live in
a town like ours you have to enunciate every word with an eye to
its ultimate effect, which is probably why so many people find it
easier to leave the town.

"If she had fifty Tommy Dodd would be too good for her," she
said crossly.

"Too good for her?" gasped Joan. "And he with a fancy-
woman in Dublin?"

"But she knows nothing about that," said Deirdre, now thoroughly alarmed.

"Doesn't she, indeed?" Joan said pityingly. " 'Tisn't because I
wouldn't know it that others wouldn't. Let me tell you, Deirdre,"
she went on, wagging a warning finger, "between the post office

and the bobbies, there's very little that isn't known in this town. How well I could meet a woman this morning that could tell me where Celia Johnson's baby is after being put out to nurse, and I'll engage Celia Johnson thinks that no one know she had a baby at all. He'd better mind himself. There's plenty of influential people were put out of business for less."

Deirdre finished her dinner in complete depression. Tommy was certainly going to be ruined, and it would be all her fault. She could never realize that others wouldn't look at things as she did; and that what for her had been the one interesting thing about Tommy, the one spot of brilliant colour in the grey bogland of his life, might be murder to others. Worse than murder, in fact, because there was at least one notorious murderer on the town council, and people fell over themselves trying to conciliate him. But love, of course, was different. There was no money in love. And the worst of it was that any time now Tommy might find out from the doctor how she had betrayed what he probably regarded as his most intimate confidences. The only thing she could think of, in her desperation, was to try and keep him away from the doctor.

That evening, when he came into the parlour, she encouraged him to talk in his usual way about the townspeople. Poor man, he didn't know the sort of things the townspeople were saying about him now!

"You didn't propose to the doctor yet, Tommy?" she asked, taking the bull by the horns.

"The who?" Tommy asked with a start.

"The doctor."

"No," Tommy said without undue depression. "I'm in no great hurry."

"Sure, of course you're not," Deirdre agreed with real relief. "You'd want to think a lot before you did a thing like that?"

"Why did you ask?" he inquired.

"I was only wondering was she the right sort for you."

"Is that so?" he asked. "Now, what makes you think she isn't, Deirdre?"

"I suppose it's just that I'm getting to know you better," said

Deirdre. "Sometimes, you get very false impressions of people. It just struck me that you'd probably want someone more domesticated."

"You might be right," he conceded, and in the same breath: "Do you like chocolates?"

She could hardly believe in her own good fortune. It would be a real achievement to get the knife out of the child's hands before he did himself any damage.

"Love them," she said with a smile.

"I have some in my room," said Tommy, and went out with great strides and took the stairs three at a time. When he returned he handed her the box of chocolates as though it were a gun.

"Go on with what you were saying," he said.

"I don't know should I," she said thoughtfully, struggling with the box, though in fact nothing but an earthquake would have stopped her. "But, you know, Tommy, I have a sort of feeling that you're not half as calculating as you think."

"Who said I thought anything of the kind?" Tommy retorted indignantly.

"You do, Tommy," she said flatly. "You think you're the smartest crook in this town, and you're not. You have a much finer nature than you realize. If you married a woman like that, you'd want to cut your throat inside six months."

"I'd be more likely to cut hers," said Tommy with a chuckle.

"You wouldn't, Tommy," Deirdre said gravely. "You see, in your heart and soul, you're really an idealist. You can't help it. You ought to have married that girl in Dublin—Elsie What's-Her-Name."

"Begor, I ought not," said Tommy with grave enjoyment.

"You ought, Tommy," said Deirdre with finality. "Whatever you may think now, the girl had courage. You don't want to admit it, because you know you treated her badly."

"Oh, indeed, I did nothing of the sort," Tommy said with conviction.

"Ah, Tommy," Deirdre cried impatiently, "why do you be always denying the better part of your nature? You know yourself you treated her badly, whatever disagreement you may have had with her. You don't want to do the decent, manly thing even when you know you ought to. That girl might have had a child."

"There was no danger."

"There's always danger. Anyway, you ought to meet her again; even to talk to her. I think you'd find you looked at the whole thing differently now. I can't help feeling, Tommy, that Elsie was the only real thing in your whole life; that all the rest of it, your life here, and your plotting and planning with the Ku Klux Klan, doesn't mean any more to you than dreaming. Do you understand me, Tommy? She was the *only* real thing."

"Begor, I hope not," he said with a laugh, striking his knee.

"Why not?"

"Because there's no such woman," he said with a guffaw.

"But you told me yourself, Tommy."

"Ah, surely you can understand a joke?"

"That's a queer sort of joke," grumbled Deirdre, so shaken by this fresh revelation that she couldn't even be certain of her own original impression of his sincerity.

"What's queer about it? 'Twould be damn queer if there was any truth in it, if I went round doing that sort of thing, making an idiot of myself. 'Tis all very well in story-books, Deirdre, but it won't do, girl, it won't do."

" 'Twould be no joke for you if someone went and repeated it," Deirdre said shortly, still incensed at the suggestion that she had mistaken a joke for a confession.

"No one would believe them, girl," said Tommy, but his face lost some of its glow.

"I wouldn't be too sure of that," Deirdre said stiffly. "Plenty of influential people were put out of business for less."

She hardly knew that she was quoting Joan, but Tommy recognized his master's voice. He might know little about love-making but he knew a lot about small towns and their inhabitants.

"Anyway, I didn't say it to anyone only you," he said humbly. "Will you marry me, Deirdre?"

"Ah, will I what?" she snapped at this fresh shock.

"Marry me? You know I never gave a damn for another girl only you. I'm telling you no lies. Ask anyone you like."

"But didn't you tell me yourself in this very room only a couple of weeks ago that 'twas the doctor you wanted to marry?" she cried angrily.

"Ah, for God's sake!" exclaimed Tommy. "You don't mean you took that seriously too. I couldn't be bothered with the old doctor. She hasn't a brain in her head. You were the only one I ever met that I respected enough to ask."

"But, Tommy," she cried almost in tears, "you said you wanted to marry her for the fifteen thousand."

Tommy looked at her in real surprise and consternation.

"And you took that seriously?" he exclaimed. "Do you know, Deirdre, I'm surprised at you. I declare to God I thought better of you. I'd have thought a woman of your discernment would know that I wasn't the sort to marry for money. If I wanted to do that I could have done it years ago. Anyway, she hasn't fifteen thousand."

"Tommy," Deirdre said desperately, "you don't mean that was all lies too."

"I don't know why you call it lies," Tommy said indignantly. "We have to say something. It seems to me there are a lot of misunderstandings. Anyway, will you marry me now?"

"I will not," snapped Deirdre ungraciously.

"Why not?" he shouted with real anger.

"Because you're too young."

"Too young? I'm fifteen years older than you."

"You're old enough to have sense," she retorted, picking up her handbag and strutting to the door. She felt hopelessly undignified. "Oh, God, for the age of the sagas!" she thought, and reaching the door, she broke down. "Ah, Tommy, what did you want to spoil it all for?" she wailed. "A fortnight ago I'd have jumped at you, but how the blazes could I marry you now? It's too ridiculous. Too ridiculous!"

GUESTS OF THE NATION

I

At dusk the big Englishman, Belcher, would shift his long legs out of the ashes and say "Well, chums, what about it?" and Noble or me would say "All right, chum" (for we had picked up some of their curious expressions), and the little Englishman, Hawkins, would light the lamp and bring out the cards. Sometimes Jeremiah Donovan would come up and supervise the game and get excited over Hawkins's cards, which he always played badly, and shout at him as if he was one of our own "Ah, you divil, you, why didn't you play the tray?"

But ordinarily Jeremiah was a sober and contented poor devil like the big Englishman, Belcher, and was looked up to only because he was a fair hand at documents, though he was slow enough even with them. He wore a small cloth hat and big gaiters over his long pants, and you seldom saw him with his hands out of his pockets. He reddened when you talked to him, tilting from toe to heel and back, and looking down all the time at his big farmer's feet. Noble and me used to make fun of his broad accent, because we were from the town.

I couldn't at the time see the point of me and Noble guarding Belcher and Hawkins at all, for it was my belief that you could have planted that pair down anywhere from this to Claregalway and they'd have taken root there like a native weed. I never in my short experience seen two men to take to the country as they did.

They were handed on to us by the Second Battalion when the search for them became too hot, and Noble and myself, being young, took over with a natural feeling of responsibility, but

Hawkins made us look like fools when he showed that he knew the country better than we did.

"You're the bloke they calls Bonaparte," he says to me. "Mary Brigid O'Connell told me to ask you what you done with the pair of her brother's socks you borrowed."

For it seemed, as they explained it, that the Second used to have little evenings, and some of the girls of the neighbourhood turned in, and, seeing they were such decent chaps, our fellows couldn't leave the two Englishmen out of them. Hawkins learned to dance "The Walls of Limerick," "The Siege of Ennis," and "The Waves of Tory" as well as any of them, though, naturally, he couldn't return the compliment, because our lads at that time did not dance foreign dances on principle.

So whatever privileges Belcher and Hawkins had with the Second they just naturally took with us, and after the first day or two we gave up all pretence of keeping a close eye on them. Not that they could have got far, for they had accents you could cut with a knife and wore khaki tunics and overcoats with civilian pants and boots. But it's my belief that they never had any idea of escaping and were quite content to be where they were.

It was a treat to see how Belcher got off with the old woman of the house where we were staying. She was a great warrant to scold, and cranky even with us, but before ever she had a chance of giving our guests, as I may call them, a lick of her tongue, Belcher had made her his friend for life. She was breaking sticks, and Belcher, who hadn't been more than ten minutes in the house, jumped up from his seat and went over to her.

"Allow me, madam," he says, smiling his queer little smile, "please allow me"; and he takes the bloody hatchet. She was struck too paralytic to speak, and after that, Belcher would be at her heels, carrying a bucket, a basket, or a load of turf, as the case might be. As Noble said, he got into looking before she leapt, and hot water, or any little thing she wanted, Belcher would have it ready for her. For such a huge man (and though I am five foot ten myself I had to look up at him) he had an uncommon shortness—or should I say lack?—of speech. It took us some time to get used to him, walking in and out, like a ghost, without a word. Especially because Hawkins talked enough for a platoon, it was strange to hear big Belcher with his toes in the ashes come out with a solitary "Excuse me, chum," or "That's right, chum." His one and only passion was cards, and I will say for him that he was a good card-player. He could have fleeced myself and Noble, but whatever we lost to him Hawkins lost to us, and Hawkins played with the money Belcher gave him.

Hawkins lost to us because he had too much old gab, and we probably lost to Belcher for the same reason. Hawkins and Noble would spit at one another about religion into the early hours of the morning, and Hawkins worried the soul out of Noble, whose brother was a priest, with a string of questions that would puzzle a cardinal. To make it worse, even in treating of holy subjects, Hawkins had a deplorable tongue. I never in all my career met a man who could mix such a variety of cursing and bad language into an argument. He was a terrible man, and a fright to argue. He never did a stroke of work, and when he had no one else to talk to, he got stuck in the old woman.

He met his match in her, for one day when he tried to get her to complain profanely of the drought, she gave him a great come-down by blaming it entirely on Jupiter Pluvius (a deity neither Hawkins nor I had ever heard of, though Noble said that among the pagans it was believed that he had something to do with the rain). Another day he was swearing at the capitalists for starting the German war when the old lady laid down her iron, puckered up her little crab's mouth, and said: "Mr. Hawkins, you can say what you like about the war, and think you'll deceive me because I'm only a simple poor countrywoman, but I know what started the war. It was the Italian Count that stole the heathen divinity out of the temple in Japan. Believe me, Mr. Hawkins, nothing but sorrow and want can follow the people that disturb the hidden powers."

A queer old girl, all right.

II

We had our tea one evening, and Hawkins lit the lamp and we all sat into cards. Jeremiah Donovan came in too, and sat down and watched us for a while, and it suddenly struck me that he had no great love for the two Englishmen. It came as a great surprise to me, because I hadn't noticed anything about him before.

Late in the evening a really terrible argument blew up between Hawkins and Noble, about capitalists and priests and love of your country.

"The capitalists," says Hawkins with an angry gulp, "pays the priests to tell you about the next world so as you won't notice what the bastards are up to in this."

"Nonsense, man!" says Noble, losing his temper. "Before ever a capitalist was thought of, people believed in the next world."

Hawkins stood up as though he was preaching a sermon.

"Oh, they did, did they?" he says with a sneer. "They believed all the things you believe, isn't that what you mean? And you believe that God created Adam, and Adam created Shem, and Shem created Jehoshophat. You believe all that silly old fairytale about Eve and Eden and the apple. Well, listen to me, chum. If you're entitled to hold a silly belief like that, I'm entitled to hold my silly belief—which is that the first thing your God created was a bleeding capitalist, with morality and Rolls-Royce complete. Am I right, chum?" he says to Belcher.

"You're right, chum," says Belcher with his amused smile, and got up from the table to stretch his long legs into the fire and stroke his moustache. So, seeing that Jeremiah Donovan was going, and that there was no knowing when the argument about religion would be over, I went out with him. We strolled down to the village together, and then he stopped and started blushing and mumbling and saying I ought to be behind, keeping guard on the prisoners. I didn't like the tone he took with me, and anyway I was bored with life in the cottage, so I replied by asking him what the hell we wanted guarding them at all for. I told him I'd talked it over with Noble, and that we'd both rather be out with a fighting column.

"What use are those fellows to us?" says I.

He looked at me in surprise and said: "I thought you knew we were keeping them as hostages."

"Hostages?" I said.

"The enemy have prisoners belonging to us," he says, "and now they're talking of shooting them. If they shoot our prisoners, we'll shoot theirs."

"Shoot them?" I said.

"What else did you think we were keeping them for?" he says.

"Wasn't it very unforeseen of you not to warn Noble and myself of that in the beginning?" I said.

"How was it?" says he. "You might have known it."

"We couldn't know it, Jeremiah Donovan," says I. "How could we when they were on our hands so long?"

"The enemy have our prisoners as long and longer," says he.

"That's not the same thing at all," says I.

"What difference is there?" says he.

I couldn't tell him, because I knew he wouldn't understand. If it was only an old dog that was going to the vet's, you'd try and not get too fond of him, but Jeremiah Donovan wasn't a man that would ever be in danger of that.

"And when is this thing going to be decided?" says I.

"We might hear tonight," he says. "Or tomorrow or the next day at latest. So if it's only hanging round here that's a trouble to you, you'll be free soon enough."

It wasn't the hanging round that was a trouble to me at all by this time. I had worse things to worry about. When I got back to the cottage the argument was still on. Hawkins was holding forth in his best style, maintaining that there was no next world, and Noble was maintaining that there was; but I could see that Hawkins had had the best of it.

"Do you know what, chum?" he was saying with a saucy smile. "I think you're just as big a bleeding unbeliever as I am. You say you believe in the next world, and you know just as much about the next world as I do, which is sweet damn-all. What's heaven? You don't know. Where's heaven? You don't know. You know sweet damn-all! I ask you again, do they wear wings?"

"Very well, then," says Noble, "they do. Is that enough for you? They do wear wings."

"Where do they get them, then? Who makes them? Have they a factory for wings? Have they a sort of store where you hands in your chit and takes your bleeding wings?"

"You're an impossible man to argue with," says Noble. "Now, listen to me—" And they were off again.

It was long after midnight when we locked up and went to bed. As I blew out the candle I told Noble what Jeremiah Donovan was after telling me. Noble took it very quietly. When we'd been in bed about an hour he asked me did I think we ought to tell the Englishmen. I didn't think we should, because it was more than likely that the English wouldn't shoot our men, and even if they did, the brigade officers, who were always up and down with the Second Battalion and knew the Englishmen well, wouldn't be likely to want them plugged. "I think so too," says Noble. "It would be great cruelty to put the wind up them now."

"It was very unforeseen of Jeremiah Donovan anyhow," says I.

It was next morning that we found it so hard to face Belcher and Hawkins. We went about the house all day scarcely saying a word. Belcher didn't seem to notice; he was stretched into the ashes as usual, with his usual look of waiting in quietness for something unforeseen to happen, but Hawkins noticed and put it down to Noble's being beaten in the argument of the night before.

"Why can't you take a discussion in the proper spirit?" he says severely. "You and your Adam and Eve! I'm a Communist, that's what I am. Communist or anarchist, it all comes to much the same thing." And for hours he went round the house, muttering when the fit took him. "Adam and Eve! Adam and Eve! Nothing better to do with their time than picking bleeding apples!"

III

I don't know how we got through that day, but I was very glad when it was over, the tea things were cleared away, and Belcher said in his peaceable way: "Well, chums, what about it?" We sat round the table and Hawkins took out the cards, and just then I heard Jeremiah Donovan's footstep on the path and a dark presentiment crossed my mind. I rose from the table and caught him before he reached the door.

"What do you want?" I asked.

"I want those two soldier friends of yours," he says, getting red.

"Is that the way, Jeremiah Donovan?" I asked.

"That's the way. There were four of our lads shot this morning, one of them a boy of sixteen."

"That's bad," I said.

At that moment Noble followed me out, and the three of us walked down the path together, talking in whispers. Feeney, the local intelligence officer, was standing by the gate.

"What are you going to do about it?" I asked Jeremiah Donovan.

"I want you and Noble to get them out; tell them they're being shifted again; that'll be the quietest way."

"Leave me out of that," says Noble under his breath.

Jeremiah Donovan looks at him hard.

"All right," he says. "You and Feeney get a few tools from the shed and dig a hole by the far end of the bog. Bonaparte and myself will be after you. Don't let anyone see you with the tools. I wouldn't like it to go beyond ourselves."

We saw Feeney and Noble go round to the shed and went in ourselves. I left Jeremiah Donovan to do the explanations. He told them that he had orders to send them back to the Second Battalion. Hawkins let out a mouthful of curses, and you could see that though Belcher didn't say anything, he was a bit upset too. The old woman was for having them stay in spite of us, and she didn't stop advising them until Jeremiah Donovan lost his temper and turned on her. He had a nasty temper, I noticed. It was pitch-dark in the cottage by this time, but no one thought of lighting the lamp, and in the darkness the two Englishmen fetched their topcoats and said good-bye to the old woman.

"Just as a man makes a home of a bleeding place, some bastard at headquarters thinks you're too cushy and shunts you off," says Hawkins, shaking her hand.

"A thousand thanks, madam," says Belcher. "A thousand thanks for everything"—as though he'd made it up.

We went round to the back of the house and down towards the bog. It was only then that Jeremiah Donovan told them. He was shaking with excitement.

"There were four of our fellows shot in Cork this morning and now you're to be shot as a reprisal."

"What are you talking about?" snaps Hawkins. "It's bad

enough being mucked about as we are without having to put up with your funny jokes."

"It isn't a joke," says Donovan. "I'm sorry, Hawkins, but it's true," and begins on the usual rigmarole about duty and how unpleasant it is.

I never noticed that people who talk a lot about duty find it much of a trouble to them.

"Oh, cut it out!" says Hawkins.

"Ask Bonaparte," says Donovan, seeing that Hawkins isn't taking him seriously. "Isn't it true, Bonaparte?"

"It is," I say, and Hawkins stops.

"Ah, for Christ's sake, chum!"

"I mean it, chum," I say.

"You don't sound as if you meant it."

"If he doesn't mean it, I do," says Donovan, working himself up.

"What have you against me, Jeremiah Donovan?"

"I never said I had anything against you. But why did your people take out four of our prisoners and shoot them in cold blood?"

He took Hawkins by the arm and dragged him on, but it was impossible to make him understand that we were in earnest. I had the Smith and Wesson in my pocket and I kept fingering it and wondering what I'd do if they put up a fight for it or ran, and wishing to God they'd do one or the other. I knew if they did run for it, that I'd never fire on them. Hawkins wanted to know was Noble in it, and when we said yes, he asked us why Noble wanted to plug him. Why did any of us want to plug him? What had he done to us? Weren't we all chums? Didn't we understand him and didn't he understand us? Did we imagine for an instant that he'd shoot us for all the so-and-so officers in the so-and-so British Army?

By this time we'd reached the bog, and I was so sick I couldn't even answer him. We walked along the edge of it in the darkness, and every now and then Hawkins would call a halt and begin all over again, as if he was wound up, about our being chums, and I knew that nothing but the sight of the grave would convince him that we had to do it. And all the time I was hoping that something would happen; that they'd run for it or that Noble would take over the responsibility from me. I had the feeling that it was worse on Noble than on me.

IV

At last we saw the lantern in the distance and made towards it. Noble was carrying it, and Feeney was standing somewhere in the darkness behind him, and the picture of them so still and silent in the bogland brought it home to me that we were in earnest, and banished the last bit of hope I had.

Belcher, on recognizing Noble, said: "Hallo, chum," in his quiet way, but Hawkins flew at him at once, and the argument began all over again, only this time Noble had nothing to say for himself and stood with his head down, holding the lantern between his legs.

It was Jeremiah Donovan who did the answering. For the twentieth time, as though it was haunting his mind, Hawkins asked if anybody thought he'd shoot Noble.

"Yes, you would," says Jeremiah Donovan.

"No, I wouldn't, damn you!"

"You would, because you'd know you'd be shot for not doing it."

"I wouldn't, not if I was to be shot twenty times over. I wouldn't shoot a pal. And Belcher wouldn't—isn't that right, Belcher?"

"That's right, chum," Belcher said, but more by way of answering the question than of joining in the argument. Belcher sounded as though whatever unforeseen thing he'd always been waiting for had come at last.

"Anyway, who says Noble would be shot if I wasn't? What do you think I'd do if I was in his place, out in the middle of a blasted bog?"

"What would you do?" asks Donovan.

"I'd go with him wherever he was going, of course. Share my last bob with him and stick by him through thick and thin. No one can ever say of me that I let down a pal."

"We had enough of this," says Jeremiah Donovan, cocking his revolver. "Is there any message you want to send?"

"No, there isn't."

"Do you want to say your prayers?"

Hawkins came out with a cold-blooded remark that even shocked me and turned on Noble again.

"Listen to me, Noble," he says. "You and me are chums. You can't come over to my side, so I'll come over to your side. That show you I mean what I say? Give me a rifle and I'll go along with you and the other lads."

Nobody answered him. We knew that was no way out.

"Hear what I'm saying?" he says. "I'm through with it. I'm a deserter or anything else you like. I don't believe in your stuff, but it's no worse than mine. That satisfy you?"

Noble raised his head, but Donovan began to speak and he lowered it again without replying.

"For the last time, have you any messages to send?" says Donovan in a cold, excited sort of voice.

"Shut up, Donovan! You don't understand me, but these lads do. They're not the sort to make a pal and kill a pal. They're not the tools of any capitalist."

I alone of the crowd saw Donovan raise his Webley to the back of Hawkins's neck, and as he did so I shut my eyes and tried to pray. Hawkins had begun to say something else when Donovan fired, and as I opened my eyes at the bang, I saw Hawkins stagger at the knees and lie out flat at Noble's feet, slowly and as quiet as a kid falling asleep, with the lantern-light on his lean legs and bright farmer's boots. We all stood very still, watching him settle out in the last agony.

Then Belcher took out a handerchief and began to tie it about his own eyes (in our excitement we'd forgotten to do the same for Hawkins), and, seeing it wasn't big enough, turned and asked for the loan of mine. I gave it to him and he knotted the two together and pointed with his foot at Hawkins.

"He's not quite dead," he says. "Better give him another."

Sure enough, Hawkins's left knee is beginning to rise. I bend down and put my gun to his head; then, recollecting myself, I get up again. Belcher understands what's in my mind.

"Give him his first," he says. "I don't mind. Poor bastard, we don't know what's happening to him now."

I knelt and fired. By this time I didn't seem to know what I was doing. Belcher, who was fumbling a bit awkwardly with the handkerchiefs, came out with a laugh as he heard the shot. It was the first time I heard him laugh and it sent a shudder down my back; it sounded so unnatural.

"Poor bugger!" he said quietly. "And last night he was so curious about it all. It's very queer, chums, I always think. Now he knows as much about it as they'll ever let him know, and last night he was all in the dark."

Donovan helped him to tie the handkerchiefs about his eyes. "Thanks, chum," he said. Donovan asked if there were any messages he wanted sent.

"No, chum," he says. "Not for me. If any of you would like to write to Hawkins's mother, you'll find a letter from her in his pocket. He and his mother were great chums. But my missus left me eight years ago. Went away with another fellow and took the kid with her. I like the feeling of a home, as you may have noticed, but I couldn't start again after that."

It was an extraordinary thing, but in those few minutes Belcher said more than in all the weeks before. It was just as if the sound of the shot had started a flood of talk in him and he could go on the whole night like that, quite happily, talking about himself. We stood round like fools now that he couldn't see us any longer. Donovan looked at Noble, and Noble shook his head. Then Donovan raised his Webley, and at that moment Belcher gives his queer laugh again. He may have thought we were talking about him, or perhaps he noticed the same thing I'd noticed and couldn't understand it.

"Excuse me, chums," he says. "I feel I'm talking the hell of a lot, and so silly, about my being so handy about a house and things like that. But this thing came on me suddenly. You'll forgive me, I'm sure."

"You don't want to say a prayer?" asks Donovan.

"No, chum," he says. "I don't think it would help. I'm ready, and you boys want to get it over."

"You understand that we're only doing our duty?" says Donovan.

Belcher's head was raised like a blind man's, so that you could only see his chin and the tip of his nose in the lantern-light.

"I never could make out what duty was myself," he said. "I

think you're all good lads, if that's what you mean. I'm not complaining."

Noble, just as if he couldn't bear any more of it, raised his fist at Donovan, and in a flash Donovan raised his gun and fired. The big man went over like a sack of meal, and this time there was no need of a second shot.

I don't remember much about the burying, but that it was worse than all the rest because we had to carry them to the grave. It was all mad lonely with nothing but a patch of lantern-light between ourselves and the dark, and birds hooting and screeching all round, disturbed by the guns. Noble went through Hawkins's belongings to find the letter from his mother, and then joined his hands together. He did the same with Belcher. Then, when we'd filled in the grave, we separated from Jeremiah Donovan and Feeney and took our tools back to the shed. All the way we didn't speak a word. The kitchen was dark and cold as we'd left it, and the old woman was sitting over the hearth, saying her beads. We walked past her into the room, and Noble struck a match to light the lamp. She rose quietly and came to the doorway with all her cantankerousness gone.

"What did ye do with them?" she asked in a whisper, and Noble started so that the match went out in his hand.

"What's that?" he asked without turning round.

"I heard ye," she said.

"What did you hear?" asked Noble.

"I heard ye. Do ye think I didn't hear ye, putting the spade back in the houseen?"

Noble struck another match and this time the lamp lit for him.

"Was that what ye did to them?" she asked.

Then, by God, in the very doorway, she fell on her knees and began praying, and after looking at her for a minute or two Noble did the same by the fireplace. I pushed my way out past her and left them at it. I stood at the door, watching the stars and listening to the shrieking of the birds dying out over the bogs. It is so strange what you feel at times like that that you can't describe it. Noble says he saw everything ten times the size, as though there were nothing in the whole world but that little patch of bog with the two Englishmen stiffening into it, but with me it was as if the patch of bog where the Englishmen were was a million miles away, and even Noble and the old woman, mumbling behind me, and the birds and the bloody stars were all far away, and I was somehow very small and very lost and lonely like a child astray in the snow. And anything that happened me afterwards, I never felt the same about again.

ETERNAL TRIANGLE

REVOLUTIONS? I never had any interest in them. A man in my position have to mind his job and not bother about what other people are doing. Besides, I never could see what good they did anybody, and I see more of that kind of thing than most people. A watchman have to be out at all hours in all kinds of weather. He have to keep his eyes open. All I ever seen out of things like that was the damage. And who pays for the damage? You and me and people like us, so that one set of jackeens can get in instead of another set of jackeens. What is it to me who's in or out? All I know is that I have to pay for the damage they do.

I remember well the first one I saw. It was a holiday, and when I turned up to the depot, I was told there was a tram after breaking down in town, and I was to go in and keep an eye on it. A lot of the staff was at the races, and it might be a couple of hours before they could get a breakdown gang. So I took my lunch and away with me into town. It was a nice spring day and I thought I might as well walk.

Mind you, I noticed nothing strange, only that the streets were a bit empty, but it struck me that a lot of people were away for the day. Then, all at once, just as I got to town, I noticed a hand-

ful of them Volunteer boys in the street. Some of them had green
uniforms with slouch hats; more of them had nothing only belts
and bandoliers. All of them had guns of one sort or another. I
paid no attention. Seeing that it was a holiday, I thought they
might be on some sort of manœuvre. They were a crowd I never
had anything to do with. As I say, I'm a man that minds his own
business.

Suddenly, one of them raises his gun and halts me.

"Halt!" says he. "Where are you bound for, mate?"

"Just down here, to keep an eye on a tram," I said, taking it in
good parts.

"A tram?" says he. "That's the very thing we want for a barricade. Could you drive it?"

"Ah, is it to have the union after me?" says I.

"Ah, to hell with the union," says a second fellow. "If you'll
drive it we'll rig it up as an armoured train."

Now, I did not like the tone them fellows took. They were making too free altogether, and it struck me as peculiar that there
wouldn't be a bobby there to send them about their business. I
went on a couple of hundred yards, and what did I see only a
second party. These fellows were wearing khaki, and I recognized
them as cadets from the college. They were standing on the steps
of the big hotel overlooking the tram, and the young fellow that
was supposed to be their officer was very excited.

"That tram is in the direct line of fire," he says. "It's not a safe
place."

"Ah, well," I said, "in my job there's a lot of things aren't safe.
I hope if anything happens me you'll put in a good word for me
with the tramway company."

Mind you, I was still not taking them seriously. I didn't know
what I was after walking into. And the first thing I did was to go
over the tram to see was there anything missing. The world is
full of light-fingered people, and a thing like that, if you only left
it for five minutes, you wouldn't know what would be gone. I
was shocked when I seen the upstairs. The glass was all broken
and the upholstery ripped.

Then the shooting began, and I had to lie on the floor, but
after a while it eased off, and I sat up and ate my lunch and read

the daily paper. There was no one around, because whenever anyone showed himself at the end of the road, there was a bang and he ran for his life. Coming on to dusk, I began to worry a bit about whether I was going to be relieved at all that day. I knew Danny Delea, the foreman, was a conscientious sort of man, and if he couldn't get a relief, he'd send me word what to do, but no one came, and I was beginning to get a bit hungry. I don't mind admitting that a couple of times I got up to go home. I didn't like sitting there with the darkness coming on, not knowing was I going to be relieved that night or the next week. But each time I sat down again. That is the sort I am. I knew the light-fingered gentry, and I knew that, firing or no firing, they were on the look-out and I wouldn't be out of that tram before one of them would be along to see what could he pick up. I would not give it to say to the rest of the men that I would leave a valuable thing like a tram.

Then, all at once, the firing got hot again, and when I looked out, what did I see in the dusk only a girl coming from behind the railings in the park and running this way and that in an aimless sort of way. She looked as if she was out of her mind with fright, and I could see the fright was more a danger to her than anything else. Mind, I had no wish for her company! I saw what she was, and they are a sort of woman I would never have much to do with. They are always trying to make friends with watchmen, because we are out at all hours. At the same time, I saw if I didn't do something quick, she'd be killed under my eyes, so I stood on the platform and shouted to her to come in. She was a woman I didn't know by sight; a woman of about thirty-five. Cummins her name was. The family was from Waterford. She was a good-looking piece too, considering. I made her lie on the floor to get out of the shooting, but she was nearly hysterical, lifting her head to look at me and lowering it not to see what was going on.

"But who in hell is it, mister?" she says. "God Almighty, I only came out for a bit of sugar for me tea, and look at the capers I'm after walking into! . . . Sacred Heart of Jesus, they're off again. . . . You'd think I was something at a fair, the way they were banging their bloody bullets all round me. Who is it at all?"

"It's the cadets in the hotel here, shooting at the other fellows beyond the park," I said.

"But why don't someone send for the police? Damn soon them fellows would be along if it was only me talking to a fellow!"

" 'Twould take a lot of police to stop this," says I.

"But what are they shooting for, mister?" says she. "Is it for Ireland?"

"Ireland?" says I. "A fat lot Ireland have to hope for from little whipper-snappers like them."

"Still and all," says she, "if 'twas for Ireland, you wouldn't mind so much."

And I declare to God but she had a tear in her eye. That is the kind of women they are. They'll steal the false teeth from a corpse, but let them lay eyes on a green flag or a child in his First Communion suit, and you'd think patriotism and religion were the only two things ever in their minds.

"That sort of blackguarding isn't going to do any good to Ireland or anyone else," says I. "What I want to know is who is going to pay for the damage? Not them. They never did an honest day's work in their lives, most of them. We're going to pay for it, the way we always do."

"I'd pay them every bloody penny I have in the world this minute if only they'd shut up and go away," she says. "For God's sake, will you listen to them!"

Things were getting hotter again. What was after happening was that some of the Volunteer fellows were after crossing the park behind the shrubbery and were firing up at the hotel. They might as well be firing at the moon. The cadets were after knocking out every pane of glass and barricading the windows. One of the Volunteers jumped from a branch of a tree over the railings and ran across the road to the tram. He was an insignificant little article with a saucy air. You could tell by his accent he wasn't from Dublin. I took him to be from somewhere in the North. I didn't like him much. I never did like them Northerners anyway.

"What are ye doing here?" he says in surprise when he seen us lying on the floor.

"I'm the watchman," says I, cutting him short.

"Begor, a watchman ought to be able to watch himself better than that," he says, and without as much as "By your leave" he up with the rifle butt and knocked out every pane of glass in the side of the tram. It went to my heart to see it go. Any other time I'd have taken him and wrung his neck, but, you see, I was lying on the floor and couldn't get up to him with the firing. I pretended not to mind, but I looked at the glass and then I looked at him.

"And who," I said, "is going to pay for that?"

"Och, Mick MacQuaid to be sure," says he.

"Ah, the gentleman is right," says the woman. "Only for him we might all be kilt."

The way she about-faced and started to soft-solder that fellow got on my nerves. It is always the same with that sort of woman. They are people you can't trust.

"And what the hell is it to anyone whether you're killed or not?" I said. "No one asked you to stop. This is the tramway company's property, and if you don't like it you can leave it. You have no claim."

"We'll see whose property this is when it's all over," says the man, and he began shooting up at the windows of the hotel.

"Hey, mister," says the woman, "is that the English you're shooting at?"

"Who else do you think 'twould be?" says he.

"Ah, I was only saying when you came in that I'd never mind if 'twas against the English. I suppose 'twill be in the history books, mister, like Robert Emmet?"

"Robert Emmet!" I said. "I'd like to know where you and the likes of you would be only for the English."

"Well, do you know," she says, as innocent as you please, " 'tis a funny thing about me, but I never cared much for the English soldiers. Of course, mind you, you'd meet nice fellows everywhere, but you'd never know where you were with the English. They haven't the same nature as our own somehow."

Then someone blew a whistle in the park, and your man dropped his rifle and looked out to see how he was going to get back.

"You're going to get your nose shot off if you go out in that, mister," says the woman. "If you'll take my advice, you'll wait till 'tis dark."

"I'm after getting into a tight corner all right," says he.

"Oh, you'll never cross that street alive, mister," she says as if she was delighted with it. "The best thing you could do now would be to wait till after dark and come round to my little place for a cup of tea. You'd be safe there anyway."

"Och, to hell with it," says he. "I have only to take a chance," and he crept down the steps and made for the railings. They spotted him, because they all began to blaze together. The woman got on her hands and knees to look after him.

"Aha, he's away!" says she, clapping her hands like a child. "Good man you are, me bold fellow. . . . I wouldn't wish for a pound that anything would happen that young man," says she to me.

"The shooting on both sides is remarkably wide," says I. "That fellow should have more sense."

"Ah, we won't know till we're dead who have the sense and who haven't," says she. "Some people might get a proper suck-in. God, wouldn't I laugh."

"Some people are going to get a suck-in long before that," says I. "The impudence of that fellow, talking about the tramway company. He thinks they're going to hand it over to him. Whoever is in, he's not going to see much of it."

"Ah, what matter?" she said. " 'Tis only youth. Youth is lovely, I always think. And 'tis awful to think of young fellows being kilt, whoever they are. Like in France. God, 'twould go to your heart. And what is it all for? Ireland! Holy Moses, what did Ireland ever do for us? Bread and dripping and a kick in the ass is all we ever got out of it. You're right about the English, though. You'd meet some very genuine English chaps. Very sincere, in their own way."

"Oh, they have their good points," says I. "I never saw much to criticize in them, only they're given too much liberty."

"Ah, what harm did a bit of liberty ever do anyone, though?" says she.

"Now, it does do harm," says I. "Too much liberty is bad. People ought to mind themselves. Look at me! I'm on this job the best part of my life, and I have more opportunities than most, but thanks be to God, I can say I never took twopenceworth belonging to my employers nor never had anything to do with a woman outside my own door."

"And a hell of a lot of thanks you'll get for it in the heel of the hunt," says she. "Five bob a week pension and the old woman stealing it out of your pocket while you're asleep. Don't I know all about it? Oh, God, I wish I was back in me own little room. I'd give all the countries that ever was this minute for a cup of tea with sugar in it. I'd never mind the rations only for the bit of sugar. Hi, mister, would you ever see me home to the doss? I wouldn't be afraid if I had you with me."

"But I have to mind this tram," says I.

"You have what?" says she, cocking her head. "Who do you think is going to run away with it?"

"Now, you'd be surprised," says I.

"Surprised?" says she. "I'd be enchanted."

"Well," I said, "the way I look at it, I'm paid to look after it, and this is my place till I'm relieved."

"But how the hell could you be relieved with this merry-go-round?"

"That is a matter for my employers to decide," says I.

"God," says she, "I may be bad but you're looney," and then she looked at me and she giggled. She started giggling, and she went on giggling, just as if she couldn't stop. That is what I say about them women. There is a sort of childishness in them all, just as if they couldn't be serious about anything. That is what has them the way they are.

So the night came on, and the stars came out, and the shooting only got louder. We were sitting there in the tram, saying nothing, when all at once I looked out and saw the red light over the houses.

"That's a fire," says I.

"If it is, 'tis a mighty big fire," says she.

And then we saw another one to the left of it, and another and another till the whole sky seemed to be lit up, and the smoke pouring away out to sea as if it was the whole sky was moving.

"That's the whole city on fire," says I.

"And 'tis getting mighty close to us," says she. "God send they don't burn this place as well. 'Tis bad enough to be starved and frozen without being roasted alive as well."

I was too mesmerized to speak. I knew what 'twas worth. Millions of pounds' worth of property burning, and no one to pour a drop of water on it. That is what revolutions are like. People talk about poverty, and then it all goes up in smoke—enough to keep thousands comfortable.

Then, all at once, the shooting got nearer, and when I looked out I saw a man coming up the road. The first impression I got of him was that he was badly wounded, for he was staggering from one side of the road to the other with his hands in the air. "I surrender, I surrender," he was shouting, and the more he shouted, the harder they fired. He staggered out into the middle of the road again, stood there for a minute, and then went down like a sack of meal.

"Oh, the poor misfortunate man!" says the woman, putting her hands to her face. "Did you ever see such barbarity? Killing him like that in cold blood!"

But he wasn't killed yet, for he began to bawl all over again, and when he got tired of holding up his hands, he stuck his feet in the air instead.

"Cruel, bloody, barbarous brutes!" says the woman. "They ought to be ashamed of themselves. He told them he surrendered, and they won't let him." And without another word, away with her off down the street to him, bawling: "Here, mister, come on in here and you'll be safe."

A wonder we weren't all killed with her. He got up and started running towards the tram with his hands still in the air. When she grabbed him and pushed him up on the platform, he still had them there. I seen then by his appearance that he wasn't wounded but drunk. He was a thin-looking scrawny man with a cloth cap.

"I surrender," he bawls. *"Kamerad."*

"Hi, mister," says the woman, "would you for the love of the suffering God stop surrendering and lie down."

"But they won't let me lie down," says he. "That's all I want is to lie down, but every time I do they makes a cockshot of me. What in hell is it?"

"Oh, this is the Rising, mister," she says.

"The what?" says he.

"The Rising," says she. "Like they said in the papers there would be."

"Who's rising?" says he, grabbing his head. "What paper said that? I want to know is this the D.T.'s I have or isn't it?"

"Oh, 'tisn't the D.T.'s at all, mister," she says, delighted to be able to spread the good news. "This is all real, what you see. 'Tis the Irish rising. Our own boys, don't you know? Like in Robert Emmet's Time. The Irish are on that side and the English are on this. 'Twas the English was firing at you, the low scuts!"

"Bugger them!" he says. "They're after giving me a splitting head. There's no justice in this bloody world." Then he sat on the inside step of the tram and put his head between his knees. "Like an engine," he says. "Have you e'er a drop of water?"

"Ah, where would we get it, man?" says the woman, brightening up when she seen him take the half pint of whisky out of his hip pocket. 'Tis a mystery to me still it wasn't broken. "Is that whisky you have, mister?"

"No water?" says he, and then he began to shudder all over and put his hand over his face. "Where am I?" says he.

"Where should you be?" says she.

"How the hell do I know and the trams not running?" says he. "Tell me, am I alive or dead?"

"Well, you're alive for the time being," says the woman. "How long we're all going to be that way is another matter entirely."

"Well, are you alive, ma'am?" says he. "You'll excuse me being personal?"

"Oh, no offence, mister," says she. "I'm still in the queue."

"And do you see what I see?" says he.

"What's that, mister?"

"All them fires."

"Oh," says she, "don't let a little thing like that worry you, mister. That's not hell, if that's what you're afraid of. That's only the city burning."

"The what burning?" says he.

"The city burning," says she. "That's it, there."

"There's more than the bloody city burning," says he. "Haven't you e'er a drop of water at all?"

"Ah, we can spare it," she says. "I think it must be the Almighty God sent you, mister. I declare to you, with all the goings-on, I hadn't a mouthful to eat the whole day, not as much as a cup of tea."

So she took a swig of the bottle and passed it to me. It is stuff I would never much care for, the whisky, but having nothing to eat, I was feeling in the want of something.

"Who's that fellow in there?" says he, noticing me for the first time.

"That's only the watchman," says she.

"Is he Irish or English?" says the drunk.

"Ah, what the hell would he be only Irish?"

"Because if he's English, he's getting none of my whisky," says the drunk, beginning to throw his arms about. "I'd cut the throat of any bloody Englishman."

Oh, pure, unadulterated patriotism! Leave it to a boozer.

"Now, don't be attracting attention, like a good man," she says. "We all have our principles but we don't want to be over-heard. We're in trouble enough, God knows."

"I'm not afraid of anyone," says he, staggering to his feet. "I'm not afraid to tell the truth. A bloody Englishman that would shoot a misfortunate man and he on the ground, I despise him. I despise the English."

Then there was a couple of bangs, and he threw up his hands and down with him like a scarecrow in a high wind.

"I declare to me God," says the woman with an ugly glance at the hotel, "them fellows in there are wound up. Are you hit, mister?" says she, giving him a shake. "Oh, begod, I'm afraid his number's up."

"Open his collar and give us a look at him," says I. By this time I was sick of the pair of them.

"God help us, and not a priest nor doctor to be had," says she. "Could you say the prayers for the dying?"

"How would I know the prayers for the dying?" says I.

"Say an act of contrition so," says she.

Well, I began, but I was so upset that I started the Creed instead.

"That's not the act of contrition," says she.

"Say it yourself as you're so smart," says I, and she began, but before she was finished, the drunk shook his fist in the air and said: "I'll cut the living lights out of any Englishman," and then he began to snore.

"Some people have the gift," says she.

Gift was no word for it. We sat there the whole night, shivering and not able to get more than a snooze, and that fellow never stirred, only for the roar of the snoring. He never woke at all until it was coming on to dawn, and then he put his head in his hands again and began complaining of the headache.

"Bad whisky is the ruination of the world," says he.

"Everyone's trouble is their own," says the woman.

And at that moment a lot of cadets came out of the hotel and over to the tram.

"Will you look at them?" says the woman. "Didn't I tell you they were wound up?"

"You'll have to get out of this now," says the officer, swinging his gun.

"And where are we going to go?" says she.

"The city is all yours," says he.

"And so is the Bank of Ireland," says she. "If I was only in my own little room this minute, you could have the rest of the city —with my compliments. Where are you off to?" she asked the drunk.

"I'll have to get the Phibsboro tram," says he.

"You could order two while you're about it," she says. "The best thing the pair of ye can do is come along to my little place and wait till this jigmareel is over."

"I have to stop here," says I.

"You can't," says the officer.

"But I must stop till I'm relieved, man," says I, getting angry with him.

"You're relieved," he says. "I'm relieving you."

And, of course, I had to do what he said. All the same, before I went, I gave him a piece of my mind.

"There's no need for this sort of thing at all," I says. "There's nothing to be gained by destroying valuable property. If people would only do what they were told and mind their own business, there would be no need for any of this blackguarding."

The woman wanted me to come into her room for a cup of tea, but I wouldn't. I was too disgusted. Away with me across the bridge, and the fellows that were guarding it never halted me or anything, and I never stopped till I got home to my own place. Then I went to bed, and I didn't get up for a week, till the whole thing was over. They had prisoners going in by droves, and I never as much as looked out at them. I was never so disgusted with anything in my life.

ORPHEUS AND HIS LUTE

Du holde Kunst . . .

THERE'S no music now like there used to be in the old days. People aren't as keen on it somehow. Then there used to be the Italian opera companies, and the chaps in the gallery sang during the intervals. I remember once a man nearly being thrown out of the gallery by the crowd because he had the bad taste to sing the tenor aria from *Martha* better than the Italian on the stage. People took opera seriously then. An opera company wouldn't come to town without a band to meet them at the railway station. Where would you hear of a band receiving an opera company now? For the matter of that, where would you hear of a proper opera company—or a band? Nowadays, it's nothing but pipers' bands—nnnaaannnaaa—no harmony, no modulation; nothing but "The Old Rustic Bridge by the Mill" played six times through. That sort of thing may be all right for Highlanders and wild people of the sort who aren't accustomed to better, but you couldn't call it music.

I put it all down to the price of porter. When porter was three halfpence a pint we could have brass bands. We can't have them now. The porter and the music went together, the way they did with the Irishtown Brass and Reed Band. That, now, was a band for you. In those days—I'm speaking of fifty years ago, of course —every parish had its band, and some of them had two bands, but Irishtown was cock of the walk. There wasn't a man in that band who wasn't reared, you might say, between bar lines, and between them they could drink Lough Erne dry. That was a well-known fact; a man would hardly be taken in that band un- less he could do something remarkable in the way of drinking.

But, of course, like everything else, drink is a thing you can take too far. The drink did for them in the long run, as it did for many a good man and many a good band. They were always collecting at the chapel gates for new uniforms or new instru- ments, and sometimes of a winter's night you'd hear a knock, and there would be two of them with a collecting box that rattled whether they wanted to rattle it or not, so that you'd have to steady it yourself to put in a copper. You'd give it, of course; you could never see real artists in the want of it, but that was the last you'd hear of the new uniforms and the new instruments, and the old rags they wore on parade hadn't a vestige of a seat in them.

People got tired of it, though. You wouldn't remember it, but in those days of the big money, it was the fashion for bands to serenade their own supporters—aldermen or M.P.'s or big butter merchants, particularly when they were giving dinner parties. It was very nice of a summer evening; the windows all wide open and the fellows in their white shirts looking out while the band in the garden played "Selections from *Traviata*." Then the band would be given refreshments in the kitchen, and the man of the house would slip the bandmaster a pound note, or maybe a five- pound note—those were the days they could do it. But in the heel of the hunt, no one would have the Irishtown band, because if they once got an innings at all, they never let up. On the least provocation they were up again, playing for their drinks, till someone gave them a halfcrown, just to be rid of them. That was the rock they perished on, because in time they lost all their rich backers, and a band without a backer is nowhere. Promenades, tournaments, or fetes—they never got anything but the leavings of the other bands.

Well, one cold wet night in February, they gathered in to the bandroom for practice. Practice! They were sitting round the fire in the jimjams, and it was two men called Butty Bowman and Ned Hegarty that were lighting the pipes for them. They couldn't reach the pipes themselves, the way their hands were shaking, and whenever a cinder fell out or the door banged downstairs, the whole lot would give one loud shriek and rise three feet in the air, chairs and all.

"Boys, boys, boys!" moaned the bandmaster, Joe Delury, rubbing his hands. "What are we going to do? What *are* we going to do?"

"Send out the conjuring box, quick," said Shinkwin, the big drummer.

"But who will we send it to?" asked the bandmaster, reaching for the poker. "Is there anyone at all in Ireland will take pity on us?"

"Send it to the pub," said Shinkwin. "Crowley's at the bridge are always good for a bob or two."

"Oh," said the bandmaster, tapping his feet, "a mouthful would do me. All I want is a cure. Here, Hegarty, take a turn at it you, now, yourself and Butty Bowman. And to make the one errand of it, take a jug or two as well."

So Hegarty and the other went off, and the rest remained, trying to bear it as best they could; some walking up and down, grinding their teeth, and some lying on the benches, shivering and moaning like men in their last agony. And every few minutes, like Sister Anne in the story, the bandmaster would go to the window and peer out through the darkness and rain like the captain of a ship on the bridge of a stormy night, with all the poor passengers crying together "Joe, Joe, are they coming yet?"

"I don't know what's detaining them men," the bandmaster said severely, drawing a deep breath through his nose. "I hope they're not drinking it themselves. I thought better of Hegarty."

It was three quarters of an hour before the doves came back to the ark and one look at them was enough. It was plain there was no land in sight. The bandmaster couldn't believe it. He had to look into the empty jug himself and then swore a holy oath and clapped his hand to his face. All at once the whole band began to moan in unison.

"Boys!" said the bandmaster suddenly.

"What is it?" asked Hegarty.

"Ye know me a long time," said Delury in a reasonable, heart-broken tone.

"We do to be sure," said Hegarty.

"And," said the bandmaster, drawing back the lapels of his coat and scowling as though he expected contradiction, "ye know I'm a musician to the eyelets of my boots."

"We do, begor," said Hegarty.

"Well," said the bandmaster with a toss of his head, "I was a man before I was a musician. Butty," he added to Bowman, "slip up to Coveney's and ask them to send down the donkey and butt. 'Tis only for half an hour, tell him."

"Erra, for what, Joe?" asked Bowman.

"Never mind the whats or the whys," shouted the bandmaster, beginning to goose-step. "Who's bandmaster here, you or me?"

Bowman could see the man wasn't himself, so away with him down to Coveney, the rag-and-bone man, for the loan of his donkey and butt, while Delury sat down and covered his ears with his hands, a picture of misery. When Bowman came back, the bandmaster gave him the key of the instrument cupboard.

"One minute," said Hegarty, the soberest of them. "Can we do this without a committee meeting?"

"Oh, we'll hold it, we'll hold it," said the bandmaster. "We're all here."

"Will I read the minutes?" asked Hegarty, who was by way of being secretary.

"Take them as read," said the bandmaster. "What's the next item on the agenda?"

"A drink," says one of the band.

"We should have a resolution or something about this," said Hegarty, shaking his head. "There could be trouble about it."

"I'm proposing it," said Shinkwin, the big drummer.

"I'm seconding it," said another.

"What?" asked Hegarty.

"Oh, whatever the bandmaster says," said Shinkwin.

"Any objections?" snaps the bandmaster. "Passed unanimously. Hurry up now, boys, or old Moon's will be shut."

With that, they scrambled downstairs with the instruments. They put them on the donkey-butt, covered them with bags and tarpaulin, and walked two by two along the footpath while a small boy drove. It was like a funeral, the speed they went at, with the rain and the darkness and the one little candle-butt burning in the lamp in front. Hegarty still went on saying he didn't like it, but no one paid much attention to him.

Old Moon, the pawnbroker in Shandon Street, thought he was having hallucinations when the whole shop filled with a brass and reed band at half past nine of a winter's night—in those days pawnshops stayed open till near midnight.

"What is it? What is it?" he snapped nervously.

"Well, Mr. Moon," said the bandmaster confidentially, resting his elbows on the counter and looking as discreet and responsible as he could, "the way it is, we want to pawn the band."

"Come on now," said Moon. "I'm a busy man. You're keeping customers out."

"But you take musical instruments, don't you?" asked the bandmaster.

"Not on the wholesale side," said Moon. "Run away now like good boys and bring me back a few of them silver watches of yours."

"But them are very valuable instruments," said the bandmaster, getting indignant.

"How much?" asked Moon.

"Ten quid," said the bandmaster, doing the Morse code on the counter.

"Five," said Moon.

"Five?" exclaimed the bandmaster, pretending to laugh but

with a sob in his voice. "Sure, the drum alone is worth more than that. Show it to him, Shinkwin," he said. "That's a beautiful drum, man. Look at the pictures on it!"

"And a hell of a lot of people are going to buy a big drum for the pictures!" said Moon.

"On the sacred word of a musician, Mr. Moon," said the band-master. "We'll release the whole lot on Saturday night. We'll want them for the practice. Be nice, Mr. Moon!" he added, start-ing to stamp. "Be nice! You can see we're in no state for argu-ment."

"Seven pound ten, so," said Moon, and not another penny would he give them if they lay down and breathed their last on him.

"One minute now," said Butty Bowman, reaching out for the money before the bandmaster could take it. "I'm treasurer of this band. How long will this last if we take it to a pub? You'll have every bummer in Irishtown on top of us inside an hour. Be said by me. We have the donkey and butt, and we'll get a couple of half-tierces and bring them back to the bandroom with us."

They did that, and when they were all in, Butty Bowman locked the bandroom door.

"Now, anyone that wants to get out can't get out," he said, "and what's more important, anyone that wants to get in can't get in, so let ye make the best of it."

Well, to make a long story short, by the following night there wasn't a ha'penny left of the seven ten, and, like Kathleen Mavourneen in the song, the grey dawn was breaking for the band.

"Boys, boys," said the bandmaster, who was shaking like an aspen leaf, "we'll have to steady up now and release the old in-struments. We have a mountain of work to do, and the other bands are practising already for St. Patrick's Day. And, as we're about it, we'll start taking the collection now."

What they collected was the sum of fourpence ha'penny.

"This won't do, boys," he said, looking grave. "That leaves us wanting seven pound nine and sevenpence ha'penny, and we want it in a hurry."

A big fling means a slow recovery, and by the week before Patrick's Day they had only five and ninepence collected.

"That means no new pieces," said the bandmaster mournfully. "And Melancholy Lane turning out in their new uniforms. We're slipping, boys, we're slipping. Tomorrow I want every man in the band collecting at the chapel gates, and if that money isn't got, bad work is what there's going to be."

To make it more solemn he had special labels printed for the collection boxes, "Great National Appeal." But the story was going the rounds, and people only laughed at them. "How much do you want for the ticket, Ned?" someone asked Hegarty. "I knew there would be bad work over this," Hegarty said mournfully. "I'm afraid our last tune is played." Some of the old supporters were very cross. "Ye'll never see a shilling of my money again," said one old gent who was a great supporter of Parnell. At the end of the day they had twenty-seven and six. The bandmaster was mortified. Naturally, he felt that it was all his fault.

"We're not slipping at all, boys," he said sadly. "We've slipped."

"Ah," said Butty Bowman, "we'll think up something yet. We'll make a house-to-house. We might be able to borrow a couple of instruments from Kilbride and play in the street like them German bands. Them fellows makes a lot of money because they play them sugary German tunes when the women are working in the house. When a woman is doing the washing is the time for getting the tears in her eyes."

"Take an oath first, then," said the bandmaster. "Not a drop of drink till we have the instruments back!"

"Not a drop," they said.

"That we might be killed stone dead."

"That we might be killed stone dead."

"Well, for the love of God, remember it," said the bandmaster.

To give them their due, they kept that promise better than ever they kept the pledge, but it did them very little good. Once people get a notion into their heads that a thing is dead, 'tis damned. Even Father Dennehy, the great priest for the bands, wouldn't give them a hand. He said they were after giving too much scandal. God rest the poor man, if he can hear the pipers' bands where he is now, he might be sorry for giving Irishtown the hard word.

On Patrick's Eve they had collected three pounds, all but a couple of pence, and away with them up to Moon's on a deputation.

"This and that, Mr. Moon," said the bandmaster with a lofty air, looking very spruce and sober in his best blue suit and a bowler hat, "we're in a rather difficult position. I know we promised to release the instruments, and we're doing our best, but circumstances are against us. If you could see your way to lend us the instruments just for the day, 'twould put great confidence in our supporters."

" 'Twould put the instruments in another pawn, you mean," said Moon with a nasty grin.

"Now, be nice, Mr. Moon!" said the bandmaster. "Be nice! We're not vagrants or robbers. We're musicians—artists—in a temporary difficulty. 'Tis common enough in the profession. We'll pay you a pound for the hire of them."

"Pay me my money and take them to hell out of this," said Moon.

"Two pounds, so," said the bandmaster. "Two pounds, and your own seven pound ten in a couple of weeks' time. What could be fairer?"

"Keeping them where they are," said Moon.

"But I tell you, if we don't put in an appearance on Patrick's Day we'll never be able to release them," said the bandmaster, beginning to get angry. "Don't treat us in this low, huxtering way. Come now, Mr. Moon, three pounds—that's every ha'penny we have and more, and we'll say a prayer for you."

"Go on to blazes out of that!" said Moon, being a Lutheran by persuasion.

"You dirty little Protestant scut!" said the bandmaster. "Hell isn't hot enough for the likes of you."

After that, Shinkwin went in, and by main persuasion got Moon to put the instruments on separate tickets. Of course, the first thing he released was his own big drum: there was feeling among the bandsmen about that, but as Shinkwin said, "What's a brass band without a big drum?" Like all big drummers, Shink-win thought he was the whole blooming band. Then they took out a trombone, a cornet, a euphonium, and two B-flat clarinets. The bandsmen were so glad to see them that they started to play then and there, and Drake, the cornet-player, gave them "The Coolin" outside the door, but the fellows whose instruments were still in prison only got hysterical. They kept rushing in, saying "Mr. Moon, Mr. Moon, throw in the old piccolo and I'll pay you on Saturday night" or "Mr. Moon, Mr. Moon, will you give us the flute if I bring you up my Sunday suit?" Even after the pawn shut, some of them remained outside, tapping at the window and calling "Mr. Moon! Hi, Mr. Moon!"

In the cold light of day, none of them could face the thought of turning out with their handful of instruments while Melancholy Lane were shaping in new uniforms, so, seeing that they couldn't play themselves, away with them in a mob to get what satisfaction they could from criticizing their neighbours. Musicians are like that as a race; very vindictive.

They got to a flight of steps where they could see and be seen. You know the way processions used to be: bands and banners and floats and drays, with Mother Erin and Brian Boru; and the National Foresters with feathers in their hats. And there was the whole band watching, and anyone that wouldn't jeer them, they'd jeer him. Not a band passed but they let a roar out of them.

That was nothing till Melancholy Lane came by playing "Defiance," a march the Irishtown fellows were very fond of. "What do you think it is?" bawls the bandmaster. "A waltz." To this day, some people say Melancholy Lane was to blame, and some say Irishtown; some say the bandmaster of Melancholy Lane gave the order "Eyes right" and some say it was pure curiosity on the part of the bandsmen, but whatever it was, there was a roar like wild beasts bursting out of a cage, and the beautiful new uniforms that Melancholy Lane took such pride in were wiping up the street.

As God did it, Butty Bowman happened to have a bit of a heavy stick with him, and with one lucky swipe he opened the head of a flute-player and made off with his flute. Then, whatever notion took him, he fell in after the procession and struck up

"Brian Boru's March" on his own. That settled it! The Irish-town fellows went mad, and they whipped off their belts and laid round them with the buckles, and one by one they started racing after Butty Bowman with cornets, piccolos, clarinets, and trombones, and the sound of each new instrument joining in gave strength to the others, while their supporters sprang up from every quarter and fell in two-deep at each side of the band to protect them.

After the procession they marched back the Stream Road, and by this time they had a force three hundred strong with them, ready to shed blood or tear iron. At the bottle-neck bend there was a cordon of policemen waiting for them. The inspector signalled them to stop. The crowd began to shout and wave sticks and the bandmaster paid no heed to the signal. The police drew their batons, but he only marched on with his head in the air. Then, about six yards from the bobbies, he swung round, marking time. As if they had it all planned, the band fell into concert formation, and before the march they were playing ended, he lifted his right hand and said: " 'Auld Lang Syne,' boys."

Then there was silence and the inspector came up to Joe.

"I have to arrest your men, Mr. Delury," he said, "and I never regretted anything more, because in my opinion ye're a great band."

"There's no reason to arrest us, inspector," said the bandmaster, growing pale. "We'll go to the Bridewell ourselves. We want no crossness. We'll finish the way we began, as artists."

And they walked to the Bridewell and surrendered without striking a blow. Of course, they were bailed out. But 'twas funny that they never got the instruments back. They never played again. That was their farewell to music all right. The St. Patrick's Temperance Society bought the instruments and the remaining tickets for a couple of pounds, and the band had one terrible night before they broke up for good.

But, sure the temperance society couldn't play for toffee. Temperance and music don't seem to go together somehow.

THE FACE OF EVIL

I could never understand all the old talk about how hard it is to be a saint. I was a saint for quite a bit of my life and I never saw anything hard in it. And when I stopped being a saint, it wasn't because the life was too hard.

I fancy it is the sissies who make it seem like that. We had quite a few of them in our school, fellows whose mothers intended them to be saints and who hadn't the nerve to be anything else. I never enjoyed the society of chaps who wouldn't commit sin for the same reason that they wouldn't dirty their new suits. That was never what sanctity meant to me, and I doubt if it is what it means to other saints. The companions I enjoyed were the tough gang down the road, and I liked going down of an evening and talking with them under the gas lamp about football matches and school, even if they did sometimes say things I wouldn't say myself. I was never one for criticizing; I had enough to do criticizing myself, and I knew they were decent chaps and didn't really mean much harm by the things they said about girls.

No, for me the main attraction of being a saint was the way it always gave you something to do. You could never say you felt time hanging on your hands. It was like having a room of your own to keep tidy; you'd scour it and put everything neatly back in its place, and within an hour or two it was beginning to look as untidy as ever. It was a full-time job that began when you woke and stopped only when you fell asleep.

I would wake in the morning, for instance, and think how

nice it was to lie in bed and congratulate myself on not having
to get up for another half hour. That was enough. Instantly a
sort of alarm-clock would go off in my mind; the mere thought
that I could enjoy half an hour's comfort would make me aware
of an alternative, and I'd begin an argument with myself. I had
a voice in me that was almost the voice of a stranger, the way it
nagged and jeered. Sometimes I could almost visualize it, and
then it took on the appearance of a fat and sneering teacher I
had some years before at school—a man I really hated. I hated
that voice. It always began in the same way, smooth and calm
and dangerous. I could see the teacher rubbing his fat hands
and smirking.

"Don't get alarmed, boy. You're in no hurry. You have another
half hour."

"I know well I have another half hour," I would reply, trying
to keep my temper. "What harm am I doing? I'm only imagining I'm down in a submarine. Is there anything wrong in that?"

"Oho, not the least in the world. I'd say there's been a heavy
frost. Just the sort of morning when there's ice in the bucket."

"And what has that to do with it?"

"Nothing, I tell you. Of course, for people like you it's easy
enough in the summer months, but the least touch of frost in the
air soon makes you feel different. I wouldn't worry trying to keep
it up. You haven't the stuff for this sort of life at all."

And gradually my own voice grew weaker as that of my tor-
mentor grew stronger, till all at once I would strip the clothes
from off myself and lie in my nightshirt, shivering and muttering: "So I haven't the stuff in me, haven't I?" Then I would go
downstairs before my parents were awake, strip, and wash in
the bucket, ice or no ice, and when Mother came down she
would cry in alarm: "Child of grace, what has you up at this
hour? Sure, 'tis only half past seven." She almost took it as a
reproach to herself, poor woman, and I couldn't tell her the reason, and even if I could have done so, I wouldn't. It was a thing
you couldn't talk about to anybody.

Then I went to Mass and enjoyed again the mystery of the
streets and lanes in the early morning; the frost which made your
feet clatter off the walls at either side of you like falling masonry,

and the different look that everything wore, as though, like yourself, it was all cold and scrubbed and new. In the winter the lights would still be burning red in the little whitewashed cottages, and in summer their walls were ablaze with sunshine so that their interiors were dimmed to shadows. Then there were the different people, all of whom recognized one another, like Mrs. MacEntee, who used to be a stewardess on the boats, and Macken, the tall postman; people who seemed ordinary enough when you met them during the day but carried something of their mystery with them at Mass, as though they, too, were reborn.

I can't pretend I was ever very good at school, but even there it was a help. I might not be clever, but I had always a secret reserve of strength to call on in the fact that I had what I wanted, and that besides it I wanted nothing. People frequently gave me things, like fountain pens or pencil-sharpeners, and I would suddenly find myself becoming attached to them and immediately know I must give them away, and then feel the richer for it. Even without throwing my weight around, I could help and protect kids younger than myself and yet not become involved in their quarrels. Not to become involved, to remain detached— that was the great thing; to care for things and for people, yet not to care for them so much that your happiness became dependent on them.

It was like no other hobby, because you never really got the better of yourself, and all at once you would suddenly find yourself reverting to childish attitudes; flaring up in a wax with some fellow, or sulking when Mother asked you to go for a message, and then it all came back; the nagging of the infernal alarm-clock, which grew louder with every moment until it incarnated as a smooth, fat, jeering face.

"Now, that's the first time you've behaved sensibly for months, boy. That was the right way to behave to your mother."

"Well, it *was* the right way. Why can't she let me alone once in a while? I only want to read. I suppose I'm entitled to a bit of peace some time?"

"Ah, of course you are, my dear fellow. Isn't that what I'm saying? Go on with your book! Imagine you're a cowboy, riding to the rescue of a beautiful girl in a cabin in the woods, and let that silly woman go for the messages herself. She probably hasn't long to live anyway, and when she dies you'll be able to do all the weeping you like."

And suddenly tears of exasperation would come to my eyes and I'd heave the story-book to the other side of the room and shout back at the voice that gave me no rest: "Cripes, I might as well be dead and buried. I have no blooming life." After that I would apologize to Mother (who, poor woman, was more embarrassed than anything else and assured me that it was all her fault), go on the message, and write another tick in my notebook against the heading of "Bad Temper" so as to be able to confess it to Father O'Regan when I went to Confession on Saturday. Not that he was ever severe with me, no matter what I did; he thought I was the last word in holiness, and was always asking me to pray for some special intention of his own. And though I was depressed, I never lost interest, for no matter what I did, I could scarcely ever reduce the total of times I had to tick off that item in my notebook.

Oh, I don't pretend it was any joke, but it did give me the feeling that my life had some meaning; that inside me I had a real source of strength; that there was nothing I could not do without and yet remain sweet, self-sufficient, and content. Sometimes, too, there was the feeling of something more than mere content, as though my body were transparent, like a window, and light shone through it as well as on it, onto the road, the houses, and the playing children, as though it were I who was shining on them, and tears of happiness would come into my eyes, and I hurled myself among the playing children just to forget it.

But, as I say, I had no inclination to mix with other kids who might be saints as well. The fellow who really fascinated me was a policeman's son named Dalton, who was easily the most vicious kid in the locality. The Daltons lived on the terrace above ours. Mrs. Dalton was dead; there was a younger brother called Stevie who was next door to an imbecile, and there was something about that kid's cheerful grin that was even more frightening than the malice on Charlie's broad face. Their father was a tall melancholy man with a big black moustache, and the nearest thing imaginable to one of the Keystone cops. Everyone was sorry for his loss in his wife, but you knew that if it hadn't been that, it would have been something else—maybe the fact that he hadn't lost her. Charlie was only an additional grief. He was always getting into trouble, stealing and running away from home; and only his father's being a policeman prevented his being sent to an industrial school. One of my most vivid recollections is that of Charlie's education. I'd hear a shriek, and there would be Mr. Dalton dragging Charlie along the pavement to school and, whenever the names his son called him grew a little more obscene than usual, pausing to give Charlie a good going-over with the belt which he carried loose in his hand. It is an exceptional father who can do this without getting some pleasure out of it, but Mr. Dalton looked as though even it were an additional burden. Charlie's screams could always fetch me out.

"What is it?" Mother would cry after me.

"Ah, nothing. Only Charlie Dalton again."

"Come in! Come in!"

"I won't be seen."

"Come in, I say. 'Tis never right."

And even when Charlie uttered the most atrocious indecencies, she only joined her hands as if in prayer and muttered "The poor child! The poor unfortunate child!" I never could understand the way she felt about Charlie. He wouldn't have been Charlie if it hadn't been for the leatherings and the threats of the industrial school.

Looking back on it, the funniest thing is that I seemed to be the only fellow on the road he didn't hate. They were all terrified of him, and some of the kids would go a mile to avoid him. He was completely unclassed: being a policeman's son, he should have been way up the social scale, but he hated the respectable kids worse than the others. When we stood under the gas lamp at night and saw him coming up the road, everybody fell silent. He looked suspiciously at the group, ready to spring at anyone's throat if he saw the shadow of offence; ready even when there wasn't a shadow. He fought like an animal, by instinct, without judgment, and without ever reckoning the odds, and he was terribly strong. He wasn't clever; several of the older chaps could beat him to a frazzle when it was merely a question of boxing or wrestling, but it never was that with Dalton. He was out for blood and usually got it. Yet he was never that way with me. We weren't friends. All that ever happened when we passed each other was that I smiled at him and got a cold, cagey nod in return. Sometimes we stopped and exchanged a few words, but it was an ordeal because we never had anything to say to each other.

It was like the signalling of ships, or, more accurately, the courtesies of great powers. I tried, like Mother, to be sorry for him in having no proper home, and getting all those leatherings, but the feeling that came uppermost in me was never pity but respect—respect for a fellow who had done all the things I would never do: stolen money, stolen bicycles, run away from home, slept with tramps and criminals in barns and doss-houses, and ridden without a ticket on trains and on buses. It filled my imagination. I have a vivid recollection of one summer morning when I was going up the hill to Mass. Just as I reached the top and saw the low, sandstone church perched high up ahead of me, he poked his bare head round the corner of a lane to see who was coming. It startled me. He was standing with his back to the gable of a house; his face was dirty and strained; it was broad and lined, and the eyes were very small, furtive and flickering, and sometimes a sort of spasm would come over them and they flickered madly for half a minute on end.

"Hullo, Charlie," I said. "Where were you?"

"Out," he replied shortly.

"All night?" I asked in astonishment.

"Yeh," he replied with a nod.

"What are you doing now?"

He gave a short, bitter laugh.

"Waiting till my old bastard of a father goes out to work and I can go home."

His eyes flickered again, and self-consciously he drew his hand across them as though pretending they were tired.

"I'll be late for Mass," I said uneasily. "So long."

"So long."

That was all, but all the time at Mass, among the flowers and the candles, watching the beautiful, sad old face of Mrs. Mac-Entee and the plump, smooth, handsome face of Macken, the postman, I was haunted by the image of that other face, wild and furtive and dirty, peering round a corner like an animal looking from its burrow. When I came out, the morning was brilliant over the valley below me; the air was punctuated with bugle calls from the cliff where the barrack stood, and Charlie Dalton was gone. No, it wasn't pity I felt for him. It wasn't even respect. It was almost like envy.

Then, one Saturday evening, an incident occurred which changed my attitude to him; indeed, changed my attitude to myself, though it wasn't until long after that I realized it. I was on my way to Confession, preparatory to Communion next morning. I always went to Confession at the parish church in town where Father O'Regan was. As I passed the tramway terminus at the Cross, I saw Charlie sitting on the low wall above the Protestant church, furtively smoking the butt-end of a cigarette which somebody had dropped, getting on the tram. Another tram arrived as I reached the Cross, and a number of people alighted and went off in different directions. I crossed the road to Charlie and he gave me his most distant nod.

"Hullo."

"Hullo, Cha. Waiting for somebody?"

"No. Where are you off to?"

"Confession."

"Huh." He inhaled the cigarette butt deeply and then tossed it over his shoulder into the sunken road beneath without looking where it alighted. "You go a lot."

"Every week," I said modestly.

"Jesus!" he said with a short laugh. "I wasn't there for twelve months."

I shrugged my shoulders. As I say, I never went in much for criticizing others, and anyway Charlie wouldn't have been Charlie if he had gone to Confession every week.

"Why do you go so often?" he asked challengingly.

"Oh, I don't know," I said doubtfully. "I suppose it keeps you out of harm's way."

"But you don't do any harm," he growled, just as though he were defending me against someone who had been attacking me.

"Ah, we all do harm."

"But, Jesus Christ, you don't do anything," he said almost angrily, and his eyes flickered again in that curious nervous spasm, and almost as if they put him into a rage, he drove his knuckles into them.

"We all do things," I said. "Different things."

"Well, what do you do?"

"I lose my temper a lot," I admitted.

"Jesus!" he said again, and rolled his eyes.

"It's a sin just the same," I said obstinately.

"A sin? Losing your temper? Jesus, I want to kill people. I want to kill my bloody old father, for one. I will too, one of those days. Take a knife to him."

"I know, I know," I said, at a loss to explain what I meant. "But that's just the same thing as me."

I wished to God I could talk better. It wasn't any missionary zeal. I was excited because for the first time I knew that Charlie felt about me exactly as I felt about him, with a sort of envy, and I wanted to explain to him that he didn't have to envy me, and that he could be as much a saint as I was just as I could be as much a sinner as he was. I wanted to explain that it wasn't a matter of tuppence ha'penny worth of sanctity as opposed to tuppence worth that made the difference, that it wasn't what you did but what you lost by doing it that mattered. The whole Cross had become a place of mystery—the grey light, drained of warmth; the trees hanging over the old crumbling walls; the tram, shaking like a boat when someone mounted it. It was the way I sometimes felt afterwards with a girl, as though everything about you melted and fused and became one with a central mystery.

"But when what you do isn't any harm?" he repeated angrily with that flickering of the eyes I had almost come to dread.

"Look, Cha," I said, "you can't say a thing isn't any harm. Everything is harm. It might be losing my temper with me and murder with you, like you say, but it would only come to the same thing. If I show you something, will you promise not to tell?"

"Why would I tell?"

"But promise."

"Oh, all right."

Then I took out my little notebook and showed it to him. It was extraordinary, and I knew it was extraordinary. I found myself, sitting on that wall, showing a notebook I wouldn't have shown to anyone else in the world to Charlie Dalton, a fellow any kid on the road would go a long way to avoid, and yet I had the feeling that he would understand it as no one else would do. My whole life was there, under different headings—Disobedience, Bad Temper, Bad Thoughts, Selfishness, and Laziness—and he looked through it quietly, studying the ticks I had placed against each count.

"You see," I said, "you talk about your father, but look at all the things I do against my mother. I know she's a good mother, but if she's sick or if she can't walk fast when I'm in town with her, I get mad just as you do. It doesn't matter what sort of mother or father you have. It's what you do to yourself when you do things like that."

"What do you do to yourself?" he asked quietly.

"It's hard to explain. It's only a sort of peace you have inside yourself. And you can't be just good, no matter how hard you try. You can only do your best, and if you do your best you feel peaceful inside. It's like when I miss Mass of a morning. Things mightn't be any harder on me that day than any other day, but I'm not as well able to stand up to them. It makes things a bit different for the rest of the day. You don't mind it so much if you get a hammering. You know there's something else in the world besides the hammering."

I knew it was a feeble description of what morning Mass really meant to me, the feeling of strangeness which lasted throughout the whole day and reduced reality to its real proportions, but it was the best I could do. I hated leaving him.

"I'll be late for Confession," I said regretfully, getting off the wall.

"I'll go down a bit of the way with you," he said, giving a last

glance at my notebook and handing it back to me. I knew he
was being tempted to come to Confession along with me, but
my pleasure had nothing to do with that. As I say, I never had
any missionary zeal. It was the pleasure of understanding rather
than that of conversion.

He came down the steps to the church with me and we went
in together.

"I'll wait here for you," he whispered, and sat in one of the
back pews.

It was dark there; there were just a couple of small, unshaded
lights in the aisles above the confessionals. There was a crowd of
old women outside Father O'Regan's box, so I knew I had a
long time to wait. Old women never got done with their confessions. For the first time I felt it long, but when my turn came
it was all over in a couple of minutes: the usual "Bless you, my
child. Say a prayer for me, won't you?" When I came out, I saw
Charlie Dalton sitting among the old women outside the con-
fessional, waiting to go in. He looked very awkward and angry,
his legs wide and his hands hanging between them. I felt very
happy about it in a quiet way, and when I said my penance I
said a special prayer for him.

It struck me that he was a long time inside, and I began to
grow worried. Then he came out, and I saw by his face that it
was no good. It was the expression of someone who is saying to
himself with a sort of evil triumph: "There, I told you what it
was like."

"It's all right," he whispered, giving his belt a hitch. "You
go home."

"I'll wait for you," I said.

"I'll be a good while."

I knew then Father O'Regan had given him a heavy penance,
and my heart sank.

"It doesn't matter," I said. "I'll wait."

And it was only long afterwards that it occurred to me that
I might have taken one of the major decisions of my life without
being aware of it. I sat at the back of the church in the dusk and
waited for him. He was kneeling up in front, before the altar,
and I knew it was no good. At first I was too stunned to feel. All

I knew was that my happiness had all gone. I admired Father
O'Regan; I knew that Charlie must have done things that I
couldn't even imagine—terrible things—but the resentment grew
in me. What right had Father O'Regan or anyone to treat him
like that? Because he was down, people couldn't help wanting
to crush him further. For the first time in my life I knew real
temptation. I wanted to go with Charlie and share his fate. For
the first time I realized that the life before me would have com-
plexities of emotion which I couldn't even imagine.

The following week he ran away from home again, took a
bicycle, broke into a shop to steal cigarettes, and, after being arrested seventy-five miles from Cork in a little village on the
coast, was sent to an industrial school.

MASCULINE PROTEST

FOR months things had been getting worse between Mother and
me. At the time I was twelve, and we were living in Boharna, a
small town twenty miles from the city—Father, Mother, Martha,
and I. Father worked in the County Council and we didn't see
much of him. I suppose that threw me more on Mother, but I
could be perfectly happy sitting with her all day if only she let
me. She didn't, though. She was always inventing excuses to get
rid of me, even giving me money to go to the pictures, which she
knew Father didn't like because I wasn't very bright at school
and he thought the pictures were bad for me.

I blamed a lot of it on Martha at first. Martha was sly, and she
was always trying to get inside me with Mother. She was always
saving, whereas I always found money burned a hole in my

pocket, and it was only to spite her that I kept a savings bank at all. As well as that, she told Mother about all the scrapes I got into. They weren't what you'd really call scrapes. It was just that we had a gang in our neighbourhood, which was the classy one of the town, and we were always having battles with the slummy kids from the other side of town who wanted to play in our neighbourhood. I was the Chief Gang Leader, and it was my job to keep them from expanding beyond their own frontiers.

Martha let on not to understand why I should be Chief Gang Leader. She let on not to know why we didn't want the slum kids overrunning our locality. Though she knew better than to tell Mother when I made Viking raids on the housekeeping money, she was always at me in a low, blood-curdling voice, following me round like a witch. "You'll be caught yet, Denis Halligan. You'll be caught. The police will be after you. You took three shillings out of Mummy's purse. God sees you!" Sometimes she drove me so wild that I went mad and twisted her arm or pulled her hair, and she went off screeching, and I got a licking.

I had managed to kid myself into the belief that one day Mother would understand; one day she would wake up and see that the affection of Dad and Martha was insincere; that the two of them had long ago ganged up against her, and that I, the black sheep, was the one who really loved her.

This revelation was due to take place in rather unusual circumstances. We were all to be stranded in some dangerous desert, and Mother, with her ankle broken, would tell us to leave her to her fate, the way they did in story-books. Dad and Martha, of course, would leave her, with only a pretence of concern, but I, in my casual way, would simply fold my hands about my knees and ask listlessly: "What use is life to me without you?" Nothing more; I was against any false drama, any raising of the voice. I had never been one for high-flown expressions like Martha: just the lift of the shoulder, the way I pulled a grass-blade to chew (it needn't be a desert), and Mother would realize at last that though I wasn't demonstrative—just a plain, rough, willing chap—I really had a heart of gold.

The trouble about Mother was that she had a genius for subjecting hearts of gold to intolerable strain. It wasn't that she was actively unkind, for she thought far too much of the impression she wanted to make to be anything like that. It was just that she didn't care a damn. She was always away from home. She visited friends in Galway, Dublin, Birr, and Athlone, and all we ever got to see of her was the flurry between one foray and the next, while she was packing and unpacking.

Things came to a head when she told me she wouldn't be at home for my birthday. At the same time, always conscientious, she had arranged a very nice treat for Martha and me. But the treat wasn't the same thing that I had been planning, when I proposed to bring a couple of fellows along and show Mother off to them, and I began to bawl. The trouble was that the moment I did, I seemed to have no reasons on my side. It was always like that with Mother; she invariably had all the reasons on her side, and made you feel contrary and a pig, but that was worse instead of better. You felt then that she was taking advantage of you. I sobbed and stamped and asked why she hadn't done that to Martha and why she was doing it to me. She looked at me coldly and said I was a pretty picture and that I had no manliness. Of course, I saw she was in the right about that too, and that there was no excuse for a fellow of my age complaining against not being treated like his younger sister, and that only made me madder still.

"Go on!" I screamed. "Who's trying to stop you? All you want is people to admire you."

I knew when I had said it that it was awful, and expected her to give me a clout, but she only drew herself up, looking twice as dignified and beautiful.

"That is a contemptible remark, Denis," she said in a biting tone. "It's one I wouldn't have expected even from you."

The way she said it made me feel like the scum of the earth. And then she went off for the evening in a car with the Clarkes, leaving Martha and me alone. Martha looked at me, half in pity, half in amusement. She was never really disappointed in Mother, because she expected less of her. Martha was born sly.

"What did I tell you?" she said, though she hadn't told me anything.

"Go on!" I said in a thick voice. "You sucker!" Then I went

upstairs and bawled and used all the dirty words I knew. I knew now it was all over between Mother and me; that no circumstances would ever occur which would show how much I loved her, because after what had happened I could not live in the same house with her again. For quite a while I thought about suicide, but I put that on one side, because the only way I could contemplate committing suicide was by shooting, and my air pistol was not strong enough for that. I took out my post-office book. I had four pounds fifteen in the bank. As I've said, it was purely out of spite against Martha, but that made no difference now. It was enough to keep me for a month or so till I found some corner where people wanted me; a plain rough-spoken chap who only needed a little affection. I was afraid of nothing in the way of work. I was strong and energetic. At the worst, I could always make for Dublin, where my grandfather and Auntie May lived. I knew they would be glad to help me, because they thought that Dad had married the wrong woman and never pretended to like Mother. When Mother had told me this I was furious, but now I saw that they were probably cleverer than I was. It would give me great satisfaction to reach their door and tell Auntie May in my plain straightforward way: "You were right and I was wrong." For the last time I looked round my bedroom and burst into fresh tears. There is something heart-rending about leaving for the last time a place where you have spent so much of your life. Then, trying to steady myself, I grabbed a little holy picture from the mantelpiece and a favourite story-book from the bookshelf and ran downstairs. Martha heard me taking out my bike and came to see. It had a dynamo lamp and a three-speed gear; a smashing bike!

"Where are you off to?" she asked.

"Never mind!" I said as I cycled off.

I had no particular feelings about seeing Martha for the last time.

Then I had my first shock, because as I cycled into Main Street I saw that all the shops were shuttered for the weekly half-holiday and I knew the post office would be shut too and I could not draw out my savings. It was the first time I felt what people so often feel in after life, that Fate has made a plaything of you. Why should I have had my final quarrel with Mother on the one day in the week when I could not get away from her? If that wasn't Fate, what was? And I knew my own weakness of character better than anyone. I knew that if I put it off until next day, the sight of Mother would be sufficient to set me servilely seeking for pardon. Even setting off across Ireland without a penny would be better than that.

Then I had what I thought was an inspiration. The city was only twenty miles away, and the General Post Office was bound to be open. I had calculated my time to and from school at twelve miles an hour; even allowing for the distance, it wouldn't take me more than two hours. As well as that, I had been to the city for the Christmas shopping, so I knew the look of it. I could get my money and stay in a hotel or have tea and then set off for Dublin. I liked that idea. Cycling all the way up through Ireland in the dark, through sleeping towns and villages; seeing the dawn break over Dublin as I cycled down the slopes of the Dublin mountains; arriving at Auntie May's door in the Shelbourne Road when she was lighting the fire—that would be smashing. I could imagine how she would greet me—"Child of grace, where did you come from?" "Ah, just cycled." My natural modesty always came out in those day-dreams of mind, for I never, under any circumstances, made a fuss. Absolutely smashing!

All the same, it was no joke, a trip like that. I cycled slowly and undecidedly out the familiar main road where we walked on Sunday, past the little suburban houses. It was queer how hard it was to break away from places and people and things you knew. I thought of letting it go and of doing the best I could to patch it up with Mother. I thought of the gang and at that a real lump rose in my throat. Tomorrow night, when my absence was noticed, there would be a new Chief Gang Leader; somebody like Eddie Humphreys who would be so prim and cautious that he would be afraid to engage the enemy which threatened us on every side. In that moment of weakness I nearly turned back. At the same moment it brought me renewed decision, for I knew that I had not been chosen Chief Gang Leader because I was a little sissy like Eddie Humphreys but because I was afraid of nothing.

At one moment my feet had nearly stopped pedalling; at the next I was pedalling for all I was worth. It was as sudden as that, like the moment when you find yourself out of your depth and two inclinations struggle in you—to swim like hell back to the shallows or strike out boldly for the other side. Up to that I had thought mainly of what was behind me; now I thought only of what was ahead of me, and it was frightening enough. I was aware of great distances, of big cloud masses on the horizon, of the fragility of my tires compared with the rough surface of the road, and I thought only of the two-hour journey ahead of me. The romantic picture of myself cycling across Ireland in the dark disappeared. I should be quite content to get the first stage over me.

For the last ten miles I wasn't even tempted to look at the scenery. I was doubled over the handlebars. Things just happened; the road bent away under me; wide green rivers rose up and slipped away again under me, castles soared from the roadside with great arches blocked out in masses of shadow.

Then at last the little rocky fields closed behind me like a book, and the blessed electric-light poles escorted me up the last hill, and I floated proudly down between comfortable villas with long gardens till I reached the bridge. The city was stretched out on the other side of the river, shining in the evening light, and my heart rose at the thought that I had at least shown Mother whether or not I had manliness. I dismounted from my bicycle and pushed it along the Main Street, looking at the shops. They were far more interesting than the shops at home, and the people looked better too.

I found the post office in a side street and went up to the counter with my savings-bank book.

"I want to draw out my money," I said.

The clerk looked at the clock.

"You can't do that, sonny," he said. 'The savings-bank counter is shut."

"When will it open again?" I asked.

"Not till tomorrow. Any time after nine."

"But can't I get it now?"

"No. The clerk is gone home now."

I slouched out of the post office with despair in my heart. I took my bicycle and pushed it wearily back to the Main Street. The crowds were still going by, but now it looked long and wide and lonesome, for I had no money and I didn't know a soul. Without a meal and a rest, I could not even set out for Dublin, if I had the heart, which I knew I hadn't. Nor could I even return home, for it was already late and I was dropping with weariness. One side of the Main Street was in shadow; the shadow seemed to spread with extraordinary rapidity, and you felt that the city was being quenched as with snuffers.

It was only then that I thought of Father. It was funny that I had not thought of him before, even when thinking of Grand-father and Auntie May. I had thought of these as allies against Mother, but I hadn't even considered him as an ally. Now as I thought of him, everything about him seemed different. It wasn't only the hunger and panic. It was something new for me. It was almost love. With fresh energy I pushed my bicycle back to the post office, left it outside the door where I could see it, and went up to the clerk I had already spoken to.

"Could I make a telephone call?" I asked.

"You could to be sure," he said. "Have you the money?"

"No, sir."

"Well, you can't make a call without the money. Where is it to?"

"Boharna," I said.

At once his face took on a severe expression.

"That's one and threepence," he said.

"And I can't ring unless I have the money?"

"Begor, you can't. I couldn't ring myself without that."

I went out and took my bicycle again. This time I could see no way out. I dawdled along the street, leaving my bicycle by the curb and gazing in shop windows. In one I found a mirror in which I could see myself full-length. I looked old and heart-broken. It was just like a picture of a child without a home, and I blinked away my tears.

Then, as I approached a public-house, I saw a barman in shirt sleeves standing by the door. I remembered that I had seen him already on my way down and that he had looked at me. He nodded and smiled and I stopped. I was glad of anyone making a friendly gesture in that strange place.

"Are you waiting for someone?" he asked.

"No," I said. "I wanted to make a phone call."

"You're not from these parts?"

"No," I said. "I'm from Boharna."

"Are you, begor?" he said. "Was it on the bus you came?"

"No," I replied modestly. "I biked it."

"Biked it?"

"Yes."

"That's a hell of a distance," he said.

"It is long," I agreed.

"What did you come all that way for?" he asked in surprise.

"Ah, I was running away from home," I said despondently.

"You were what?" he asked in astonishment. "You're not serious."

"But I am," I said, very close to tears. "I did my best, but then I couldn't stick it any longer and I cleared out." I turned my head away because this time I was really crying.

"Oh, begor, I know what 'tis like," he said in a friendlier tone. "I did it myself."

"Did you?" I asked eagerly, forgetting my grief. This, I felt, was the very man I wanted to meet.

"Ah, indeed I did. I did it three times what's more. By that time they were getting fed up with me. Anyway, they say practice makes perfect. Tell me, is it your old fellow?"

"No," I said with a sigh. "My mother."

"Ah, do you tell me so? That's worse again. 'Tis bad enough to have the old man at you, but 'tis the devil entirely when the mother is against you. What are you going to do now?"

"I don't know," I said. "I wanted to get to Dublin, but the savings bank is shut, and all my money is in it."

"That's tough luck. Sure, you can't get anywhere without money. I'm afraid you'll have to go back and put up with it for another while."

"But I can't," I said. " 'Tis twenty miles."

" 'Tis all of that, begor. You couldn't go on the bus?"

"I can't. I haven't the money. That's what I asked them in the post office, to let me ring up Daddy, but they wouldn't."

"Where's your daddy?" he asked, and when I told him: "Ah, we'll try and get him for you anyway. Come on in."

There was a phone in the corner, and he rang up and asked for Daddy. Then he gave me a big smile and handed me the receiver. I heard Daddy's voice and I nearly wept with delight.

"Hullo, son," he said in astonishment. "Where on earth are you?"

"In the city, Daddy," I said modestly—even then I couldn't bring myself to make a lot of it, the way another fellow would.

"The city?" he repeated incredulously. "What took you there?"

"I ran away from home, Dad," I said, trying to make it sound as casual as possible.

"Oh!" he exclaimed and there was a moment's pause. I was afraid he was going to get angry, but his tone remained the same. "Had a row?"

"Yes, Dad."

"And how did you get there?"

"On the bike."

"All the way? But you must be dead."

"Just a bit tired," I said modestly.

"Tell me, did you even get a meal?"

"No, Dad. The savings bank was shut."

"Ah, blazes!" he said softly. "Of course, it's the half day. And what are you going to do now?"

"I don't know, Dad. I thought you might tell me."

"Well, what about coming home?" he said, beginning to laugh.

"I don't mind, Dad. Whatever you say."

"Hold on now till I see what the buses are like. . . . Hullo! You can get one in forty minutes' time—seven ten. Tell the conductor I'll be meeting you and I'll pay your fare. Will that be all right?"

"That's grand, Dad," I said, feeling that the world was almost right again.

When I finished, the barman was waiting for me with his coat on. He had got another man to look after the bar for him.

"Now, you'd better come and have a cup of tea with me before your bus goes," he said. "The old bike will be safe outside."

He took me to a café, and I ate cake after cake and drank tea and he told me about how he'd run away himself. You could see he was a real hard case, worse even than I was. The first time, he'd pinched a bicycle and cycled all the way to Dublin, sleeping in barns and deserted cottages. The police had brought him home and his father had belted hell out of him. They caught him again the second time, but the third time he'd joined the army and not returned home for years.

He put me and my bicycle on the bus and paid my fare. He made me promise to tell Dad that he'd done it and that Dad owed me the money. He said in this world you had to stand up for your rights. He was a rough chap, but you could see he had a good heart. It struck me that maybe only rough chaps had hearts as good as that.

Dad was waiting for me at the bus stop, and he looked at me and laughed.

"Well, the gouger!" he said. "Who ever would think that the son of a good-living, upright man like me would turn into a common tramp."

All the same I could see he was pleased, and as he pushed my bike down the street he made me tell him all about my experiences. He laughed over the barman and promised to give me the fare. Then, seeing him so friendly, I asked the question that had been on my mind the whole way back on the bus.

"Mummy back yet, Dad?"

"No, son," he said. "Not yet. She probably won't be in till late."

What I was really asking him, of course, was "Does she know?" and now I was torn by the desire to ask him not to tell her, but it choked me. It would have seemed too much like trying to gang up against her. But he seemed to know what I was thinking, for he added with a sort of careful casualness that he had sent Martha to the pictures. I guessed that that was to get her out of the way so that she couldn't bring the story to Mother, and when we had supper together and washed up afterwards, I knew I was right.

Mother came in before we went to bed, and Father talked to her just as though nothing had happened. He was a little bit more forthcoming than usual, but that was the only indication he gave, and I was fascinated, watching him create an understanding between us. It was an understanding in more ways than one, because it dawned on me gradually that, like myself and the barman, Dad too had once run away from home, and for some reason—perhaps because the bank was shut or because he was hungry, tired, and lonely—he had come back. People mostly came back, but their protest remained to distinguish them from all the others who had never run away. It was the real sign of their manhood.

I never ran away after that. I never felt I needed to.

THE MAN OF THE HOUSE

As a kid I was as good as gold so long as I could concentrate. Concentration, that was always my weakness, in school and everywhere else. Once I was diverted from whatever I was doing, I was lost.

It was like that when the mother got ill. I remember it well; how I waked that morning and heard the strange cough in the kitchen below. From that very moment I knew something was wrong. I dressed and went down. She was sitting in a little wickerwork chair before the fire, holding her side. She had made an attempt to light the fire but it had gone against her.

"What's wrong, Mum?" I asked.

"The sticks were wet and the fire started me coughing," she

said, trying to smile, though I could see she was doubled up with pain.

"I'll light the fire and you go back to bed," I said.

"Ah, how can I, child?" she said. "Sure, I have to go to work."

"You couldn't work like that," I said. "Go on up to bed and I'll bring up your breakfast."

It's funny about women, the way they'll take orders from anything in trousers, even if 'tis only ten.

"If you could make a cup of tea for yourself, I'd be all right in an hour or so," she said, and shuffled feebly upstairs. I went with her, supporting her arm, and when she reached the bed she collapsed. I knew then she must be feeling bad. I got more sticks—she was so economical that she never used enough—and I soon had the fire roaring and the kettle on. I made her toast as well; I was always a great believer in buttered toast.

I thought she looked at the cup of tea rather doubtfully.

"Is that all right?" I asked.

"You wouldn't have a sup of boiling water left?" she asked.

" 'Tis too strong," I agreed, with a trace of disappointment I tried to keep out of my voice. "I'll pour half it away. I can never remember about tea."

"I hope you won't be late for school," she said anxiously.

"I'm not going to school," I said. "I'll get you your tea now and do the messages afterwards."

She didn't say a word about my not going to school. It was just as I said; orders were all she wanted. I washed up the breakfast things, then I washed myself and went up to her with the shopping basket, a piece of paper, and a lead pencil.

"I'll do the messages if you'll write them down," I said. "I suppose I'll go to Mrs. Slattery first?"

"Tell her I'll be in tomorrow without fail."

"Write down Mrs. Slattery," I said firmly. "Would I get the doctor?"

"Indeed, you'll do nothing of the kind," Mother said anxiously. "He'd only want to send me to hospital. They're all alike. You could ask the chemist to give you a good strong cough bottle."

"Write it down," I said, remembering my own weakness. "If I

haven't it written down I might forget it. And put 'strong' in big letters. What will I get for the dinner? Eggs?"

That was really only a bit of swank, because eggs were the one thing I could cook, but the mother told me to get sausages as well in case she was able to get up.

It was a lovely sunny morning. I called first on Mrs. Slattery, whom my mother worked for, to tell her she wouldn't be in. Mrs. Slattery was a woman I didn't like much. She had a big broad face that needed big broad features, but all she had was narrow eyes and a thin pointed nose that seemed to be all lost in the breadth of her face.

"She said she'll try to get in tomorrow, but I don't know will I let her get up," I said.

"I wouldn't if she wasn't well, Gus," she said, and she gave me a penny.

I went away feeling very elevated. I had always known a fellow could have his troubles, but if he faced them manfully, he could get advantages out of them as well. There was the school, for instance. I stood opposite it for a full ten minutes, staring. The schoolhouse and the sloping yard were like a picture, except for the chorus of poor sufferers through the open windows, and a glimpse of Danny Delaney's bald pate as he did sentry-go before the front door with his cane wriggling like a tail behind his back. It was nice too to be chatting to the fellows in the shops and telling them about the mother's cough. I made it out a bit worse to make a good story of it, but I had a secret hope that when I got home she'd be up so that we could have sausages for dinner. I hated boiled eggs, and anyway I was already beginning to feel the strain of my responsibilities.

But when I got home it was to find Minnie Ryan with her. Minnie was a middle-aged woman, gossipy and pious, but very knowledgeable.

"How are you feeling now, Mum?" I asked.

"I'm miles better," she said with a smile.

"She won't be able to get up today, though," Minnie said firmly.

"I'll pour you out your cough bottle so, and make you a cup of tea," I said, concealing my disappointment.

"Wisha, I'll do that for you, child," said Minnie, getting up.

"Ah, you needn't mind, Miss Ryan," I said without fuss. "I can manage all right."

"Isn't he great?" I heard her say in a low wondering voice as I went downstairs.

"Minnie," whispered my mother, "he's the best anyone ever reared."

"Why, then, there aren't many like him," Minnie said gloomily. "The most of the children that's going now are more like savages than Christians."

In the afternoon my mother wanted me to go out and play, but I wouldn't go far. I remembered my own weakness. I knew if once I went a certain distance I should drift towards the Glen, with the barrack drill-field perched on a cliff above it; the rifle range below, and below that again the mill-pond and mill-stream running through a wooded gorge—the Rockies, Himalayas, or Highlands according to your mood. Concentration; that was what I had to practise. One slip and I should be among those children that Minnie Ryan disapproved of, who were more like savages than Christians.

Evening came; the street-lamps were lit and the paper-boy went crying up the road. I bought a paper, lit the lamp in the kitchen and the candle in the bedroom, and read out the police-court news to my mother. I knew it was the piece she liked best, all about people being picked up drunk out of the channels. I wasn't very quick about it because I was only at words of one syllable, but she didn't seem to mind.

Later Minnie Ryan came again, and as she left I went to the door with her. She looked grave.

"If she isn't better in the morning I think I'd get a doctor to her, Gus," she said.

"Why?" I asked in alarm. "Would you say she's worse?"

"Ah, no," she said, giving her old shawl a tug, "only I'd be frightened of the old pneumonia."

"But wouldn't he send her to hospital, Miss Ryan?"

"Ah, he might and he mightn't. Anyway, he could give her a good bottle. But even if he did, God between us and all harm, wouldn't it be better than neglecting it? . . . If you had a drop of whisky you could give it to her hot with a squeeze of lemon."

"I'll get it," I said at once.

Mother didn't want the whisky; she said it cost too much; but I knew it would cost less than hospital and all the rest of it, so I wouldn't be put off.

I had never been in a public-house before and the crowd inside frightened me.

"Hullo, my old flower," said one tall man, grinning at me diabolically. "It must be ten years since I saw you last. One minute now—wasn't it in South Africa?"

My pal, Bob Connell, boasted to me once how he asked a drunk man for a halfcrown and the man gave it to him. I was always trying to work up courage to do the same, but even then I hadn't the nerve.

"It was not," I said. "I want a half glass of whisky for my mother."

"Oh, the thundering ruffian!" said the man, clapping his hands. "Pretending 'tis for his mother, and he the most notorious boozer in Capetown."

"I am not," I said on the verge of tears. "And 'tis for my mother. She's sick."

"Leave the child alone, Johnny," the barmaid said. "Don't you hear him say his mother is sick?"

Mother fell asleep after drinking the hot whisky, but I couldn't rest. I was wondering how the man in the public-house could have thought I was in South Africa, and blaming myself a lot for not asking him for the halfcrown. A halfcrown would come in very handy if the mother was really sick. When I did fall asleep I was wakened again by her coughing, and when I went in, she was rambling in her speech. It frightened me more than anything that she didn't recognize me.

When next morning, in spite of the whisky, she was no better, the disappointment was really terrible. After I had given her her breakfast I went to see Minnie Ryan.

"I'd get the doctor at once," she said. "I'll go and stop with her while you're out."

To get a doctor I had first to go to the house of an undertaker who was a Poor Law guardian to get a ticket to show we couldn't pay, and afterwards to the dispensary. Then I had to rush back, get the house ready, and prepare a basin of water, soap, and a towel for the doctor to wash his hands.

He didn't come till after dinner. He was a fat, slow-moving, loud-voiced man with a grey moustache and, like all the drunks of the medical profession, supposed to be "the cleverest man in Cork if only he'd mind himself." From the way he looked, he hadn't been minding himself much that morning.

"How are you going to get this now?" he growled, sitting on the edge of the bed with his prescription pad on his knee. "The only place open is the North Dispensary."

"I'll go, doctor," I said at once.

" 'Tis a long way," he said doubtfully. "Would you know where it is?"

"I'll find it," I said confidently.

"Isn't he a great help to you?" he said to the mother.

"The best in the world, doctor," she sighed with a long look at me. "A daughter couldn't be better to me."

"That's right," he told me. "Look after your mother while you can. She'll be the best for you in the long run. . . . We don't mind them when we have them," he added to Mother, "and then we spend the rest of our lives regretting them."

I didn't think myself he could be a very good doctor, because, after all my trouble, he never washed his hands, but I was prepared to overlook that since he said nothing about the hospital.

The road to the dispensary led uphill through a thickly populated poor locality as far as the barrack, which was perched on the hilltop, and then it descended between high walls till it suddenly almost disappeared over the edge of the hill in a stony pathway flanked on the right-hand side by red-brick corporation houses and on the other by a wide common with an astounding view of the city. It was more like the back-cloth of a theatre than a real town. The pathway dropped away to the bank of a stream where a brewery stood; and from this, far beneath you, the opposite hillside, a murmuring honeycomb of factory chimneys and houses, whose noises came to you, dissociated and ghostlike, rose steeply, steeply to the gently rounded hilltop with a limestone spire, and a purple sandstone tower rising out of it and piercing the clouds. It was so wide and bewildering a view that it was never all lit up at the same time; sunlight wandered across it as across a prairie, picking out a line of roofs with a brightness like snow or delving into the depth of some dark street and outlining in shadow the figures of climbing carts and straining horses. I felt exalted, a voyager, a heroic figure. I made up my mind to spend the penny Mrs. Slattery had given me on a candle to the Blessed Virgin in the cathedral on the hilltop for my mother's speedy recovery. I felt sure I'd get more value in a great church like that so close to heaven.

The dispensary was a sordid hallway with a bench to one side and a window like a railway ticket office at the end of it. There was a little girl with a green plaid shawl about her shoulders sitting on the bench. She gave me a quick look and I saw that her eyes were green too. For years after, whenever a girl gave me a hasty look like that, I hid. I knew what it meant, but at the time I was still innocent. I knocked at the window and a seedy, angry-looking man opened it. Without waiting to hear what I had to say he grabbed bottle and prescription and banged the shutter down again without a word. I waited a minute and then lifted my hand to knock a second time.

"You'll have to wait, little boy," the girl said quickly.

"Why will I have to wait?" I asked.

"He have to make it up," she explained. "He might be half an hour. You might as well sit down."

As she obviously knew her way round, I did what she told me.

"Where are you from?" she went on, dropping the shawl, which she held in front of her mouth the way I had seen old women do it whenever they spoke. "I live in Blarney Lane."

"I live by the barrack," I said.

"And who's the bottle for?" she asked.

"My mother."

"What's wrong with her?"

"She have a bad cough."

"She might have consumption," the little girl said cheerfully. "That's what my sister that died last year had. My other sister have to have tonics. That's what I'm waiting for. 'Tis a queer old world. Is it nice up where ye live?"

I told her about the Glen, and she told me about the river out to Carrigrohane. It seemed to be a nicer place altogether than ours, the way she described it. She was a pleasant talkative little girl and I never noticed the time passing. Suddenly the shutter went up and a bottle was banged on the counter.

"Dooley!" said the man, and the window was shut again.

"That's me," said the little girl. "My name is Nora Dooley. Yours won't be ready for a long time yet. Is it a red or a black one?"

"I don't know," said I. "I never got a bottle before."

"Black ones is better," she said. "Red is more for hacking coughs. Still, I wouldn't mind a red one now."

"I have better than that," I said. "I have a lob for sweets."

I had decided that, after all, it wouldn't be necessary for me to light a candle. In a queer way the little girl restored my confidence. I knew I was exaggerating things and that Mother would be all right in a day or two.

The bottle, when I got it, was black. The little girl and I sat on the steps of the infirmary and ate the sweets I'd bought. At the end of the lane was the limestone spire of Shandon; all along it young trees overhung the high, hot walls, and the sun, when it came out in hot, golden blasts behind us, threw our linked shadows onto the road.

"Give us a taste of your bottle, little boy," she said.

"Can't you have a taste of your own?" I replied suspiciously.

"Ah, you couldn't drink mine," she said. "Tonics is all awful. Try!"

I did, and I spat it out hastily. It was awful. But after that I couldn't do less than let her taste mine. She took a long drink out of it, which alarmed me.

"That's beautiful," she said. "That's like my sister that died last year used to have. I love cough bottles."

I tried it myself and saw she was right in a way. It was very sweet and sticky, like treacle.

"Give us another," she said.

"I will not," I said in alarm. "What am I going to do with it now?"

"All you have to do is put water in it, out of a pump. No one will know."

Somehow, I couldn't refuse her. Mother was far away, and I was swept from anchorage into an unfamiliar world of spires, towers, trees, steps, and little girls who liked cough bottles. I worshipped that girl. We both took another drink and I began to panic. I saw that even if you put water in it, you couldn't conceal the fact that it wasn't the same, and began to snivel.

"It's all gone," I said. "What am I going to do?"

"Finish it and say the cork fell out," she said, as though it were the most natural thing in the world, and, God forgive me, I believed her. We finished it, and then, as I put away the empty bottle, I remembered my mother sick and the Blessed Virgin slighted, and my heart sank. I had sacrificed both to a girl and she didn't even care for me. It was my cough bottle she had been after all the time from the first moment I appeared in the dispensary. I saw her guile and began to weep.

"What ails you?" she asked in surprise.

"My mother is sick, and you're after drinking her medicine, and now if she dies, 'twill be my fault," I said.

"Ah, don't be an old cry-baby!" she said contemptuously. "No one ever died of a cough. You need only say the cork fell out—'tis a thing might happen to anyone."

"And I promised the Blessed Virgin a candle, and spent it on sweets for you," I cried, and ran away up the road like a madman, holding the empty bottle. Now I had only one hope—a miracle. I went into the cathedral to the shrine of the Blessed Virgin and, having told her of my fall, promised a candle with the next penny I got if only she would make Mother better by the time I got home. I looked at her face carefully in the candlelight and thought it didn't seem too cross. Then I went miserably home. All the light had gone out of the day, and the echoing hillside had become a vast, alien, cruel world. Besides, I felt terribly sick. It even struck me that I might die myself. In one way that would be a great ease to me.

When I reached home, the silence of the kitchen and the sight of the empty grate showed me at once that my prayers had not been heard. Mother was still sick in bed. I began to howl.

"What is it at all, child?" she cried anxiously from upstairs.

"I lost the medicine," I bellowed from the foot of the stairs, and then dashed blindly up and buried my face in the bedclothes.

"Ah, wisha, wisha, if that's all that's a-trouble to you, you poor misfortunate child!" she cried in relief, running her hand through my hair. "I was afraid you were lost. Is anything the matter?" she added anxiously. "You feel hot."

"I drank the medicine," I bawled, and buried my face again.

"And if you did itself, what harm?" she murmured soothingly. "You poor child, going all that way by yourself, without a proper dinner or anything, why wouldn't you? Take off your clothes now, and lie down here till you're better."

She rose, put on her slippers and an overcoat, and unlaced my shoes while I sat on the bed. Even before she was finished I was asleep. I didn't hear her dress herself or go out, but some time later I felt a cool hand on my forehead, and saw Minnie Ryan peering down at me.

"Ah, 'tis nothing, woman," she said lightly. "He'll sleep that off by morning. Well, aren't they the devil! God knows, you'd never be up to them. And indeed and indeed, Mrs. Sullivan, 'tis you should be in bed."

I knew all that. I knew it was her judgment on me; I was one of those who were more like savages than Christians; I was no good as a nurse, no good to anybody. I accepted it all. But when Mother came up with her evening paper and sat reading by my bed, I knew the miracle had happened. She'd been cured all right.

JUDAS

"Sure you won't be late, Jerry?" said the mother and I going out.

"Am I ever late?" said I, and I laughed.

That was all we said, Michael John, but it stuck in my mind. As I was going down the road I was thinking it was months since I'd taken her to the pictures. Of course, you might think that funny, but after the father's death we were thrown together a lot. And I knew she hated being alone in the house after dark.

At the same time I had my own troubles. You see, Michael John, being an only child I never knocked round the way other fellows did. All the fellows in the office went out with girls, or at any rate they let on they did. They said "Who was the old doll I saw you with last night, Jerry? You'd better mind yourself, or you'll be getting into trouble." To hear them you'd imagine there was no sport in the world, only girls, and that they'd always be getting you into trouble. Paddy Kinnane, for instance, talked like that, and he never saw the way it upset me. I think he thought it was a great compliment. It wasn't until years after that I began to suspect that Paddy's acquaintance with girls was about of one kind with my own.

Then I met Kitty Doherty. Kitty was a hospital nurse, and all the chaps in the office said a fellow should never go with hospital nurses. Ordinary girls were bad enough, but nurses were a fright —they knew too much. I knew when I met Kitty that that was a lie. She was a well-educated superior girl; she lived up the river in a posh locality, and her mother was on all sorts of councils and committees. Kitty was small and wiry; a good-looking girl, always in good humour, and when she talked, she hopped from one thing to another like a robin on a frosty morning.

I used to meet her in the evening up the river road, as if I was walking there by accident and very surprised to see her. "Fancy meeting you!" I'd say or "Well, well, isn't this a great surprise!" Mind you, it usually was, for, no matter how much I was expecting her, I was never prepared for the shock of her presence. Then we'd stand talking for half an hour and I'd see her home. Several times she asked me in, but I was too nervous. I knew I'd lose my head, break the china, use some dirty word, and then go home and cut my throat. Of course, I never asked her to come to the pictures or anything of the sort. She was above that. My only hope was that if I waited long enough I might be able to save her from drowning or the white slavers or something else dramatic, which would show in a modest and dignified way how I felt about her. At the same time I had a bad conscience because I knew I should stay at home more with the mother, but the very thought that I might be missing an opportunity of fishing Kitty out of the river would spoil a whole evening on me.

That night in particular I was nearly distracted. It was three weeks since I'd seen Kitty. I was sure that, at the very least, she was dying and asking for me, and that no one knew my address. A week before, I had felt I simply couldn't bear it any longer, so I had made an excuse and gone down to the post office. I rang up the hospital and asked for Kitty. I fully expected them to say in gloomy tones that Kitty had died half an hour before, and got the shock of my life when the girl at the other end asked my name. I lost my head. "I'm afraid I'm a stranger to Miss Doherty," I said with an embarrassed laugh, "but I have a message for her from a friend."

Then I grew completely panic-stricken. What could a girl like Kitty make of a damned, deliberate lie like that? What else was it but a trap laid by an old and cunning hand? I held the receiver out and looked at it as if it was someone whose neck I was going to wring. "Moynihan," I said to it, "you're mad. An asylum, Moynihan, is the only place for you."

I heard Kitty's voice, not in my ear at all, but in the telephone booth as though she were standing before me, and nearly dropped the receiver in terror. Then I raised it and asked in what I thought of as a French accent: "Who is dat speaking, please?" "This is Kitty Doherty," she replied impatiently. "Who are you?"

That was exactly what I was wondering myself. "I am Monsieur Bertrand," I went on cautiously. "I am afraid I have the wrong number. I am so sorry." Then I put down the receiver carefully and thought how nice it would be if only I had a penknife handy to cut my throat with. It's funny, but from the moment I met Kitty I was always coveting sharp things like razors and penknives.

After that an awful idea dawned on me. Of course, I should have thought of it before, but, as you can see, I wasn't exactly knowledgeable where girls were concerned. I began to see that I wasn't meeting Kitty for the very good reason that Kitty didn't want to meet me. What her reason was, I could only imagine, but imagination was my strong point. I examined my conscience to see what I might have said to her. I remembered every remark I had made. The reason was only too clear. Every single remark I had made was either brutal, indecent or disgusting. I had talked of Paddy Kinnane as a fellow who "went with dolls." What could a pure-minded girl think of a chap who naturally used such a phrase except—what unfortunately was quite true—that he had a mind like a cesspit.

But this evening I felt more confident. It was a lovely summer evening with views of hillsides and fields between the gaps in the houses, and it raised my spirits. Perhaps I was wrong; perhaps she hadn't noticed or understood my filthy conversation, perhaps we might meet and walk home together. I walked the full length of the river road and back, and then started to walk it again. The crowds were thinning out as fellows and girls slipped off up the lanes or down to the river-bank, courting. As the streets went out like lamps about me, my hopes sank lower and lower. I saw clearly that she was avoiding me; that she knew I was not the quiet, good-natured fellow I let on to be but a volcano of brutality and lust. "Lust, lust, lust!" I hissed to myself, clenching my fists. I could have forgiven myself anything but the lust.

Then I glanced up and saw her on a tram. I instantly forgot about the lust and smiled and waved my cap to her, but she was looking ahead and didn't see me. I raced after the car, intending to jump onto it, to sit in one of the back seats on top where she would not see me, and then say in astonishment as she got off "Fancy meeting you here!" But as if the driver knew what was in my mind, he put on speed, and the old tram went tossing and screeching down the one straight bit of road in the town, and I stood panting in the roadway, smiling as though missing a tram were the best joke in the world, and wishing all the time that I had a penknife and the courage to use it. My position was hopeless!

Then I must have gone a bit mad—really mad, I mean—for I started to race the tram. There were still lots of people out walking, and they stared after me in an incredulous way, so I lifted my fists to my chest in the attitude of a professional runner and dropped into what I fondly hoped would look like a comfortable stride and delude them into the belief that I was in training for a big race. By the time I was finished, I *was* a runner, and full of indignation against the people who still continued to stare at me.

Between my running and the tram's halts I just managed to keep it in view as far as the other side of town. When I saw Kitty get off and go up a hilly street, I collapsed and was only just able to drag myself after her. When she went into a house on a terrace, I sat on the high curb with my head between my knees until the panting stopped. At any rate I felt safe. I could afford to rest, could walk up and down before the house until she came out, and accost her with an innocent smile and say "Fancy meeting you!"

But my luck was dead out that night. As I was walking up and down, close enough to the house to keep it in view but not close enough to be observed from the windows, I saw a tall man strolling up at the opposite side of the road and my heart sank. It was Paddy Kinnane.

"Hallo, Jerry," he chuckled with that knowing grin he put on whenever he wanted to compliment you on being discovered in a compromising situation. "What are you doing here?"

"Just waiting for a chap I had a date with, Paddy," I said, trying to sound casual.

"Looks more as if you were waiting for an old doll, to me," Paddy said flatteringly. "Still waters run deep. When are you supposed to be meeting him?"

Cripes, I didn't even know what the time was!

"Half eight," I said at random.

"Half eight?" said Paddy. " 'Tis nearly nine now."

"Ah, he's a most unpunctual fellow," I said. "He's always the same. He'll turn up all right."

"I may as well wait with you," said Paddy, leaning against the wall and taking out a packet of cigarettes. "You might find yourself stuck by the end of the evening. There's people in this town that have no consideration for anyone."

That was Paddy all out: a heart of gold; no trouble too much for him if he could do you a good turn—I'd have loved to strangle him.

"Ah, to hell with him!" I said impatiently. "I won't bother waiting. It only struck me this minute that I have another appointment up the Western Road. You'll excuse me now, Paddy. I'll tell you all about it another time."

And away I went hell-for-leather to the tram. I mounted it and went on to the other terminus, near Kitty's house. There, at least, Paddy Kinnane could not get at me. I sat on the river wall in the dusk. The moon was rising, and every quarter of an hour a tram came grunting and squeaking over the old bridge and went black-out while the conductor switched his trolley. Each time I got off the wall and stood on the curb in the moonlight, searching for Kitty among the passengers. Then a policeman came along, and, as he seemed to be watching me, I slunk slowly off up the hill and stood against a wall in shadow. There was a high wall at the other side of the road as well, and behind it the roof of a house was cut out of the sky in moonlight. Every now and then a tram came in and people passed, and the snatches of conversation I caught were like the warmth from an open door to the heart of a homeless man. It was quite clear now that my position was hopeless. If Kitty had walked or been driven she could have reached home from the opposite direction. She could be at home in bed by now. The last tram came and went, and still there was no Kitty, and still I hung on despairingly. While one glimmer of a chance remained I could not go home.

Then I heard a woman's step. I couldn't even pretend to myself that it might be Kitty until she suddenly shuffled past me with that hasty little walk of hers. I started and called her name. She glanced quickly over her shoulder and, seeing a man emerge from the shadow, took fright and ran. I ran too, but she put on speed and began to outdistance me. At that I despaired. I stood on the pavement and shouted after her at the top of my voice.

"Kitty! Kitty, for God's sake, wait!"

She ran a few steps farther and then halted incredulously. She looked back, and then turned and slowly retraced her steps.

"Jerry Moynihan!" she whispered in astonishment. "What are you doing here?"

I was summoning strength to tell her that I had happened to be taking a stroll in that direction and was astonished to see her when I realized the improbability of it and began to cry instead. Then I laughed. It was hysteria, I suppose. But Kitty had had a bad fright and, now she was getting over it, she was as cross as two sticks.

"What's wrong with you, I say?" she snapped. "Are you out of your mind or what?"

"But I didn't see you for weeks," I burst out.

"I know," she replied. "I wasn't out. What about it?"

"I thought it might be something I said to you," I said desperately.

"What did you say?" she asked in bewilderment, but I couldn't repeat the hideous things I had already said. Perhaps, after all, she hadn't noticed them!

"How do I know?"

"Oh, it's not that," she said impatiently. "It's just Mother."

"Why?" I asked almost joyously. "Is there something wrong with her?"

"Ah, no, but she made such a fuss about it. I felt it wasn't worth it."

"A fuss? What did she make a fuss about?"

"About you, of course," Kitty said in exasperation.

"But what did I do?" I asked, clutching my head. This was worse than anything I had ever imagined. This was terrible!

"You didn't do anything, but people were talking about us. And you wouldn't come in and be introduced like anyone else. I know she's a bit of a fool, and her head is stuffed with old nonsense about her family. I could never see that they were different to anyone else, and anyway she married a commercial traveller herself, so she has nothing to talk about. Still, you needn't be so superior."

I felt cold shivers run through me. I had thought of Kitty as a secret between God, herself, and me and assumed that she only knew the half of it. Now it seemed I didn't even know the half. People were talking about us! I was superior! What next?

"But what has she against me?" I asked despairingly.

"She thinks we're doing a tangle, of course," snapped Kitty as if she was astonished at my stupidity, "and I suppose she imagines you're not grand enough for a great-great-grandniece of Daniel

O'Connell. I told her you were above that sort of thing, but she wouldn't believe me. She said I was a deep, callous, crafty little intriguer and I hadn't a drop of Daniel O'Connell's blood in my veins." Kitty giggled at the thought of herself as an intriguer, and no wonder.

"That's all she knows," I said despairingly.

"I know," Kitty agreed. "She has no sense. And anyway she has no reason to think I'm telling lies. Cissy and I always had fellows, and we spooned with them all over the shop under her very nose, so I don't see why she thinks I'm trying to conceal anything."

At this I began to laugh like an idiot. This was worse than appalling. This was a nightmare. Kitty, whom I had thought so angelic, talking in cold blood about "spooning" with fellows all over the house. Even the bad women in the books I had read didn't talk about love-making in that cold-blooded way. Madame Bovary herself had at least the decency to pretend that she didn't like it. It was another door opening on the outside world, but Kitty thought I was laughing at her and started to apologize.

"Of course, I had no sense at the time," she said. "You were the first fellow I met that treated me properly. The others only wanted to fool around, and now, because I don't like it, Mother thinks I'm into something ghastly. I told her I liked you better than any fellow I knew, but that I'd grown out of all that sort of thing."

"And what did she say to that?" I asked fiercely. I was beginning to see that imagination wasn't enough; that all round me there was an objective reality that was a thousand times more nightmarish than any fantasy of my own. I couldn't hear enough about it, though at the same time it turned my stomach.

"Ah, I told you she was silly," Kitty said in embarrassment.

"Go on!" I shouted. "I want to know."

"Well," said Kitty with a demure grin, "she said you were a deep, designing guttersnipe who knew exactly how to get round featherpated little idiots like me. . . . You see, it's quite hopeless. The woman is common. She doesn't understand."

"Oh, God!" I said almost in tears. "I only wish she was right."

"Why do you wish she was right?" Kitty asked with real curiosity.

"Because then I'd have some chance of you," I said.

"Oh!" said Kitty, as if this was news to her. "To tell you the truth," she added after a moment, "I thought you were a bit keen at first, but then I wasn't sure. When you didn't kiss me or anything, I mean."

"God," I said bitterly, "when I think what I've been through in the past few weeks!"

"I know," said Kitty, biting her lip. "I was a bit fed up too."

Then we said nothing for a few moments.

"You're sure you mean it?" she asked suspiciously.

"But I tell you I was on the point of committing suicide," I said angrily.

"What good would that be?" she asked with another shrug, and this time she looked at me and laughed outright—the little jade!

I insisted on telling her about my prospects. She didn't want to hear about my prospects; she wanted me to kiss her, but that seemed to me a very sissy sort of occupation, so I told her just the same, in the intervals. It was as if a stone had been lifted off my heart, and I went home in the moonlight, singing. Then I heard the clock strike, and the singing stopped. I remembered the mother's "Sure you won't be late?" and my own "Am I ever late?" This was desperation too, but of a different sort.

The door was ajar and the kitchen in darkness. I saw her sitting before the fire by herself, and just as I was about to throw my arms round her, I smelt Kitty's perfume and was afraid to go near her. God help us, as though that would have told her anything!

"Hullo, Mum," I said with a nervous laugh, rubbing my hands. "You're all in darkness."

"You'll have a cup of tea?" she said.

"I might as well."

"What time is it?" she said, lighting the gas. "You're very late."

"I met a fellow from the office," I said, but at the same time I was stung by the complaint in her tone.

"You frightened me," she said with a little whimper. "I didn't know what happened you. What kept you at all?"

"Oh, what do you think?" I said, goaded by my own sense of guilt. "Drinking and blackguarding as usual."

I could have bitten my tongue off as I said it; it sounded so cruel, as if some stranger had said it instead of me. She turned to me with a frightened stare as if she were seeing the stranger too, and somehow I couldn't bear it.

"God Almighty!" I said. "A fellow can have no life in his own house."

I went hastily upstairs, lit the candle, undressed, and got into bed. A chap could be a drunkard and blackguard and not be made to suffer what I was being made to suffer for being out late one single night. This, I felt, was what you got for being a good son.

"Jerry," she called from the foot of the stairs, "will I bring you up your cup?"

"I don't want it now, thanks," I said.

I heard her sigh and turn away. Then she locked the doors, front and back. She didn't wash up, and I knew that my cup of tea was standing on the table with a saucer on top in case I changed my mind. She came slowly upstairs and her walk was that of an old woman. I blew out the candle before she reached the landing, in case she came in to ask if I wanted anything else, and the moonlight came in the attic window and brought me memories of Kitty. But every time I tried to imagine her face as she grinned up at me, waiting for me to kiss her, it was the mother's face that came up instead, with that look like a child's when you strike him for the first time—as if he suddenly saw the stranger in you. I remembered all our life together from the night my father died; our early Mass on Sunday; our visits to the pictures, and our plans for the future, and Christ! Michael John, it was as if I was inside her mind while she sat by the fire waiting for the blow to fall. And now it had fallen, and I was a stranger to her, and nothing I could ever do would make us the same to one another again. There was something like a cannon-ball stuck in my chest, and I lay awake till the cocks started crowing. Then I could bear it no longer. I went out on the landing and listened.

"Are you awake, Mother?" I asked in a whisper.

"What is it, Jerry?" she replied in alarm, and I knew that she hadn't slept any more than I had.

"I only came to say I was sorry," I said, opening the door of her room, and then as I saw her sitting up in bed under the Sacred Heart lamp, the cannon-ball burst inside me and I began to cry like a kid.

"Oh, child, child, child!" she exclaimed, "what are you crying for at all, my little boy?" She spread out her arms to me. I went to her and she hugged me and rocked me as she did when I was only a nipper. "Oh, oh, oh," she was saying to herself in a whisper, "my storeen bawn, my little man!"—all the names she hadn't called me in years. That was all we said. I couldn't bring myself to tell her what I had done, nor could she confess to me that she was jealous: all she could do was to try and comfort me for the way I'd hurt her, to make up to me for the nature she had given me. "My storeen bawn!" she said. "My little man!"

MY FIRST PROTESTANT

It was when I was doing a line with Maire Daly that I first came to know Winifred Jackson. She was my first Protestant. There were a number in our locality, but they kept to themselves. The Jacksons were no exception. The father was a bank manager, a tall, thin, weary-looking man, and the mother a chubby, pious woman who had a lot to do with religious bazaars. I met her once with Winifred and liked her. They had one son, Ernest, a medical student who was forever trying to get engaged to some trollop who had caught his fancy for the moment—a spoiled pup if ever there was one.

But Winifred caused her parents far more concern than he did. They probably felt she had to be taken seriously. She and Maire were both learning the piano from old Streichl, and they became great friends. The Dalys' was a grand house in those days. The father was a builder; a tall, thin, sardonic man who, after long and bitter experience, had come to the conclusion that the whole town was in a conspiracy against him, and that his family—all but his wife, whom he regarded as a friendly neutral—was allied with the town. His wife was a handsome woman, whose relations with the enemy were far closer than her husband ever suspected. As for the traitors—Joe, Maire, Brenda, and Peter, the baby—they had voices like trumpets from shouting one another down and exceedingly dirty tongues to use when the vocal cords gave out.

Joe was the eldest; a lad with a great head for whisky and an even better one for books if only he had taken them seriously, but it was a convention of the Daly family to take nothing seriously but money and advancement. Like a lot of other conventions this one didn't bear much relation to the fundamental facts. The only exception to the convention was Peter, who later became a Jesuit, and Peter had something in common with a submarine. He was a handsome lad with an enormous brow and bright blue eyes; he sometimes saluted you with a curt nod, but more often cut you dead, being submerged. For weeks he sat in his room, reading with ferocity, and then suddenly one night decided to come up for air and a little light conversation, and argued like a mad dog until two in the morning. That, the Dalys said flatly, was what reading did for you.

Yet it was a wonderfully pleasant house on a Sunday evening when the children and their friends were in, and old Daly concluded an armistice with us for the evening. There was always lashings of stuff; the Dalys, for all their shrewdness, could do nothing in a small and niggardly way. If you borrowed a cigarette from one of them, you were quite liable to be given a box of a hundred, and attempting to repay it might well be regarded as a deadly insult. Brenda, the younger girl, slouched round with sandwiches and gibes; Joe sang "Even Bravest Heart may Swell" with an adoring leer at "Loving smile of sister kind"; while Maire, who played his accompaniment, muttered furiously: "Of all the bloody nonsense! A puck in the gob was all that we ever got."

"Really," Winifred said with a sigh as I saw her home one night, "they are an extraordinary family."

I didn't take this as criticism. Having been brought up in a fairly quiet home myself, I sometimes felt the same bewilderment.

"Isn't that why you like them?" I asked.

"Is it, do you think?" she said with surprise. "I dare say you're right. I wish Daddy thought the same."

"What does he object to?" I asked.

"Oh, nothing in particular," she replied with a shrug. "Just that they're the wrong persuasion. Haven't I nice girls of my own class to mix with? Don't I realize that everything said in that house is reported in confession? . . . Is it, by the way?" she added eagerly.

"Not everything."

"I hardly thought so," she added dryly. "Anyhow, they can confess everything I say to them."

"You're not afraid of being converted?" I asked.

"Oh, they're welcome to try," she said indifferently. "Really, people are absurd about religion."

I didn't say that some such ambition was not very far from Mrs. Daly's mind. I had seen for myself that she liked Winifred and thought she was good company for Maire, and it was only natural that a woman so big-hearted should feel it a pity that such a delightful girl dug with the wrong foot. It probably wasn't necessary to say it to Winifred. There was little about the Dalys which she wasn't shrewd enough to observe for herself. That was part of their charm.

On the whole her parents did well to worry. What had begun as a friendship between herself and Maire continued as a love affair between herself and Joe. It came to a head during the summer holidays when the Dalys took a house by the sea in Crosshaven and Winifred stayed with them. I went down for occasional week-ends, and found it just like Cork, and even more so. By some mysterious mental process of his own, Mr. Daly had worked out that, as part of a general conspiracy, the property-owners of Crosshaven charged high rents and then encouraged you to dissipate the benefits of your seaside holiday by depriving you of your sleep, and insisted on everybody's being in bed at eleven o'clock of a summer night, so, with the connivance of the neutral power, we all slipped out again when he was asleep, for a dance in some neighbour's house, a moonlight swim or row, or a walk along the cliffs. I was surprised at the change in Winifred. When first I had seen her, she was prim and demure, and, when anyone ragged her out of this, inclined to be truculent and awkward. Now she had grown to accept the ragging that was part of the Dalys' life, and evolved a droll and impudent expression which gave people the impression that it was she who was making fun of them. Naturally, this was far more effective.

"She's coming on," I said to Maire one evening when we were lying on the cliffs.

"She's getting more natural," admitted Maire. "At first she'd disgrace you. It wasn't bad enough wanting to pay for her own tea, but when she tried to give me the penny for the bus I thought I'd die with shame. God, Dan, do you know I was so flabbergasted I took it from her."

The picture of Maire taking the penny made me laugh outright, for she too had all the Daly lavishness, and there was nothing flashy about it; it was just that the story of their lives was written like that, in large capital letters.

"It's all very well for you," said Maire, who didn't know what I was laughing at, "but that family of hers must be as mean as hell."

"Not mean," I said. "Just prudent."

"Prudent! Pshaw!"

"Where is she now?"

"Spooning with Joe, I suppose. They're doing a terrible line. She'd be grand for him. She wouldn't stand for any of his nonsense."

"Is that the sort Joe is?" I asked, closing my eyes to enjoy the sun.

"He's as big a bully as Father," said Maire, busily tickling my nose with a blade of grass. "God, the way Mother ruins that fellow!—she expects us to let him walk on us. Aren't Protestants great, Dan?"

"We'll see when her family hears she's walking out with Joe," I said.

"Oh, I believe they're kicking up hell about that already," she said, throwing away one blade and picking up another to chew, a most restless woman. I looked round and she was sitting with one leg under her, staring away towards the sea. "They think he was put on to her by the Pope."

"And wasn't he?"

"Is it Mother?" laughed Maire. "God help us, you wouldn't blame her. Two birds with one stone—a wife for Joe and a soul for God."

I watched Winifred's romance with sympathy, perhaps with a reminiscence of Romeo and Juliet in my mind, perhaps already with a feeling of revolt against the cliques and factions of a provincial town. But for a time it almost appeared to mean more to me than my own relationship with Maire.

One autumn evening when I was coming home from the office I saw Winifred emerge from a house on Summerhill. She saw me too and waved, before she came charging after me with her long legs flying. She always remained leggy even in middle age; a tall, thin girl with a long, eager face, blue eyes, and fair hair. When she caught up on me she took my arm. That was the sort of thing I liked in her; the way she ran, the way she grabbed your arm; her capacity for quick, spontaneous moments of intimacy without any element of calculation in them.

"How's Joe?" I asked. "I haven't seen him this past week."

"No more have I," she replied lightly.

"How's that?" I asked gravely. "I thought you'd be giving us a night by this time."

"Ah, I don't think it'll ever come to that, Dan," she replied in the same tone, but without any regret that I could see.

"You're not going to disappoint us?" I asked, and I fancy there must have been more feeling in my voice than in hers.

"Well, we've discussed it, of course," she said in a businesslike tone, "but it seems impossible. He can't marry me unless I become a Catholic."

"Can't he?" I aked in surprise.

"Well, I suppose he couldn't be stopped, but you know how it would affect his business."

"I dare say it would," I said, and mind you, it was the first time the idea of that had crossed my mind—I must have been even more sentimental than I know, even now. "But you could get a dispensation."

"Yes, if I agreed to have the children brought up as Catholics."

"And wouldn't you?"

"Really, Dan, how could I?" she asked wearily. "It's all that the parents threatened me with from the beginning. I suppose it was wrong of me really to start anything with Joe, but I couldn't walk out on them now."

"It's your life, not theirs," I pointed out.

"Even so, Dan, I have to consider their feelings, just as Joe has to consider his mother's. She wouldn't like to see her grandchildren brought up as Protestants, and they feel just the same. You may think their opinions are wrong, but it would hurt them just as much as if they were right."

"I think the sooner people with opinions like those get hurt, the better," I said with a queer feeling of disappointment.

"Oh, I know," she retorted, flaring up at me like a real little termagant. "You're just like Joe. You're the normal person, I'm the freak; consequently, you expect me to make all the sacrifices."

We were passing the Cross at the time, and I stopped dead and looked at her. Up to this I had never, I thought, felt so intensely about anything.

"If that's the sort you think I am, you're very much mistaken," I said. "If you were my girl I wouldn't let God, man, or devil come between us."

Her face suddenly cleared and she gave my arm a little squeeze.

"You know, Dan, I almost wish I was," she said in a tone that restored all our intimacy.

Anyone who didn't know her would have taken it for an invitation, but even then, emotional as I felt, I knew it was nothing of the sort. I had a great admiration for her; I knew she'd make an excellent wife for Joe, and I couldn't help feeling that there was something wrong about letting religion come between them.

The following evening I went for a walk with Joe up the Western Road and we had it out.

"I had a talk with Winnie last night," I said. "I hope you won't think me interfering if I mention it to you."

"I know anything you said would be kindly meant, Dan," he replied reasonably.

That was one nice thing about Joe. However much of a bully he might be, you didn't have to skirmish for position with him. It had something to do with the capital letters that the Dalys used as if by nature. They had no time for trifles.

"I think she's very fond of you, Joe," I said.

"I think the same, Dan," he agreed warmly, "and 'tisn't all on one side. I needn't tell you that."

"You couldn't come to some agreement with her about religion?" I asked.

"I'd like to know what agreement we could come to," he said. "I can talk to you about it because you know what it means. You know what would happen the business if I defied everybody and married her in a register office."

"But you want her to do it instead, Joe," I said.

" 'Tisn't alike, Dan," he said in his monumental way. "And you know 'tisn't alike. This is a Catholic country. Her people haven't the power they had. It might mean ruin to me, but it would mean nothing to her."

"That only makes it worse," I said. "You want her to give up a religion that may mean something to her for one that doesn't mean anything to you, only what harm it can do you."

"I never said it meant nothing to me," he said without taking offence. "But you've shifted your ground, Dan. That's a different proposition entirely. We were talking about my responsibility to provide for a family."

"Very well then," I said, seeing what I thought a way out of it. "Tell her that! Tell her what you've told me; that you'll marry her your way and take the responsibility for what happens, or marry her her way and let her take the responsibility."

"Aren't you forgetting that it would still be my responsibility, Dan?" he asked, laying a friendly hand on my shoulder.

"And because it is, she won't take it," I said warmly.

"Ah, well, Dan," he said, "she mightn't be as intelligent as you about it, and then I'd have to face the consequences."

"That's not the sort of girl she is at all," I said.

"Dan," he said whimsically, "I'm beginning to think you're the one that should marry her."

"I'm beginning to think the same," I said huffily.

We didn't discuss the subject again, but I'd still take my oath that if he had done what I suggested she'd have pitched her family to blazes and married him. All a girl like that wanted was proof that he cared enough for her to take a risk, to do the big thing, and that was what Joe wouldn't do. Capital letters aren't enough where love is concerned. I don't blame him now, but at that age when you feel that a friend should be everything I felt disillusioned in him.

Winifred wasted no tears over him, and in a few months she was walking out in a practical way with a school-teacher of her own persuasion. She still called at the Dalys', but things weren't the same between them. Mrs. Daly was disappointed in her. It seemed strange to her that an intelligent girl like Winifred couldn't see the error of Protestantism, and from the moment she knew there was to be no spectacular public conversion, she gave it up as a bad job. She told me she had never approved of mixed marriages, and for once she got me really angry.

"All marriages are mixed marriages, Mrs. Daly," I said stiffly. "They're all right when the mixture is all right."

And then I began to notice that between Maire and myself the mixture had ceased to be all right. It was partly the feeling that the house was not the same without Winifred there. These things happen to people and to families; some light in them goes out, and afterwards they are never the same again. Maire said the change was in me; that I was becoming conceited and argumentative; and she dropped me.

I was sore about that for months. It wasn't Maire I missed so much as the family. My own home life had been quiet, too quiet, and I had loved the capital letters, the gaiety and bad tempers. I had now drifted into another spell of loneliness, but loneliness with a new and disturbing feeling of alienation, and Cork is a bad place for one who feels like that. It was as though I could talk to nobody. One Sunday, instead of going to Mass, I walked down the quays and along the river. It was charming there, and I sat on a bench under the trees and watched the reflection of the big painted houses and the cliffs above them at the opposite side of the river, and wondered why I hadn't thought of doing this before. I made a vow that for the future I'd bring a book. A long, leisurely book.

I had been doing that for months when one day I noticed a man who turned up each Sunday about the same time as myself. I knew him. He was a teacher from the South Side, with a big red face and a wild mop of hair. We chatted, and the following Sunday when we met again he said in an offhand way:

"You seem to be very fond of ships, Mr. Hogan?"

"Mr. Reilly," I said, "those that go down to the sea in ships are to me the greatest wonder of the Lord."

"Oh, is that so?" he said without surprise. "I just wondered when I saw you here so much."

That morning I was feeling a bit depressed, and I didn't care much who knew my reason for being there.

"It happens to be the most convenient spot to the church where my family think I am at the moment," I said with a touch of bitterness.

"I fancied that from the book you have under your arm," he said. "I wouldn't let too many people see that book if I was you. They might misunderstand you." Then as he noticed another man we had both seen before come towards us, he added with amusement: "I wonder would he, by any chance, be one of us too?"

As a matter of fact, he was. It was remarkable, after we all got to know one another, the number of educated men who found their way down the Marina Walk on Sunday mornings. Reilly called us "the Atheists' Club" but that was only swank, because there was only one atheist. Reilly and myself were agnostics, and the rest were anticlericals or young fellows with scruples. All this revealed itself gradually in our Sunday-morning arguments. It was also revealed to me that I was not the only young man in town who was lonely and unhappy.

After Winifred married I visited her a few times, and her husband and I got on well together. He was a plump, jolly, good-humoured man, fond of his game of golf and his glass of whisky, and he and she seemed to hit it off excellently. They had two sons. Joe Daly never gave her any cause to regret him, because, though his business prospered, he proved a handful for the girl who married him. Drink was his trouble and he bore it with great dignity. At one time half the police in Cork seemed to be exclusively occupied in preventing him from being charged with drunkenness, and, except for one small fine for being on unlicensed premises after hours—a young policeman was to blame and he was transferred immediately—he never was charged.

But, of course, we all drifted apart. Ten years later when I heard that Winifred's husband was dead, I went to the funeral for the sake of old times, but I knew nobody there and slipped away again before it reached the cemetery.

A couple of months later I strolled back from the Atheists' Club one Sunday morning as Mass was ending to pick up two orthodox acquaintances who I knew would attend it. It was a sunny day. The church, as usual, was crammed, and I stood on the pavement watching the crowds pour down the steps. Suddenly I glimpsed Winifred passing under the portico at right angles in the direction of the back entrance. She had the two children with her. It was the sight of these that convinced me I wasn't imagining it all. I made a dash through the crowd to reach her, and when she saw me her face lit up. She caught my hands—it was one of those instinctive gestures that at once brought back old times to me.

"Dan!" she cried in astonishment. "What on earth brings you here?"

"Young woman," I said, "I'm the one that should ask that question."

"Oh, that's a long story," she said with a laugh. "If you're coming back my way I might tell you. . . . Run along, Willie!" she called to the elder boy, and he and his brother went ahead of us up the steps.

"So you took the high jump!" I said.

"Ah, there's nothing to keep me back now," she said with a shrug. "Daddy and Mummy are dead, and you know how much Ernest cares."

"Well, you still seem quite cheerful," I said. "Almost as cheerful as a roaring agnostic like me."

"Ah, but look at you!" she said mockingly, taking my hand again quite without self-consciousness. "A bachelor, with nothing in the world to worry you! Why on earth wouldn't you be cheerful?"

I nearly told her why but thought better of it. It was complicated enough as it was. But for the first time I understood how her life had gone awry. A woman always tries to give her children whatever it is she feels she has missed in life. Sometimes you don't even know what it is till you see what she is trying to give them. Perhaps she doesn't know herself. With some it's money, with others it's education; with others still, it is love. And the kids never value it, of course. They have never really known the loss of it.

And there, as we sat over our drinks in the front room of her little house, two old cronies, I thought how strange it was that the same thing should have blown us in opposite directions. A man and woman in search of something are always blown apart, but it's the same wind that blows them.

THE SORCERER'S APPRENTICE

THEIR friends said that whenever Jimmy Foley named the day, Una MacDermott slipped a disk. They had been keeping company for five years, and at least half a dozen times they had been on the point of marriage, only to be put off by another row. Jimmy blamed this on Una, who was an only child, and whose father, according to him, simply ruined her. Una blamed it on

Jimmy's mother, and declared loudly that Irish mothers were a menace to their sons. Their friends thought it a pity, because they got so much pleasure discussing which of them was in the wrong that you felt they would never be short of subjects to talk about.

Una was a warm-hearted, excitable, talkative girl with a great flow of gossip. Jimmy was more reserved; a handsome man who dressed according to his looks, serious and rather pompous, though with great skittishness when he chose to relax. He was the centre of a small planetary system of flappers, and these, Una said, were part of the trouble. Not that she was jealous, but they did spoil him, and after a trying day at the office he arrived at her house with a dying air, too dispirited to talk, and thought she had nothing better to do than to prop his head and feed him chocolates.

This was bad enough, but even when she fed him chocolates, he still didn't seem prepared to let her have views of her own. She didn't want much in the way of views, for she was an intensely pious girl, always in and out of churches; but she did like to gossip, and even this Jimmy denied her out of respect for what he called "facts." The "facts" of course, were the facts as admitted by Jimmy's newspaper, which was exceedingly orthodox. Anything more was scandal. She had only to tell some story against a minister for him to knit his brows and ask: "Where did you hear that, if I may ask?" On occasion, he even rang up the city editor in Dublin to confirm the story. The city editor, of course, never confirmed it.

After three rows in one week, Una decided again that they were entirely unsuited to one another and took a train to Dublin to stay with her friends the Sheehys, who had a flat on the South Side. Joan Sheehy was Una's oldest friend. When Una stayed with them, she got into Una's bed, and they lay awake half the night, discussing every problem of love and marriage in the most concrete terms. Joan had been a nurse, so she knew all the terms. Sometimes her husband got bored or cold, sleeping alone, and staggered in to them half asleep with a pillow in his hand, but talk about love always bored him, and in a few minutes he was usually snoring while they went on with their discussion in excited whispers.

But for a full year Una had been getting less and less sympathy from Joan, who had begun to suspect that the delay in the marriage was being caused by Una rather than by Jimmy, and that she had no intention of marrying at all. Una swore she had, but Joan didn't believe her.

"Ah, for goodness' sake, girl," she said, "it's about time you stopped making excuses and settled down. You're thirty, and if you go on like this much longer, you won't have any alternative."

"But I haven't an alternative now, Joanie," Una said earnestly. "Honestly, how can I marry a man that I fight with every week?"

"Well, it's good training for fighting with him every day," said Joan. "And I'm tired of the way you grouse about your men. It doesn't matter who they are—you're bound to find something wrong with them. There was Ned Buckley," she went on, ticking them off on her fingers. "He was the best of the bunch, but he had no religion. Doyle, the fellow with the shop on the Grand Parade, had too much. He was at Mass every morning, so he got on your nerves. Michael Healy had a lovely voice, but he drank. Now for the last five years we're hearing about Jimmy. I suppose there's something wrong with every man if you go at him with a microscope. You're turning into a proper old maid, Una, that's what's happening you."

This was precisely what alarmed Una herself whenever she thought of it, and, to disprove the charge, she set out to flirt violently with the Sheehys' friend Denis O'Brien. Charm came natural to Una, but when she wanted to be charming, she could knock a man out in the first round. And Denis didn't look as though he had many defences. He was forty-five, an age when every man becomes fair game for flattery. He was separated from his wife. As well as that, he was poor and plain. He had a plump, bright, beaming face, with a small dark moustache, a high, bald forehead, and a quiet voice with insinuating manners. He was lonely; he did not get much in the way of solid meals, so he came a good deal to the Sheehys, who were very fond of him. He was clearly delighted with Una, encouraged her to rattle on in her usual excitable, forthright way—the way that irritated Jimmy so much—and then poked good-natured fun at her. When he had gone, Joan warned Una that Denis wasn't quite so defenceless as he appeared.

This was quite sufficient to rouse Una's interest in him. When, two evenings later, he called in the Sheehys' absence, she invited him in and deliberately encouraged him to make love to her. He needed little in the way of encouragement. When they fell to discussing love, he took the line which always irritated her when people introduced it: that of treating love as a sort of natural expression of the personality. You couldn't be yourself while you repressed this tendency. She listened to him with grave disapproval. When she told him of her difficulties with Jimmy, he irritated her further by taking Jimmy's side and giving her precisely the same line as Joan had already given her—she even suspected that he might be a mouthpiece for Joan.

"Well, you see, Una," he said in that insinuating, sermonizing way of his, "you have to take a chance. There's no such thing in marriage as absolute security. You can be friends with a man for twenty years and think you know all about him, but when you marry him, you find out things about him you never even guessed. It's a gamble, however you do it. Sooner or later you'll have to take a chance, and you should take it before you get too set in your ways."

"Haven't you ever regretted taking a chance, Denis?" she asked mockingly.

"Well, no, dear," he said after a moment's hesitation. "I can't say I have. It's no use trying to be wise before the event, you know, not in matters like that."

"It's no use throwing your judgment out the window either," she retorted.

"No," he agreed quietly, "I wouldn't ask you to do that. But you've used your judgment, so far as it takes you, and now it won't take you any farther. It's only when you find you've let opportunity slip that you really start to throw your judgment out of the window. Think of all the women you know who made fools of themselves in their thirties."

"And the men who made fools of themselves in their forties," she said maliciously, but he only slapped his knee in delight and said: "Doesn't Jimmy ever knock you about, Una?"

She repeated this conversation to Joan, omitting the love-making, but Joan didn't seem to be flattered at Denis's giving the same advice as herself. She didn't like the way Una carried her personal problems to anyone who would listen; she felt it was almost a way of ridding herself of them and of the urge to get married.

"You mean you were talking to *Denis* about Jimmy?" she asked incredulously.

"Oh, just generally," Una replied with a blush.

"God help your husband if you go round talking of him like that after you're married," Joan added dryly.

Next evening Una went to the pictures with Denis and they returned to his flat for coffee. She felt slightly self-conscious with him. He never wore a hat; his greying hair was long behind his big bald brow, and his trousers, which he never seemed to press, flapped about his heels. The flat depressed her too: two large rooms on the ground floor, a dirty toilet without a bolt in the hallway, and a communal bathroom three floors up. It had the tidy and joyless look of bachelor quarters anywhere. But it was pleasant to sit in the dusk by the large window and watch the lights come on like stars in the great pink mass of a city square, and tell him about all the young men who had courted her from the age of sixteen on. Denis was a good listener, and everything she told him moved him to some comment. When she talked of Jimmy, he repeated his advice with even more conviction. This time it struck her as positively funny, because he had his arm about her waist. Jimmy wouldn't exactly approve of this oily old clerk as an advocate.

"You see, Una," he said in his earnest paternal way, "it's no good telling me what you think of Jimmy now. You're just at a dead end with him. You'll think differently when you're married, because you'll change and he'll change as well."

"As much as all that?" she cried in mock alarm.

"Pretty much," he replied gravely. "And it won't be all for the better, of course. It may even be for the worse."

"And all after one night?" she went on in the same *gamine* tone.

"Not after one night, Una," he replied reproachfully. "Maybe not till after a good many nights—and days. You're making too much of the night altogether."

"Denis, am I an old maid?"

"No, dear," he went on, refusing to be interrupted. "The way I see it, girls like you with plenty of life, if you're not married by the time you're thirty, you start exaggerating because your mind's gone off in one direction and your body in another. You talk far too much about sex. That's because you should be enjoying it instead. And that's why I think Jimmy and you quarrel as you do. You have to get your mind and body working together, the way they did when you were a kid."

He was a very unusual man, she decided; he talked in a solemn, silky, almost clerical tone, with a touch of mysticism, yet here he was at the same time making love to her, and the inconsistency gave it all a sort of fairytale quality.

When she reached home, Joan talked severely to her. She and her husband were very fond of Denis and were now convinced that Una was leading him on, amusing herself with him. Here she was, running away from a most desirable young man to whom she should have been married years before, and running round with a married man who was lonely, disappointed, and poor and had to work in a small job in a government office to provide the alimony he had to pay because of a previous indiscretion. Someone was going to be hurt, and it wasn't she.

Una had a good deal of conscientiousness as well as natural good sense, and instead of quarrelling with Joan she thanked her and promised to behave better. The more she thought of it, the more she saw Joan was right, and that she had only been flirting with Denis, quite regardless of the consequences to him. She was also rather flattered at the idea that it was she and not Denis who was doing the flirting.

Next evening, she gave the same sales-talk to Denis with a slight change of emphasis. With great frankness she pointed out his irresponsibility and lack of regard for the future of his children. He listened to her quietly with bowed head until she mentioned the children, and then he flashed her a quick, angry look and said: "Let the kids out of it, Una, please." She was so satisfied with her own maturity of judgment that she rang up Jimmy and told him gaily that she had had a proposition from a married man with two children.

"Some people have all the luck," he replied darkly.

"Why?" she asked in surprise. "What's wrong with the flappers?"

"Not biting this weather," he said.

Next morning she woke with a slight feeling of discomfort. When she thought about it she realized that it was caused by Denis's look when she spoke to him of his children. Something about the look suggested that he must think her not only a coquette but a hypocrite as well. She rang him up to invite him for a walk. Now that she had the situation in hand, she saw no reason why they should not be friends and regretted the words that might have caused him pain.

At midnight she found herself in bed with him, lying in a most extraordinary position, which made her giggle to herself, and realized that Joan's warning had not been superfluous. What a dozen men with ten times his attraction had failed to do, he had managed without the slightest difficulty. At one he was fast asleep and snoring in the little single bed under the window. She rose, dressed, and looked for a long time at the innocent round red face with the mouth slightly open and said aloud in a scandalized tone: "His mistress." Then she looked at herself in the mirror and frowned. She tiptoed out of the room, closed the front door quietly behind her, and was startled by the echo of her own footsteps from the other side of the square, like those of the secondary personality who had taken her place and was now returning furtively from her midnight adultery. "Adultery," she added in the same hushed voice. She felt very solemn and wanted the quiet of her own room, where she could meditate on the strangeness of her own conduct without being disturbed by his snores or the touch of his body. She was alarmed and disillusioned: alarmed that she had deliberately behaved in such an irrational and shocking way, and disillusioned because it had produced no effect on her. If this was what was supposed to change people's characters, they must be considerably more susceptible than she was.

When she woke, it was with a full sense of the possible consequences and she flew into a panic. She decided that she would marry Jimmy at once. She had now reached a stage where she could not trust herself without being married. She rang him up to tell him she was returning next day. He sounded relieved and she felt relieved herself, as though she were escaping from a great danger. She went into town and spent a lot of money on a really beautiful pull-over for him. This and the crowds in the sunlight in Stephen's Green reassured her and covered up the memory of those stealthy echoing footsteps in the dark and silent square.

They reassured her so much that at last she could see no point in rushing home. After all, it was a new experience, something that people generally agreed was essential to the character, and the least she could do was to give it a chance. She returned to Denis's to cook dinner for him that evening. This, too, was an experience that she wanted to have, just to see what marriage to him would have been like. He seemed touched by the sight of her, making a muck of his clean kitchen. "Eh, girl," he said fondly, "you look a different woman in that apron. You look quite beautiful." She felt it. She was much happier this way than without her clothes. Denis was not a good lover as Jimmy was; he never made her feel exalted as Jimmy did; but he did make her feel comfortable, as though they had been married for years. And what impressed her most was that she had no more sense of guilt than if they had been married. It struck her that in a girl of such strict principles, a girl who never coddled herself but set off to early Mass, winter and summer, this was most remarkable and must mean something, if only she knew what.

Instead of going home in a hurry, she spent an extra week in Dublin, visiting museums and galleries and going on excursions with Denis. She ceased to be embarrassed by his baldness and his baggy trousers. She realized that, wherever they went, there was always about him an air of quiet distinction which marked him out. Poor but intelligent, he knew every object of interest within twenty miles of the city. It was a revelation to see it in his company.

At the station, when she threw her arms about his neck, the Sheehys exchanged glances of alarm. They had known something was happening, but not this. She kept her tears for the train. Then, after it had passed Maryboro, and Dublin was well behind, she cheered herself with the thought of her return, and was her old gay self when her father met her.

It was pleasant and restful to slip back into the familiar routine of evenings with Jimmy, the walks out the Lee Road and the visits to the pictures, but even the pull-over did not entirely wipe out her feeling of guilt, so she tried to make it up to him in other ways. She felt unusually mature and motherly, and capable at last of coping with his moods. For the first time, thanks to Denis, she realized how many of their quarrels had been caused by her own unsettled state, and resolved that they must not fall back into the same pattern. She even made discoveries about Jimmy. He wasn't an easy man to understand because he didn't understand himself. He was touchy about orthodoxy because he wasn't happy with it himself. There was a critical side of Jimmy which he never gave rein to. So when he had what he considered a trying day and needed sympathy, she let him put his head on her lap and stroked his hair while he moaned about his intolerable existence. When he frowned at one of her hasty conclusions, she withdrew it immediately. It was really quite easy, though she had never realized it until Denis made it plain to her; a mere matter of technique that never really impinged upon her own freedom of judgment, and she wondered at the crises she had needlessly provoked because of such trifles. Jimmy noticed the change in her and said suspiciously that her holiday seemed to have done her good.

"I suppose it's really that fellow, O'Brien," he growled, "with the—how many is it?—five children."

"Some day I'm afraid I'll have to confess everything, love," she replied with a mocking grin, and hugged herself at the thought of how little poor Jimmy knew. As she walked through the main streets, exchanging gossip with her friends, she seemed to hear those echoing footsteps in the silent square, romantic now and far away, and thought what her friends would say if only they knew. Una MacDermott! You're not serious. Her poor father would drop dead.

Then one night she and Jimmy had a thundering row. It began quite innocently, in an argument about a current political scandal, something about a distillery. Political scandals always seemed to involve a distillery or two. Jimmy would not admit that there was any scandal at all, and finally, in a rage, Una stamped out, swearing that she would never speak to him again; that he didn't know what manliness was. By the time she reached home it had dawned on her that the old pattern had reasserted itself exactly as before. And this time it definitely wasn't only her unsettled state. Jimmy was unsettled too, and it was only too plain that he took the wrong side and stuck to it because in life he had taken the wrong side and was unable to detach himself from it. But it wasn't to be supposed that he would find a feminine equivalent of Denis or even listen to her if he did.

"Steady up, girl!" she told herself. "Somebody in this establishment has to have a sense of responsibility."

Before she went to bed she rang up Jimmy and proposed going to Glengarriff for the week-end. It was a favourite haunt of theirs. She was syrupy, as though she had forgotten all about their quarrel, and Jimmy was sour as though he had no intention of allowing her to forget, but he said in a weary tone that if she really wanted to go so badly, he didn't mind. When Jimmy's orthodoxy was challenged he seemed to revert to the age of twelve.

However, the trip down put him in better humour, as it always did, and when they walked along the village street and watched the moon rising over Cab Du, he was in high spirits. While the ripples broke the moon's reflection in the water till it looked like a great tree of leaves, they lingered over the wall, chatting to the boatmen of the first arrivals among the summer visitors.

When he said good-night to her in her room, she pulled his head down to hers and asked in a low voice: "Aren't you going to stay with me, Jimmy?" He grew very red. "Are you sure you want me to?" he replied. For answer, she turned her back on him and pulled her frock over her head. He still stood there, embarrassed and silent, till she embraced him. She felt in control of the situation again. All the nonsense between them was over. She would soon force him to admit the connection between his smugness and his celibacy. And as a lover there was no comparison between him and Denis. There never had been. Jimmy wasn't only a lover; he was a sweetheart whom she had known for years, whose ways she understood and whose honesty she trusted. She felt a pleasure with him she had never felt with Denis, and when they lay quietly, listening to the ripples on the beach and watching the moonlight streak about the blind, she patted his leg and explained in whispers what imbeciles they had been and how close they had gone to wrecking their relationship. Jimmy agreed drowsily.

Next morning he got up and dressed before the maids were about, and Una sat cross-legged on the bed, watching him in admiration. He raised the blind, and she noticed his unusual gravity as he stared over the bay.

"What's the day going to be like?" she asked brightly.

"I wasn't looking," he replied in a faraway voice without looking round. "I was thinking that perhaps we'd better get married as soon as we can. Don't you think so?"

The proposal did not upset her so much as the funereal tone in which it was spoken.

"Oh," she replied blithely but with a sinking heart, "do you think so?"

He leaned his shoulder against the window-frame, and the morning light caught his handsome, big-boned, gloomy face and brought out the deep vertical lines between his eyes.

"We don't want to have to rush into it," he said. "Your people wouldn't like it. Neither would mine."

"I dare say not," she said doubtfully, and then gazed anxiously at him. "You're not disappointed, are you?"

He turned a penetrating look on her. "Aren't you?"

"Me?" she cried, between astonishment and laughter. "Good Lord, no! I think it's marvellous."

"Perhaps disappointment is the wrong word," he said in the same faraway voice, and nodded over his shoulder towards the door. "But we don't want much more of this."

"You mean it's—furtive?"

"Oh, and wrong," he said wearily.

"Wrong?"

By way of reply, he shrugged his shoulders with the broken-down air he wore after a bad day at the office. Translated, it meant: "If you can't see that!"

"Well, it's better than fighting, isn't it?" she asked wistfully. "We know one another long enough, anyway."

"That only makes it worse," he said coldly. "Having stuck it so long, we should have been able to stick it a bit longer. After all, we're not just out for a good time."

He sounded as though he were explaining the policy of his paper. At any other time his tone would have set her at his throat, but now she winced. It was true enough. Their squabbles and misunderstandings had been merely part of the normal behaviour of two grown people who contemplated a lifetime of each other's society and were sensitive to the trifles that threatened their happiness. There had been nothing wrong with them but her own misinterpretation. She sprang out of bed and threw her arms round him.

"Oh, for Heaven's sake, Jimmy, don't blame yourself for this," she cried in an agony of maternal feeling. "This was all my fault."

"No, it wasn't," he said miserably, turning his head away and dropping his editorial air. "It was mine."

"It wasn't, Jimmy, it wasn't," she said eagerly, shaking her head. "I brought you here with that intention. I know I'm a fool. I know I don't know anything about it. You can't imagine what a bitch I am."

"Oh, you're not," he replied in the same tone, his body as stiff as that of a small boy in a fit of the glooms. "It's just that you're so changed. I don't seem to be able to get at you as I used."

"But that's exactly why I wanted you to make love to me, Jimmy," she cried. "I can't get at you either."

"Yes," he added with a sob of jealous rage. "And it's all that damn fellow in Dublin. He's the one who changed you."

"You're wrong there, Jimmy," she cried earnestly, taking him by the shoulders and making him look her between the eyes. "I swear you're wrong. I'm not in the least changed, and he didn't do anything to me. You do believe me, don't you? You know I wouldn't let him do that?" Then the falsehood touched the chord of hysteria in her and she began to sob, pulling wildly at her hair. "Oh, I'm a fool. I do my best, but I don't know anything. And you're right. It is awful."

"Not awful," he said, weeping. "It's just that it's not the right thing for us."

And again she saw the situation through his eyes—as something beautiful that had been irretrievably spoiled by an hour of boredom and dissatisfaction, and which could never be the same again, because innocence had gone out of it.

When he left her, she threw herself on the bed and wept in earnest. She was finished. She had done her best and everything had been wrong. The morning light brightened her room and revealed to her her own wickedness and folly. She knew that, whatever about her deception of him, Jimmy would never forgive her lies. She could not marry him while any possibility existed of his discovering the truth.

Yet, even while she wept, she seemed to see Denis, his plump face aglow with good-natured laughter, and hear his silky, insinuating voice. So she imagined she could get along without him now, did she? She thought there was nothing left for her to learn? She felt so resentful that she stopped crying, put her fists under her chin, and glared at the wall before her while she argued it out with herself. After all, where had she gone wrong? What lesson was it she had failed to learn properly? Was it her fault or was it Jimmy's?

"Oh, damn!" she said suddenly. She sprang up, dressed in a hurry and rushed downstairs to the telephone. She had some minutes to wait for her call and stamped nervously up and down the hall with her eye on the stairs, afraid that Jimmy might appear. Then the bell rang and a meek, sleepy voice answered her. She could almost see the narrow bed against the wall with the telephone on a table at its head and hear the bells in the square, calling people to Mass, and her heart overflowed. All the time she had thought that she was learning the business of love, but now she knew every man and woman is a trade in himself, and he was the only trade she knew.

DON JUAN (RETIRED)

ONE summer evening, Joe French, the insurance agent, went into Cassidy's pub. He went in for the drink only because the after-noon was warm and he felt thirsty. He was a tall, well-built young man with a broad, smooth, pleasant face, popular with everyone, very pious, and going a shade bald in front. He dressed well, spoke well, and had never drifted into any of the sloppy ways of young men in Irish country towns. He had had one disappoint-ment with a girl called Celia Goodwin, whom he had been walk-ing out with for years and who had finally run off with a com-mercial traveller. Celia was a nice girl but a bit unstable. Apart from this, Joe's life had been uneventful enough.

There were two people in the pub: the barman, Jimmy Mat-thews, and a motor-driver called Spike Ward. Jimmy had his elbows on the counter and was studying the daily paper. When French came in, he looked up in a startled way. Jimmy was the leader of the local Republicans, and it may have been this that gave him the air of something peeping out of a burrow. He was tall, with a haggard face like a coffin, a rather modish mop of black hair going white at the temples, and a pair of pince-nez which gave him a cast-iron intellectual expression. French re-spected him as a studious and respectable man but regretted that his politics made him so hostile to the Church. Spike was a flabby-looking man with a plump face, tired eyes, and a cigarette dan-gling from the corner of his mouth. He was a town character, a fellow who had had opportunities and thrown them away on drink and women. People blamed for it the fact that he had had a good baritone voice which had brought him into contact with undesirables—singers and actors.

" 'Tis hot, Joe," said Jimmy, rubbing his hands briskly as if he meant it was cold, and cocking his ear for the order—he was slightly deaf. "A pint?"

"A pint, Jimmy," said French. "Have a drink with me."

"Never touch it, Joe," said Jimmy, leaning his two palms on the counter and bending nearly half-way across it. Jimmy was a man of the most ungainly attitudes, as though his politics had got into his joints.

"I dare say you see enough of it?"

"I see too blooming much of it," said Jimmy candidly, readjusting his pince-nez.

"I suppose you could never manage to finish that, Spike?" French asked good-naturedly. Spike, who had been sitting before an almost empty glass, looked at it thoughtfully.

"I doubt it, Joe," he replied without a smile. "That was one of the two things my poor mother always warned me against."

"And I suppose the other was women," said French with a nod to Jimmy. Spike's face lit up with a sad smile, as much at the thought of the drink as at the word "women."

"Ah, how did you know?" he drawled wonderingly.

"Oh, my Lord!" Jimmy said in disgust. "Is that blooming man talking about women again?"

"Was it I brought up the subject of women, Joe?" Spike asked reproachfully.

"You thundering rogue!" shouted Jimmy, busy with the beer engine. "Do you ever do anything else? Sitting there all day on your fat ass, bragging and boasting!"

"Bragging and boasting?" Spike asked plaintively. "I said a couple of words and I'm accused of bragging and boasting!"

"Ah, what else is it?" Jimmy snapped impatiently. "And I wouldn't mind," he added in the candid tone of a factory hooter, "but 'tis all blooming lies."

"Go on!" Spike said wonderingly with an air of great interest, as if only now were he discovering the full extent of Jimmy's malice. "So I'm a liar as well! Is there anything else now while you're at it?"

"My sweet Lord!" cried Jimmy, pointing to a corner of the bar. "Didn't I hear you there last night, spinning yarns about Lady Something-or-other up in the Glen that you said wanted to bring you back to London with her?"

"And wasn't I a fool not to go with her instead of wasting the best years of my life in this misfortunate hole?" Spike moaned. "What the hell is there here for anyone?"

"There's free drinks if you know how to scrounge them," Jimmy replied bitterly. "Getting all the blooming fools of the town paying for them for you. I wish to God I could knock it down as easy. . . . Thanks, Joe. . . . And I wouldn't mind," he added vigorously, "if you were a decent-looking man itself, but a little jackeen like you that's only two hands higher than a duck." He flashed a joyous look at French and threw back his head with a loud guffaw. "Only two hands higher than a duck," he repeated as he made an adroit half-turn to the till, raised his half-closed eyes reflectively while doing the sum, and held his fingers poised above the keys of the cash register as though about to perform a piano solo.

"Now, there's no need to be personal," Spike said, rising slowly and with great dignity.

"Thanks, Joe," Jimmy said again. He twiddled at his pince-nez, folded his arms, and looked Spike up and down. "You ought to be thoroughly ashamed of yourself," he said severely, "talking like that about a woman of birth and education."

"Tut-tut-tut," clucked Spike pityingly. "What has birth to do with it?"

"What is it so, Spike?" asked French.

"Oh, education, of course," said Jimmy with another guffaw, toppling back stiffly against the shelves with his arms still folded. "They like Spike's cultured conversation."

"Ah, education has nothing to do with it either, man," Spike said wearily. "Women are the same wherever they come from."

"Of course, some of those society women are pretty rotten," said French.

"Oh, shocking! Shocking!" Jimmy agreed gravely with a shake of his head.

"They're what?" Spike asked incredulously, putting down his

glass and approaching French as though he hadn't heard him properly. "What's that you said?"

"Well, you have only to look at the papers," said French.

"Joe," Spike said imploringly, "I beg and beseech you not to mind what you read in the papers. You'll soon be as bad as this man here for the papers. He's getting softening of the brain from them. Sure, women are the same the wide world over, society women and every other sort of women."

"Are you going to stand the man a drink?" shouted Jimmy.

"Maybe you think I can't," said Spike with a sneer.

"I think you're too blooming close," said Jimmy.

"Go on!" drawled Spike with quiet irony. "That's a charming character you're giving me. I'm a bragger and a boaster; I'm a liar, and now I'm close as well! See what it is to have friends!" He took out a halfcrown and laid it solemnly on the counter. "Bite it and see if it's all right," he said scornfully. "But I'm surprised at you, Joe," he said pityingly. " 'Pon my word, I'm surprised."

"But I'm only trying to get a few tips from you, man," said French with a grin.

"I hope they're better than the tips he gives for the horses," said Jimmy.

"Seeing that you know as much about women as you do about horses, I don't think 'twould be much use to you," retorted Spike.

"Isn't it amazing, Joe," Jimmy said eagerly, "isn't it positively amazing that we have a respectable woman left in the town with him?"

"But I have to live in the town, man," said Spike regretfully.

"And you're not going to tell us the secret?" said French.

"What secret?"

"How you have them all tumbling over you. How well they don't do it to Jimmy and me!"

"Two good-looking men, begor!" said Jimmy with another guffaw.

"There ye go again!" Spike said sadly. "A thing is only human nature; ordinary flesh and blood; the same in the highest and the lowest; and ye go on as if 'twas something a man ought to get patented."

"Or insured," chuckled French, but Spike ignored the facetious-
ness.

"A woman wants to be respected as a woman, the way a man
wants to be respected as a man," he went on meditatively. "There's
nothing more in it. I was thinking just as you came in of a certain thing that happened myself a good while ago. It must be
twenty years. 'Twas just the way I was going up to Dublin by
train. While we were waiting in Limerick a girl got into the
carriage. Ye'd know her if I told ye her name, so I won't. At the
time I didn't know it myself. She was a fine, well-educated, good-
looking girl—her father had a big shop, as a matter of fact. That
girl puzzled the wits out of me. There were only the two of us
in the compartment, so, naturally, to pass the time, I started cod-
acting with her. Well, she got into a corner from me and gave
me dog's abuse. 'Tis unknown the names she called me. I didn't
mind that. I mean, girls out of convent schools have the queerest
notions. But after I argued a bit with her and got her friendly
again, I was surprised at the way she carried on. 'Twasn't only
the things she did, but the things she said. Some of them I
wouldn't like to repeat even in this bar."

"Go on!" said French.

"So I began to wonder," continued Spike. "It struck me that
she knew more than her prayers, and when she told me the name
of the hotel she was going to, I decided I'd take a chance and go
there too. We got in a bit late, and we had a cup of tea, and then
it was time for bed. I couldn't get anywhere with her. 'Twas all
talk, talk, talk. I couldn't get near her, so away with me to bed,
thinking I was after wasting my good money on the hotel. Hotels
weren't much in my line, I needn't tell you.

"I declare to my God, at two o'clock in the morning didn't she
come into my room, as bold as brass! I woke up, and the light was
on, and there she was with her head tossed back. Oh, a lovely
figure she had!"

"I'd improve it for her," Jimmy said fiercely. "A dirty thing!"

"Now, that's what you might think," Spike said with a sad
smile, "and that's where you'd be wrong. It wasn't till I saw that
I was hurting her that it began to dawn on me. 'Is this your first

time?' I said. 'Why?' she said. 'What did you think I was?'
Cripes, by that time I didn't know what to think.

"Anyhow, as I say, she stayed the night, and next day I went
back home. But whatever the hell it was, I couldn't stop thinking
about her. That girl haunted me. It's funny with a man, the impression it makes on him, being a girl's first. You know, no matter
what happens her after, that's going to mark her for life. A girl
can forget anything else only that. Now, you might think I'm a
bad man," he added with a mournful smile at French, "but I'm
not as bad as that. God knows, I hadn't much at the time, but I
wrote to that girl and asked her to meet me. I wanted to marry
her."

"You didn't!" said French.

"I did," said Spike. "I saw her in Limerick one night. We went
to a café and had a cup of tea, and I asked her."

"And what did she say?" asked French.

"She said: 'No, thanks, Spike, but all the same I'm glad you
asked me.'"

"What a fool she was!" snorted Jimmy.

"So I said: 'Why did you do it?'" Spike went on, ignoring
him, "and she said: 'I knew when I started fighting you that I
was really fighting myself, and that I'd never have any peace till
I stopped.' Wasn't that a funny thing for her to say?"

"Extraordinary," said French.

"And I said: 'What are you going to do now?' She just
shrugged her shoulders and said: 'I'm a woman now. Whatever
turns up, I can deal with it.' Hardly a week of my life passes but
I think of that girl. 'I'm a woman now.' And she hardly more
than a child."

"A queer old child!" said Jimmy. "She had sense enough not to
marry you." Then, as it gradually dawned on him that Spike had
done it again, that some magic had come into the stale, stuffy
public-house, and that he and French had hung on his words
like any of the poor caubogues of the town, seeking enlighten-
ment, he affected an air of contempt. "Anyway, what is it only
more of your lies?" he said.

"Lies?" Spike said angrily.

"What else is it?"

"After all," said French without malice, "We have only your own word for it."

"And what do you expect?" Spike drawled scornfully. "A signed receipt?"

"We want you to prove it, man," Jimmy said boisterously, pouring out fresh drinks. "What's the good of you coming in here, day after day, telling us about all the women you say fell in love with you when we don't know whether they did or not? Can't you prove it?"

"There was a time I could prove it," Spike said with a smile of reminiscence, but all the same he was taken aback.

"But what's the use of that when you can't prove it now?" shouted Jimmy.

"I'm not the man I was twenty years ago," Spike replied with noble pathos.

"Nor never were, Spike," Jimmy said flatly. "You might as well admit it. You never were."

"We could have a bet on that," said French. "We'll lay you a quid you won't prove it within the next three days."

"A quid?" repeated Spike with a trapped air. "Maybe you'd come down to something within my means."

"We will," Jimmy chortled. "We'll make it ten bob, and I'll put up five of it. But you'll have to prove it," he said sternly. We're not going to pay out our good-looking ten bob for another of your tall yarns." And off he went in another guffaw, thinking of the grand story he'd have for the customers that night.

Spike grew very red. He was thinking the same. It wasn't only that a lot of Spike's little comforts depended on the impression he made on the poor caubogues of the town for whom he was a window that looked out on the great world. He enjoyed it himself. He knew he told occasional lies. He knew he tried to make it artistic. He loved to be thinking and talking of it. He finished his drink slowly and turned to go.

"Take care but I would," he said lightly.

"You'd better," bellowed Jimmy good-humouredly. "Or you need never show your nose in this bar again. . . . I have you now, you blooming chancer!" he yelled joyously after Spike.

"Just to show you what a man is like," Spike said contemptuously over his shoulder. "Freeing Ireland!" he said with a pitying look at French. "A pack of old women that can't even free themselves." He turned from the pavement to hurl a final shaft at Jimmy. "Who am I calling a woman to?" he drawled. "A woman is a thing you can get some pleasure out of, but what pleasure is there in you? You're neither fish, flesh, nor good red herring."

"I'll be with you, Spike," said French as he finished his drink.

"And don't forget to bring us back the proofs, Spike," Jimmy bawled after them. All the way down the main street they could hear him chortling to himself. He obviously thought it a great joke.

It was an unusual experience for French to be walking down the town with Spike, but he was still under the spell. He wanted him to tell about the English lady up the Glen who had wanted to bring him home with her, but Spike wouldn't. He was too mad. His pride had been hurt. He went on with a red face, answering only in impatient monosyllables.

Suddenly, at the end of the town, he stopped. A good-looking red-headed girl was coming towards them.

"Hold on a minute!" he said, his face clearing suddenly. "I want to have a word with this girl. I met her before somewhere. Where the hell was it, or what is her name? Mary—Mary—'twill come to me."

"Would you sooner I'd go on?" asked French, suddenly awkward, remembering the bet.

"Oh, hang on, hang on," Spike said casually. "It mightn't be any good. . . . Hallo, Mary," he added in a peculiar unctuous drawl, a broad smile flickering across his melancholy, beery face as he raised his battered old bowler with antique courtesy. "It's ages since I saw you. Where were you?"

"See you later, Spike," French said in confusion, and went on.

He looked round only when he reached the bend in the road and then saw Spike and the girl following him, deep in conversation. Spike seemed different as though someone had oiled his hinges. The light was turning and the little plantation by the roadside was filling with a tangle of shadows. The two stood for a while, talking, the smoke of the town rising behind them; then the girl gave a hasty glance round and crossed the wall into the plantation. Spike followed. They did it so quickly that French almost lost sight of them. He waited a few minutes, then strolled idly back, glancing into the plantation. After that, he sat on a wall by the road and lit his pipe. He had a lot to think about. He realized that Spike's romances were not all romances; that there were women who behaved as he described them behaving. He thought of the girl from Limerick, but in place of her shadowy figure he put that of Celia Goodwin. It had now become easy to imagine it. He could see her on the train, in the hotel, in the bedroom at two in the morning with her head defiantly thrown back, and finally in the café, telling Spike that she was a woman at last and refusing to marry him. Something that had always been unintelligible to him had at last become a reality, and it was exactly as though he had discovered how she had been unfaithful to him and with whom. It was a shock; a different sort of shock from what it had been five years before, but a shock just the same.

It was nearly an hour before Spike came out with the girl. They got over the wall hastily and separated without a word or a backward glance. The girl squared her shoulders and set off down the road, head in air, as though admiring the scenery in the evening light. Spike approached French, his face as grave and smug as a greyhound's or a parish priest's. There was a look of mock humility on it as though at any moment he were going to say he had done nothing but what any man would have done under the circumstances.

"I suppose we might as well be going back," he said modestly.

"I suppose so," said French, and then, growing red, took a ten-shilling note from his wallet. "I owe you that, I think," he said.

He felt very embarrassed about it, but Spike took the whole affair and put it on an everyday level.

"You're quite satisfied about that?" he asked anxiously, looking first at the note and then at French as though wondering whether conscience would allow him to accept it.

"Oh, quite," said French.

A ROMANTIC

ONE of Mick Dowling's friends whom I became friendly with was a railway clerk known as Frenchy. At first I assumed his name must be "French" till he corrected me. His real name was Miah Hennessey. He had something like a fixation on Mick. Not only was Mick a university man, which Miah was convinced he would have been himself only for the poverty of his family; he was tall and handsome, with a broad, unimpassive face that reflected a tolerant but unsusceptible mind. He was a character not easily swayed; a man who looked neither back nor sideways; a realist who took everything with a grain of salt—even Miah.

And Miah certainly needed a bagful. He was a big, powerful, pasty-faced man who alternated between bouts of laziness and energy. He was exceedingly popular, being both kindly and un-assuming; which was just as well for him because he was some-thing of a know-all, and could not help understanding everyone's problems better than they understood them themselves. There was nothing of the specialist's aridity about Miah; he was alter-nately gardener, builder, mechanic, and cook, and he threw as much energy into one of those peripheral activities as most peo-ple put into the central passion of their lives. It was only natural that he should occasionally overlook the trifling affairs of the Great Southern and Western Railway Company.

When he tired of his job, he simply invented an excuse for a call in town and dropped in on Mick, who was usually hard at work.

"Are you back again, Hennessey?" he would growl. "You do

no work yourself, and you'd like to prevent anyone else doing it."

But when it came to ragging, Miah, with his fluent enthusiasms, was always more than a match for him.

"You'd better mind yourself, Mick," he would say in a grave and gentle tone, putting his hand lightly on Mick's arm and whispering. "Sometimes you frighten me. You're so steady that by the time you're forty it will take two bottles of whisky to relax you. Mark my words, Mick, you're heading for a really terrible breakdown."

Miah's real passion, the thing he really knew—better than anyone in Ireland, as he modestly assured us—was France. France and the French. That was how he came by the nickname. For a man who had hardly ever been outside Cork, he spoke French with what seemed to me a remarkable purity of accent; at least, I flattered myself that I could recognize its purity. The other clerks thought he was dotty, but none of them would take the trouble to find out. He knew France, and in France everything was really better, just as he said: the climate, the food, the drink, the movies, the books, the girls—particularly the girls. He begged Mick and me on no account to make up our minds on the subject of girls till we had sampled the French ones.

Mick was really very fond of him in practice though he disapproved of him in principle. I never quite knew whether it was the practice or the principle that really swayed Mick; all I knew was that he would take things from Miah which would have shocked him coming from me. I suppose the truth is that they were complementary types, and that Mick gave Miah a sense of stability, while Miah gave Mick a sense of the variety and richness of life he felt he lacked. In private he told me that Miah had a streak of genius. Then, because he rarely made any statement without qualification, he added gloomily that, of course, Miah was as mad as a hatter.

When we went out together, Miah worked himself into ecstasies, trying to induce us to drink claret instead of stout. He sipped reverently, closed his eyes, and murmured lines of love poetry in French; and I, gathering that wine was the secret of French lightness, logic, and love-making, felt my palate being schooled, but after one mouthful of claret Mick returned to stout and refused to give wine a second chance. He said it reminded him too much of Parrish's Food. On another occasion, Miah produced a battered packet of French cigarettes which some tobacconist had procured for him, and begged us to say honestly, if given our chance, we would ever smoke anything else. His eyes as he watched us were soft with tears, and I couldn't find it in my heart to say the damn things made me sick, but Mick, having smoked the first one down to the butt, said he'd give up smoking if that was the only alternative. Miah got us tied up with extraordinary and most alarming women to whom he introduced us under false names, but though Mick was exceedingly tolerant and allowed himself to be referred to as Joe Murphy, nobody could ever divert him even for half an hour from his own Babiche. He was a man who never looked either back or sideways. He continued to nag at Miah to do something practical for himself, and Miah, with a glass of sour claret before him and an unwholesome cigarette between his lips, smiled sadly and asked if Mick meant that he should get himself appointed station-master of Ballydehob. His own ideas for the future were never less than magnificent if only they had remained the same for two days running.

Then, one day, when he wasn't feeling as full of bounce as usual, he would break down—really break down, I mean—and with his head in his hands lament that he was wasting his life and must leave the railway and take up some career with reasonable hopes of advancement. Mick was the only one who could work him up to this point, but even Mick couldn't keep him up to it, and a few days later Miah would be doing a wonderful turn, imitating his own tears and Mick's wooden countenance for any of our friends he happened to run into. Mick would pretend to be annoyed, but it was rarely more than pretence.

"Get out, you fat slug!" he would growl at Miah. "You'll get the sack one of these days, and you'll laugh at the other side of your puss."

"Oh, no, Mick," Miah would say serenely. "I won't get the sack. You'll get the sack, and you'll be so upset that you'll have a nervous breakdown and take to the bottle. That's the only thing that worries me. Now, if you'd be said by me and drink wine—"

Mick and I sometimes discussed whether he really enjoyed the wine and the smelly cigarettes or was only kidding himself. Mick in his growling, critical mood maintained that it was only part of an act that was becoming second nature; but I sometimes wondered which was the act, and whether stout, Virginia cigarettes, Sunday Mass, and Babiche were quite so substantial as they sometimes seemed. I knew Mick would always prefer the local drink and the local doll, always make the best of his circumstances, but I doubted my own capacity for doing so.

Then, like the rest of us, Miah got limed in nature's snare by one Susie Morgan. In that particular matter it would be hard to say who really got caught, for Susie lived in a small terrace house with three brothers and two sisters, and was so overcome by the yarn Miah spun her that she hadn't a chance of behaving like a self-respecting snare. He wooed her in a haze of euphoria. He was going to the university to pass an exam in something or other (he was never sure what), and take a job in the south of France (he was never sure where), and have what he called "a villa" of his own where the sun would shine on them during all but fourteen days of the year (it had been established statistically) for the rest of their natural lives. No wonder the poor girl felt it was God sent him. Meanwhile, it was a joy to hear him criticize the bad way everything was done in Cork and describe the wonderful clotheslines with pulley-blocks they would have in their own back yard. She believed it all and married him.

Mick and I were both a bit soft on Susie, and Miah encouraged it. Frenchwomen were notoriously broad-minded, and it probably gave him the illusion of being married to one, though it had no such effect on us. Susie was small and slight; she had a long, eager face like an energetic version of a Pre-Raphaelite madonna, with long, fair hair brushed down at either side. She really was quite mad on Miah, but she couldn't let him alone. They had scarcely set up house when she began interrupting him to ask about the clotheslines.

"I'll try and manage a half day for it next week, Susie," he said gently in the tone you'd use to a child who wanted you to play with him.

"But we need them badly, Miah. Couldn't you do it now?"

"How could I, Susie?" he asked with a touch of severity. "Don't you realize that I have to get the pulley-blocks?"

"Really, Miah!" she exclaimed, clasping her hands anxiously. "The way you go on about those old pulley-blocks! Couldn't you put up an ordinary line for me, so?"

"An ordinary line would only be a waste of time, dear," he said sadly. "Anything that's worth doing is worth doing well."

When Susie got one of her brothers to put up the lines for her, Miah was hurt. He said with tears in his eyes that he hadn't thought she was so hard. Then he got a fit of energy and did the job properly—a really fine job that any woman might well be proud of—and even put up a cupboard in the kitchen for her. But even this didn't satisfy Susie. Next thing she wanted was shelves.

Miah was rather disappointed in Susie. It seemed to him that Irishwomen could never rise above shelves. You threw good-looking young fellows in their way, but they only mothered them and tried to make them take cod-liver oil. They wouldn't let you rest of an evening, but wanted you to chop wood or fetch coal or put a washer on the tap. They even followed you to the lavatory when you had ensconced yourself there with an illustrated magazine and nagged at you through the keyhole. A man had nothing like the same peace with his wife as he had with his mother. It is a discovery that many Irishmen have made from time to time.

When he first told Susie about snails in France she held up her hands in horror and said beseechingly: "Miah, don't go on please! You're only making it up." When he went out into the garden and collected a canful of what he said were "genuine *Bourguignons*" she went into screaming hysterics. "Miah, take them away! Take them away, I tell you. I'm going to be sick."

"I'm not going to do anything with them yet," he shouted angrily. "You have to starve them first."

"Starve them? What a thing to do! I won't have them in the house at all, I tell you."

"All right, all right," he said in disgust. "I'll leave them in the yard."

"You will not leave them in the yard, Miah. I won't stay in the house unless you take them away."

So Miah had to take the can of snails to his mother and get her to starve them. She blinked, tut-tutted, and called him "a mad divil," but she did as he asked her. Miah ate them all alone with great reverence and pride and said unctuously that they were delicious. All they needed was the right wine.

Miah was genuinely disappointed in Susie. Of course, he asked a lot of her. No man living within a few hundred yards of his mother can help feeling at times that he has married the wrong woman, but I see now that Miah would have been disappointed in anyone. Mick said that Susie was a girl in a million. Miah said mournfully that she was frigid. She showed a regrettable tendency to prefer real shelves to imaginary ones, a thing Miah couldn't imagine in any really passionate woman. She would have preferred real Cork babies with common accents to imaginary ones in the south of France who spoke French perfectly from childhood, but Miah, seeing all he had lost in his mother, had no intention of letting Susie's attentions be subdivided till they were safe in France. It was too dangerous. She wouldn't eat snails and she wouldn't make love according to the textbooks Miah brought home. He had tried Fig. 18 with her on the rug in front of the fire, and it was even worse than the snails. For days he went round with a sulky air, and told her mournfully that if this was how she felt about him, she would have done better not to marry him. He talked the same way to us. That is what I mean by his influence on Mick. Mick had never heard of Fig. 18, and anyone else who had tried to tell him about it would probably have got a sock in the jaw.

As protection against the perpetual wail for new shelves, Miah did what many a good man before him has done and fell ill. He complained of headaches. His mother blamed Susie's cooking for them, but it wasn't the cooking; it was the shelves. Their place had now been taken by doctors, and Susie was nagging him to get his headaches seen to till he broke down and told her he wouldn't because he already knew he had a tumour on the brain.

"God bless us and save us, Miah!" Susie said despairingly. "Wouldn't you get it seen to?"

"If my suspicions are right, dear," he said tragically, "nobody can do anything."

"But can't you make sure, at least?" begged Susie.

"Do you think I could live, knowing I was going to die a horrible death inside a few months?" he asked, giving her a ghastly smile of reproach.

"Hell's cure to you!" Susie's brothers said when she got them to put up the shelves for her. "Why couldn't you marry a decent tradesman instead of a blooming gas-bag like him? Snails, be-god!"

None of the Morgan family ever really got over the snails. They said it showed that Miah wasn't all there.

As walks were the only thing that relieved his tumour, he was less and less at home in the evenings. By this time Mick was married himself and living with Babiche and their child in a nice little suburban house, which he worked like a black on. Miah's walks were mostly in that direction, and Mick put him to work as though he hadn't a tumour at all. Miah was suffi-ciently fond of Mick to overlook this, though privately he told me that Mick was ruining Babiche and the child. I could well believe that, for Mick was one of those powerful, easy-going, con-siderate husbands who will ruin any family and enjoy it. This was where I disagreed with Miah, who was already turning it into a romantic novel and assured me that, like himself, Mick was disappointed in marriage, and if only he had the nerve, would break away from Babiche and clear out to England or America. Miah disliked Babiche. She not only answered Mick back; she answered Miah back as well. She did worse. She told him that she regretted not being married to him instead of Mick, as it deprived her of the opportunity of wringing his neck. That, as Miah said with a sad shake of his head, was enough to show anybody the sort of woman she was, and he kept on pertina-ciously trying to get Mick to admit that she was frigid too, and that life in the little house on College Road was hell. If this was so, Mick managed to conceal it pretty well.

To everyone's surprise, it was not Miah but Susie who eventu-ally fell ill. Her condition was hopeless from the start. But the really curious thing was the change that came over Miah. He seemed to become a different man, quiet, conscientious, and industrious. Even his mother-in-law admitted it—"Search the world over and you wouldn't find a husband like him." He, who normally couldn't be induced to spend an evening in his own home, hurried back each evening from the office and did most of the cooking and cleaning. For months he nursed Susie with genuine devotion, and after her death he collapsed on Mick and blamed himself for it.

"Nonsense, man!" Mick said sharply. During Susie's illness he had developed a new respect for Miah. "If I did for Babiche what you did for Susie, I'd look for a medal."

"It's not the same thing, Mick," Miah said hopelessly. "Susie died a disappointed woman. I disappointed her."

His mother returned to keep house for him, and did so till her own death five years later, but Miah's moody fits grew more protracted, his fits of enthusiasm more exalted. Two short holidays in France did nothing to settle him. Mick was very concerned for him. He tried to get him to marry again, but Miah either felt he could never replace Susie or was afraid of fresh responsibilities. Then Mick decided that the only hope for him was to get a job in France.

"It's just like anything else," he said to me. "We all have high notions and nothing but experience can cure us. A few months working in France and he'd be very glad to settle down at home."

But this wasn't as easy as it sounded. Apart from knowing French, Miah had no particular qualifications for a job in France, and even if he had, Cork was no place to hear of one.

Then, one day, passing from one bay to the next, Miah did something no one was supposed to do in theory and everybody did in practice: he crossed over the buffers of a stationary train. It didn't remain stationary, and he was picked out from beneath it with his left arm mangled unmercifully. He was still conscious, and was put lying on some bales of cloth while the ambulance was sent for. Once again that astonishing man had a surprise in store for everybody. Miah, who worked himself into hysterics over an imaginary pain in the head, suffered agonies with quiet courtesy. It was Susie's illness all over again, as though real suffer-

ing, real grief, came as a relief to him after what he had endured
in his imagination.

It did not last, of course. He lost his arm. Mick and I visited
him regularly in hospital, and he seemed to enjoy being there
and having nothing to do all day but dream. There was a lot of
pother about the compensation, and he enjoyed that too. There
was nothing he liked more than composing withering letters to
the railway company, though his solicitor showed a disappointing lack of appreciation of the style. Miah's attention had now
been turned to the law; he thought he might take it up himself
and was sure there should be an opening for a lawyer with style.
This was about as far as he got in planning for the future, and
Mick was very worried about it.

"I'll be all right, Mick," Miah said to comfort him. Then he
gave Mick a penetrating look and his voice dropped to an in-
cantatory monotone. "Has it ever occurred to you, Mick, that
all this was intended?"

"Intended to make you work?" Mick asked with a grin.

"No, Mick. Intended to leave me free. Didn't it occur to you
that it's almost as if somebody intended to shake me out of the
rut I was getting into and force me to lead the life I should have
been leading?"

But Mick was lacking in those perceptions and intuitions
which seem to come to others from a world outside themselves.

"No, it didn't," he growled, rubbing his temple thoughtfully.
"It strikes me that you're going to find it hard to live on whatever
you get."

"I'll be able to live all right on it in France, Mick," Miah said
with serene confidence.

"You won't be able to live on it anywhere."

"But you don't understand, Mick," Miah said with genuine
pity. "It's different in France. Everything is cheaper there."

Mick was really alarmed. He did not mind the idea of Miah's
going to France—as I have said, it seemed to him the only solution—but he had begun to notice what he described as "a bit
of a crack" in Miah's character; his plunges from enthusiasm to
despair were becoming more marked; and he was afraid that

this might be Miah's way of escaping from the consciousness of his crippled state and would be followed by a depression worse than anything that had gone before.

"I wish you'd be practical," he said gloomily.

"Oh, but I am practical, Mick," Miah said excitedly. "It's you who're not practical. I could live like a rajah on less than that in France. I have it all worked out."

"I hope it keeps fine for you."

"Oh, but it will, Mick," gurgled Miah, and his fat face glowed. "That's what it does in the south of France. You see, the trouble with you is that you're doing what you've always done—inventing obstacles."

"I haven't noticed any shortage of obstacles."

"But what else are you doing, Mick?" asked Miah with love and admiration mingled in his tone with wonderment at Mick's obstinacy. "A man like you, who could be earning thousands, sticking in a hole like this for a couple of lousy hundred! I'm not an old man. I can work even with one hand. I might even marry again," he went on with growing enthusiasm. "The French are wonderful housekeepers; you have no idea. And you and Larry could come out and stay with us, and we'd sit on the terrace of an evening and drink our couple of bottles of wine. Wouldn't it be marvellous?"

And, of course, he managed temporarily to convince us, as he had so often convinced us before, and we wandered back through greasy streets under an indiarubber sky, wondering how we could stick a hole like Cork for the rest of our days. Some little town in the south of France which we had never seen was running through our minds—oh, nothing very ambitious; like Miah we did not ask much of life: some little town like Carpentras or Tarascon which formed an image of grace and completeness and made all our surroundings seem trivial. Mick was doing very well for himself; he had attracted the attention of someone in the Department of Education and would end up as a school-inspector, but in Ballydehob, not in Carpentras.

When Miah came out of hospital he was in no hurry to go. He took to dropping in on us at work, just to let us know how things should be done. We both lacked system, it seemed. He also took his time about disposing of the house and furniture, but even these went at last, and one day when Mick called to bring him home with him, he found Miah sitting on a box in the empty kitchen, weeping. Mick felt like tears himself, though he wasn't the sort to show it. It was only now that we were losing him that we realized how much Miah had meant to us, how much of our lives he had made tolerable by his fantasies. The city would be a more depressing place without him. Mick even admitted to me with a sly grin that he was beginning to think Miah was right and that he really was a disappointed man.

They took his bags over to Mick's house. Miah had always sneered at the house, but he didn't sneer now. He even developed a capacity for amusing himself with the children—there were now two of these—and became something of a hero with them. He admitted that Mick had a nice little home and that Babiche was a good wife, a very good wife, even if she did answer back. What use was a wife without a bit of spirit?

"Of course, Mick," he said sadly, "you always knew how to respect her. I never really began to respect Susie till I lost her."

When we saw him off at the station he was weeping. We found it hard enough to keep our own faces bright as the train slid out under the tunnel with the great sandstone cliff and the houses on top. Already we imagined it emerging at the other side of the city, at Rathpeacon, among the green fields, as if in a different world, and something of our youth gone with it. In a small place like Cork funerals are frequently less harrowing than separations: one has no illusion that the dead are enjoying themselves in one's absence.

But we weren't yet done with Miah's surprises. He stayed in London to visit some cousins whose existence he had never before seemed aware of. Next he was in Birmingham, looking for a job there. He was waiting for the fine weather to go to France. It was all very strange.

It took us weeks to realize the truth. Miah simply had no intention of going to France. He had never any intention of going there. All his life he had been using it as an escape from a reality which was too oppressive for him, and now that it threatened to become a reality itself, he could not face it. But it was not until the fine weather came that we really admitted to ourselves that only that his home was broken up and himself too tired to start again, he would have been back with us by the first boat.

Instead, he hung on for a year, betwixt and between, till gradually he sank into a tramp—oh, none of your down-and-outs, of course; a comfortable tramp who knew where to go and what to do, but all the same a tramp, driven on by some restlessness beyond human reason.

Eventually, to the romantic, reality itself becomes romance, but not until he has let it slip from his hands. That is the romantic's tragedy.

THE CUSTOM OF
THE COUNTRY

I

It is remarkable the difference that even one foreigner can make in a community when he is not yet accustomed to its ways, the way he can isolate its customs and hold them up for your inspection. Things that had been as natural to you as bread suddenly need to be explained, and the really maddening thing is that you can't explain them. After a while you begin to wonder if they're real at all. Sometimes you doubt if you're real yourself.

We saw that with the new factory when they brought over an English foreman named Ernest Thompson to teach the local workers the job. It was not that people didn't like Ernie. They did. He was a thoroughly obliging chap, more particularly in confidential matters that our people wouldn't like to discuss among themselves, and a number of respectable married couples, as well as some that were neither married nor respectable, were under obligations to him which they would have found it dangerous to admit. Nor was it that he was stand-offish, because, in fact, he wanted to be in on everything, from the way you made love to your wife to the way the mountainy men made poteen, and he was never without ideas for improving the one or the other. There wasn't much he didn't know something about, and quite a lot of things he let on to know everything about. But for all that he could give you useful tips about mending a car or building a house, he put you off at the same time by the feeling you had that if he was natural, then there must be something wrong with you.

Take, for instance, the time when he started walking out with Anna Martin. Anna was a really nice girl even if she was a bit innocent. That is never much harm in a girl you care for. Anna's innocence showed even in her face, plump, dark, childish, and all in smooth curves from the bulging boyish forehead to the big, dimpled chin, with the features nesting in the hollows as if only waiting for a patch of sunlight to emerge.

Her mother, a widow woman of good family who had had the misfortune to marry one Willie Martin, a man of no class, kept a tiny huckster shop at a corner of the Cross. She was a nice, well-preserved, well-spoken little roly-poly of a woman with bad feet which gave her a waddle, and piles, which made her sit on a high hard chair, and she sat for the greater part of the day in the kitchen behind the shop with her hands joined in her lap and an air of regret for putting the world to the trouble of knowing her, though all the time she was thinking complacently of the past glories of her family, the Henebry-Hayeses of Coolnaleama. Mrs. Martin had a sallow face that looked very innocent down the middle and full of guile round the edges, like a badly ironed pillowcase, and appeared so refined and ethereal that you thought her soul must be made of shot silk. Anna knew her mother's soul was made of stouter stuff. She was a woman of great principle, and if Anna bought a dress in a fashionable Protestant shop, she had to pretend it was bought in a Catholic one. It was not that her mother would create scenes; she was not a woman for scenes, but back the Protestant frock would go if she had to bring it herself. The coffee they drank tasted mouldy, but it was Catholic coffee. She didn't believe in digging with the wrong foot; it was linked somewhere in her mind with family pride and keeping to your own class, and until the last maid left, having smashed the last bit of family china off the kitchen wall, and denounced "the Hungry Hayeses," as she called them, to the seventh generation of horse-stealers and land-grabbers, Mrs. Martin had never ceased in her humble deprecating way to persuade them to wear cap and apron, serve from the left, and call Anna "miss."

That she had failed was entirely the doing of the Mahoneys, two mad sisters who kept another small shop farther up towards the chapel and corrupted her maids with tea and scandal. They were two tall, excitable women, one with the face of a cow and the other with the face of a greyhound, and the greyhound had a son who was going in for the priesthood. The madness of the Mahoneys took a peculiar form which made them think themselves as good as the Henebry-Hayeses of Coolnaleama; a harmless enough illusion in itself if only they didn't act as though it were true. When Mrs. Martin had Anna taught to play the violin, they had Jerry taught to play the piano (the scandal was dreadful, because the piano wouldn't go through their front door and up the stairs, and had to be hoisted aboard like a cow on a hooker). When Anna and Jerry were both to have played at a concert in the convent, the Mahoneys, by a diabolical intrigue, succeeded in getting her name omitted from the program, and Mrs. Martin refused to let Anna play at all and dragged her from the hall by the hand. Sister Angela, Mrs. Martin's friend, agreed that she was perfectly right, but Anna bawled the whole night through and said her mother had made a show of her. Even at that age Anna had no sense of what was fitting.

Then Jeremiah Henebry-Hayes, Mrs. Martin's brother, came home from the States and stayed with her, driving off each day to Killarney, Blarney, or Glengarriff in a big car with the Stars and Stripes flying from the bonnet, and the madness of the Mahoneys reached such a pitch that they brought home a dis-

solute brother of their own from Liverpool and hired a car for
him to drive round in. They couldn't get rid of him after, and it
was Mrs. Martin who gave him the couple of cigarettes on tick.
She was never paid, but it was worth it to her.

It was no easy life she had of it at all, with the Mahoneys sending in their spies to see if she was selling proprietary stuff at cut
prices, but it must be said for the commercial travellers that they
knew a lady when they saw one, and tipped her off about the
Mahoneys' manœuvres.

Finally Ernest Thompson made the shop his home. Mrs. Martin's cooking was good, and he returned the compliment in scores
of ways from mending the electric light to finding cures for her
piles. She couldn't get over his referring to the piles, but, of
course, he wasn't Irish. She was very amiable with him, and
waddled round after Anna, correcting her constantly over her
shoulder in a refined and humorous way; not, as Anna well
knew, in any hope of improving her, but just to show Ernest
that she knew what was becoming.

"Well, well!" she exclaimed in mock alarm at one of Anna's
outbursts of commonness. "Where on earth do you pick up
those horrible expressions, Anna? I wonder do young ladies in
England talk like that, Mr. Thompson?"

"I should say there aren't many young ladies anywhere who
can talk like Anna," Ernest said fondly.

"Oh, my!" cried Mrs. Martin, deliberately misunderstanding
him and throwing up her hands in affected fright. "You don't
mean she's as bad as that, Mr. Thompson?"

"Anna is a very exceptional girl, Mrs. Martin," he replied
gravely.

"Ah, I don't know," sighed Mrs. Martin, looking doubtfully
at Anna as though she were some sort of beast she wouldn't like
to pass off on a friend. "Of course, she should be all right," she
added, ironing out another crease or two in the middle of her
face. "She comes of good stock, on one side anyway. I don't
suppose you'd have heard of the Henebry-Hayeses?" she added
with quivering modesty. "You wouldn't, to be sure—how could
you?"

Ernest skirted this question, which seemed to involve a social gaffe of the first order, like not knowing who the Habsburgs were.

"Of course," Mrs. Martin went on, almost going into convulsions of abnegation, "I believe people nowadays don't think as much of breeding as they used to, but I'm afraid I'm terribly old-fashioned."

"You're not old-fashioned at all, Ma," said Anna, who knew all the vanity that her mother concealed behind her girlish modesty. "You're antediluvian."

"Of course, her father's people were what we in Ireland call self-made," added Mrs. Martin, revenging herself in a ladylike way. "I suppose you can see it breaking out in her at times."

On the whole, though Mrs. Martin wasn't an enthusiastic woman, she was inclined to approve of Ernest. At any rate he was socially more presentable than an Irishman of the same class. Only a woman as refined as herself would be likely to notice that he wasn't quite the thing. That showed how little Mrs. Martin really knew about people, for even while he was listening deferentially to her account of the Henebry-Hayeses, Ernest was plotting in connection with Anna things that would have made the Henebry-Hayeses turn in their graves. Ernest was lonely, he was accustomed to having women; he knew all the approaches. He took Anna for drives, filled her with gin, talked to her in the most intimate fashion of his experiences with other women, but he found that he was really getting nowhere with her. Anna's innocence would have stopped a cavalry charge.

She didn't even understand what he was getting at until one night when the two of them were walking in a lane up the hill with the valley of the city far below them. Ernest felt if Anna had any romance in her at all that this should touch her. He suggested that they go away for a week-end together.

"But what do you want to go away for a week-end for, Ernie?" drawled Anna in the accent which her mother said was like the wind up a flue.

"Because I want to make love to you, Anna," he replied in a voice that throbbed like an organ.

"And what do you think you're doing now?" Anna asked gaily.

"Don't you want me to make love to you?" he asked earnestly, seizing her by the wrists and looking deep into her eyes. "We love one another, don't we? What more do we need?"

"Ah, merciful God, Ernie!" she cried in panic, understanding him at last. "I couldn't do that. I couldn't."

"Why not, Anna?" He was almost sobbing.

"Because 'twould be a sin."

"Is love like ours a sin?"

"What the hell has love to do with it? 'Tis always a sin unless people are married."

"Always?"

"Always."

He looked at her doubtfully for a few moments as though he were trying to hypnotize her and then dropped her hands mournfully and with finality.

"Oh, well, if you feel like that about it!"

She saw he had expected something different and that he was now disappointed and hurt. She took out her cigarettes and offered him one, more by way of peace-offering than anything else. By way of peace-offering, he also refused it. She saw then he was really mad with her. He stood against the wall, his hands by his sides, looking up at the sky, and the match-flame showed his plump, dark, handsome face with the injured expression of a child who has been told he can't have an apple. Anna felt terrible about it.

"I suppose you think I'm not fond of you now?" she drawled miserably, turning up her face to let out a column of smoke.

"I don't go by what people think," Ernest said stiffly without even looking at her. "I can only go by how they behave."

"Because I am, if you want to know," she said trying to keep back her tears. "And, God knows, I wouldn't tell you a lie."

"I don't suppose it's altogether your fault," Ernest said in the same stiff, judicial tone. "I dare say you're inhibited."

"I dare say I am," agreed Anna, who didn't know what he was talking about, but was prepared to plead guilty to anything if only it made him happy. "I suppose 'tis only the custom of the country. Would an English girl do it?"

"If she loved a man," Ernest said hollowly, studying the Milky Way.

"And what would her family say?"

"They wouldn't be consulted," said Ernest. "A woman's life is her own, isn't it?"

It was as well for Mrs. Martin that she couldn't hear that. It was as well for Ernest that the dead generations of Henebry-Hayeses in Coolnaleama graveyard couldn't hear it. Men had died at their hands for less than that.

II

In spite of this rebuff Ernest continued to call and to see Anna outside of work. He borrowed a car, and took her and her mother for long drives into the country. By this time Mrs. Martin had become quite resigned to the thought of him as a husband for her daughter. So few Irishmen of good family would look at a girl without money, and if Anna had to marry outside what Mrs. Martin regarded as her class, it was as well for her to marry a foreigner whose origins would be obscured by his manners.

"Of course, he's not what I'd call a gentleman," she said with resignation, "but then, I suppose we can't have everything."

"Well, I'm not a lady either," retorted Anna, "so we suit one another fine."

"It's nice to hear it from your own lips anyway," giggled her mother in her genteel way of bridling up.

"Well, I'm not, and that's the holy bloody all of it," said Anna. "I'm not a lady, and I couldn't be a lady, and it's no use trying to make me a lady."

"The language is delightful," chirruped her mother with the affected lightness that always drove Anna mad. "I hope you talk like that to them when you're in England. They're sure to love it."

"Who said I was going to England?" bawled Anna, growing commoner than ever under the provocation. "He never asked me yet."

"Well, I hope when he does that you won't forget you're supposed to be a Catholic as well as a lady," her mother said, waddling off to bed.

"A Catholic?" cried Anna in alarm. "What difference does that make?"

"Oh, none in the world," her mother said cheerfully over her shoulder. "Only you can't marry him unless he turns."

"Oh, Christ!" moaned Anna.

"I beg your pardon, Anna," her mother said, huffing up in the doorway, a picture of martyred gentility. "Did I hear you say something?"

"I said I might as well stuff my head in the gas oven," said Anna despairingly.

"Ah, well," said her mother complacently, "I dare say he'll turn. Most men do."

But Anna, lying awake, could not treat the matter so lightly. Every morning she was up at seven, gave her mother tea in bed before going to early Mass, did the shopping, and minded the shop three nights a week, and a girl doesn't behave like that unless she has a man so much on her mind that whatever she does seems to be done under his eye, for his approval, as though she were living in a glasshouse. "I have it bad all right," she thought in her common way. But even her commonness seemed different when Ernest was there. She had been brought up to look on it as a liability, but Ernest made it seem like a talent.

As well as that, she already had a bad conscience about the week-end she had denied him. She might be inhibited, but her maternal instinct was very strong, and she was haunted by the picture of Ernest looking up at the stars, on the point of tears, and all because of her, and she felt it could never, never be right to deprive someone you cared for of any little pleasure he valued. To suggest that she should now refuse to marry him unless he became a Catholic seemed to her the end.

A fortnight later they were in the sitting-room that overlooked the Cross, a stuffy little room where all the Henebry-Hayes treasures were kept, when he suddenly proposed to her. Her heart sank. She got up hastily and looked in the glass, then lit a cigarette and threw herself in an armchair with her legs crossed, a boyish pose that her mother would certainly have denounced as vile, but Anna was too wrought up even to imagine what her mother would have said.

"I don't know that I can, Ernie," she said in a businesslike tone.

"What's the difficulty?" Ernest asked, leaning forward with his pudgy hands clasped and a new look of anxiety on his face.

"It's hard to explain, Ernie," she said, taking a puff of her cigarette and managing to look as brassy as three film stars.

"Why, Anna?" he asked, growing pale. "Is there another man?"

"Ah, not at all," she said impatiently, wishing to God he wouldn't always act the know-all and try to get in a jump ahead of you to maintain his pose of omniscience.

"You needn't be afraid to tell me, you know," he said soothingly. "It doesn't matter. It doesn't matter even if you've got a kid already."

"A what?" she asked with a start.

"A kid. Lots of girls do."

"They don't in this country," she said, growing red. "It's not that at all. It's—well, you see, I'm a Catholic."

"A Catholic?" Ernest exclaimed with great interest and real pleasure. "Are you really, Anna? I thought you were an R.C."

"It's the same thing."

"Are you sure?" he asked doubtfully. He hated to be caught out on a matter of fact.

"Positive. And it seems I just can't marry a Protestant."

"But why not?" he asked with a smile. "I don't mind."

"No, but other people do. I don't understand the half of it myself. It's Ma—she's simply dotty on religion. She can tell you."

"I'll talk to your mother," Ernest said in a low murmur that was full of meaning. She could see from the battle-light in his eyes that he was looking forward to the scene.

Mrs. Martin was sitting by the fire in the kitchen, and when they came in, she fluttered about Ernest in great concern, but for once he was too angry for ceremony. He took a kitchen chair and rested one knee on it, smiling crookedly like a sunset in a stormy sky.

"Mrs. Martin," he began in a low, complaining tone, "Anna tells me she can't marry me because of my religion. Is that true?"

"Oh," Mrs. Martin cried joyously, not forgetting her own manners in spite of his bad ones, "are you going to be married,

Ernest? Well, well, this is a surprise! I think she's very lucky, Ernest; I do, indeed, and I hope you'll be very happy."

"So do I," Ernest said with another wry smile, refusing to let go of the chair and embrace her tenderly the way she expected, "but I don't see how we can."

"Ah, that's nothing," Mrs. Martin said with a shrug and a giggle. "Where there's a will there's a way, Ernest. We'll soon get over that. Of course," she added, just to show him how simple it was, "if you were a Catholic, you could be married in the morning."

"No doubt," Ernest said remorselessly, "but, you see, I'm not. I was brought up Church of England, and I see nothing particularly wrong with it."

"Why would you?" Mrs. Martin said tolerantly. "I had some very dear friends who were Church of England. Indeed, they were better than a good many of our own. You might even be able to get a dispensation," she added, going on her knees with the poker, a tactical position that enabled her to look at him and look away as best suited her.

"A dispensation," repeated Ernest. "What's that?"

"It's really permission from the Pope." She gave him a rapid glance over her shoulder. "You understand, of course—I needn't tell you that—the children would have to be brought up Catholics."

"It's nothing to me how they're brought up," said Ernest. "That's Anna's look-out."

"We could try it," Mrs. Martin said doubtfully, and Anna knew from her tone that they wouldn't. Ernest, poor lamb, was man enough to stand up to her mother, but not smart enough to see how he was being outflanked by the old witch. He had given too much ground, and now that Mrs. Martin had shaken him, she was not going to be satisfied with a compromise like a dispensation. A son-in-law who dug with the wrong foot, indeed! She was out to make a convert of him, and Anna knew he hadn't a chance against her. "Wouldn't that fire melt you?" Mrs. Martin added with a sigh. "Of course," she went on, lifting herself back into her chair and joining her hands in her lap, " 'twouldn't be much of a marriage."

"Why not?" asked Ernest. "What's wrong with it?"

"You'd have to be married out of the diocese," Mrs. Martin said cheerfully, not concealing the fact that she looked on a marriage where the Mahoneys couldn't see it as not much better than open scandal. "You can imagine what the neighbours would say! Wisha, do you have people like that in England, Ernest?" she asked in amusement.

"God Almighty!" Anna said with chagrin to see her sweetheart so impotent, "wouldn't you think mixed marriages were catching? A wonder they wouldn't put us up in the fever hospital as they're about it!"

Mrs. Martin saw the cause of religion being abandoned by her daughter because of human weakness.

"Of course, Ernest," she went on with the meek air she wore when she was really piqued, "if that's how Anna feels, I don't see why ye wouldn't get married in a registry office. I suppose 'tis as good as anything else."

"Mrs. Martin," Ernest said with great dignity, dominating her, or at any rate imagining he was doing so, "I don't want Anna to do anything she doesn't think right, but I have principles too, remember. My religion means as much to me as hers to her."

"I hope it means a good deal more, Ernest," Mrs. Martin said abjectly, getting in an extra poke at Anna under his guard. "I'd be long sorry to think that was all it meant to you. But you see, Ernest," she added with a humility that bordered on farce, "there is a difference. We look on ourselves as the One True Church."

"And what do you think we look on ourselves as?" Ernest asked. "Mrs. Martin," he went on appealingly with a throb of manly pathos in his voice, "why should you despise a man merely because he worships at a different altar?"

"Oh, I wouldn't say we despised anybody, Ernest," Mrs. Martin said in alarm, fearing that she might have gone too far. Then her tone grew grave again. "But 'tisn't alike, you know."

"Isn't it?"

"No, Ernest," she said, shaking her head. "The Catholic Church was founded by our Blessed Lord when He appointed St. Peter to be His vicar on earth. St. Peter is not quite the same thing as Henry VIII, Ernest."

She looked at Ernest with a triumphant little smile, but it was revealed to her that Ernest didn't know the first thing about Henry VIII—the history of his own country at that. Indeed, he seemed to take her remark as some sort of a slight on royalty.

"Why not, Mrs. Martin?" he asked with a quelling glance.

"And all the wives, Ernest?" she asked meekly.

"Doesn't that depend on the wives, Mrs. Martin?" Ernest replied, refusing to be subdued. "Some men are luckier than others in the women they marry. You know, Mrs. Martin," he went on, getting into his stride, "I don't think you should judge a man's conduct unless you know all about his circumstances. People are sometimes nothing like so bad as they're made out to be. Often they're very good people who find themselves in circumstances beyond their own control. . . . Anyhow, I'm marrying Anna, even if I have to become a Mohammedan, but at the same time I must say that I consider it unnecessary and unfair. I shouldn't be honest with myself or you unless I made that protest."

"Ah, well," Mrs. Martin said without rancour as she spread the tablecloth for supper, "maybe you'll think differently when you know us a bit better. And indeed, Ernest," she added with a wounded laugh which showed that she thought Ernest rather lacking in good taste, "I hope you'll find we're a cut above Mohammedans."

Anna had to butt in to prevent Ernest from glorifying Mohammedans. That was one of the troubles about a man who knew everything like Ernest; he was so confoundedly tolerant that he was always wanting to quarrel with those who weren't.

III

Next evening Anna brought him to the convent, a large hospital on a hill overlooking the town. There was a statue of the Sacred Heart on the lawn, a statue of the Blessed Virgin in the hall, and at the end of the corridor a coloured statue of St. Joseph. Ernest tried to walk with a masculine swing, but skated on the polished floor, got red, and swore under his breath. When they entered a parlour with open windows, a bookcase, and a picture of the Holy Family, he looked so sorry for himself that Anna's heart was wrung.

"And you won't forget to call her 'sister,' Ernie, will you?" she whispered appealingly.

"I'll try, Anna," Ernest said wearily, slumped in his chair with his head hanging. "I can't guarantee anything."

The door opened and in bounced Mrs. Martin's friend, Sister Angela, beaming at them with an array of prominent teeth. She had a rather good-looking, emaciated face with a big-boned nose, and an intensely excitable manner exacerbated by deafness. Mrs. Martin said in her modest way that quite a lot of people looked on Sister Angela as one of the three great intellects of Europe, which she seemed to think was much the same thing as her other favourite remark that "poor Sister Angela was very simple, very childish." She had been for years the bosom friend of an old parish priest who had visions, and was now collecting evidence to get him beatified. She had cut up and distributed his nightshirts among the poor as relics, and one leg of his trousers, turned into a belt, was supposed to have converted one of the city drunkards into a model husband.

She wrung both their hands simultaneously, beaming sharply from one to the other with a birdlike cock of her head. Like all deaf people she relied as much upon expression as upon speech.

"Anna, dear!" she said breathlessly. "So delighted when your mother told me! And this is your fiancé! Quite a handsome man. What's his name? Speak up!"

Anna shouted.

"Thompson?" Sister Angela cried, beaming again as though this were a most delightful and unexpected coincidence. "He's not one of us, your mother says?" she added, lowering her voice and still clinging to Ernest's hand. "What persuasion is he?"

"Church of England," said Anna.

"No, no, not a bit," said Sister Angela, shaking her head vigorously.

"I said he was Church of England," bawled Anna.

"Oooh! Church of England?" hooted Sister Angela, her face lighting up. Anna noticed she had really lovely eyes. "So near and yet so far," she chuckled. "But we never have any difficulty," she added with a firm shake of her head. "Last month," she bellowed, beaming at Ernest, "we had a sun-worshipper."

"You didn't!" exclaimed Anna. "And did he turn?"

"I didn't like him," Sister Angela said, clamping her lips and shaking her head as she stared into the fireplace. She had a tendency to drop out of conversations as unexpectedly as she had burst in on them. "He was a mechanic. You'd think he'd know better. So silly!" She beamed at Anna again. "I wouldn't say he was sincere, would you?"

"I'll leave ye to it," Anna said in a panic, well knowing that at any moment Ernest was liable to break into an impassioned defence of sun-worshippers. In fact, he had already told her it was a religion that greatly appealed to him. He wouldn't like to hear it described as silly. When she turned to smile at him from the door, she failed to catch his eye, and it grieved her to see the trapped look on his handsome, sulky face.

She waited for him in a little paper-shop opposite the convent. When he emerged, she knew at once that things had gone wrong by the way he kept his head down and failed to raise his hat to her.

"Well?" she asked gaily. "How did you get on?"

"It's hard to say," he said moodily, striding on without looking at her. "I've listened to some tall stories in my life, but she takes the biscuit."

"But what did she say?" wailed Anna.

"She had nothing to say," Ernest replied with gloomy triumph. "I refuted her on every single point."

"She must have loved that."

"She didn't. Women never appreciate clear, logical discussion. You'd think if Catholicism meant so much, that they'd have men teaching it."

"And did you call her 'sister'?"

"No. She didn't sound much like a sister to me. She said: 'I thought you were Church of England,' and I said: 'I was brought up Church of England, but for many years I have been a disciple of Abou Ben Adhem. She hadn't even heard of Abou Ben Adhem!"

"Go on!" Anna said desperately. "And who was he when he was at home?"

"Abou Ben Adhem?" Ernest exclaimed. "He was the man

who said to the angel: 'Write me as one who loved his fellow men.' Abou Ben Adhem has been the great religious inspiration of my life," he added reverently.

"Well, I hope he inspires you now," said Anna. "That one will be after you with a carving knife."

Ernest, who knew so much, had no idea how serious the situation had now become. When he saw Anna so depressed, he changed, and adopted a lofty and patronizing air, said he'd make things all right next day; it was just that he hadn't been feeling well and women were so illogical. For the future, he'd swallow everything Sister Angela told him. Anna told him he simply didn't know what he was talking about, and for once her mother agreed. Mrs. Martin, who had been married to one of them, knew only too well the harm a man with a loose tongue could do himself with neighbours like the Mahoneys round. She treated it as a major crisis, put on her best things, and went off to the convent herself.

When she returned, she looked more apologetic than ever, and fluttered about the house, fussing over trifles with an air of crucified humility, till she got on Anna's nerves.

"Well?" Anna bawled glumly when she could bear it no longer. "Aren't you going to tell us what she said?"

"Sister Angela?" Mrs. Martin breathed lightly. "She's not seeing anybody."

"Go on!" Anna said with a cold hand on her heart. "Why not?"

"She was too upset," Mrs. Martin said almost joyously. "She won't be able to go on with the instruction. He wasn't Church of England at all, but some religion they'd never heard of."

"I know," said Anna. "An Abou Ben Something."

"Ah, well," said her mother with resignation, "if 'twas any decent sort of a religion they'd know about it. They think it's probably something like the Dippers. Of course, I knew he wasn't a gentleman. Reverend Mother gave me the name of a Dominican theologian, but she thinks herself you'd better have no more to do with him."

"How soft she has it!" blazed Anna. "Giving him up just to suit her!"

"Maybe you'd better instruct him yourself," giggled her mother.

"I will," said Anna. "And make a better job of it than them."

She put on her coat and strode blindly out without a notion of where she was going. It was dark night by this time, and she walked up the hill past the Mahoneys' shop and said as she did so: "Blast ye, anyway! Ye're just as bad." Then she found herself beside the church, a plain, low, towerless church which lay on top of the hill with all its soft lights burning like the ark left high on top of Mount Ararat. The thought that she might never come down the steps of it in wreath and veil gave her courage. She knew there was a new curate in the presbytery, and that he was young like herself.

When the housekeeper showed her in, he was sitting before the fire, listening to the wireless, a handsome young man with a knobbly face. He got up, smiling, one hand in his trousers pocket, the other outstretched.

"I'm Anna Martin," Anna said, plunging straight into her business, "and I'm engaged to an English bloke that's over here at the new factory. He wants to turn, but he can't make head or tail of what the nuns tell him."

"Sit down and tell me about him," said the curate amiably, turning off the wireless. "Will you have a fag?"

"I will," said Anna, crossing her legs and opening her coat. "As true as God," she said, her lip beginning to quiver, "I'm nearly dotty with it."

"What religion is he?" asked the curate, holding out a lighted match to her.

"An Abou Ben Something," replied Anna, screwing up her eyes from the smoke. "You never heard of it?"

"I did not," said the curate. "I thought you said he was English."

"He is, too," said Anna. "I don't know much about it. 'Tis something about loving your neighbour—the usual stuff! And damn little love there is when you start looking for it," she added bitterly.

"Do you take a drink?" asked the curate.

"I do," said Anna, who thought he was a pet.

"Don't worry any more about it," he advised, pouring her out a glass of sherry. "We'll make him all right for you."

"You'll have no trouble as long as you don't mind what he says," Anna said eagerly. "He's the best fellow in the world only he likes to hear himself talk."

" 'Tis a good man's fault," said the curate.

Next evening, outside the presbytery gate, Anna gave Ernest his final instructions. Desperation had changed her. She was now masterful and precise to the point of vindictiveness, and Ernest was unusually subdued.

"And mind you're to call him 'father,' " she said sharply.

"All right, all right," said Ernest sulkily. "I won't forget."

"And whatever the hell you do, don't contradict him," said Anna. "There's nothing they hate like being contradicted."

Then, feeling she had done everything in her power, she went into the little church to say a prayer. Afterwards she met Ernest outside, and had every reason to feel gratified. He and the curate had got on like a house afire.

"Isn't he a delightful fellow?" Ernest chuckled enthusiastically. "And what a brain! It's positively a pleasure to argue with him." Ernest was himself again, his face shining, his eyes popping. "You see, Anna, I told you that woman had no brains."

After that it was almost impossible to keep him away from the presbytery, instruction or no instruction. He courted the curate with considerably more warmth than he courted Anna. He repaired the curate's shotgun and practically rewired the whole presbytery, and in return the curate told him all the things he wanted to know about clerical life. Ernest even began to see himself as a priest; celibacy, which to him might have been a major obstacle, was explained when you realized how free it left you to deal with other people's sex life, and Ernest enjoyed other people's sex life almost more than he did his own. Ernest was nothing if not broad-minded.

One Saturday afternoon, six weeks later, he made his profession of faith and renounced all his previous heresies, including Abou Ben Adhemism, made his first confession, was baptized, and received absolution for all the sins of his past life. Unfortunately, the Mahoneys had got hold of the convent version of it and were putting it about that he was a Turk. Mrs. Martin countered this by exaggerating, in her deprecating way, his wealth, rank, and education—of course, his family was only upper middle class and his salary only a thousand a year, but then, you couldn't expect everything.

He cut a splendid figure coming from the altar with Anna, in a new suit specially bought for the occasion, his hands joined and a look of childish beatitude on his big, fat, good-natured face.

IV

It was too good to be true, of course. It all became clear to Anna on the boat to Holyhead when Ernest disappeared into the saloon and only emerged half-seas-over. She had never seen him drunk before and she didn't like it. He was hysterical, jubilant, swaggering, and there was a wild look in his eyes.

"What's wrong, Ernie?" she said impatiently, staring hard at him.

"Wrong?" replied Ernest with a shrill laugh. "What could be wrong?"

"That's what I want to know," Anna said quietly. "And I'm not going any farther with you till I do know."

"Why?" he asked in the same wild tone. "Do I look like someone there was something wrong with?"

"You look as if you were scared out of your wits," Anna said candidly.

That sobered him. He leaned over the side of the boat, flushed and wry-faced as though he were going to be sick. The sunlit water was reflected up onto his big, heavy-jowled face, and he no longer looked handsome. He scarcely looked human.

"You didn't pinch anything, did you?" she asked anxiously.

"No, Anna," he replied, beginning to sob, "it's not that."

"I suppose you're going to tell me that you're married already?"

He nodded a couple of times, too full for speech.

"That's grand," she said with bitter restraint, already hearing the comments of the Mahoneys. "And kids, I suppose?"

"Two," sobbed Ernest, and buried his head in his arms.

"Sweet of you to tell me," she said, growing white.

"Well, can you blame me?" he asked wildly, drawing himself up with what was almost dignity. "I loved you. I knew from the first moment that you were the only woman in the world for me. I had to have you."

"Oh, you had me all right, Ernie," said Anna, unable, even at this most solemn moment of her life, to be anything but common.

But in spite of all his pleadings she refused to go beyond Holyhead with him. Her childhood training had been too strong, and though she might be common, she wouldn't deliberately do anything she thought really wrong. She felt sure she was going to have a baby: that was the only thing lacking to her degradation. And it all came of going with foreigners.

In the weeks that followed, she almost came to admire her mother. It was bad enough for Anna, but for her mother it was unredeemed catastrophe. Unless Father Jeremiah Mahoney not only left the Church but left it to live with a married woman or a Negress—a thing Mrs. Martin was too conscientious even to desire—the war between herself and the Mahoneys was over. But she wasn't going to let herself be dislodged on that account. Under all the convent-school fatuity was the stout, sensible peasant-stuff. She even approved of Anna's decision to give no information to the police, who were after Ernest. Even the prospect of a baby she accepted as the will of God—anything that couldn't be concealed from the Mahoneys seemed to be her definition of the will of God.

But Anna couldn't take things in that spirit. Undoubtedly the whole neighbourhood was humming with spite. When she went into town she ran the gauntlet of malicious eyes and tongues. "She knew, she knew! Sure, of course, she knew! Didn't Sister Angela warn them what he was? All grandeur and false pride. She wanted to say she could get a husband—a pasty-faced thing like that." But it wasn't only the spite. Every second day she got some heart-rending appeal from Ernest not to let him down and threatening to kill himself. She knew she shouldn't open his letters, but she couldn't keep off them. She read and re-read them. That is what I mean by the influence of a foreigner. Things that had been as natural as breathing to Anna suddenly began to seem queer. She didn't know why she was doing them or why anyone

else expected her to do them. Under the strain her character began to change. She grew explosive.

One night she had been sitting in the back kitchen, listening to
her mother and a neighbour whispering in the shop, and when
the neighbour left, Anna came to the inner door and leaned
against the jamb with folded arms, blowsy and resentful.

"Who was the 'poor Anna' ye were talking about?" she asked
casually.

"Ah, indeed, Anna, you may well ask," sighed her mother.

"But why 'poor'?" Anna went on reasonably. "I didn't marry a
boozer that knocked me about like that old one did. I'm going to
have a kid, which is more than a lot of the old serpents will ever
have."

"I'm so glad you appreciate it," her mother said waspishly. "I
hope you tell everyone. They'll be all delighted you're not downhearted about it."

"Why?" asked Anna. "Am I supposed to be downhearted?"

"Why should you be?" said her mother. "Haven't you every
reason for being cheerful?"

"That's exactly what I was thinking," Anna said in a heart-
breaking drawl. "It just crossed my mind that I wasn't suited to
this place at all." Then, as she heard her own voice speaking, she
was aghast. "Cripes!" she thought in her common way. "There
goes the blooming china." She was exactly like the last maid giving notice after breaking the last of the Henebry-Hayes china off
the kitchen wall. She realized that at that moment there was not
a drop of Henebry-Hayes blood left in her veins; from head to
foot she was pure Martin; a woman of no class. "I'm not grand
enough for this place," she went on recklessly. "I think I'll have
to go somewhere I'm better suited."

She was suddenly filled with a great sense of liberation and
joy. The strain of being a real Henebry-Hayes is something you
cannot appreciate until it is lifted. Then she went upstairs and
wrote to Ernest, telling him when to expect her.

Under the circumstances, it was perhaps the best thing she
could have done. Once those foreign notions have found their
way into your mind, it is impossible ever to expel them entirely
afterwards.

THE LITTLE MOTHER

I

IN MY youth there was a family that lived up Gardiner's Hill in Cork called Twomey. It consisted of father, mother, and three pretty daughters, Joan, Kitty, and May. The father was a small builder, honest, hard-working, unbusinesslike, and greatly esteemed. The mother was a real beauty, tall, attractive, and sentimental, who wept profusely over the wrongs of Ireland, romantic love, and the sufferings of the poor. At least once a day Mick Twomey, coming in and finding a beggar eating his dinner on a chair outside the front door, or warming himself in the kitchen over the fire, denounced her imbecility, but in secret he adored her, and told his daughters that there wasn't a woman in the world like her.

The girls were as wild as they make them; they were spoiled; there was no doubt of that. May, being only thirteen, couldn't be really wild, but there was something about her gentle smile and insinuating air which indicated that this was only a pleasure deferred. Joan, the eldest, had a broad, humorous face, an excitable manner, and a great flow of gab. Kitty, the second girl, was an untidy, emotional sort, who took more after her mother than the others and was her father's pet. Mrs. Twomey couldn't control them. She would fly into a wild rage against one of them, and threaten to tell their father, and then remember an identical occasion in her own girlhood and laugh at her own naughtiness and her dead mother's fury till, the immediate occasion of her emotion forgotten, she went about the house singing sentimental songs like "Can you recall that night in June?"

She shamelessly searched their rooms and handbags for love-letters, ostensibly because it was her duty, but really because they reminded her of the letters she had received herself when she was a girl and of the writers, now married, scattered, or dead. She was usually so enchanted by them that she never bothered to inquire whether or not the writers were suitable companions for her daughters. She tried to read some of them to her husband, not realizing that all men hate to be reminded of their adolescent follies. "For God's sake, don't be encouraging them in that sort of nonsense!" he snapped. But what was nonsense to him was the breath of life to Mrs. Twomey. She loved it on Sunday evenings when the gas was lit in the little front room, and the oil lamp was placed in the middle of the big round table to give light to the piano, and the girls' friends dropped in for a cup of tea and a singsong. She hung on there till she couldn't decently do so any longer, beaming and asking in stage-whispers: "What do you think of Dick Gordon? People say he's not steady, but there's something very manly about him."

Naturally, Dick Gordon, Joan's boy, was the one whose letters she appreciated the most. He was tall and handsome and bony, with a great back to his head, walked with a swagger, talked with verve, and sang "Toreador" and "The Bandolero" in a reckless baritone. The neighbours were quite right in saying he wasn't steady. He took a drink, was known to have knocked about with bad women, drove a motor bicycle, and brought Joan off to Crosshaven on it for week-ends. What was worse, he didn't go to Mass or the Sacraments, and seemed to be entirely lacking in any sense of shame about it. But he was also lacking in any desire to force his views on others. He was an engineer, a well-read boy, and explained to Joan that early in life he had come to the conclusion that people were in a conspiracy to prevent him enjoying himself, and determined to evade it. It wasn't on principle. He had no principles that anybody could see, and was perfectly respectful of everybody else's, so long as they let him alone.

Dick was not only Joan's sweetheart, but the ideal of the other two girls. Kitty didn't have a boy of her own; she always had a number of them, but none of them came up to Dick's standard. He mightn't be steady, but who at that age ever wanted a sweetheart to be steady? "Here, Joan," she would say, producing a love-letter for her sister, "did you ever read such blooming nonsense as Sonny Lawlor writes?" And while she and Joan compared and argued, May hung round wistfully and asked: "Can't I look?"

Then one day death laid its hand on the family. Mrs. Twomey died suddenly, and for weeks the girls' beauty was masked by mourning and tears. Mick was so stunned that he behaved almost as though it were somebody else's loss rather than his own. On the day they buried her, he took Kitty and May by the hand and presented them to Joan with a curious formality.

"You'll have to be a mother to them now, Joan, girl," he said in a low voice. "They have no one else."

II

The little ceremony made an extraordinary impression on Joan. That night, as she knelt by her bed, she made a solemn vow to be everything to her father and sisters that her mother had been. She had no illusions about its being an easy task, and it filled her with a certain mournful pride. It was as though within a few hours her whole nature had changed; as though she no longer had a father and sisters, only a husband and children: as though, in fact, her girlhood had suddenly become very far away.

Father and sisters, too, realized the seriousness of the occasion and at first gave her every help. On Friday night her father counted out the housekeeping money to her in front of the others and said humbly: "That's eighty-five bob, Joan. Ten for pocket money and five for the club. Think you'll be able to manage?" The girls were so awe-stricken that they hardly dared ask her for money, and it was she who had to press it on them.

But that phase didn't last. She discovered a change even in herself. The excitement in her blood when dusk fell on the fields and trees behind the little terrace house and the gas lamp was lit at the street corner was no longer the same. It was always qualified by her new sense of responsibility. When Kitty was out with a boy, Joan realized that it wasn't any longer an adventure she could share with her on her return, but a burden she could share only with her father. Dick was very quiet and anxious to be helpful, but he couldn't understand her anxiety about Kitty. He knew that Kitty was giddy, but he didn't see what a responsibility it imposed on her. She didn't expect anything unreasonable, only that Kitty should be in at proper hours, but Kitty seemed to resent this far more from her than she had resented it from her mother. "Here, what's coming over you?" she asked pertly. "Who do you think you are?" She even said that Joan was getting too big for her boots. There were times when Joan felt old and tired. Children never understood the responsibilities of their parents and guardians. They never realized the way budgets had to be balanced so that the loss of an umbrella or the breaking of a teapot could leave you worried and distraught for days. When she remembered how often she had blamed her own gentle and self-sacrificing mother on that very score, she wept.

To give her strength to get through the day she took to going to Mass every morning. The neighbours, who saw it only from outside, were enormously impressed by the way a flighty girl of eighteen developed into a mature, responsible young woman who saw that meals were cooked, clothes washed and mended, and bills paid on time. But Kitty and May realized that they had lost a sister and caught a tartar. It was true that Joan had always had a touch of the Reverend Mother about her; had been serious and bossy and attempted to make up in knowingness for the affection which had been diverted onto her younger sisters. But this had only been swank. In all essential matters she had remained part of the juvenile conspiracy—treating their parents as enemies, raiding their stores, and defeating their intelligence system.

Now that she had deserted to the enemy, she was worse than any parent because she knew all their tricks—the whole secret set-up of school-books, fees, carfares, clothes, and boy friends—and they could do nothing without her knowledge. Now it was their intelligence system that was dislocated. Whenever they wanted something out of the ordinary, they had to tell her why and they had to tell the truth. They did, but they resented it far more than they resented her occasional fits of panic and meanness, because it derogated from their femininity, and in the intervals of scolding and wheedling they lapsed into a mute and sullen conspiracy which she felt was quite unjustified.

All the family learned things from the new situation, but Joan, who was the heart of it, learned the most. She discovered that it was far from being the romantic change of parts which she had at first imagined, and not at all a matter of her father and herself on the one hand and "the children," as she liked to call them, on the other. Her father had a secret life of his own, which was not at all easy to penetrate. At first, when she discussed her difficulties with him, she was flattered by the mournful candour with which he responded, giving her chapter and verse for his earnings, and she loyally and vigorously denounced to shopkeepers and neighbours the thoughtlessness of customers who left big accounts outstanding. Besides, no matter how hard up he might be, he always managed to find her a something extra, wherever he got it or whatever he had to sacrifice to obtain it. Sometimes the sacrifice was so patent that she begged him to take it back, but he shook his head mournfully and replied: "No, no, child. You need it more than I do. I can get along."

But in time she began to suspect that the candour was fallacious and the sacrifice imaginary—the accounts varied too much. It was hard to believe, and it hurt her to believe it, but it had to be faced: her father was not truthful. What she was too young to see was that it had to be so; a man's income and expenditure are necessarily up to a point subjective, for you must leave room for optimism and pessimism, and to tie him to mere figures is to deny him a temperament. Joan wanted an objective income because it was she who was blamed when things went short. Kitty even went so far as to call her "a mean bitch," and Joan, to keep from weeping, drew herself up and said with dignity: "I'm afraid you're not old enough to understand Daddy's difficulties, Kit."

But even if she couldn't break down her father's secrets, nothing her sisters did could be kept from her. One day, when she was really worried about making ends meet, she saw Kitty open her handbag and turn over a handful of silver. Her first scared thought was that Kitty might have stolen it.

"Where did you get all that money, Kit?" she asked.

"What money?" Kitty asked with an attempt at brazenness, though she turned pale. "I have no money."

"Don't try to fool me. That money in your bag."

"But 'tis only a couple of pence—look!" Kitty wailed, opening her handbag and taking out a few coppers. Joan had had time to realize that she hadn't stolen it. She hadn't stolen it, but she was going to spend it on the pictures or on buying cigarettes for some young waster she was going out with, while Joan was left to worry.

"Would you like to show me your bag so?" she asked icily.

"Why would I show you my bag?" Kitty asked indignantly.

"You got that money from Father," Joan said.

"I did not get it from Father," shouted Kitty, now thoroughly scared as she saw the source of her independence threatened. "I got it from Aunt Molly, as you're so blooming inquisitive."

Joan didn't even bother to reply. She felt too bitterly about it. Now she understood a certain air of independence that "the children" had worn for months. Their father had been keeping them in funds. In spite of the credit she had earned among the neighbours, in spite of her struggles to keep the house going, he conspired with them as though she were some sort of ogre who denied them the necessities of life. She could see it all exactly as if it were some man who was being unfaithful to her. It never occurred to her to excuse him because he had been equally generous to her during her mother's life, because he had always responded fondly when she came to him, bubbling with her secret crises, because, in fact, he was the sort of man who was at his best only when you went to him in a scrape. Any form of regular commitment was torture to him because it had no emotional overtones, but he loved the little occasions that enabled him to show the real warmth of his heart.

When she challenged him with it, he was horrified. It would never have occurred to him that anyone could possibly put such a cruel construction on his innocent generosity. He had never seen it that way at all. He didn't have to go to the neighbours to know what sort of job she was making of the home. It was just that he loved them all!

He argued, he pleaded; he even lost his temper and threatened to hand over the housekeeping to Kitty, but Joan was remorseless. He had been unfaithful to her and she was disillusioned; and, like every other deceived wife, she knew that her disillusionment was a weapon which would keep him in order for the rest of his days with her. Never again would he betray her. He wouldn't have the nerve. Kitty might weep on him for a new dress, but he would only mumble apologies about "the troubles of poor Joan," and even when she went beyond the beyonds and tackled him about the amount he spent on drink—a thing her mother would never have dared to do—he was humble and apologetic. He had never behaved so abjectly to his wife, but then, she had spurts of sentiment which he well knew how to take advantage of. All he had to do to get around Mrs. Twomey was to mention some fellow he had met who had spent a holiday in Killarney, where he and she had spent their honeymoon, and within a half an hour Mrs. Twomey was washing up while she sang in a sweet cracked voice "By Killarney's lakes and fells." He had no such hold over Joan. Now she had three quivering victims, a thing that might have gone to the head of a less emotional girl than she was.

III

It horrified her to see how badly they had all been brought up. Until then, when she heard criticism of their wildness, she had only mocked at the neighbours and said that they were jealous. Now that she found herself in the neighbours' camp, she saw how right they had been. No attempt had ever been made to correct herself and her sisters until she had taken things into her own hands. She could not blame her mother for this and found it hard to attach anything so substantial as blame to an unstable character like her father. It must, she thought, be plain, crude original sin. There were even moments when she wondered whether God in His infinite wisdom had not been compelled to remove her mother to bring her to a proper sense of responsibility —a common stage in the development of spiritual pride.

But Dick Gordon was the one who really saw the profound change that was taking place in her. Till her mother died, she had seen no harm in him; neither her parents nor herself had taken his atheism seriously, and her father had even said that every intelligent young fellow went through the same thing; it had given her a feeling of broad-mindedness to listen to his dashing, cynical talk. But now she had only to imagine him saying the same sort of things to Kitty to realize that there are two ways of looking at a man.

It troubled her a lot; she prayed a good deal, and tried to break off with him gently by diminishing the number of occasions when she went out with him, but there was a curious thickness about Dick that made him come back again and again. Finally she had to speak to him seriously about it, but it was with real regret and pity.

"I think, Dick, boy, we've got to give up going with one another," she said with a gentle smile.

"Go on!" Dick said lightly, raising his head and looking at her curiously. "Why do you think that?"

"Well, you see, I have certain responsibilities, and I don't see how we can ever get married."

"I have a few responsibilities myself, and we never expected to be able to get married in a hurry."

"But this is a long job, Dick—years and years."

Dick shrugged his shoulders uncomprehendingly.

"Well, if we have to wait, we have to wait. If you find someone that suits you, you have to put up with the inconveniences."

"But that's the trouble, Dick," she said, realizing that she was not going to escape without open discussion. "I don't think we do suit one another."

He still refused to be shaken. Dick was an engineer, and he tended to treat life very like a delicate machine. If something went wrong, you opened it up and fixed it, and then it worked again.

"How long have you thought that, Joan?"

"For quite a while."

"Since your mother's death?"

"I dare say."

"Well, I know it upset you; that's only to be expected, but it's also only to be expected that you'll get over it."

"I don't think so, Dick. Not so far as that goes. You see, I was young and giddy, and I didn't realize how much certain things meant to me. Religion, for instance. I couldn't marry a man who didn't believe the same things as I do."

Dick shrugged his shoulders. "It hasn't affected you very much up to this."

"No, Dick, but it could."

"Could!" he repeated with light mockery. He was bewildered. He couldn't help feeling that religion had nothing to do with it; that a cog wasn't engaging somewhere or a plug wasn't sparking. He continued to argue. At last he rose with a shrug.

"Oh, well," he said, "if that's how you feel about it."

He was really very fond of Joan and enjoyed knocking about the house, so he was quite incredulous at her dropping him. It was a thing to hurt the feelings of any man, but Dick was worse than hurt, he was bewildered. From his limited, logical, liberal point of view, the thing didn't make sense. Sometimes he even wondered whether there wasn't something in religion after all, and whether he wasn't a freak of nature whom any sensible girl must naturally drop. At other times it seemed to him that Joan was becoming slightly touched, and that it was his duty to speak to her father about it. Either way you took it, it seemed monstrous. He knew the wild side of Joan better than anyone else, and loved it in his own limited way, and he could not understand how it could disappear like that, overnight, leaving nothing behind but a soured, censorious old maid. He talked lightly to Kitty about it.

"It's all pride, Dick," she said violently. "It's all rotten pride and vanity."

He was a creature of habit, and he continued to come to the house; to rag May, who adored him, and chat with Mick Twomey, who liked his manliness. When Joan refused to make it up, he shrugged his shoulders and flirted with Kitty instead. To put the crowning touch on it, Kitty fell head and ears in love with him; she could scarcely believe that the ideal of her early girlhood was now at her feet, and Kitty in love could be observed not only by Joan but by half the road. When she was kept five minutes late for an appointment, she burst into tears and threatened suicide.

Then Joan grew really angry. This was a development she hadn't intended at all, and Kitty was far too young and too spoiled to understand her objections. She chose to think that the breach between Joan and Dick had been caused by Dick's resentment at the change in her, and that her objections to Dick going with herself were merely jealousy. Joan, intensely aware of the purity of her own motives, found it hard to realize what was going on in Kitty's head.

"I suppose it's because you can't have him yourself you don't want anyone else to have him?" blazed Kitty.

"I don't give a button who has him," Joan said flatly. "I just don't want you to have anything to do with him, that's all."

"Ah, we know all about that."

"What on earth do you mean, child?" asked Joan.

"Where do you get your women from?" retorted Kitty. "I'm not such a child as all that. You pretend you don't want him; other people might think 'twas the way he didn't want you."

Joan looked at Kitty in stupefaction. It was only now she was beginning to realize the change in her own character. Six months before, that skinny little brat wouldn't have dared to tell Joan that any man in the world preferred herself to Joan without Joan's showing her pretty soon the mistake she was making. Even then she could feel a certain temptation to take Dick back, just to teach the little fool a good lesson about the nature of men and the facts of life. But it was only for a moment.

"You're welcome to think it, if it gives you any satisfaction," she said coldly.

In spite of it, Kitty continued to defy her, and Dick, with that unshakable self-confidence of his, continued to come to the house and behave exactly as though nothing whatever had happened, beyond the change from herself to Kitty. He even did with Kitty the sort of things he had done with herself, and took her off on the pillion of his motor bicycle to Crosshaven for the week-end without saying a word to her about it. This was really too much for Joan, who had no faith whatever in Kitty's capacity for keeping out of mischief, and she complained to her father.

Now, Mick was a bad man to complain to, because he was full

of pity for humanity in general and young fellows of Dick's age in particular. He too thought she was jealous—it was extraordinary, the number of people who got that impression.

"Ah, listen, Joan," he said with an anguished air, "wouldn't you make it up with him, whatever he did to you?"

"Honestly, Daddy," she protested, "he did nothing to me."

"Whatever ye did to one another so."

"But I tell you we did nothing to one another. It's just that I don't think Dick and I are suited to one another. He doesn't go to Mass. I don't think he has a proper sense of responsibility. And Kitty is much too young and too giddy to be mixing round with that Crosshaven crowd. She's bound to drink too much, and Dick will only encourage her. I tell you, unless we put a stop to it, she'll be ruined within a year."

"Ah, God, Joanie," muttered her father with a distraught air, "I was very like Dick at that age. He's only knocking round with Kitty to spite you. It only shows how fond of you he is. Damn it, I nearly married your Aunt Molly after one row I had with your poor mother, God rest her."

In fact, though he did speak to Kitty, he only made matters worse, for he mumbled that he didn't know what was after coming over Joan, but she was mad jealous of anyone who looked crosswise at Dick Gordon—nothing, it seemed, could convince him of the nobility of Joan's motives—and that it would be very unkind of Kitty to go between them. Kitty, who had a violent temper, flew off the handle, told him no one could live in the house since her mother's death; that it was all his fault because he let Joan do what she liked, and swore that if he wasn't careful, she'd leave and get a job in Dublin. She scared him so badly that he withdrew to his bedroom and sulked in protest against both of them.

But Joan wasn't to be beaten so easily. One day she called at the office where Dick Gordon worked. He brought her into the waiting-room, looking quite pleasant and collected, and stood at the fireplace with his hands behind his back.

"Dick," she said sweetly, "I want to ask a favour of you."

"Sure," said Dick with his usual amiability. "Fire ahead."

"It's about Kitty."

He pursed his lips and tossed his head deprecatingly. He knew now that he was in for a scene.

"What about her?"

"Please, Dick, for my sake, will you stop taking her out?"

"Why should I stop taking her out?"

"Because it's upsetting her, and you know you don't really care about her."

Hands still behind his back, he drew himself up on his heels.

"It seems to be upsetting more than her," he said pleasantly.

"It is, if you want to know," she replied quietly. "You're only doing it to spite me."

"You have a very high opinion of yourself, haven't you?" he asked with a laugh.

"You don't have to talk to me like that," she said reproachfully.

"I don't have to talk to you at all, if it comes to that," he retorted indifferently.

She knew that the indifference was only assumed, and that he would have welcomed the chance of a good breakdown like anyone else.

"You know you think a great deal of me, and I think the same of you," she said appealingly. "Why won't you do this for me?"

Joan could be angelic when it suited her, and it suited her then. She didn't leave till he had given his promise, though he gave it grudgingly, feeling that in some way he was being exploited. Even then he insisted on telling Kitty himself. Kitty wept for hours and then packed her bag and announced that she was leaving for Dublin at once. Her father was very upset, but Joan, still indignant at Kitty's defiance, assured him that this was the best way of bringing "the child" to her senses. Left to herself for a while in lodgings, she would soon learn the value of a good home.

IV

There was more peace after she left, and to everyone's surprise Joan became friendly with another fellow, a civil servant named Chris Dwyer. Chris was the very opposite of Dick Gordon; a pale, pious, harassed young fellow with an angular, irritable sense of humour and a passion for music. Where Dick swaggered

into any group, entirely at his ease, Chris arrived with a bundle
of gramophone records under his arm and a politeness and pleasure which he couldn't keep up and which gradually gave place
to an air of doubt and distress. Even when he was playing one
of his beloved records on the gramophone, he clasped his hands
and watched the gramophone feverishly, as though he expected
that at any moment it would come out with a wrong note. He
lived in Sunday's Well—a classy quarter—was of a good family
which had come down in the world, and devoted himself to the
care of his mother, a woman of such invincible refinement that
she couldn't even understand what had happened to her income.
Chris couldn't enlighten her much, for he understood it all so
well that to explain anything at all, he had to begin with the history of banking.

Joan confided in Chris her troubles with her sisters, and Chris,
after a certain amount of hesitation, admitted that he, too, had
serious difficulties with his older brothers, Bob and Jim, neither
of whom seemed to have any sense of responsibility. Between
family confidences and a love of music, he and Joan seemed made
for one another, the only obstacle being that each had so many
responsibilities that there did not seem to be the slightest prospect
of their ever being able to get married; but even this common
element of frustration formed something of a bond, and in their
conscientious way, going to concerts and walking up the Lee
Fields in the evening, they were profoundly happy in one another's company.

But Joan's troubles with her sisters were very far from being
ended. By the time May was seventeen, she was a handful, and a
much bigger handful than Kitty. Kitty had a temper and wept
on the least provocation, but May was a girl of extraordinary
sweetness, with a disposition as clear as her complexion. You
could hear Kitty getting into a scrape a mile off, but May merely
glided into it like a duck into water. It was her natural element.
She was cool, resourceful, and insinuating, and frequently turned
the tables on Joan, who was none of these things. For instance,
she could appeal to Joan's sense of humour, which was fatal to
her dignity. Or she could get her to talk about her own troubles
and then advise her as though she and not Joan were the elder.

May could be involved in a police-court case and, in some way Joan couldn't understand, it would all be turned into a warning against Chris Dwyer. May had never got over her early hero-worship of Dick Gordon, and everything about Chris annoyed her: his dark suits and white shirts, his clumsy attempts to please her, and the intensity with which he bowed his head and clasped his long, thin hands while listening to a Beethoven quartet. May didn't know much about music, but she felt that it was never worth all that strain.

"Ah, listen, Joan," she would say peremptorily, "take that fellow by the scruff of the neck and drag him up to the priest yourself. You'll never get married at all if you leave it to him."

"But we haven't a chance of getting married anyhow, girl," Joan would say with resignation. "Between his mother and Daddy, it looks as if we have another twenty years to wait."

"But even if Chris buried his mother tomorrow, he'd find an old aunt that had to be looked after," May would say with exasperation. "I'm warning you, Joan—that fellow is a born grandmother. He's not your sort at all."

May was like quicksilver: you had her cornered, and then, before you knew what was happening, she had you cornered. She slipped in and out of the Ten Commandments as if they were ten harmless old aunts, not in the least trying to discredit them—on the contrary, she thought them delightful, in the manner of characters in a Jane Austen novel, and deeply resented anyone's speaking disrespectfully of them—but she never gave them more than the affection and respect due to ancient monuments.

May's principal achievement—no small one for a girl living at home in a small city like Cork—was to become involved with a married man. Timmy MacGovern was a fat, greasy man with a long lock of black hair that fell over his left eye, small merry eyes, a jovial air, and small, unsteady feminine feet that positively refused to support his weight. He rarely went anywhere except by car, and even when he dislodged himself from the car he usually tried out the feet first to see if they were still functioning.

He was the commercial representative of several big firms, and in line for the Dublin management of one, which must have been largely due to his charm, for he was very rarely in his office on the Grand Parade, and when he was, he either sat at his desk as though he were sitting for his portrait, or thudded to and from the window, riffling his hair and interrupting his adoring secretary, till somebody came to bring him out for a drink. Usually this was Tony Dowse, who had some undefined job in the County Council that left him free to go and come as he pleased. He was as big a man as Timmy, with a pasty face and an anxious air, and always adopted a protective attitude to Timmy. He was very fond of Timmy, but regarded him as the last word in fantasy and excitability. While Timmy riffled his hair and knit his black brows in a thunderous frown, Tony flapped his fat hands feebly. "You take things to the fair, MacGovern," he would moan, curling his long, mournful upper lip in distaste. "If 'tisn't women, 'tis ghosts." (Timmy was a strong believer in ghosts and had seen a number of them in his time, but Dowse blamed it all on his excitability and unreasonableness. Dowse had never seen a ghost, and except for one distressing little episode with a girl at the age of sixteen he had never had anything to do with women.) Timmy was a born boon companion, had a small army of admirers, and brought light and laughter to any pub he chose to patronize. Among his other accomplishments, he was an out-and-out Voltairean, a part that was possible for him, as Tony Dowse remarked, only because nobody believed him. "If that was me or you," Tony would say, shaking his head over the injustice of it, "we'd be for the long drop. They think Timmy is only cod-acting."

This was an injustice to Timmy, who had genuine aspirations after a fuller life; aspirations you wouldn't understand until you met his wife, one of the Geraghty girls from Glenareena. "The Grip of the Geraghtys" was a proverbial saying in that part of the country. Eily MacGovern was a small, thrifty, pious, unimaginative woman whom Timmy was supposed to have married for her money—another example of the way people are misjudged, because he really married her for her voice. But the voice was all the romance there was in Eily. The soul of order, she had given Timmy a small house in the suburbs, with small rooms that were a clutter of small useless tables which Timmy was always falling over, and a son and daughter as neatly matched as the two china dogs on her parlour mantelpiece. Timmy was a conscientious husband and father, but he would often look at his family in their surroundings and shake his head as if he wondered who had been putting spells on him. Eily had nursed him through a dozen different ailments, all mortal. Timmy, an imaginative man, never got any disease that wasn't mortal, and when he had a gastric attack, he took to his bed in a state of icy terror, while Eily, who never ceased to marvel at the ways of imaginative men, said with a stunned air to Tony Dowse: "And they call *us* the weaker sex!"

May, who loved imaginative men, was delighted with Timmy's big frame and robust humour, his songs and stories and bawdy jokes. Then—just like the second figure on the weather-clock that pops out on the approach of rain—out came the second Timmy, a bewildered man with aspirations after a fuller life, and complained of Eily and denounced the pettiness of Cork, and begged May to leave everything and come away with him; even if they had nothing, and no home but the lonesome roads of Ireland.

It was just like Timmy, who couldn't walk half a mile with his poor feet, to talk about the roads, but May thought the way he described them was something beautiful, with castles and fairs and tinkers and asses, just as though he had served his time to them, and at once she saw herself swinging a shawl and dragging a barefoot child behind her while they tramped the boglands in the warm days of June. There was no humbug about May's ambitions. She had a genuine streak of the vagrant in her, and a real liking for the extremes that give a sharp edge to sensation—hunger and thirst and cold and weariness. It had always seemed to her that people attached too much importance to security, and that the happiest souls in the world were the tinkers who built their campfires by the road and stretched old bags across the shafts of their carts by way of tents.

But when Joan heard that Timmy and May had been practising the simple life in the mountain country outside Macroom, sitting in pubs and talking to tinkers, she thought May must have taken leave of her senses. She searched May's room till she found Timmy's letters, and read them in a state of utter incredulity. She knew from of old that all love-letters were silly, but these were mad. They would go on for a paragraph in a jerky style like a broken-down Ford, and then suddenly soar into passages of inspired rhetoric in which Timmy declared that when he was with May the real world didn't exist any longer for him, and there was nobody and nothing only the two of themselves. They were so queer that she hardly knew what to say to May about them.

"Tell me, May," she asked that evening, "what's going on between Timmy MacGovern and you?"

"How do you mean, going on?" May asked with mock ingenuousness.

"Ah, stop playing the innocent with me," Joan said impatiently. "You know quite well what I mean."

"Nothing's been going on to get in a bake like that about," May said reproachfully.

"I read his letters to you."

"Well, you know all about it, so."

"You should be proud of them," Joan said bitterly.

"They suit me all right."

"They'd probably suit Mrs. MacGovern too. Listen, May, what are you going to do about this thing?"

"We didn't decide that yet," May said with a slight touch of guilt as though she didn't quite know how she had come to let such opportunities slip. "I dare say eventually I'll go and live with him."

"You'll what, May?" Joan asked in a dangerous tone.

"Ah, not here, of course," May added impatiently. "I mean when he gets his transfer to Dublin. He might even have to get a job in London. People in this country are so blooming narrow-minded. They get in a rut by the time they're eighteen, any of them that weren't in one to begin with."

At any moment now Joan felt May would tell her that Ireland didn't exist any longer either, nothing only Timmy and herself.

"Are you in your right mind, May Twomey?" she asked.

"Now, Joan, it's no use your talking that schoolgirl stuff to me," snapped May. "It's not because Chris Dwyer was born in a rut."

"What has Chris Dwyer to do with it?"

"Chris Dwyer has you driven out of your mind," said May

hotly. "You're becoming as big an old maid as he is. You ought to be old enough to talk sensibly about things like this. Timmy made a mistake in his marriage, that's all. Lots of men do. He has either to put up with Eily Geraghty for the rest of his life or make a fresh start."

"Well, he's making a still bigger mistake if he thinks he's going to make a fresh start on you," said Joan.

"We'll see about that," said May with a shrug. She was apparently beginning to think that Joan didn't exist either.

First Joan complained to her father. As usual he behaved as though the person who made the complaint was at least equally guilty with the offender. It was the attitude of a man born weak, who hates to have his peace of mind disturbed. "Oh, for Christ's sake!" he said, and shambled in to May. He told May it was a happy day for her poor mother the day she died, and then went on to threaten her as though her mother were still alive and May was breaking her heart. May, who loved him even more than the Ten Commandments, listened to him with respect, but within ten minutes she had him admitting that there were damn few women in the world like her poor mother, God rest her, and that only for what people might say, you wouldn't blame their husbands, whatever they did. He then went off to bed, apparently under the impression that he had restored order in the household.

But Joan had no intention of being satisfied with that sort of moral cowardice. Next afternoon she bearded Timmy in his office. Timmy had his usual look of having dropped in for a chat with his secretary. He was obviously very pleased to see Joan, and smiled with the whole array of his discoloured teeth as he led her into the back office. It was a small room with a window opening on a vent. He closed the window carefully and sat down, riffling his hair. On the desk before him was a photograph of May, looking romantic against a mountain. It was most improbable that he left it there permanently; more likely he had taken it out to remind himself that offices weren't real either, but it gave Joan a fresh grievance.

"I think I'd better take charge of this, Timmy," she said, opening her handbag.

"What do you mean, Joan?" Timmy asked, rising with a look of alarm. It was a divided look, for the eyes frowned but the teeth still grinned wistfully beneath them.

"If you can't protect my sister's reputation, I must, Timmy," Joan said briskly. "Now, if you'd give me her letters—"

"Her letters?"

"Yes."

"But I haven't them, Joan."

"Nonsense, Timmy. You know you wouldn't have the nerve to keep them at home."

"I'm sorry you feel like this about it, Joan," he said gravely, twiddling nervously with the spring of his pince-nez.

"I don't see what other way I can feel," she replied frankly.

"I don't think you'd be so severe if you knew the sort of life I have to lead, Joan," he said, his eyes clouding with tears. "I don't want you to think I'm complaining of Eily. I'm not. She was always a good wife, according to her lights, and I'm grateful; but there was never any understanding between us. When I met May, I knew she was the only girl in the world for me. I love that girl, Joan," he added with manly simplicity. "I'd die for her this minute."

"I'm sorry, Timmy," Joan said coldly, "but I can't help your disagreements with Mrs. MacGovern. I didn't come here to discuss them. I came to get my sister's letters, and to warn you that the next time you see her or write to her, I'll go straight to your wife and then to the parish priest."

Joan was bluffing, and she knew it. She was playing it as if she were haggling over a pound of vegetables in the market. Timmy, like the rest of us, was vulnerable, but there were few in a stronger position to resist threats of that sort. If he had stuck to his guns, there was very little Joan could have done which wouldn't have brought more trouble on herself than on him, but, scared by the hysteria in her tone, he didn't realize it. That is the worst of poetic sentiments; they so rarely stand up to a well-played bluff.

"You wouldn't do that to us, Joan?" he asked, growing pale.

Joan strode to the door with an actressy air.

"The child has no other mother," she said with her hand on

the handle and the door half-open. "I have to be a mother to her."

This was another bluff, for at that moment Joan's sentiments were very far from being maternal, but it worked. Timmy grabbed her and closed the door again. He was, as Tony Dowse said, an excitable man. He begged her to be reasonable, not to be so uncompromising—nothing would happen beyond an occasional meeting and letter.

"The first time I see another letter of yours with May, I go straight to your wife," she said.

That did it. Timmy shed a few tears, but he produced the bundle of letters, and Joan went down the stairs and along the Grand Parade in the afternoon sunlight, full of triumph and miserable as hell. She had a stocky figure with a permanent roll on it, and she bowed and called greetings to her friends, and at the same time wished she were dead. Like most of the men who came her way, Timmy was a coward. If only he had had the courage to tell her go to blazes, the story might have had a different ending, for she loved a man of spirit. Having denounced Timmy to his face as a vile seducer, she was now filled with the desire to go back and denounce him as an old molly. She knew if she had been in love with anybody as Timmy was supposed to be in love with May, and written him all those poetic letters about reality not existing for her, she wouldn't have been scared off by the threats of any relative, least of all a girl. "Schoolgirl stuff," indeed! She'd show May which of them was the schoolgirl.

That evening, as they were washing up after supper, May gave her her opportunity. Very gently, as though she were ashamed of the way she had spoken earlier, she asked if there was anything else Joan wished her to do, as she had promised to meet Timmy and some friends at a hotel in town for a drink. She spoke as though Joan were already a confidante and partner.

"I'm afraid you won't be seeing any more of Timmy MacGovern, May," Joan replied in a hesitating tone which was intended to represent regret. And at that moment she did feel rather sorry for "the child."

"Won't I?" May asked with amusement, taking up the challenge.

"I doubt it," Joan said candidly.

"You mean you'd like me to try?" May asked quietly, putting down the dish she had been drying. By this time Kitty would probably have broken it on Joan's head, but May's fantasy was of a kind which could not be easily affected from outside.

"Oh, I'm not trying to stop you, girl," said Joan with a shrug, and went into the sitting-room. She came back with her handbag, took out the picture of May, and tossed it on the table with the air of an old card-sharper producing the missing ace. "Don't you think you'd better have that back?" she asked mildly.

May grew a little more serious, but she was not one to be swept off her feet by any sort of histrionics.

"Where did you pinch that?" she asked lightly.

This time it was Joan who had to restrain herself from flinging something at May. Instead, she smiled and took out the bundle of letters.

"And those," she said mockingly.

May picked one up and looked at it casually. Then she glanced at Joan.

"Check," she said. "Now tell us what it's all about."

Then as May swung her legs from a corner of the kitchen table, Joan described her interview with Timmy. She didn't exaggerate her own part in it. She didn't need to with the evidence of Timmy's weakness of character staring them both in the face. By the time she had finished, Joan had talked herself into good humour again. "To tell you the truth, May," she said candidly, "I think you're a hundred times too good for him."

"I'm beginning to think the same myself," said May, and Joan knew that she meant it. If Timmy came crawling to her now, May wouldn't have him. Not after that humiliation. Schoolgirls were queer like that. Joan knew. She had been one herself—an awful long time ago, it seemed.

That was the end. Timmy took to his bed with thrombosis; Eily Geraghty nursed him and marvelled again at men's reputation for endurance; Tony Dowse visited him and found him sitting up with a shawl round his head, weeping and waving his hands.

"It's the old mistake, MacGovern," Tony said, showing his big teeth in a mournful smile. "I knew what was going to happen.

It's just like that ghost in Glengarriff. It's all imagination, all imagination."

But May's imagination was playing about a tall and sulky young man who played golf and drove a small sports car. She tried to interest him in a caravan and talked a lot to him about tinkers, but he wasn't even interested. In this world one can't have everything.

V

Joan had to confide her troubles to somebody, so, even though she felt it was letting down the family, she told Chris the details of May's affair with Timmy MacGovern. Chris appreciated the gravity of the situation, was disgusted at Timmy, and admired Joan's courage, but he wasn't as scandalized as she had feared. He even admitted that at one time there had nearly been a nasty scandal about his brother Bob. "Bob?" Joan cried in stupefaction. "But I thought Bob was a saint." "That's what we thought too," said Chris, and described the horror of the early-morning call from an old policeman with whom he was friendly and who wanted it hushed up, and the scene at the Bridewell, where some of those who were plaster saints by day were bailed out at night. She respected his reserve in not having told her sooner. Apparently every family, even the most respectable, had things to hide. Respectability, far from being a dull and quiet virtue, was like walking a tight-rope.

Indeed, there are few pleasures more satisfying than those of normality. To walk out of an evening from your normal happy home with a normal respectable young man, and realize that the head of his department, though a Sanskrit scholar, lives in a home where the dirt and confusion created by eight children make life intolerable, and that the second assistant, though a man of genius, is also a dipsomaniac, makes you feel that if cleanliness isn't next to godliness, respectability certainly is. Joan was only beginning to realize her luck and to see that Chris was not only good but beautiful.

But she wasn't yet done with family troubles. May showed a disappointing lack of gratitude for the favour that Joan had done her in breaking off her relations with Timmy MacGovern. She wasn't the sort of girl to make herself unhappy by being cold or distant, but Joan had the feeling that there was watchfulness behind that pleasant manner of hers. A week or two before she married the golfer, she passed Joan a letter from Kitty.

"I don't know that this is any business of yours," she said dryly, "but it looks to me as if Daddy should be told."

It certainly looked as if somebody should be told, for Kitty announced in the calmest way in the world that she was having a baby by a student called Rahilly. He was apparently a young fellow of very fine character, but with no job and entirely dependent on his parents. Joan read the letter and saw ruin staring her in the face. She realized that if Kitty had a baby, it was doubtful if Chris could marry her, and Kitty's chance of ever getting married would be nil. That was one of the drawbacks of respectability—the odds were so high.

"I suppose you're going to tell Jimmie all about this?" she asked.

"Why wouldn't I?" May asked in surprise.

"If you do," said Joan, "don't be surprised if your marriage is broken off in a hurry."

She hoped she might have scared May out of the assumption that her future in-laws would consider Kitty's plight the best of good news. But her father was no better. Weak as usual, he wanted to take all the blame on himself—as much of it as he didn't by implication shoulder off onto her.

"I can't blame the girl, Joan," he said, shaking his head mournfully from side to side. "It was all my fault for letting her go. That would never have happened if she was in her own home. What is she, after all, but a child, and away there among strangers?"

Joan could have told her father pretty shrewdly what Kitty was, but she thought it better not to. His only solution seemed to be to bring Kitty home, let her have her baby there, and face the shame of it as best they could. Joan knew that was no solution. She decided she must talk to Chris about it, and that evening she met him outside his office and they went to a restaurant.

She didn't have to explain anything to him. No sooner had she begun than she saw by his face that he was already foreseeing even more disaster than was apparent to herself.

"Your father should go to Dublin and see this fellow himself," he said with a frown.

"But you know what will happen? They'll go out and have a drink and Father will sympathize with him."

He said nothing to that and talked tangentially for about ten minutes about how difficult things were in the office. Then he asked with something like embarrassment: "Would you like me to go?"

"No, thanks, Chris," she said, shaking her head. "You might be able to deal with this fellow, but you couldn't deal with Kitty. You don't know what a handful she is. If you think someone must go, I'll go myself."

"I wish you hadn't to," he said. "It's going to be very unpleasant."

"Don't I know it?" she said with a sigh.

Next afternoon she set off for Dublin and was met at Kingsbridge Station by a sullen and resentful Kitty. While they crossed the bridge to the bus stop, Kitty asked with no great interest after her father, May, and the neighbours, and Joan answered good-humouredly. But as they passed the Four Courts, Kitty, affecting innocence, asked what had brought her.

"Well, I hope I came up to meet your future husband, Kit," Joan replied quietly.

"Not blooming likely!" said Kitty.

"What on earth do you mean, Kitty?" Joan asked sternly.

"I know what you want, you jealous thing!" Kitty muttered fiercely with the throb of tears in her voice. "You want to interfere between me and Con the way you interfered between me and Dick Gordon and between Timmy MacGovern and May. I know all about it. You're not going to be let."

"I suppose you'll tell me next I shouldn't have interfered between Timmy MacGovern and May," Joan asked sweetly.

"I don't see what the hell business it was of yours," Kitty retorted hotly.

"I'd soon be told what business it was if I had to meet your young man's family with a scandal like that hanging over us," said Joan. "I hope you're not going to tell me that he's married?"

No, he wasn't married, but, as it turned out, it was almost as bad. Joan met him that night in a cinema restaurant. He came in with a heap of books under his arm, a thin, dyspeptic, worried-looking lad with spectacles.

"Really, Miss Twomey," he began, "I'm terribly sorry about all this. I really am."

"I'm sure of it," Joan agreed sweetly, "but what we've got to discuss now is what we're going to do about it."

"I know," he said. "I don't think about anything else. I keep racking my brains, but I simply don't seem to be able to think of anything."

"Well, I presume at least that you're going to marry her?"

"You're presuming a lot," Kitty cut in. "It isn't as easy as all that."

"Would you mind telling me what the objections are?"

"Well, it's my parents," he wailed. "It would be an awful shock to them."

"And I suppose you think it hasn't been a shock to my father?" she asked sternly.

"Con doesn't mean that at all," Kitty put in hotly.

"Then what does he mean?"

"I mean, Miss Twomey, that I haven't got anything, and if I did marry Kitty we'd have to keep it dark or my parents might throw me out."

"That would be a very peculiar sort of marriage, Mr. Rahilly."

He shrugged his shoulders, looking more crushed than ever, and his eyes wandered all over the restaurant as though in search of counsel.

"I don't think Kitty's father would like that sort of marriage at all," she added firmly.

"Well, I can't say I like it, but I don't see what else we can do."

"And who's to support Kitty until you've finished college and got a job." Con clutched his head and looked at Kitty, but even Kitty didn't seem to be able to help him in this dilemma. Joan could see that he was an intolerably weak character, entirely under the thumb of his parents; that he wasn't even considering seriously the possibility of a secret marriage, and that even this she would not succeed in achieving unless she dealt with him firmly. "I suppose you mean my father can support her while she hides away in furnished lodgings like a criminal, all to spare your parents the shock. Really, I think you're as irresponsible as Kitty, if not worse."

"It's easy for you to talk," Kitty said bitterly. "You don't know his mother."

"Well, she can't eat him, Kitty."

"That remains to be seen, Miss Twomey," he said, and she flashed an angry look at him, but he seemed to be quite serious. "As Kitty says, you don't know her."

"Well, I'm going to get to know her within the next couple of days," said Joan. "I'll leave it to you to prepare her."

He threw up his hands in despair.

"You're not going to get to know her," said Kitty. "This is my business, not yours."

"Very well, Kitty. Then I'll wire for Father, and he can deal with you. As a matter of fact," she added untruthfully, "he'd be here now, only for me."

"Then I can give up all hope of continuing at college," Con said, giving it up as a bad job. "I don't mind. I probably wouldn't have been any good as a doctor anyway. I suppose I can be a clerk, if anyone will take me. As you can see, I'm not the type for a labourer."

Joan thought she had never seen such a weak specimen of an entirely degenerate type. She wasn't at all sure but that it would be better for everybody if she didn't interfere. The following evening she took the bus to the Rahillys' house. It was an old-fashioned terrace house on the strand with a great view of the bay and Howth. The door was opened for her by Mr. Rahilly, a red-faced, boozy man with pleasant manners. Mrs. Rahilly was sitting in the front room by the window. Mr. Rahilly introduced them and then disappeared.

Mrs. Rahilly was a plump, pasty-faced woman with rather syrupy manners. To give herself courage, Joan talked in a loud breezy tone, but it came back to her with a hollow echo. She was in a quandary and knew it. To treat the matter too gravely would imply such a reflection on Kitty that Mrs. Rahilly might make it an excuse for refusing to agree to it at all, while if she treated it too lightly, she might conclude that Joan was of the same kind.

"Well, I'm sure I'm very sorry, Miss Twomey," the older woman said effusively. "But I don't see there's anything I can do about it. I had to pinch and scrape to send Con to college, and if it was to save my life, I couldn't do more."

"But surely you'll agree that they must get married," Joan said eagerly.

"Well, indeed, I'm sure I'd be delighted," said Mrs. Rahilly; "that's if your family can support them."

"We have nothing," replied Joan, realizing that she wasn't going to get a shilling.

"Nor more have we," said Mrs. Rahilly as if it was a great joke.

"Then I suppose they must only do what others did before them," Joan said in chagrin. "Kitty can't support a child on her own."

"She might find she has to support a husband and child," said Mrs. Rahilly. "There's no use putting a tooth in it, Miss Twomey, but Con would be no head to her. His father was a weak man—I can say that to you—it was the drink with him; there's no use in denying it. But Con is weaker still. I never thought I'd rear him. It is the digestion with him. He has every delicacy in his own home, but he cannot keep it down. What chance has a boy like that of providing for a wife and child? It's foolishness, Miss Twomey—foolishness!"

Joan was beginning to think that much as she disliked Mrs. Rahilly, they were in agreement about this at least. She was very angry with Kitty and refused to tell her what had happened. "I know what happened all right," Kitty said. "You met your match at last," and this made Joan angrier still. But when Con turned up to Kitty's lodging next day he was resolute for the marriage. Joan had no great faith in his resolution. It was desperation rather than courage. Bad as poverty was, it now had less terrors for him than life with Mother.

When all this was fixed, Joan brought Kitty home to prepare for the wedding. She didn't speak to her all the way down on the train. Her interview with Mrs. Rahilly still rankled. She refused to let her father have anything to say to her either, and except for confidences with May, Kitty was treated as an outcast, an abandoned woman who had brought disgrace on them all. Joan was still very doubtful whether when the moment came, Con Rahilly would have the nerve to defy his mother, and she had to prepare her father and Chris for the worst. She watched every letter which Kitty received, sure that each one must contain the bad news.

This was the beginning of what Kitty called Joan's hypocrisy, though at no time did Joan ever feel in the least hypocritical. It was only that during those difficult months her attitude to Chris changed completely. She became more dependent on him. She asked his advice about everything. She clung to him with a passion that surprised herself. It surprised Chris too, but if he had any qualms about it, he put it down to the strain that she was enduring. Having suffered so much himself, he was prepared to be tolerant of her.

To everybody's astonishment, Con arrived the evening before the wedding. To Joan he seemed a different young man. He had packed his bag and walked out of the house alone. His father had shaken him silently by the hand and slipped him a five-pound note, but his mother had refused to leave her room or admit him to say farewell. The father of a college friend had made a small job for him. He had rented one furnished room in Lower Leeson Street. His friends had treated the whole thing as no better than suicide, and he took them off with great gusto while he cracked ghastly jokes about starvation, which Joan found tasteless. But to her surprise, her father took an instant liking to him. He laughed at Con's grim jokes and took him aside to offer to raise a loan for him. When Con refused, he told Joan that Kitty had picked the best of the bunch.

Joan didn't at all share her father's views, but she didn't try to disillusion him, because his satisfaction seemed to round off her task. Now that her sisters were both married, she felt she had kept the promise made after her mother's death, and proposed to devote the rest of her days to Chris. She proclaimed joyously that they were now getting married too, just as quick as they could. They would live in Dublin because he must have the chance of hearing good music. Every obstacle was brushed aside.

Chris's mother would have to live with Bob; her father would either have to live with May or fend for himself. There was to be no further talk of her responsibilities or of Chris's. To her surprise, her father agreed enthusiastically.

"That's just the way I see it too, Joan," he said emotionally. "There's nothing I'd hate so much as to see you turning into an old maid. You're a great girl, a great girl. I'm glad you're getting a good, steady fellow like Chris. Young Gordon was a nice chap too, but he wasn't your sort, and you're better off with someone like yourself."

Mick might almost be said to have overdone it, but I am afraid the truth is he was almost light-headed with relief. I suppose you have to have as good a daughter as Joan to realize what a blessing it is when she marries and takes herself off. A man with marriageable daughters never has a house he can call his own. If it was only an old barn, you would prefer to have it to yourself.

So she and Chris bought a little bungalow in the hills behind Dublin; a new house without even a cottage near, and with a wonderful view across the city to the Mourne Mountains and over the bay to Howth, and indulged themselves in the solitude they both longed for. They rarely visited or had visitors, and Joan's letters described their solitary evenings, watching the lights come on in the city beneath and listening to the Beethoven quartets right through on the gramophone.

It sounded idyllic, but Kitty and Con got a different impression one evening when they were cycling through Rathfarnham and dropped in unexpectedly. Con was something of a surprise to everybody except Mick Twomey. Though so modest that he scarcely dared express an opinion of his own, he had developed into an extraordinarily acute businessman. Joan was sure he was doing it out of spite, though whether against her or his mother she wasn't sure. At any rate, he and Kitty now had a small house of their own and were talking of buying a car. He stood at the window and generously admired the view while Joan, in her vivacious way, enthused about the calm of the bungalow and the voices of the birds in the early morning. Kitty said nothing. She thought Joan's bungalow was the last word in inconvenience: an emotional girl with no side, she was very fond of the noise of buses, and thought there was an awful lot of nonsense talked about birds. Suddenly she heard a sound that made her start.

"What's that?" she asked incredulously. "A baby?"

Joan smiled, looking rather uncomfortable, and Chris rose with an anguished air.

"I'll see to him, Joan," he volunteered.

He went out and the crying ceased. For several minutes the others stared at one another. Then, in turn, they all grew red. At last Joan grinned insinuatingly.

"We have to keep it dark on Chris's account," she explained apologetically, as though it were all Chris's doing and he had given birth to the baby himself. "Of course, it could be used against him in the civil service."

"That's right," Con said with complete gravity. "You can't be too careful. There's an awful lot of hypocrisy in this country."

"Are you telling us there's hypocrisy?" Kitty asked bitterly as she rose.

"You might as well stay and have something to eat as you're at it," Joan said with more warmth than she had previously shown. "It's a relief that you know about it, because now you can come whenever you like."

"Quartets are not enough," said Con.

"Ah, you'd be dead for want of someone to talk to," said Joan.

"We'd better be going back to our own brat," Kitty said, just managing to keep her temper. "He's probably bawling the house down by now."

All the way downhill she pedalled madly, keeping well ahead of her husband. "God Almighty!" she said bitterly when he caught up on her, "the rest of us can have babies but she can only have quartets. Did you hear her—herself and her birds? That one was crooked from the cradle."

Con only thought it a great joke. May was the same when Kitty wrote and told her. "What name did she call him?" she replied. "Is it Gordon or Dick?" Kitty, who knew that the child could be no one but Chris's, found it a puzzling question.

THE MAD LOMASNEYS

I

NED LOWRY and Rita Lomasney had, one might say, been lovers from childhood. The first time they had met was when he was fourteen and she a year or two younger. It was on the North Mall on a Saturday afternoon, and she was sitting on a bench under the trees; a tall, bony string of a girl with a long, obstinate jaw. Ned was a studious young fellow in a blue and white college cap, thin, pale, and spectacled. As he passed he looked at her owlishly and she gave him back an impudent stare. This upset him—he had no experience of girls—so he blushed and raised his cap. At that she seemed to relent.

"Hullo," she said experimentally.

"Good afternoon," he replied with a pale smile.

"Where are you off to?" she asked.

"Oh, just up the dike for a walk."

"Sit down," she said in a sharp voice, laying her hand on the bench beside her, and he did as he was told. It was a lovely summer evening, and the white quay walls and tall, crazy, claret-coloured tenements under a blue and white sky were reflected in the lazy water, which wrinkled only at the edges and seemed like a painted carpet.

"It's very pleasant here," he said complacently.

"Is it?" she asked with a truculence that startled him. "I don't see anything very pleasant about it."

"Oh, it's very nice and quiet," he said in mild surprise as he raised his fair eyebrows and looked up and down the Mall at the old Georgian houses and the nursemaids sitting under the trees. "My name is Lowry," he added politely.

"Oh, are ye the ones that have the jeweller's shop on the Parade?" she asked.

"That's right," replied Ned with modest pride.

"We have a clock we got from ye," she said. " 'Tisn't much good of an old clock either," she added with quiet malice.

"You should bring it back to the shop," he said in considerable concern. "It probably needs overhauling."

"I'm going down the river in a boat with a couple of chaps," she said, going off at a tangent. "Will you come?"

"Couldn't," he said with a smile.

"Why not?"

"I'm only left go up the dike for a walk," he said complacently. "On Saturdays I go to Confession at St. Peter and Paul's, then I go up the dike and back the Western Road. Sometimes you see very good cricket matches. Do you like cricket?"

"A lot of old sissies pucking a ball!" she said shortly. "I do not."

"I like it," he said firmly. "I go up there every Saturday. Of course, I'm not supposed to talk to anyone," he added with mild amusement at his own audacity.

"Why not?"

"My mother doesn't want me to."

"Why doesn't she?"

"She comes of an awfully good family," he answered mildly, and but for his gentle smile she might have thought he was deliberately insulting her. "You see," he went on gravely in his thin, pleasant voice, ticking things off on his fingers and then glancing at each finger individually as he ticked it off—a tidy sort of boy—"there are three main branches of the Hourigan family: the Neddy Neds, the Neddy Jerrys, and the Neddy Thomases. The Neddy Neds are the Hayfield Hourigans. They are the oldest branch. My mother is a Hayfield Hourigan, and she'd have been a rich woman only for her father backing a bill for a Neddy Jerry. He defaulted and ran away to Australia," he concluded with a contemptuous sniff.

"Cripes!" said the girl. "And had she to pay?"

"She had. But, of course," he went on with as close as he ever seemed likely to get to a burst of real enthusiasm, "my grand-father was a very well-behaved man. When he was eating his dinner the boys from the National School in Bantry used to be brought up to watch him, he had such beautiful table manners. Once he caught my uncle eating cabbage with a knife and he struck him with a poker. They had to put four stitches in him after," he added with a joyous chuckle.

"Cripes!" the girl said again. "What did he do that for?"

"To teach him manners," Ned said earnestly.

"He must have been dotty."

"Oh, I wouldn't say so," Ned exclaimed in mild surprise. Everything this girl said came as a shock to him. "But that's why my mother won't let us mix with other children. On the other hand, we read a good deal. Are you fond of reading, Miss—I didn't catch the name."

"You weren't told it," she said, showing her claws. "But if you want to know, it's Rita Lomasney."

"Do you read much, Miss Lomasney?"

"I couldn't be bothered."

"I read all sorts of books," he said enthusiastically. "And as well as that, I'm learning the violin from Miss Maude on the Pa-rade. Of course, it's very difficult, because it's all classical music."

"What's classical music?" she asked with sudden interest.

"*Maritana* is classical music," he replied eagerly. He was a bit of a puzzle to Rita. She had never before met anyone with such a passion for handing out instruction. "Were you at *Maritana* in the opera house, Miss Lomasney?"

"I was never there at all," she said curtly.

"And *Alice Where Art Thou* is classical music," he added. "It's harder than plain music. You see," he went on, composing signs in the air, "it has signs on it like this, and when you see the signs, you know it's after turning into a different tune, though it has the same name. Irish music is all the same tune and that's why my mother won't let us learn it."

"Were you ever at the opera in Paris?" she asked suddenly.

"No," said Ned. "I was never in Paris. Why?"

"That's where you should go," she said with airy enthusiasm.

"You couldn't hear any operas here. The staircase alone is bigger than the whole opera house here."

It seemed as if they were in for a really informative conversation when two fellows came down Wyse's Hill. Rita got up to meet them. Lowry looked up at them and then rose too, lifting his cap politely.

"Well, good afternoon," he said cheerfully. "I enjoyed the talk. I hope we meet again."

"Some other Saturday," said Rita.

"Oh, good evening, old man," one of the two fellows said in an affected drawl, pretending to raise a top hat. "Do come and see us soon again."

"Shut up, Foster!" Rita said sharply. "I'll give you a puck in the gob."

"Oh, by the way," Ned said, coming back to hand her a number of the *Gem* which he took from his coat pocket, "you might like to look at this. It's not bad."

"Thanks, I'd love to," she said insincerely, and he smiled and touched his cap again. Then with a polite and almost deferential air he went up to Foster. "Did you say something?" he asked.

Foster looked as astonished as if a kitten had suddenly got on its hind legs and challenged him to fight.

"I did not," he said, and backed away.

"I'm glad," Ned said, almost purring. "I was afraid you might be looking for trouble."

It came as a surprise to Rita as well. Whatever opinion she might have formed of Ned Lowry, fighting was about the last thing she would have associated him with.

II

The Lomasneys lived in a house on Sunday's Well, a small house with a long, sloping garden and a fine view of the river and city. Harry Lomasney, the builder, was a small man who wore grey tweed suits and soft collars several sizes too big for him. He had a ravaged brick-red face with keen blue eyes, and a sandy, straggling moustache with one side going up and the other down, and his workmen said you could tell his humour by the side he pulled. He was nicknamed "Hasty Harry." "Great God!" he fumed when his wife was having her first baby. "Nine months over a little job like that! I'd do it in three weeks if I could only get started." His wife was tall and matronly and very pious, but her piety never got much in her way. A woman who had survived Hasty would have survived anything. Their eldest daughter, Kitty, was loud-voiced and gay and had been expelled from school for writing indecent letters to a boy. She had copied the letters out of a French novel but she failed to tell the nuns that. Nellie was placider and took more after her mother; besides, she didn't read French novels.

Rita was the exception among the girls. There seemed to be no softness in her. She never had a favourite saint or a favourite nun; she said it was soppy. For the same reason she never had flirtations. Her friendship with Ned Lowry was the closest she ever got to that, and though Ned came regularly to the house, and the pair of them went to the pictures together, her sisters would have found it hard to say whether she cared any more for him than she did for any of her girl acquaintances. There was something in her they didn't understand, something tongue-tied, twisted, and unhappy. She had a curious raw, almost timid smile as though she felt people desired no better sport than hurting her. At home she was reserved, watchful, almost mocking. She could listen for hours to her mother and sisters without once opening her mouth, and then suddenly mystify them by dropping a well-aimed jaw-breaker—about classical music, for instance—before relapsing into a sulky silence; as though she had merely drawn back the veil for a moment on depths in herself which she would not permit them to explore.

After taking her degree, she got a job in a convent school in a provincial town in the west of Ireland. She and Ned corresponded and he even went to see her there. He reported at home that she seemed quite happy.

But this didn't last. A few months later the Lomasney family were at supper one evening when they heard a car stop, the gate squeaked, and steps came up the long path to the front door. Then came the sound of a bell and a cheerful voice from the hall.

"Hullo, Paschal, I suppose ye weren't expecting me?"

" 'Tis never Rita!" said her mother, meaning that it was but that it shouldn't be.

"As true as God, that one is after getting into trouble," Kitty said prophetically.

The door opened and Rita slouched in, a long, stringy girl with a dark, glowing face. She kissed her father and mother lightly.

"Hullo," she said. "How's tricks?"

"What happened you?" her mother asked, rising.

"Nothing," replied Rita, an octave up the scale. "I just got the sack."

"The sack?" said her father, beginning to pull the wrong side of his moustache. "What did you get the sack for?"

"Give us a chance to get something to eat first, can't you?" Rita said laughingly. She took off her hat and smiled at herself in the mirror over the mantelpiece. It was a curious smile as though she were amused by the spectacle of what she saw. Then she smoothed back her thick black hair. "I told Paschal to bring in whatever was going. I'm on the train since ten. The heating was off as usual. I'm frizzled."

"A wonder you wouldn't send us a wire," said Mrs. Lomasney as Rita sat down and grabbed some bread and butter.

"Hadn't the tin," replied Rita.

"Can't you tell us what happened?" Kitty asked brightly.

"I told you. You'll hear more in due course. Reverend Mother is bound to write and tell ye how I lost my character."

"But what did you do, child?" her mother asked placidly. Her mother had been through all this before, with Hasty and Kitty, and she knew God was very good and nothing much ever happened.

"Fellow that wanted to marry me," said Rita. "He was in his last year at college, and his mother didn't like me, so she got Reverend Mother to give me the push."

"And what has it to do with Reverend Mother?" Nellie asked indignantly. "What business is it of hers?"

"That's what I say," said Rita.

But Kitty looked suspiciously at her. Rita wasn't natural; there was something wild about her, and this was her first real love affair. Kitty just couldn't believe that Rita had gone about it the same as anyone else.

"Still, I must say you worked pretty fast," she said.

"You'd have to in that place," said Rita. "There was only one possible man in the whole village and he was the bank clerk. We called him 'The One.' I wasn't there a week when the nuns ticked me off for riding on the pillion of his motor-bike."

"And did you?" asked Kitty.

"I never got the chance, girl. They did it to every teacher on principle to give her the idea that she was well watched. I only met Tony Donoghue a fortnight ago—home after a breakdown."

"Well, well, well!" her mother exclaimed without rancour. "No wonder his poor mother was upset. A boy that's not left college yet! Couldn't ye wait till he was qualified anyway?"

"Not very well," said Rita. "He's going to be a priest."

Kitty sat back with a superior grin. Of course, Rita could do nothing like anyone else. If it wasn't a priest it would have been a Negro, and Rita would have made theatre of it in precisely the same deliberate way.

"A what?" asked her father, springing to his feet.

"All right, don't blame me!" Rita said hastily. "It wasn't my fault. He told me he didn't want to be a priest. It was his mother was driving him into it. That's why he had the breakdown."

"Let me out of this," said her father, "before I—"

"Go on!" Rita said with tender mockery (she was very fond of her father). "Before you what?"

"Before I wish I was a priest myself," he snarled. "I wouldn't be saddled with a family like I am."

He stumped out of the room, and the girls laughed. The idea of their father as a priest appealed to them almost as much as the idea of him as a mother. Hasty had a knack of stating his grievances in such a way that they inevitably produced laughter. But Mrs. Lomasney did not laugh.

"Reverend Mother was perfectly right," she said severely. "As if it wasn't hard enough on the poor boys without girls like you throwing temptation in their way. I think you behaved very badly, Rita."

"All right, if you say so," Rita said shortly with a boyish shrug of her shoulders, and refused to answer any more questions.

After her supper she went to bed, and her mother and sisters sat on in the front room discussing the scandal. Someone rang and Nellie opened the door.

"Hullo, Ned," she said. "I suppose you came up to congratulate us on the good news?"

"Hullo," Ned said, smiling with his mouth primly shut. With a sort of automatic movement he took off his coat and hat and hung them on the rack. Then he emptied the pockets with the same thoroughness. He hadn't changed much. He was thin and pale, spectacled and clever, with the same precise and tranquil manner, "like an old Persian cat," as Nellie said. He read too many books. In the last year or two something seemed to have happened him. He didn't go to Mass any longer. Not going to Mass struck all the Lomasneys as too damn clever. "What good news?" he added, having avoided any unnecessary precipitation.

"You didn't know who was here?"

"No," he replied, raising his brows mildly.

"Rita!"

"Oh!" The same tone. It was part of his cleverness not to be surprised at anything.

"She's after getting the sack for trying to run off with a priest," said Nellie.

If Nellie thought that would shake him she was mistaken. He merely tossed his head with a silent chuckle and went in, adjusting his pince-nez. For a fellow who was supposed to be in love with her since they were kids, he behaved in a very peculiar manner. He put his hands in his trousers pockets and stood on the hearth with his legs well apart.

"Isn't it awful, Ned?" Mrs. Lomasney asked in her deep voice.

"Is it?" Ned purred, smiling.

"With a priest?" cried Nellie.

"Now, he wasn't a priest, Nellie," said Mrs. Lomasney reprovingly. " 'Tis bad enough as it is without making it any worse."

"Suppose you tell me what happened," suggested Ned.

"But we don't know, Ned," cried Mrs. Lomasney. "You know what that one is like in one of her sulky fits. Maybe she'll tell you. She's up in bed."

"I'll try," said Ned.

Still with his hands in his pockets, he rolled after Mrs. Lomasney up the thickly carpeted stairs to Rita's little bedroom on top of the house. She left him on the landing and he paused for a moment to look out over the river and the lighted city behind it. Rita, wearing a pink dressing-jacket, was lying with one arm under her head. By the bed was a table with a packet of cigarettes she had been using as an ashtray. He smiled and shook his head reprovingly at her.

"Hullo, Ned," she cried, reaching him a bare arm. "Give us a kiss. I'm quite kissable now."

He didn't need to be told that. He was astonished at the change in her. Her whole bony, boyish face seemed to have gone mawkish and soft and to be lit up from inside. He sat on an armchair by the bed, carefully pulling up the bottoms of his trousers, then put his hands in his trousers pockets again and sat back with crossed legs and shoulders slightly hunched.

"I suppose they're all in a floosther downstairs?" Rita asked with amusement.

"They seem a little excited," said Ned with bowed head cocked a little sideways, looking like a wise old bird.

"Wait till they hear the details and they'll have something to be excited about," said Rita grimly.

"Why?" he asked mildly. "Are there details?"

"Masses of them," said Rita. "Honest to God, Ned, I used to laugh at the glamour girls in the convent. I never knew you could get like that about a fellow. It's like something busting inside you. Cripes, I'm as soppy as a kid!"

"And what's the fellow like?" Ned asked curiously.

"Tony Donoghue? His mother had a shop in the Main Street. He's decent enough, I suppose. I don't know. He kissed me one night coming home. I was furious. I cut the blooming socks off him. Next evening he came round to apologize. I never got up or asked him to sit down or anything. I suppose I was still mad with him. He said he never slept a wink. 'Didn't you?' said I. 'It didn't trouble me much.' Bloody lies, of course. 'I did it because I was fond of you,' says he. 'Is that what you told the last one too?' said I. Then he got into a wax too. Said I was calling him a liar. 'And aren't you?' said I. Then I waited for him to hit me, but, begor, he didn't, and I ended up sitting on his knee. Talk about the Babes in the Wood! First time he ever had a girl on his knee, he said, and you know how much of it I did."

They heard a step on the stairs and Mrs. Lomasney smiled benevolently at them both round the door.

"I suppose 'tis tea Ned is having?" she asked in her deep voice.

"No, I'm having the tea," said Rita. "Ned says he'd sooner a drop of the hard tack."

"Oh, isn't that a great change, Ned?" cried Mrs. Lomasney.

" 'Tis the shock," Rita explained lightly, throwing him a cigarette. "He didn't think I was that sort of girl."

"He mustn't know much about girls," said Mrs. Lomasney.

"He's learning now," said Rita.

When Paschal brought up the tray, Rita poured out tea for Ned and whisky for herself. He made no comment. Things like that were a commonplace in the Lomasney household.

"Anyway," she went on, "he told his old one he wanted to chuck the Church and marry me. There was ructions, of course. The people in the shop at the other side of the street had a son a priest. She wanted to be as good as them. So away with her up to Reverend Mother, and Reverend Mother sends for me. Did I want to destroy the young man's life and he on the threshold of a great calling? I told her 'twas they wanted to destroy him. I asked her what sort of priest Tony would make. Oh, 'twas a marvellous sacrifice, and after it he'd be twice the man. Honest to God, Ned, the way that woman went on, you'd think she was talking about doctoring an old tomcat. I told her that was all she knew about Tony, and she said they knew him since he was an altar boy in the convent. 'Did he ever tell you how he used to slough the convent orchard and sell the apples in town?' says I. So then she dropped the Holy Willie stuff and told me his ma was after getting into debt to put him in for the priesthood, and if he chucked it, he'd never be able to get a job at home to pay it back. Three hundred quid! Wouldn't they kill you with style?"

"And what did you do then?" asked Ned with amusement.

"I went to see his mother."

"You didn't!"

"I did. I thought I might work it with the personal touch."

"You don't seem to have been very successful."

"I'd as soon try the personal touch on a traction engine, Ned. That woman was too tough for me altogether. I told her I wanted to marry Tony. 'I'm sorry,' she said; 'you can't.' 'What's to stop me?' said I. 'He's gone too far,' says she. 'If he was gone farther it wouldn't worry me,' says I. I told her then what Reverend Mother said about her being three hundred pounds in debt and offered to pay it back to her if she let him marry me."

"And had you the three hundred?" Ned asked in surprise.

"Ah, where would I get three hundred?" she replied ruefully. "And she knew it too, the old jade! She didn't believe a word I said. After that I saw Tony. He was crying; said he didn't want to break his mother's heart. As true as God, Ned, that woman had as much heart as a traction engine."

"Well, you seem to have done it in style," Ned said approvingly as he put away his teacup.

"That wasn't the half of it. When I heard the difficulties his mother was making, I offered to live with him instead."

"Live with him?" asked Ned. Even he was startled.

"Well, go away on holidays with him. Lots of girls do it. I know they do. And, God Almighty, isn't it only natural?"

"And what did he say to that?" asked Ned curiously.

"He was scared stiff."

"He would be," said Ned, wrinkling up his nose and giving his superior little sniff as he took out a packet of cigarettes.

"Oh, it's all very well for you," Rita cried, bridling up. "You may think you're a great fellow, all because you read Tolstoy and don't go to Mass, but you'd be just as scared if a girl offered to go to bed with you."

"Try me," Ned said sedately as he lit her cigarette for her, but somehow the notion of suggesting such a thing to Ned only made her laugh.

He stayed till quite late, and when he went downstairs the girls and Mrs. Lomasney fell on him and dragged him into the sitting-room.

"Well, doctor," said Mrs. Lomasney, "how's the patient?"

"Oh, I think the patient is coming round nicely," said Ned.

"But would you ever believe it, Ned?" she cried. "A girl that wouldn't look at the side of the road a fellow was at, unless 'twas to go robbing orchards with him. You'll have another drop of whisky?"

"I won't."

"And is that all you're going to tell us?" asked Mrs. Lomasney.

"Oh, you'll hear it all from herself."

"We won't."

"I dare say not," he said with a hearty chuckle, and went for his coat.

"Wisha, Ned," said Mrs. Lomasney, "what'll your mother say when she hears it?"

" 'All *quite* mad,' " said Ned, sticking his nose in the air and giving an exaggerated version of what Mrs. Lomasney called "his Hayfield sniff."

"The dear knows, I think she's right," she said with resignation, helping him with his coat. "I hope your mother doesn't notice the smell of whisky from your breath," she added dryly, just to show him that she couldn't be taken in, and then stood at the door, looking up and down, as she waited for him to wave from the gate.

"Ah," she sighed as she closed the door behind her, "with the help of God it might be all for the best."

"If you think he's going to marry her, I can tell you now he's not," said Kitty. "I'd like to see myself trying it on Bill O'Donnell. He'd have my sacred life. That fellow only enjoys it."

"Ah, God is good," her mother said cheerfully, kicking a mat into place. "Some men might like that."

III

Inside a week Kitty and Nellie were sick to death of the sight of Rita round the house. She was bad enough at the best of times, but now she just brooded and mooned and snapped the head off you. In the afternoons she strolled down the dike and into Ned's little shop, where she sat on the counter, swinging her legs and smoking, while Ned leaned against the side of the window, tinkering at the insides of a watch with some delicate instrument. Nothing seemed to rattle him. When he had finished work, he changed his coat and they went out to tea. He sat at the back of the teashop in a corner, pulled up the legs of his trousers, and took out a packet of cigarettes and a box of matches, which he placed on the table before him with a look that almost commanded them to stay there and not get lost. His face was pale and clear and bright, like an evening sky when the last light has drained from it.

"Anything wrong?" he asked one evening when she was moodier than usual.

"Just fed up," she said, thrusting out her jaw.

"What is it?" he asked gently. "Still fretting?"

"Ah, no. I can get over that. It's Kitty and Nellie. They're bitches, Ned; proper bitches. And all because I don't wear my heart on my sleeve. If one of them got a knock from a fellow she'd take two aspirins and go to bed with the other one. They'd have a lovely talk—can't you imagine? 'And was it then he said he loved you?' I can't do that sort of stuff. And it's all because they're not sincere, Ned. They couldn't be sincere."

"Remember, they have a long start on you," Ned said smiling.

"Is that it?" she asked without interest. "They think I'm batty. Do you?"

"I've no doubt that Mrs. Donoghue, if that's her name, thought something of the sort," replied Ned with a tight-lipped smile.

"And wasn't she right?" asked Rita with sudden candour. "Suppose she'd agreed to take the three hundred quid, wouldn't I be in a nice pickle? I wake in a sweat whenever I think of it. I'm just a blooming chancer, Ned. Where would I get three hundred quid?"

"Oh, I dare say someone would have lent it to you," he said with a shrug.

"They would like fun. Would you?"

"Probably," he said gravely after a moment's thought.

"Are you serious?" she whispered earnestly.

"Quite."

"Cripes," she gasped, "you must be very fond of me."

"It looks like it," said Ned, and this time he laughed with real heartiness, a boy's laugh of sheer delight at the mystification he was causing her. It was characteristic of Rita that she should count their friendship of years as nothing, but his offer of three hundred pounds in cash as significant.

"Would you marry me?" she asked frowningly. "I'm not proposing to you, only asking," she added hastily.

"Certainly," he said, spreading out his hands. "Whenever you like."

"Honest to God?"

"Cut my throat."

"And why didn't you ask me before I went down to that kip? I'd have married you then like a shot. Was it the way you weren't keen on me then?"

"No," he replied matter-of-factly, drawing himself together like an old clock preparing to strike. "I think I've been keen on you as long as I know you."

"It's easily seen you're a Neddy Ned," she said with amusement. "I go after mine with a scalping knife."

"I stalk mine," said Ned.

"Cripes, Ned," she said with real regret, "I wish you'd told me sooner. I couldn't marry you now."

"No?"

"No. It wouldn't be fair to you."

"Isn't that my look-out?"

"It's my look-out now." She glanced round the restaurant to make sure no one was listening and then went on in a dry voice, leaning one elbow on the table. "I suppose you'll think this is all cod, but it's not. Honest to God, I think you're the finest bloody man I ever met—even though you do think you're an atheist or something," she added maliciously with a characteristic Lomasney flourish in the cause of Faith and Fatherland. "There's no one in the world I have more respect for. I think I'd nearly cut my throat if I did something you really disapproved of—I don't mean telling lies or going on a skite," she added hastily, to prevent misunderstandings. "They're only gas. Something that really shocked you is what I mean. I think if I was tempted to do anything like that I'd ask myself: 'What would that fellow Lowry think of me now?'"

"Well," Ned said in an extraordinarily quiet voice, squelching the butt of his cigarette on his plate, "that sounds to me like a very good beginning."

"It is not, Ned," she said sadly, shaking her head. "That's why I say it's my look-out. You couldn't understand it unless it happened to yourself; unless you fell in love with a girl the way I fell in love with Tony. Tony is a scut, and a cowardly scut, but I was cracked about him. If he came in here now and said: 'Come on, girl, we're going to Killarney for the week-end,' I'd go out and buy a nightdress and toothbrush and be off with him. And I wouldn't give a damn what you or anybody thought. I might chuck myself in the lake afterwards, but I'd go. Christ, Ned," she exclaimed, flushing and looking as though she might burst into tears, "he couldn't come into a room but I went all mushy inside. That's what the real thing is like."

"Well," Ned said sedately, apparently not in the least put out —in fact, looking rather pleased with himself, Rita thought—"I'm in no hurry. In case you get tired of scalping them, the offer will still be open."

"Thanks, Ned," she said absent-mindedly, as though she weren't listening.

While he paid the bill, she stood in the porch, doing her face in the big mirror that flanked it, and paying no attention to the crowds, coming homeward through streets where the shop windows were already lit. As he emerged from the shop she turned on him suddenly.

"About that matter, Ned," she said, "will you ask me again, or do I have to ask you?"

Ned just refrained from laughing outright. "As you like," he replied with quiet amusement. "Suppose I repeat the proposal every six months."

"That would be the hell of a long time to wait if I changed my mind," she said with a thoughtful scowl. "All right," she said, taking his arm. "I know you well enough to ask you. If you don't want me by that time, you can always say so. I won't mind."

IV

Ned's proposal came as a considerable comfort to Rita. It bolstered up her self-esteem, which was always in danger of collapse. She might be ugly and uneducated and a bit of a chancer, but the best man in Cork—the best in Ireland, she sometimes thought—wanted to marry her, even after she had been let down by another man. That was a queer one for her enemies! So while her sisters made fun of her, Rita considered the situation, waiting for the best possible moment to let them know she had been proposed to and could marry before either of them if it suited her. Since her childhood Rita had never given anything away without extracting the last ounce of theatrical effect from it. She would tell her sisters, but not before she could make them sick with the news.

That was a pity, for it left Rita unaware that Ned, whom she respected, was far from being the only one who liked her. For instance, there was Justin Sullivan, the lawyer, who had once been by way of being engaged to Nellie. He hadn't become engaged to her, because she was as slippery as an eel, and her fancy finally lit on a solicitor called Fahy whom Justin despised with his whole heart and soul as a light-headed, butterfly sort of man. But Justin continued to visit the house as a friend of the girls. There happened to be no other house that suited him half as well, and besides he knew that sooner or later Nellie would make a mess of her life with Fahy, and his services would be required.

Justin, in other words, was a sticker. He was a good deal older than Rita, a tall, burly man with a broad face, a brow that was rising from baldness as well as brains, and a slow, watchful, ironic air. Like many lawyers, he tended to conduct conversation as though the person he was speaking to were a hostile witness who had either to be coaxed into an admission of perjury or bullied into one of mental deficiency. When Justin began, Fahy simply clutched his head and retired to sit on the stairs. "Can't anyone shut that fellow up?" he would moan with a martyred air. Nobody could. The girls shot their little darts at him, but he only brushed them aside. Ned Lowry was the only one who could even stand up to him, and when the pair of them argued about religion, the room became a desert. Justin, of course, was a pillar of orthodoxy. "Imagine for a moment," he would declaim in a throaty rounded voice that turned easily to pomposity, "that I am Pope." "Easiest thing in the world, Justin," Kitty assured him.

He drank whisky like water, and the more he drank, the more massive and logical and orthodoxly Catholic he became.

At the same time, under his truculent air he was exceedingly gentle, patient, and understanding, and disliked the ragging of Rita by her sisters.

"Tell me, Nellie," he asked one night in his lazy, amiable way, "do you talk like that to Rita because you like it, or because you think it's good for her?"

"How soft you have it!" Nellie cried. "We have to live with her. You haven't."

"That may be my misfortune, Nellie," said Justin with a broad smile.

"Is that a proposal, Justin?" asked Kitty shrewdly.

"Scarcely, Kitty," said Justin. "You're not what I might call a good jury."

"Better be careful or you'll have her dropping in on your mother, Justin," Kitty said maliciously.

"Thanks, Kitty," Rita said with a flash of cold fury.

"I hope my mother would have sufficient sense to realize it was an honour, Kitty," Justin said severely.

When he rose to go, Rita accompanied him to the hall.

"Thanks for the moral support, Justin," she said in a low voice, and then threw her overcoat over her shoulders to go as far as the gate with him. When he opened the door they both stood and gazed about them. It was a moonlit night; the garden, patterned in black and silver, sloped to the quiet roadway, where the gas lamps burned with a dim green light, and in the farther walls gateways shaded by black trees led to flights of steps or to steep-sloping avenues which led to moonlit houses on the river's edge.

"God, isn't it lovely?" Rita said in a hushed voice.

"Oh, by the way, Rita," he said, slipping his arm through hers, "that was a proposal."

"Janey Mack, they're falling," she said, giving his arm a squeeze.

"What are falling?"

"Proposals."

"Why? Had you others?"

"I had one anyway."

"And did you accept it?"

"No," Rita said doubtfully. "Not quite. At least, I don't think I did."

"You might consider this one," Justin said with unusual humility. "You know, of course, that I was very fond of Nellie. At one time I was very fond of her indeed. You don't mind that, I hope. It's all over and done with now, and there are no regrets on either side."

"No, Justin, of course I don't mind. If I felt like marrying you I wouldn't give it a second thought. But I was very much in love with Tony too, and that's not all over and done with yet."

"I know that, Rita," he said gently. "I know exactly what you feel. We've all been through it." If he had left it at that everything might have been all right, but Justin was a lawyer, which meant that he liked to keep things absolutely shipshape. "But that won't last forever. In a month or two you'll be over it, and then you'll wonder what you saw in that fellow."

"I don't think so, Justin," she said with a crooked little smile, not altogether displeased to be able to enlighten him on the utter hopelessness of her position. "I think it will take a great deal longer than that."

"Well, say six months, even," Justin went on, prepared to yield a point to the defence. "All I ask is that in one month or six, whenever you've got over your regrets for this—this amiable young man" (momentarily his voice took on its familiar ironic ring), "you'll give me a thought. I'm old enough not to make any more mistakes. I know I'm fond of you, and I feel pretty sure I could make a success of my end of it."

"What you really mean," said Rita, keeping her temper with the greatest difficulty, "is that I wasn't in love with Tony at all. Isn't that it?"

"Not quite," Justin said judiciously. Even if he'd had a serenade as well as the moonlight and the girl, it couldn't have kept him from correcting what he considered to be a false deduction. "I've no doubt you were very much attracted by this—this clerical Adonis; this Mr. Whatever-his-name-is, or that at any rate you thought you were, which in practice comes to the same thing, but

I also know that that sort of thing, though it's painful enough while it lasts, doesn't last very long."

"You mean yours didn't, Justin," Rita said tartly.

"I mean mine or anybody else's," Justin said pompously. "Because love—the only sort of thing you can really call love—is something that comes with experience. You're probably too young yet to know what the real thing is."

As Rita had only recently told Ned that he didn't yet know what the real thing was, she found this rather hard to stomach.

"How old would you say you'd have to be?" she asked viciously. "Thirty-five?"

"You'll know soon enough—when it hits you," said Justin.

"Honest to God, Justin," she said, withdrawing her arm and looking at him with suppressed fury, "I think you're the thickest man I ever met."

"Good night, my dear," said Justin with perfect good humour, and he raised his cap and took the few steps to the gate at a run.

Rita stood gazing after him with folded arms. At the age of eighteen to be told that there is anything you don't know about love is like a knife in your heart.

V

Kitty and Nellie grew so tired of her moodiness that they persuaded her mother that the best way of distracting her mind was to find her another job. A new environment was also supposed to be good for her complaint, so Mrs. Lomasney wrote to her sister who was a nun in England, and the sister found her work in a convent there. Rita let on to pay no attention, though she let Ned see something of her resentment.

"But why England?" he asked wonderingly.

"Why not?" replied Rita challengingly.

"Wouldn't any place nearer do you?"

"I suppose I wouldn't be far enough away from them."

"But why not make up your own mind?"

"I'll probably do that too," she said with a short laugh. "I'd like to see what's in theirs first though."

On Friday she was to leave for England, and on Wednesday

the girls gave a farewell party. This, too, Rita affected to take no great interest in. Wednesday was the half-holiday, and it rained steadily all day. The girls' friends all turned up. Most were men: Bill O'Donnell of the bank, who was engaged to Kitty; Fahy, the solicitor, who was Justin's successful rival for Nellie; Justin himself, who simply could not be kept out of the house by anything short of an injunction, Ned Lowry, and a few others. Hasty soon retired with his wife to the dining-room to read the evening paper. He said all his daughters' young men looked exactly alike and he never knew which of them he was talking to.

Bill O'Donnell was acting as barman. He was a big man, bigger even than Justin, with a battered boxer's face and a Negro smile, which seemed to well up from depths of good humour with life rather than from any immediate contact with others. He carried on loud conversations with everyone he poured out drink for, and his voice overrode every intervening tête-à-tête, and challenged even the piano, on which Nellie was vamping music-hall songs.

"Who's this one for, Rita?" he asked. "A bottle of Bass for Paddy. Ah, the stout man! Remember the New Year's Day in Bandon, Paddy? Remember how you had to carry me up to the bank in evening dress and jack me up between the two wings of the desk? Kitty, did I ever tell you about that night in Bandon?"

"Once a week for the past five years, Bill," said Kitty philosophically.

"Nellie," said Rita, "I think it's time for Bill to sing his song. 'Let Me like a Soldier Fall,' Bill!"

"My one little song!" Bill said with a roar of laughter. "My one and only song, but I sing it grand. Don't I, Nellie? Don't I sing it fine?"

"Fine!" agreed Nellie, looking up at his big, beaming moon-face shining at her over the piano. "As the man said to my mother, 'Finest bloody soprano I ever heard.'"

"He did not, Nellie," Bill said sadly. "You're making that up. . . . Silence, please!" he shouted joyously, clapping his hands. "Ladies and gentlemen, I must apologize. I ought to sing some-

thing like Tosti's 'Good-bye,' but the fact is, ladies and gentlemen, that I don't know Tosti's 'Good-bye.' "

"Recite it, Bill," said Justin amiably.

"I don't know the words of it either, Justin," said Bill. "In
fact, I'm not sure if there's any such song, but if there is, I ought
to sing it."

"Why, Bill?" Rita asked innocently. She was wearing a long
black dress that threw up the unusual brightness of her dark,
bony face. She looked happier than she had looked for months.
All the evening it was as though she were laughing to herself.

"Because 'twould be only right, Rita," said Bill with great
melancholy, putting his arm about her and drawing her closer
to him. "You know I'm very fond of you, don't you, Rita?"

"And I'm mad about you, Bill," said Rita candidly.

"I know that, Rita," he said mournfully, pulling at his collar
as though to give himself air. "I only wish you weren't going,
Rita. This place isn't the same without you. Kitty won't mind my
saying that," he added with a nervous glance at Kitty, who was
flirting with Justin on the sofa.

"Are you going to sing your blooming old song or not?"
Nellie asked impatiently, running her fingers over the keys.

"I'm going to sing now in one minute, Nellie," Bill said
ecstatically, stroking Rita fondly under the chin. "I only want
Rita to know the way we'll miss her."

"Damn it, Bill," Rita said, snuggling up to him with her dark
head on his chest, "if you go on like that I won't go at all. Tell
me, would you really prefer me not to go?"

"I would prefer you not to go, Rita," he replied, stroking
her cheeks and eyes. "You're too good for the fellows over
there."

"Oh, go on doing that," she said hastily, as he dropped his
hand. "It's gorgeous, and you're making Kitty mad jealous."

"Kitty isn't jealous," Bill said fondly. "Kitty is a lovely girl
and you're a lovely girl. I hate to see you go, Rita."

"That settles it, Bill," she said, pulling herself free of him with
a determined air. "I simply couldn't cause you all that suffering.
As you put it that way, I won't go."

"Won't you, just?" said Kitty with a grin.

"Now, don't worry your head about it any more, Bill," said Rita briskly. "It's all off."

Justin, who had been quietly consuming large whiskies, looked round lazily.

"Perhaps I ought to have mentioned," he boomed, "that the young lady has just done me the honour of proposing to me and I've accepted her."

Ned Lowry, who had been enjoying the scene between Bill and Rita, looked at him for a moment in surprise.

"Bravo! Bravo!" cried Bill, clapping his hands with childish delight. "A marriage has been arranged and all the rest of it—what? I must give you a kiss, Rita. Justin, you don't mind if I give Rita a kiss?"

"Not at all, not at all," replied Justin with a lordly wave of his hand. "Anything that's mine is yours, old man."

"You're not serious, Justin, are you?" Kitty asked incredulously.

"Oh, I'm serious all right," said Justin. "I'm not quite certain whether your sister is. Are you, Rita?"

"What?" Rita asked as though she hadn't heard.

"Serious," repeated Justin.

"Why?" asked Rita. "Trying to give me the push already?"

"We're much obliged for the information," Nellie said ironically as she rose from the piano. "Now, maybe you'd oblige us further and tell us does Father know."

"Hardly," said Rita coolly. "It was only settled this evening."

"Well, maybe 'twill do with some more settling by the time Father is done with you," Nellie said furiously. "The impudence of you! How dare you! Go in at once and tell him."

"Keep your hair on, girl," Rita advised with cool malice and then went jauntily out of the room. Kitty and Nellie began to squabble viciously with Justin. They were convinced that the whole scene had been arranged by Rita to make them look ridiculous, and in this they weren't very far out. Justin sat back and began to enjoy the sport. Then Ned Lowry struck a match and lit another cigarette, and something about the slow, careful way in which he did it drew everyone's attention. Just because he was not the sort to make a fuss, people realized from his

strained look that his mind was very far away. The squabble
stopped as quickly as it had begun and a feeling of awkwardness
ensued. Ned was too old a friend of the family for the girls not
to feel that way about him.

Rita returned, laughing.

"Well?" asked Nellie.

"Consent refused," growled Rita, bowing her head and pulling
the wrong side of an imaginary moustache.

"What did I say?" exclaimed Nellie, but without rancour.

"You don't think it makes any difference?" Rita asked dryly.

"I wouldn't be too sure of that," said Nellie. "What else did
he say?"

"Oh, he hadn't a notion who I was talking about," Rita
said lightly. " 'Justin who?' " she mimicked. " 'How the hell do
you think I can remember all the young scuts ye bring to the
house?' "

"Was he mad?" asked Kitty with amusement.

"Hopping."

"He didn't call us scuts?" asked Bill in a wounded tone.

"Oh, begor, that was the very word he used, Bill," said Rita.

"Did you tell him he was very fond of me the day I gave him
the tip for Golden Boy at the Park Races?" asked Justin.

"I did," said Rita. "I said you were the stout block of a fellow
with the brown hair that he said had the fine intelligence, and
he said he never gave a damn about intelligence. He wanted me
to marry the thin fellow with the specs. 'Only bloody gentleman
that comes to the house.' "

"Is it Ned?" cried Nellie.

"Who else?" said Rita. "I asked him why he didn't tell me that
before and he nearly ate the head off me. 'Jesus Christ, girl, don't
I feed ye and clothe ye? Isn't that enough without having to
coort for ye as well? Next thing, ye'll be asking me to have a
few babies for ye.' Anyway, Ned," she added with a crooked,
almost malicious smile, "you can always say you were Pa's
favourite."

Once more the attention was directed to Ned. He put his
cigarette down with care and sprang up with a broad smile, holding out his hand.

"I wish you all the luck in the world, Justin," he said.

"I know that well, Ned," boomed Justin, catching Ned's hand in his own two. "And I'd feel the same if it was you."

"And you too, Miss Lomasney," Ned said gaily.

"Thanks, Mr. Lowry," she replied with the same crooked smile.

VI

Justin and Rita got married, and Ned, like all the Hayfield Hourigans behaved in a decorous and sensible manner. He didn't take to drink or break the crockery or do any of the things people are expected to do under the circumstances. He gave them a very expensive clock as a wedding present, went once or twice to visit them and permitted Justin to try and convert him, and took Rita to the pictures when Justin was away from home. At the same time he began to walk out with an assistant in Halpin's; a gentle, humorous girl with a great mass of jet-black hair, a snub nose, and a long, pointed melancholy face. You saw them everywhere together.

He also went regularly to Sunday's Well to see the old couple and Nellie, who wasn't yet married. One evening when he called, Mr. and Mrs. Lomasney were at the chapel, but Rita was there, Justin being again away. It was months since she and Ned had met; she was having a baby and very near her time, and it made her self-conscious and rude. She said it made her feel like a yacht that had been turned into a cargo boat. Three or four times she said things to Ned which would have maddened anyone else, but he took them in his usual way, without resentment.

"And how's little Miss Bitch?" she asked insolently.

"Little Miss who?" he asked mildly.

"Miss—how the hell can I remember the names of all your dolls? The Spanish-looking one who sells the knickers at Halpin's."

"Oh, she's very well, thanks," Ned said primly.

"What you might call a prudent marriage," Rita went on, all on edge.

"How's that, Rita?"

"You'll have the ring and the trousseau at cost price."

"How interested you are in her!" Nellie said suspiciously.

"I don't give a damn about her," Rita with a shrug. "Would Señorita What's-her-name ever let you stand godfather to my footballer, Ned?"

"Why not?" Ned asked mildly. "I'd be delighted, of course."

"You have the devil's own neck to ask him after the way you treated him," said Nellie. Nellie was interested; she knew Rita and knew that she was in one of her emotional states, and was determined on finding out what it meant. Ordinarily Rita, who also knew her sister, would have delighted in thwarting her, but now it was as though she wanted an audience.

"How did I treat him?" she asked with amusement.

"Codding him along like that for years, and then marrying a man that was twice your age."

"Well, how did he expect me to know?"

Ned rose and took out a packet of cigarettes. Like Nellie he knew that Rita had deliberately staged the scene and was on the point of telling him something. She was leaning very far back in her chair and laughed up at him while she took a cigarette and waited for him to light it.

"Come on, Rita," he said encouragingly. "As you've said so much you might as well tell us the rest."

"What else is there to tell?"

"What you had against me."

"Who said I had anything against you? Didn't I distinctly tell you when you asked me to marry you that I didn't love you? Maybe you thought I didn't mean it."

He paused for a moment and then raised his brows.

"I did," he said quietly.

She laughed.

"The conceit of that fellow!" she said to Nellie, and then with a change of tone: "I had nothing against you, Ned. This was the one I had the needle in. Herself and Kitty were forcing me into it."

"Well, the impudence of you!" cried Nellie.

"Isn't it true for me?" Rita said sharply. "Weren't you both trying to get me out of the house?"

"We weren't," Nellie replied hotly, "and anyway that has

nothing to do with it. It was no reason why you couldn't have married Ned if you wanted to."

"I didn't want to. I didn't want to marry anyone."

"And what changed your mind?"

"Nothing changed my mind. I didn't care about anyone, only Tony, but I didn't want to go to that damn place, and I had no alternative. I had to marry one of you, so I made up my mind that I'd marry the first of you that called."

"You must have been mad," Nellie said indignantly.

"I felt it. I sat at the window the whole afternoon, looking at the rain. Remember that day, Ned?"

He nodded.

"The rain had a lot to do with it. I think I half hoped you'd come first. Justin came instead—an old aunt of his was sick and he came for supper. I saw him at the gate and he waved to me with his old brolly. I ran downstairs to open the door for him. 'Justin,' I said, grabbing him by the coat, 'if you still want to marry me, I'm ready.' He gave me a dirty look—you know Justin! 'Young woman,' he said, 'there's a time and place for everything.' And away with him up to the lavatory. Talk about romantic engagements! Damn the old kiss did I get off him, even!"

"I declare to God!" said Nellie in stupefaction.

"I know," Rita cried, laughing again over her own irresponsibility. "Cripes, when I knew what I was after doing I nearly dropped dead."

"Oh, so you came to your senses?" Nellie asked ironically.

"What do you think? That's the trouble with Justin; he's always right. That fellow knew I wouldn't be married a week before I didn't give a snap of my fingers for Tony. And me thinking my life was over and that was that or the river! God, the idiots we make of ourselves over men!"

"And I suppose 'twas then you found out you'd married the wrong man?" Nellie asked.

"Who said I married the wrong man?" Rita asked hotly.

"I thought that was what you were telling us," Nellie said innocently.

"You get things all wrong, Nellie," Rita replied shortly. "You jump to conclusions too much. If I did marry the wrong man I wouldn't be likely to tell you—or Ned Lowry either."

She looked mockingly at Ned, but her look belied her. It was plain enough now why she wanted Nellie as an audience. It kept her from admitting more than she had to admit, from saying things which, once said, might make her own life impossible. Ned rose and flicked his cigarette ash into the fire. Then he stood with his back to it, his hands behind his back, his feet spread out on the hearth.

"You mean if I'd come earlier you'd have married me?" he asked quietly.

"If you'd come earlier, I'd probably be asking Justin to stand godfather to your brat," said Rita. "And how do you know but Justin would be walking out the señorita, Ned?"

"Then maybe you wouldn't be quite so interested whether he was or not," said Nellie, but she didn't say it maliciously. It was now only too plain what Rita meant, and Nellie was sorry for her.

Ned turned and lashed his cigarette savagely into the fire. Rita looked up at him mockingly.

"Go on!" she taunted him. "Say it, blast you!"

"I couldn't," he said bitterly.

A month later he married the señorita.

A SENSE OF RESPONSIBILITY

I

MICK and Jack Cantillon lived up our road when I was a young fellow. They were very much alike in general appearance, small, stout, and good-natured, but there the resemblance stopped.

Mick was a thundering blackguard, while Jack was a slow, quiet, conscientious chap. Naturally, Mrs. Cantillon—a tall, mournful, pious woman with the remains of considerable good looks—adored Mick and despised Jack. She liked men to be manly; she liked the way Mick, after drinking the housekeeping money or being arrested for being drunk and disorderly, approached her with his arms out and said mockingly "Mother, forgive your erring son." Even when Jack had a drop taken, he didn't regard himself as being in error, and was out to work the next morning, head or no head; he seemed to have no religious feelings at all, wouldn't be bothered going to a mission or retreat, and expected the poor woman to keep accounts. Accounts were things Mrs. Cantillon couldn't keep.

Jack was a great friend of another young man called Farren, and the two of them went everywhere together, though they were as much unlike as lads could be. Farren was tall and handsome, with a clear, delicate, tubercular complexion. He was quick-witted and light-hearted. Having been brought up in a household of women, sent to work in an office full of women, he seemed at times to be half a woman himself. He certainly seemed happier with women than with most men. Meeting some well-to-do educated young lady from Sunday's Well who swallowed all her words in the best Sunday's Well manner, he called her "sweetheart," and when she'd got over the shock of that, coaxed her into telling him how changed her boy friend seemed to be since he'd come back from Paris. Farren was just like another girl with her; so understanding, sympathetic, and light in touch that it didn't strike her till later that this was the only thing feminine about him, and by that time it was usually too late. As a result women were always trying to get him over the phone, and the things he said about them were shocking. Not that he meant them to be, but there was something almost treasonable about the way he talked so intimately of them, and some men didn't like it because it so resembled eavesdropping.

Apart from Farren, Jack's great friends were the Dwyers, a large, loud-voiced family. The father was a small building contractor, known to his wife as "poor Dwyer," whose huffy shyness had never permitted him to get anywhere in life. His wife had ten times his brains and he lectured her as if she were an idiot, and she put up with it as if she were. She was a big, buxom, bonny woman, very devout and very caustic. They had three boys and three girls, and Jack went drinking and bowl-playing with the boys and dancing with the girls until the latter held a council about him and decided, as he was completely incapable of making up his own mind, that they had better do it for him. It was decided that he should marry Susie, the middle girl. Annie, the youngest, whom he was supposed to favour, was compensated with a blue frock.

If Jack noticed anything peculiar about the way Susie was thrust on him, he didn't say much. He never said much anyway. Soon after, the Dwyers had plenty of opportunity for observing how close Jack could be when it suited him.

Mick, you see, had married a girl called Madge Hunt, a good-natured, stupid, sentimental woman who adored him. She was shocked at the harshness of his employers, who actually expected him to be at work six days out of every week, and at the intolerable behavior of people he owed money to, who expected him to pay it back, whether he had it or not. A couple of years of marriage to Mick improved her sense of reality enormously. She became hard as nails, cold and knowing. Then Mick was killed, not too gloriously, in a motoring accident, and Madge had to go out and work as a charwoman.

Jack was very upset by Mick's death. He took to calling regularly on Madge and her little boy. The Dwyers at first saw nothing wrong with this; a decent grief is a very respectable thing, and the Dwyers were nothing if not respectable. But Jack's concern bordered on insincerity. And it didn't stop there. The eldest of the Dwyer girls, Babs, who heard everything, heard from the Mrs. MacDunphy who employed Madge that Jack had made her give up the daily work and was supplying the equivalent of her wages out of his own pocket. According to Mrs. MacDunphy, this was to go on till her son left school. What Mrs. MacDunphy had said was "There's a good brother-in-law for you!" What Babs said was "How well I wouldn't find some old fool to keep me!" But what her mother said was "That's very queer behaviour in a man who's walking out with Susie." It was the first glimpse she'd caught of that side of Jack's character, and she didn't like it.

She wanted Susie to have it out with him, but Susie flew in a panic and said she'd be afraid. Mrs. Dwyer wasn't afraid. Anyone who employed one of the Dwyer family could rely on her to see that the goods came up to scratch, and she wasn't the sort to tolerate a slight on her daughter.

"I hear you're looking after Madge Hunt while the little fellow is at school, Jack," she said pleasantly one evening when she managed to get Jack alone.

Jack looked embarrassed. He didn't like his charities to be known.

"There isn't much I can do for her," he said apologetically. "But it isn't good for the little fellow to have to be left with strangers every day."

" 'Tis hard," she agreed. "I dare say it won't make it too easy for you to settle down yourself," she added.

"I dare say not," agreed Jack.

"Isn't it a long time to ask Susie to wait, Jack?" she asked reproachfully.

"It's longer than I like to wait myself, Mrs. D.," he said, knocking out his pipe. "I have some hopes I might get a rise, but I can't be certain. Of course, if Susie got a better chance, I wouldn't stand in her way."

"I think we'd better leave it at that, Jack," she replied with the least trace of pompousness. Whatever else Mrs. Dwyer might be, she was not pompous, but she had the mortifying feeling that she was being bested by an amateur without a trump in his hand. Madge Hunt, who wasn't even intelligent, could get round Jack and she couldn't.

"I'd have nothing more to do with that fellow, Susie," she told her daughter unemotionally. "He hasn't enough manliness to make anyone a good husband. The Cantillons all take after their mother."

But Susie wasn't like that at all. She was gentle and a nagger; alarmed at the idea that Jack did not appreciate her, she was more concerned with making him change his mind than maintaining her dignity.

So she began in the most flagrant way to throw herself at Pat

Farren's head. She didn't really like Pat; she could not like any man with a reputation of his sort, and he knew more than Susie approved of about her little weaknesses. It's all very well, a man dancing attendance on you, but not when he shows that he knows what's going on in your mind. Susie couldn't have a grievance without Pat's seeing it first. At the same time she wanted Jack to see that others besides himself could appreciate her.

Another man would have withdrawn from a situation of such profound delicacy, but Pat lacked all niceness of feeling. He thought it the funniest thing ever. He was delighted with Susie's conviction that nobody knew what she was doing, and was passionately inquisitive to know how far she'd go with it. It was just the sort of situation that appealed to him because it showed up a woman's character like a searchlight. If Susie had known, she would have died of mortification, but he even discussed it with Jack. When the three of them were together he acted it for all he was worth.

"Are you coming home with me, Susie?" he would say, throwing his arms about her. "I can't live another day without you."

"I can't, sure," Susie would cry, half-pleased, half-terrified by his manner.

"Is it that fellow you're afraid of?" he would say, pointing at Jack.

"He'd kill me!"

"That fellow? He doesn't care a snap of his fingers about you. I'm the one that really loves you."

"Go on out of that, ye pair of whoors!" Jack would cry with tears of laughter in his eyes.

In Crosshaven, where the Dwyers had a cottage for the summer and where Pat spent most of his time, the flirtation continued, and Susie even began to enjoy it. But it seemed to have no effect on Jack. She began to wonder whether her mother mightn't be right, and if Jack was a man at all.

Coming on to Christmas, Pat fell ill and had to be operated on. Susie had never seen Jack so upset. He spent every afternoon at the hospital. She discovered from Pat's mother that he had offered to guarantee a loan to get his friend to Switzerland. But it was too late for that. Pat died the week after Christmas. Jack took to visiting the Farrens as he had visited Madge Hunt, and busied himself with tidying up Pat's small business interests. But it was far worse than the business of Mick's death. He kept a picture of Pat on his mantelpiece, and sometimes when Susie called she found him glancing at it and realized that she was interrupting some sort of colloquy between him and the picture. As time went on and she saw that it had become a sort of fixation with him, she became more concerned. It was morbid; she felt it was her duty to put a stop to it, but she could not get him to listen to ordinary reasonable criticism of Pat. Either he looked pained and changed the subject or he told her gently that she didn't understand. The latter charge really riled Susie. After all, which of them had been made love to by Pat?

"You're very foolish," she said in a distant tone. "You let people influence you too much. Now, I'd never let anyone influence me like that, not even a man. Pat was amusing enough, but you never realized how shallow he was."

"Now, Susie, don't let's argue," he said with a slight pained smile. "Pat had a very fine brain."

"Ah, he was very insincere, Jack," Susie said with a frown and a shake of the head.

"Pat was sincere enough in his own way. It wasn't your way or my way. We all have different ways of being sincere."

"Ah, for goodness' sake," she exclaimed with a superior air. "Pat was all right as long as he was with you, but he let you down the moment your back was turned. My goodness, didn't I know him?"

"You didn't, Susie. Pat made fun of us, as he made fun of everybody, but he'd never do anything to harm a friend. He didn't even know what it was."

Then Susie realized that she must make the sacrifice of her life. Nothing else would ever shake Jack out of his absorption in his dead friend.

"That's all you know," she said in a low voice, her lip trembling at the thought of her own nobility.

"I know as much as anyone."

"I suppose so, you know that Pat and myself were—living together?" she asked with a long underhung look while she tried to keep her voice level.

"You were what?" Jack exclaimed testily.

Susie broke down.

"Oh, it's all very well for you to criticize," she sobbed, "but it's your own fault for keeping me dragging on like this from year to year. How soft you have it! Any other girl would do the same."

"Not making you a saucy answer, Sue," Jack said irritably, "I don't give a damn what you do, but I'm not going to have you going round telling lies about a man who can't defend himself."

"Lies?" she cried indignantly.

"What the hell else is it?"

"It is not lies," she cried, really furious with him this time. "The impudence of you! I suppose you think no one could do a thing like that to you. Well, Pat Farren did, and I can hardly blame him. You're not natural. My mother said it. You don't even know the temptations people have."

"And as I said before, I don't give a damn," Jack said, almost wagging his finger at her as though she were nothing but a schoolgirl kicking up a scene at a funeral. "But it could cause great pain to Pat's people to have stories like that going round about him. So don't do it again, like a good girl."

Susie realized with stupefaction that whether he believed her or not, he would still continue to think it more important not to cause pain to Farren's parents than to consider her warnings. What made it worse was that she could not tell them at home what the quarrel was about. They would never realize the magnitude of the sacrifice she had made to bring Jack round to a sense of reality. Either they would believe her and regard her as a monster, or they wouldn't and regard her as a fool. She went home in a state approaching hysterics and said that Jack was a most appalling man, a most unnatural man. Her mother said quietly: "Well, girl, you can't say you weren't warned," which was about the most useless thing she could have said, for the more Susie was warned against Jack, the more interesting he became to her. It was inquisitiveness more than anything else.

When a girl ceases to be inquisitive about a man, she is finished with him.

It was five years before he was in a position to marry her, and by that time Susie's spirit was broken. He had become a habit with her. It was no use pretending that Mrs. Dwyer was pleased; she had sized the man up, once for all, but as Susie seemed so set on him, she supposed she must only do her best to put up with him. By this time Jack was chief clerk in the carrier's where he worked, and they were fairly comfortable. They bought a nice house on a terrace only a stone's throw from the Dwyers', and produced two children, a girl and a boy. It seemed as if everything was running smooth for them at last. Almost too smooth for Susie's comfort. She had never really got over the way Jack had slighted her great sacrifice. According to her mood, she had two entirely different versions of her relations with Pat. The first and general one was that it had been entirely innocent —which it had; the second was that it had been nothing of the sort—which was equally true, according to the way you viewed it. When she was in good humour—which was most of the time—there had been nothing between Pat and herself except what she called "old nonsense"; when she was out of sorts, she had had a dark past, forced on her entirely by Jack, and had made a magnificent gesture in confessing it to him, only to have it dismissed as childishness. And when she felt like this, and had repeated it in confession as a sin of her past life which she particularly regretted, and remembered her own nobility, grief and fury rose in her till she made Jack a thorough, good, old-fashioned scene in which she wept and screamed and called him an old molly. Jack, with his feet on the mantelpiece and a book or paper in his hands, would look up at her with concern from time to time over his spectacles and make some reasonable masculine protest, which only started her off again. Finally it would get too much for him. He would dash down his paper, say "F— you!" in a choking voice, and go out to get drunk. The first time he did this, Susie was thrilled, but she soon discovered that Jack's emotional vocabulary was limited to one word, which he used only under extreme provocation, and once he had done this, he had nothing more to say for himself.

II

Then, at the height of their married happiness, the worst happened. Mrs. Cantillon, having managed to exhaust her small means and entangle herself in a labyrinth of tiny debts, none of which could be explained at less than novel length, was threatened with eviction. Jack was profoundly worried. He went to Madge Hunt for advice. Madge was the only woman whose judgment he really trusted.

"Well, it seems to me you'll just have to be a bit of a bastard for once in your life, Jack," she said.

"Would I have to take lessons for that?" he asked gently.

"The first lesson is that you ought to put your mother in a home," she said coldly.

He shook his head.

"That's what I mean," she said with a shrug. "If you weren't the sort who couldn't be sensible, I wouldn't be sitting here on my bottom advising you to be sensible. You know she'll make a wreck of your house."

"I fancy she'll try," he agreed with a sombre nod.

"Don't kid yourself, Jack, she will. The only thing you can do is ask her to come here. There's a room here, and she's welcome to it on your account. But my bet is she'll go to the workhouse first."

Then Madge saw him go off despondent, and thought in her cynical way that he was probably the one man in the world she could have been happy with.

But she had seen through Mrs. Cantillon, for those, more or less, were the words Mrs. Cantillon used. First she looked at Jack with a timid smile as if wondering if he was in earnest. Then she explained in her simple, homely way that Madge had killed poor Mick before his time; that though at the time she had lied herself black in the face for the child's sake, everyone knew poor Mick had committed suicide, and that, though as a Christian she had long forgiven and forgotten all that, the daily contact with her son's murderess would be more than a sensitive woman like herself could bear. Mrs. Cantillon, for all her silliness, was a woman of infinite perception. She saw that in the matter of mischief-making, Madge Hunt was a woman you'd get nowhere with; a hard, cynical woman who would see through an old lady's tricks before she even began them, while Susie, as well as being a much better cook, would be clay in her hands.

Mrs. Dwyer, a woman of small silliness and excellent perception, saw the situation in the same light. She warned Susie that Mrs. Cantillon would drive her out of her home by hook or by crook. She went further. Seeing Susie's complete lack of gumption, she spoke to Jack himself about it. This time there was no pleasantness. The gloves were off so far as she was concerned.

"I don't think you realize the danger of in-laws in your house, Jack," she said severely.

"I think I do, Mrs. D.," said Jack with a sigh.

"I don't think so, Jack," she said, her voice growing hard, "or you wouldn't offer your mother a home with Susie and the children. I've seen more of that sort of thing than you have, and I never yet saw it come to any good. People may mean no harm, but they make mischief just the same."

"Mrs. Dwyer," Jack said almost appealingly, "even my mother's worst enemy wouldn't accuse her of meaning no harm," and for a moment Mrs. Dwyer's eyes twinkled. She knew Mrs. Cantillon too.

"That's all the more reason she shouldn't share a house with Susie, Jack," she said remorselessly. "When you married Susie, you took on certain responsibilities to her. Young people have to have their disagreements, and they have to have them in some sort of privacy. I never interfered, good or bad, between Susie and you because I know what it leads to. Marriage is a secret between two people. 'Tis at an end when outsiders join in."

"If you think I'd be likely to side with anyone in the world against Susie!" Jack exclaimed, almost with a groan.

"You mightn't be able to help it, Jack. 'Tis all very well talking, but your mother is your mother."

"If that day came, I could always cut my throat," said Jack with something like passion. "But old people have to live, Mrs. Dwyer." "They have, Jack," she said almost with resignation, "but they haven't the same claims as young people, and there's no good denying it. For everybody's sake, your mother would be better in a home. I have to think of Susie."

"And I have to think of Susie and my mother," said Jack with an embarrassed smile.

"I think you may have to choose between them, Jack," Mrs. Dwyer said quietly.

"There are certain things you have no choice about, Mrs. Dwyer," he said gloomily, and again she realized with irritation that this intolerably weak man, this sucker who was allowing himself to be imposed on by his mischievous and selfish mother, had some source of strength that made him immune from being imposed upon by a woman of character like herself.

"Well, don't blame me if you wreck your home, Jack," she said with finality.

From that on, she refused to visit Jack's house again, and though the children came regularly to see her, and Jack himself came every Sunday morning after Mass and she received him warmly, the old relationship was at an end. She had too much pride to let herself be flouted.

It must be admitted that she had miscalculated Mrs. Cantillon's style though not her content. Mrs. Cantillon made hell of the home all right, but not in the straightforward way a woman of Mrs. Dwyer's character expected. She made no attempt to make Susie's life impossible. She contented herself with making Jack's impossible. The imbecility of women like Mrs. Cantillon has an aspect that is never far removed from genius. She knew Jack's weaknesses in a way Susie had never known them. She remembered with sentimental attachment childish humiliations he had suffered. She knew that though a married man and a father, he had always remained temperamentally a bit of a bachelor, remote from the stresses of courtship and marriage. Perhaps it is only bachelors who can have a sense of responsibility. He had lived all his life in one small corner of Cork, nodding and smiling to his neighbours without ever knowing more about them than was necessary for congratulation or sympathy. He had managed to head Susie off intimacies, but it would have taken a tank to head off his mother. To her, the great joy in life was knowing everybody's business.

She knew that after his day's work he liked to change cere-monially into old trousers and read or play with the children, so she began to jolly him into taking Susie out. On the surface it was the height of good nature, and Susie, who found long-extin-guished flutterings revive in her, took it at its face value and seconded her mother-in-law.

"Ah, what other use is there for an old woman like me," asked Mrs. Cantillon with a mournful smile, "except to let ye free to enjoy yeerselves?"

The extraordinary thing was that as the home grew more wretched, Susie came to depend more and more on her mother-in-law. She even had arguments with her mother about it. Mrs. Dwyer believed that Jack was weak, but nothing would persuade her but that his mother was bad to the heart. Susie argued with her. She said it wasn't Mrs. Cantillon at all; Mrs. Cantillon wasn't bad when you came to know her; it was Jack. She came to see that in all the disagreements between them, it was Jack with his monstrous selfishness who had been at fault. It seemed he had always been that way, even as a boy—hard-natured. She listened eagerly to Mrs. Cantillon's tales of Mick, who had none of Jack's faults, and though her own memory told her differently, she allowed herself to be persuaded that, even admitting every-thing, Mick was the better man. "Ah, poor Mick," Mrs. Cantillon said with the tears in her eyes, "in spite of his little faults, you couldn't begrudge him anything." If Madge Hunt had decided she had married the wrong brother, Susie was now well on the way to believing the same. Even Jack's one dirty word had ceased to cover the situation. He stayed out in the evenings, boozing.

III

One day Susie came in to find the children crying and Mrs. Cantillon sprawled at the foot of the stairs unconscious. For two days she hung on while Jack waited at the hospital. Mrs. Dwyer came to look after the children, and it was clear when they met that the old quarrel was over. In fact, it had been over for a long time, for it impressed her that Mrs. Cantillon had succeeded in moving Susie but not him. At the funeral he pretended no great grief, and Susie, who automatically broke down at all funerals, received the sympathy of a number of women who believed her to be the daughter of the deceased. This made her furious, and she said that Jack would show no more nature for her than he had for his mother.

Mrs. Dwyer had troubles of her own to think of at the time. Jim, the last of the boys, had married, and she was on her own. This, according to herself, was the day she had always been waiting for, and she plunged into a life of dissipation, going to the pictures, playing cards, and refusing to mind her grand-children. "Wisha, aren't I right?" she asked Jack. "Aren't I fussing round them long enough? 'Tis time I had a bit of enjoyment out of life." Then she developed arthritis. Susie came to nurse her, and after that it became clear to the family that their mother's short-lived period of independence was over. She could not be left in the house alone. She would have to go and live with one of the boys—a bitter humiliation for a strong-minded woman.

Tim, an easy-going fellow, would have had her willingly, but easy-going fellows get easy-going wives, and it wasn't likely that Mrs. Dwyer, who boasted that she had never seen the day when a properly cooked dinner was not served in her house, would long put up with Nora and her perpetual round of frying.

Ned's wife had six children, and there would be no room for her unless they took a bigger house. Jim, being just married, had only the minimum of furniture, and it would take a considerable capital expenditure to set him up. It wasn't that they didn't love their mother or wouldn't have died for her if occasion arose, but none of them wanted to be the sucker when a little hesitation might mean a considerable easing of the sacrifice asked of them.

Susie, who had a heart for everyone's troubles, understood it perfectly and wept for all of them equally, but her sister, Babs, told them they were a bloody pack of wasters and went upstairs to tell their mother the same. "How often did I say it to you?" she demanded. "You ruined that gang. One of us could get nothing in this house, and that's all the thanks you get for it."

Babs was a forthright girl who could always be relied upon to make things as difficult as possible for everyone else. Her mother only listened to her splutterings with sly amusement.

"The Lord lighten their burdens!" she said dryly. "As if I'd be under an obligation to any of them!"

"Well, what are you going to do, woman?" asked Babs.

"Don't bother your head about what I'm going to do," said her mother with a wave of her hand. "I'm going up to the Little Sisters where I can be properly looked after. I had all that arranged six months ago. Do you think, after all my years, I'm going into another woman's house to play second fiddle to her? I am not."

The whole family realized when this was reported to them that it was precisely what they'd always imagined their mother would do, and, much as they regretted it, they were almost relieved. The only person who was not was Jack. When Susie told him he stretched his legs to the fire, pulled on his pipe, and looked grave.

"That will kill her, Susie," he said at last.

"Do you think so really, Jack?" she asked wonderingly.

"I'm sure of it."

"But anyway it's not as bad as having to live with an in-law."

"Why?" he asked. "Do you think she's going to escape other women by going into a home?"

"I suppose not," said Susie, beginning to be troubled again herself. "But what can you do with her? You know what she's like when she has her mind made up."

"I wonder if she has her mind made up," he said doubtfully.

The following evening he went for a long walk, up Montenotte and back by Mayfield. On his way home he called at the Dwyers'. Babs was there, and her mother instantly ordered her out to make tea for him. Marriage made no difference to the Dwyer girls. Inside her door they instantly reverted to a dependent position. Mrs. Dwyer never had had any regard for the principle of women's rights. "If they'll give me enough money, they can have their rights," she had said, and only voted to humour her husband. " 'Tis alike to me which of them gets in," was her view.

"I hear you're going up to the Little Sisters?" said Jack as they sat over the fire together.

"Arrah, of course I am, child," she replied lightly. "You know what I always thought of in-laws."

"I do," he replied with a grin.

"And can't you imagine me turned loose on them? Not, between ourselves, Jack Cantillon, that I'm not a better woman than any of them."

"No one said you weren't."

"God knows," she went on with resignation, "I don't know what sort of women are they turning out. They're good for nothing only raising their elbows and resting their backsides. That wife of Tim's—I don't know is she ever right. If I was a man and a woman offered me sausages for my dinner, I'd take the frying-pan to her. I declare to God I would."

"You wouldn't come to Susie and me?" he asked, dropping his voice. "You'd be no trouble. The room is there since the mother died."

"Was Susie talking about it?" she asked sharply.

"She was not," Jack replied with vigour, answering two questions; one which had been implied but not asked, the other not even implied. The implied question was "Are you encouraging Susie to patronize me?" "Of course, Susie must have the last word," he added, answering the question which existed only in his own mind.

"Wisha, Jack, boy," she said, dropping her defences, "I'm easy where I go. I had my day, and I must only be satisfied. At the same time, mind you, I like to be asked. I suppose we all have our bit of vanity."

"You're well entitled to it," he said with a laugh. "Will you come?"

"I will not come, Jack, thanks all the same. Ye had enough of in-laws to last ye the rest of yeer lives—not criticizing your poor mother, God rest her, whatever I might have said when she was alive. 'Tis only when you come to it yourself that you realize. Besides," she added with sudden candour, "I wouldn't give it to say to the boys."

"I thought of that," Jack agreed with a nod. "I don't think they'd mind if you let me put it up to them first. I think I might get round them. You see, we are a bit better off than they are, and I don't think they'd stand in the way of making you more comfortable."

She looked at him closely to see if he was smiling, and realized that there was no intentional irony behind his remarks. She gave a sudden shrug.

"To tell you the God's truth, Jack," she said, "I'd hate to be in an institution. I'd nearly sooner put up with Tim's wife. I could never get on with nuns, God forgive me. Half the time I don't think they're natural. Mind, Jack, I'll be no acquisition to you. I'll do my best but I won't promise you anything. Old people get very selfish. You have no idea. You'd be waiting here for a cup of tea, and if half Cork died, you wouldn't care till you got it. And isn't it only natural?" she asked, cocking an argumentative eyebrow. "What else have we to look forward to?"

Of course, it had to be done tactfully, and even then created a few scenes and some protests, but somehow, from the moment it was mentioned, it seemed the family had always known it would happen that way. Their mother would be impossible in an institution unless she were made matron at once. Jack was steady; he was fairly well-to-do; he was the born burden-carrier, and in the matter of money would be much easier to deal with than any member of the family.

Curiously, as things turned out, Mrs. Dwyer proved a real acquisition, at least to Jack. The thought that she hadn't to go into a home seemed to give her a new lease of life, and almost up to her death she was livelier than Susie. The first evening Jack came home from work, she had his old trousers warming on a chair at the fire and made him change there instead of in the bedroom. "Wisha, at my age, as if I couldn't look at a man with his trousers off! Do you want me to go out?" "I don't." "Wisha, why would you?" Mrs. Dwyer looked after him as if he were a child, trying to judge what he really wanted—never an easy thing with a man so bottled-up. She was so pleased not to be treated as an imbecile the way "poor Dwyer" treated her that she even tried to develop an interest in politics to please him. When Susie started her first big row with him, her mother said sharply: "Susie, what way is that to talk to Jack?" and Susie broke down and went upstairs to weep. When Jack made to follow her, Mrs.

Dwyer said firmly: "Stop where you are, Jack. You only make her worse."

She went upstairs to deal with Susie herself. She knew Jack didn't like it; she knew he hated anybody's interfering between himself and Susie, but she also knew how women should be treated, which he never would.

"The trouble with you is that you don't know a good man when you see one," she told Susie dryly. "I only wish to God I had a husband like him—not criticizing poor Dwyer."

"God is good," sniffed Susie. "I mightn't last long between the pair of ye."

But Susie had enough respect for her mother to realize that she was right, and even after Mrs. Dwyer's death she no longer looked elsewhere for a model of what men should be. On her deathbed Mrs. Dwyer asked to be buried with Jack and Susie. She didn't ask it with any particular emotion, and even at that Jack was surprised, for she was a woman who loathed sentiment, disliked anyone who professed to ideals above money and security, and had always pretended complete indifference to where they slung her when her time was up, but he promised just the same.

He also broke his promise, but she would hardly have held that against him, because she knew how he hated to inflict unnecessary pain. All he had to remember her by was the undertaker's bill, which he kept and looked at from time to time. It puzzled him that he who had always hated his own mother should care so much for her. He didn't think it right that anyone else should share in the funeral expenses, and, fortunately, no member of the family wanted to contest the privilege with him.

COUNSEL FOR ŒDIPUS

To sit in court and watch a case between wife and husband is like seeing a performance of *Œdipus*. You know that no matter what happens the man hasn't a chance. A colt will consider it a matter of conscience to pass a filly, and a court of law is the same. Even the man's own counsel will be ashamed of him and envy counsel for the wife, who, whatever she did or didn't do, has the ear of the court. As for judges—every single one that I've known had a mother fixation.

But the worst thing of all is that even the man is divided against himself. Now, take the day when Nickie Joe Dougherty was defending a big countryman called Lynam, whose wife was suing him for legal separation and accusing him of cruelty and adultery. The adultery was admitted, and all that was needed to prove the cruelty was to put Tom Lynam in the box. He was a big, good-looking man with a stiff, morose manner; one of those men who are deceptively quiet and good-humoured for months on end and then lay you out with a stick for a casual remark about politics.

His wife was a trim, mousy little female about half his height and a quarter his weight, with an anxious face and a gentle, bedraggled air. She cocked her little head while she listened to her counsel's questions, as though they were uttered in a foreign language, and replied to them in something of the same way, raising her colourless little voice and illustrating her answers with pathetic, half-completed gestures. It reminded you of fourth-form French. All the same, it gave impressiveness to the picture she drew of her husband, drunk and violent, smashing everything in the kitchen on her. You could see O'Meara, the judge, adored her. "Come over here where we can hear you, ma'am," he said, pointing to a seat on the bench beside him, and he leaned one elbow on the bench, crossed his legs, and studied her. Poor O'Meara was a bad case; he had blood pressure as well as a mother fixation. Once or twice, as she gave her evidence, she glanced sadly and pityingly at her husband, who stared back at her with a gloomy hatred that was awe-inspiring. Most men, hearing how they have beaten and strangled their wives, even if they never laid a finger on them, don't know where to look—the poor devils are wondering what everyone thinks of them—but here was a man who watched his wife as if he was wondering why the blazes he hadn't taken a hatchet and finished the job as he was at it.

"And what did he say then?" asked Kenefick, her counsel.

"He called me—do I have to say that?" she asked with a wistful girlish look at O'Meara.

"Oh, not at all, not at all, ma'am," he said hastily. "Write it down," and pushed pencil and paper towards her. She wrote as she talked, slowly and carefully, raising her eyes sightlessly as she thought of all the cruel things her husband had said to her. Then she passed the paper apologetically to the judge, who glanced at it and passed it down to counsel. Tom Lynam, his face black with fury, leaned forward and whispered something to his solicitor, Matt Quill, but Matt only shook his head. If Matt had had his way, he'd have settled the case out of court.

"Did he say anything else?" asked Kenefick.

"Only if I didn't get out of the house in five minutes, sir, that he'd do to me what the Jews did to Jesus."

"What the Jews did to who?" O'Meara asked incredulously.

"Jesus, my lord," she replied, bowing her head reverently at the Holy Name. "Our Blessed Lord, you know. Crucify me, he meant."

"Huh!" snorted O'Meara with his blood pressure going up several degrees.

"Tell my lord what happened then," prompted Kenefick.

"So then I told him I could not go out at that hour of night, and the state of feebleness I was in," Mrs. Lynam continued with growing animation, "and he dragged me off the sofa and twisted my wrist behind my back." She illustrated "wrist" and "back" with another feeble gesture which she didn't complete.

"And did he know the state you were in?"

"Sure, how could he not know it?" cried Mrs. Lynam with her little hands outspread. "I wasn't able to get up from the sofa the whole day. That was what he had against me, of course. He wouldn't believe I was sick. Shamming he said I was."

"And what did he do?"

"Oh, he kicked me."

"Where was this?"

Her hand went to her back again, and she blushed. "Oh, in the—"

"No, no, no. I don't mean that. Where did this occur? What direction did he kick you in?"

"Oh, out the front door, sir," she replied hastily. "I fell on the path. Tommy—that's our little boy—knelt alongside me and began to cry, and my husband told him if he didn't get to bed, he'd do the same to him."

"He'd do the same to Tommy. How old is the child?"

"Five, sir, the 14th of February."

"And your husband made no effort to see were you injured in the fall?"

"Oh, indeed he didn't, sir," she replied with a smile like a rainbow—an optical illusion between two downpours. "Only to give me another kick off the path and into the flower-bed."

"And didn't you, at any time, make some appeal to him to cease this cruel treatment?" demanded Kenefick, stepping up his voice to indignation.

"Oh, indeed, I did, sir," she replied, responding sadly with a shake of her head. Whatever brand of French she spoke, it was clearly going down well, and she was beginning to enjoy it herself. "I asked him did he think I was in a fit state to go crawling across the fields in the dark to a neighbour's house, but he only used a filthy expression and banged the door in my face."

"And those were the marks that you showed next day to Dr. O'Mahony?"

"They were, sir. The same. A week he made me stop in bed with them."

"Tell me, ma'am," the judge interrupted, "this second kick he gave you—the one that sent you off the path into the flower-bed —where were you when he did that?"

"Oh, on the ground, my lord. I was too bad to get up. Half the way across the fields, I was crawling like that, on my hands and knees."

After this it was scarcely necessary to prove her husband's be-haviour with Nora MacGee, a woman of notorious bad character, for in fact she had had a child by him and his paternity was not denied. He had even visited her and nursed the child himself.

"And did you ask him to give up seeing this woman?"

"Why then, indeed, I did, sir. A dozen times if I did it once."

"And what did he say?"

"He said he wouldn't give up seeing a Lynam child for all the Hanafeys that were ever pupped, sir. The Hanafeys are my family," she added with her rainbow smile.

At this, Kenefick sat down as though he could not bear to prolong the poor woman's agony further, and Mickie Joe rose. Now, it cannot be pretended that, the best day he ever was, Mickie Joe was much of a lawyer or made a good appearance in court. Mickie Joe had begun life as a schoolmaster, but aban-doned it, first for politics and then for the law. He really loved the art of oratory, and his soul filled with emotion whenever he spoke of the great orators of old who swayed vast audiences with the power of their voices, but Mickie Joe's own voice was like the whistle of a train, and the only effect he had ever had on an audience was to make them laugh. He had a long, thin, mourn-ful face, and big, blackberry-coloured sunken eyes, and he looked at you over his pince-nez as though at any moment he might burst into tears. Everybody loved Mickie Joe, everybody tried to throw business in his way, but nobody ever took him seriously. He had a tendency which was very obvious in the Lynam case to identify himself with his client, a thing no real lawyer will do. A client is a fact, and a true lawyer hates facts. A lawyer is like an actor who can never bother about what sort of play he appears in, but tells himself some little story to cover as many of the incidents as he can be bothered to remember. The only thing he hates is to be reminded—for instance by the author—what the real story is about.

But Mickie Joe got up bursting with indignation, and even O'Meara smiled at the picture of Mickie Joe, who never said a cross word to anybody, identifying himself with this uproarious, drunken farmer. He felt Tom Lynam had been wronged and was bent on proving it. What made it funnier was that he began with a series of questions which nobody understood, which only reflected further Mrs. Lynam's virtue and his client's beastliness, but which he asked with a bitter reserve. Mrs. Lynam wasn't afraid of him. No woman was ever afraid of Mickie Joe. She answered steadily and quietly. Yes, she had been educated in a convent. Yes, she was a great friend of Sister Dominic. And of Father O'Regan, the parish priest. Yes, she had asked their advice before beginning proceedings against her husband. Yes, she was a member of the Women's Sodality and the Children of Mary.

Then Mickie Joe began to expand, and it became clear what his purpose had been. But it also looked as though Mickie Joe had lost his reason. It's bad enough to attack a woman, but to attack her because she's a pious woman is to go looking for trouble.

"And when you were at the Women's Sodality," he asked icily, looking at her between the wig and the pince-nez, "who got your husband's supper?"

"Sometimes he got it himself."

"And the children's supper?"

"Of an odd time."

"And when you were out at Mass, he got his breakfast, I suppose?"

"Unless he wanted to wait till I got in."

"But you always got it for him when you came in?"

"Always, except when I wasn't able."

"And I take it you weren't always able?"

"Well, no," she admitted candidly. "Not always." She still didn't take him seriously.

"You were able to go to Mass," he said, drawling every word, "but you were not able to get your husband's breakfast? Is that what you're telling my lord?"

"Sometimes I went to Mass when I wasn't able, either," she replied with a noble pathos which would have silenced another man but not Mickie Joe.

"You went to Mass when you weren't able," he repeated with a bitter smile, "but you didn't get your husband's breakfast when you weren't able. Is that what you mean?"

"I think I ought to explain that," she said, beginning to get flurried. "I'm not strong. I have a pain in my back. I hurted it years ago in a fall I got. Dr. O'Mahony treated me."

"Mrs. Lynam, do you also suffer from headaches?"

"I do. Bilious," she replied, pointing to her stomach.

"Really, Mr. Dougherty," said O'Meara wearily, "if a headache is an offence we're all bad characters."

Of course, by this time O'Meara was champing at the bit, waiting to get on with his judgment. For a judge with a mother fixation to listen to evidence at all when he wants to rush to the rescue of some poor afflicted female is an ordeal in itself, but it made it worse that all there was between himself and it was a poor fish like Mickie Joe. But for once Mickie Joe did not give way. He looked at the judge reprovingly over his pince-nez and replied in a wail:

"My lord, if the petitioner is presented to the court as something out of a medical museum, I have nothing more to say."

"Oh, go on, Mr. Dougherty, go on!" said O'Meara, but all the same he grew red. He was beginning to notice like the rest of us that Mickie Joe had ceased to be a figure of fun, but no more than ourselves did he realize what was happening. The truth was that there is only one person who can stand up to a man with a mother fixation, and that is a woman-hater. Exactly as O'Meara wanted to get at that big hulk of a man in the court, Mickie Joe wanted to get at that gentle, pious little woman sitting up beside the judge with her hands in her lap. And, in a queer way, his dislike was beginning to affect people's opinion. It wasn't only that you couldn't any longer patronize Mickie Joe. You couldn't any longer see her the way you had seen her first. Whether it was right or wrong, another picture was beginning to emerge of a woman who was both ruthless and designing and who ruled her great brute of a husband by her weakness. This was only one stage of his ruin. In the next she would be living in comfort in a terrace house on his earnings, while he dragged out an impoverished and lonely existence.

Lynam himself began to perk up, and, instead of looking at his wife, looked at the people round him. The court had gradually begun to fill up, the way it does when a case gets interesting. He still scowled, but now he seemed to be challenging the people in court to say if he wasn't justified.

"Did you and your husband do much visiting together, Mrs. Lynam?" Mickie Joe asked gently.

"Well, you can't do much with two children, sir, can you?" she asked with soft reproach.

"That depends, ma'am," he said with a mournful smile. "A lot of people seem to be able to do it."

"I dare say they have servants," she said nervously.

"Strange to say, ma'am, friendships have been known to persist even in the humblest homes," sighed Mickie Joe with a smile like a glacier.

"I'm sure I don't know how they manage it, then."

"There are such things as neighbours, ma'am."

"Well, you can't be always asking the neighbours."

"No," he said bitterly. "You can ask them to put you up after a quarrel with your husband, but you can't ask them to mind your children. And how much attention do the children need? What age is your little girl, ma'am?"

"She's ten."

"And she couldn't look after the little fellow and herself?"

"Well, I can explain that," she said with a nervous glance at the judge. "You see, they don't get on, and you couldn't leave little Tommy with her, on account of that."

"You mean, she would beat him?" Mickie Joe asked sternly.

"Well, not beat him exactly," said Mrs. Lynam, getting more rattled than ever. "But she might be tormenting him."

"Mrs. Lynam," he asked gravely, "is it the way you didn't like to ask the neighbours or the neighbours didn't like to be asked?"

"I don't know why you say that," she said, shaking her head. "The children don't like going to strange houses, and you wouldn't blame them."

"Do you mean that, ma'am, or do you mean they did not like going to houses where they would have to behave themselves? Mrs. Lynam, isn't it true that your children are too spoiled and vicious to be left in the home of any reasonable person?"

"No," she replied shrilly, starting in her seat. "Certainly not. I never heard such a thing."

But Tom Lynam himself looked at his counsel with such an expression of astonishment that it was clear to everyone that intuitively Mickie Joe had stumbled on the truth. He knew it himself too, and for the first time a smile of satisfaction played about his thin, mournful lips.

"Did many of your husband's friends visit you?"

"Some of them did, yes."

"He had a lot of friends at the time he married you, hadn't he?"

"He had. A few."

"And at the time of this break-up, how many of them were still coming to the house?"

The witness's eyes sought out one tall man sitting at the back of the court.

"I'm sure I couldn't say," she replied doubtfully. "There was one of them at any rate."

"The local St. Sebastian, I presume?"

"The local—I beg your pardon; I didn't catch."

"Mrs. Lynam, every married man has at least one friend who sticks to him, even in spite of his wife's attempts to separate them," Mickie Joe said savagely. "What happened his other friends?"

"I'm sure I don't know."

"Mrs. Lynam, why did they stop coming to your house? Was it, for instance, that when they came for a meal, you sent your husband out to do the shopping?"

"Only a couple of times," she said excitedly. "And that is a thing that might happen to anybody. No matter how careful a housekeeper you were, you couldn't remember everything."

"And I dare say that while he was out, you left them there to entertain themselves?" he asked with a wicked smile.

"Only if I was putting the children to bed, sir," she said sanctimoniously.

"And I suppose, too, that when this last remaining friend of your husband—this Last Rose of Summer left blooming alone—came to bring him out, say, to the greyhounds, it sometimes happened that they couldn't go?"

"Well, I explained about my back," she said earnestly.

"You did, ma'am, fully," said Mickie Joe cruelly. "We are now better acquainted with your back than with any other portion of your anatomy. And we may take it that your husband and his friend had to stay at home and mind the children instead of enjoying themselves."

"I'm sure they enjoyed themselves more than I did," she said. "They played cards a lot. They're both very fond of cards."

But Tom Lynam was still staring incredulously at Mickie Joe. The tall man at the back of the court had grown red. He smiled and nodded amiably to the judge, to the counsel, and even to the pressmen. The Last Rose of Summer, a shy, neighbourly sort of man, was clearly enjoying the publicity. Lynam leaned forward and whispered something to his solicitor, but Quill only frowned and brushed him off. Quill was beginning to see the power and pathos of the play Mickie Joe was producing and no more than any other man of the theatre had he time to spare for the author's views.

"Tell me, ma'am," Mickie Joe asked, "how long is it since you had relations with your husband?"

"Since I what?" she asked in a baby voice, her head raised expectantly.

"Since you went to bed with him, if you like."

"Oh, I forgot to mention that," she said hastily. "He doesn't sleep with me, of course. He has a bedroom of his own."

"Oh, he has a bedroom of his own, has he?" Mickie Joe asked with a new light in his eye. "We'll come back to that. But that wasn't the question I asked just now. The question I asked was how long it was since you had relations with him."

"Well, with my back," she began, raising her hand illustratively to her hip.

"Never mind your back now, ma'am. It's not your back we're talking about at the moment. How long is it?"

"Oh, I suppose about two years," she replied pertly.

"Or more?"

"It could be."

"No doubt it left no impression on your mind," said Mickie Joe. "But when you asked your husband not to have further relations with Mrs. MacGee, you weren't inviting him to have them with you?"

"He never asked me."

"And when he was at Mrs. MacGee's, nursing his child by her, he was in the only decent sort of home he had," said Mickie Joe with a throb of pathos in his voice that, for once, didn't make anybody laugh. "Would it be true to say that you don't think much of married life, ma'am?"

"Oh, I wouldn't say that," she replied vigorously. "The Church, of course, takes a very high view of it."

"I was referring to you, ma'am, not to the Church. Now, weren't you always baaing and bleating to Sister Dominic about the drawbacks of married life?"

"I went to her for advice," Mrs. Lynam replied anxiously. She was beginning to be doubtful of the impression she was creating, and small wonder.

"On your oath, ma'am," shouted Mickie Joe, "didn't you say to Sister Dominic that you never had a happy day after you left the convent?"

"Did I?" Mrs. Lynam asked nervously with a finger to her chin.

"Didn't you?"

"I don't remember. But I might, when I was upset."

"And to Father O'Regan, when you were trying to set him against your unfortunate, decent husband?"

"I never tried to set anyone against him," she retorted indignantly. "All I asked Father O'Regan was to ask him to be more natural."

"Natural?"

"Reasonable, I mean. Ah, 'tis all very well to be talking, Mr. Dougherty. That may be all right for young people, but 'tis no way for people like us to be behaving."

The tables were turned now with a vengeance. Tom Lynam had ceased to look at anyone now but his wife, and at her he looked with an expression of overpowering gravity. He seemed to be saying: "I told you what would happen and you wouldn't believe me. Now look at the result." He knew as everyone else did that she had failed to prove her case, and that even the police-men at the back of the court who had wives of cast iron were looking reproachfully at the gentle, insinuating little woman who was being revealed as a grey, grim, discontented monster with a mania for power.

When the court adjourned, Mickie Joe's cross-examination wasn't over, but he could easily have closed there, for even O'Meara's mother fixation could find nothing to fix on in the petitioner's case. She was probably the only person in court who didn't realize she had lost, but even she was badly shaken. She grabbed her handbag and waddled quickly down the court, looking neither to right nor to left. As she passed, her husband looked reproachfully at her, but she refused to catch his eye. Sud-denly to everyone's astonishment he jumped up and followed her. The lawyers followed too without delay. They were afraid that in their moment of triumph he would snatch the victory from them by finishing the job in the hall. Instead, when they went out he was standing before her, talking in a low, pleading voice. She, with an actressy air, was listening, but half turned away from him as if caught in flight. Finally he approached Quill and Mickie Joe with a frown on his handsome face.

"Nellie and me are settling this between us," he muttered.

"You're what?" Quill asked in consternation. "But damn it, man, you have it won."

"I know that," Lynam replied in an apologetic mutter, "and I'm very grateful, but I wouldn't like her to have to answer any more questions. She thinks I told you all the things you men-tioned. You know yourself I didn't."

Mickie Joe was fit to be tied. He stared at his client over his pince-nez.

"You mean you're going back to live with that woman?" he asked coldly.

"I am."

"And you know that within forty-eight hours she'll be making your life a misery again?"

"If she does itself, we'll settle it between us," Tom Lynam re-torted in a low voice, though his anger could be heard rumbling beneath, like a volcano.

"You certainly will," Mickie Joe said with icy fury. "You will not get me to assist you. A man tries to help you, but it is only talent thrown away. Go and commit suicide in your own way. I have nothing further to do with you."

"There's a pair of us there," Lynam exploded. "I don't know where you got your information, but you can go back to the people that told you and tell them to mind their own business. I won't let you or anyone talk to my wife that way."

Quill almost had to separate them. Two madder men he had rarely seen. But from the window of the barristers' room he and Mickie Joe saw the Lynams depart together, she small and sprightly, he tall and morose, and realized that never would they see justice done to a man in a court of law. It was like Œdipus. You couldn't say whether it was the Destiny that pursued the man or the man the Destiny; but you could be quite sure that nothing in the world would ever keep the two of them apart.

A TORRENT DAMNED

I

CITY men are never much good in a small town like ours. They lack tenacity. Grip is a good dog, but Holdfast is a better.

Take Tom Looney, for instance. Tom was a chemist who had served his time in Dublin and decided to put the bit of money his father had left him into a business of his own. There being as many chemists as publicans in Asragh, where he came from, he thought it better to place his talents at our disposal. This was before Johnny Desmond opened his shop and we had no proper chemist. You couldn't call Gorman a chemist; the man was more of a sleepwalker, taking down his shutters at eleven in the morning, and then putting up a notice to say he'd be back at twelve. Of course, he had no competition, so he couldn't be bothered.

Looney thought it was as easy as falling off a stool, that all he had to do was to open his doors and the whole countryside would flock in to him. That shows how little he knew about it. Mind you, he was a nice young fellow, tall and dark and good-looking, with a pleasant manner and as obliging as they make them. He felt it was up to him. He was a man with an aim in life; he wanted to get on, and no trouble was too much for him. He would work till midnight if he had to, and then deliver the prescriptions himself on a bicycle. Being good-looking in a dark, strained, ferocious way which gave you the impression that he wouldn't stop short at murder, he did well in the flapper trade with face packs and lipsticks, for flappers are the same everywhere; they belong to no society and will buy what they want from anyone they fancy without regard for the consequences. But he did not get the good, substantial country trade that Gorman got. A farmer cannot afford to buy a packet of cigarettes except by way of an investment, and, no matter how nice or obliging he might be, a foreigner from Asragh without wife, brother, father, or friends is no investment for anyone.

Looney could not understand this. His heart was set on selling the farmers cattle medicines, and he could not see why they wouldn't give him a trial. He was a nervous young man, always concerned about his own deficiencies, and thought it must be the way his youthful appearance was against him, so he started to grow a moustache. Moustaches on young men are always a sign of neurosis. But all the moustache did for him was to complete the conquest of Maudie Moynihan in O'Brien's Ladies Outfitters.

Maudie was a sweet girl; rather delicate, with hair between black and red, a snub nose, and a mouth as big and soft as a tearose—the sort of mouth you can't keep off once you get used to it. As it was the first time she had met a man with an aim in life, she went off the deep end about him. There was nothing steady about it, and Maudie knew this and respected him the more for it. The first time he actually kissed her he stood back and apologized profusely, and explained that he could not afford to think of love or marriage, and that if he ever did marry, it would have to be someone with money. She found his honesty captivating; she recognized that he was a man with an aim in life, and though the aim did not then include her, it made him endlessly interesting to her. When they were not making love, they talked about his career. That is one of the great advantages of a man with an aim in life; he never leaves you short of a topic of conversation.

Maudie would slip into the shop and her first whispered endearment would be "How's business?"

Tom would answer with a shrug and a look of mortal agony.

"Oh, dear!" she'd say, and her face falling. "And you'd think a place like this would be worth a fortune."

"That's what I thought," Tom would mutter despairingly, and steal a glance at the little hand-mirror he kept on the counter to see how his moustache was coming on. Even for a young man, it was shocking; it was scraggy and so fair as to be almost invisible in certain lights. Feeling that no farmer would ever trust the fate of his cows to a man without a proper moustache, Looney would spill the stuff he was pouring out, say "Damn! Damn! Damn!" and bare his teeth.

So far as anyone could console him for his failure, Maudie did, but she was also useful in other ways, by indicating the things where he went wrong from the point of view of the town. It was gradually being borne in on Looney that the town had ways of its own, and that if a man said no more than "Good evening" to you, it was just as well to have a native round to translate it.

"That was ever and always the trouble with this place," Maudie said one day. "They grumble because there isn't a place to get a cup of tea, and then when Miss Redmond started the teashop, none of them would go near it."

"Why not?" Looney asked in surprise.

"Because she was a Protestant. Oh, dear, I do think they take things too far. I could never be as narrow as that."

But she had given Tom an idea, and as well as encouraging his moustache, he took to going to morning Mass, weekly Communion and Benediction at the convent, and joined two sodalities. He showed himself so fervent that it was even put about that he had failed for the priesthood, and a lot of the flappers who had thought him a dangerous and romantic fellow were so disgusted that they took their custom to Asragh. (That is what I mean about the instability of the flapper trade.)

"Oh, they're awful," sighed Maudie, referring to her fellow townsmen. "Really, the way they go on about poor Mr. Dorgan, the bank manager, would sicken you."

"How's that?" asked Tom, who got all his intimate information through her and found it as astonishing as something you'd read about an African tribe.

"Oh, I'm sure it's all old talk, but you know the way they go on about funerals. They're mad on funerals. They'll remember for years who was there and who wasn't—as if it mattered! They say poor Mr. Dorgan wears a black suit and a black tie for deposits, but only the tie for a current account, and he doesn't turn up at all if there's an overdraft. I'd never believe that, would you, Tom?"

But by this time Tom was ready to believe anything, and began to see that he might be neglecting an important side of his business, so he started to put in an appearance at funerals, properly dressed. Even this didn't do. It is one thing for an established man like a bank manager to ignore the conventions, but another thing entirely for an upstart from outside the town to pay too much attention to them, and there were people to say Tom went too far. When they met, Dorgan, who was anything but the object of pity that Maudie made him out to be, frequently gave Tom digs about what he called his "Jew's trousers" and made him feel self-conscious and out of place. It didn't matter what you did—if you didn't turn up it was held against you; if you turned up in your ordinary clothes it was held against you, and if you came properly dressed you were wearing Jew's trousers. It made Tom irritable and touchy. Once or twice when he went off for drinks with the other mourners, he drank too much and refused to listen to proper criticism of his native town, a place, as everybody knows, which has always suffered from swelled head. He said in a squeaky voice that he couldn't see why anyone ever wanted to

leave Asragh. It was the finest town in the world. If he liked it
so much, people wanted to know, why didn't he go back there?

That was what he often asked himself. Why did he have to
have an aim in life? Why had he not been content with Asragh,
with its Georgian crescents and its river, its peace and civiliza-
tion? In this benighted hole, whatever he did was wrong, and it
was as though the whole population—priests, nuns, and bank
managers—was sitting back, laughing at him. "Damn! Damn!
Damn!" About that time he read a psychology book which made
him realize that his mother was entirely to blame. She had said
to him that he had no brains and that he would eventually die
in the workhouse. She was responsible for having destroyed his
self-confidence.

"I wouldn't take it to heart, Tom," Maudie told him. "You
have to give them a year or two to get used to you."

"If I'm here in a year or two," he retorted. "And, by God, if I
am, I'll give them something to get used to."

II

One day he was in the shop when a good-looking, well-spoken
girl came in for face cream, and, scenting a likely new customer,
he nearly fell over himself advising her. When she had gone, a
poor woman looked after her and said: "You know who that is,
Mr. Looney, don't you?"

"No," Tom said inquisitively. "Who?"

"Hilda Doherty. Her father is Mr. Doherty, the chairman of
the County Council. The man that gets that lassie won't get her
empty-handed."

Looney's heart soared like a thoroughbred at a gate. This was
the nearest thing he had ever known to love at first sight. It
wasn't love for Hilda, or even for her fortune; it was a pure,
passionate, disinterested devotion to her father, a man he had
never laid eyes on. When next Hilda called he didn't let her
leave the shop till she'd asked him to her home.

He went there in style in a hired car—true love never counts
pennies. Mr. Doherty was a big, pasty-faced man with a great
flow of talk. He was an old Tory who believed in table wines,
cricket, and horses, and was accordingly greatly detested by Re-

publicans. By some mischance, they had neglected to shoot him while the shooting was good, and now he did not hesitate to denounce them publicly as hooligans, corner boys, and men of no property. Unfortunately, the County Council exacted from him the same manners as those he denounced, and he tended to entertain guests in his charming little Regency house rather like a buccaneer aboard a pirate vessel, and his amiable thundering and roaring made Tom jump in his seat. However, Tom, who was very good with machinery, mended his car for him, and it was arranged that Hilda and himself should have dinner together next time they came to town.

It was quite a romance. Maudie knew all about it and was dreadfully upset, all the more because she knew Tom was upset himself. He was very self-conscious about his relationship with Hilda, and either in joke or in bitter earnest couldn't keep from saying that he wasn't interested in anything but money. Maudie knew he was being unfair to himself, that he was far less venal than any other man she knew but his career wouldn't let him live as he wanted to live. This was how she came to chum up with a girl like Kitty Hunt. Kitty was a lively little spark who also had an aim in life and made no secret of it. She intended to marry well, and knew it was a sport, like big-game hunting, in which you had to use heavy weapons and take big risks. She was vastly entertained by Maudie's ingenuousness, and started to walk her out and tell her something about life.

At least, she succeeded in diverting Maudie with her talk about big-game hunting, for at Kitty's caricature of her great, beautiful love for Tom she was halted dead, like a baby with a rattle, and temporarily ceased weeping to follow the coloured bauble with her eyes. Then—also like a baby—remembering her grief, she bawled louder than ever.

"Ah, but Mr. Looney isn't a bit like that, Kitty," she protested.

"How is he different?" Kitty asked with a tolerant smile.

"He is, he is. You have no idea. I was never in the least interested in any of the fellows here. They think of nothing only themselves."

"And what does he think about?" Kitty asked without rancour.

"Marrying money."

"But it isn't the money, Kitty," Maudie cried despairingly. "That's what you don't understand. He's above all that. You feel it the minute you get to know him. There's something big about Mr. Looney."

"There is," Kitty said mockingly. "His ears."

It wasn't true about Tom's ears, and Kitty was really more impressed than she let on to be. In all of us, even those with an aim in life, there is a certain doubt about our own judgments and a quality about other people's praise of a third party which gives it a sort of objective firmness. That is why clever women always tend to deprecate publicly the things they value most. It throws possible rivals off the scent.

It must be said in Tom's favour that Hilda Doherty was a really nice girl, though a lot slower off the mark than Maudie. She was gentle, but at the same time distrustful and nervous, and like all women of that sort, inclined to a gentle sort of nagging that needed a solider temperament than Tom's to prey on. Her father was mad on horses—symbol of the real old Irish gentry— and Hilda had to ride, to satisfy him, though she was nervous of riding and was always falling off. Tom was not nervous of horses—not in that way. He just hated horses. He hated them with a holy hate as spoiled, vicious, useless animals and made a personal enemy of anyone he came near. When he was in good humour he looked a horse in the eye and told it just what he thought of it, and when he wasn't he envied horses because he was always wanting to kick them. Being an excellent mechanic, he disliked anything he couldn't open up and repair as he could a bicycle or a car.

But he recognized that the horses stood to him better than the moustache. That, and the friendship of Michael Doherty. New customers began to come in, and he found himself able to stop attending so many funerals. Even Dorgan, the bank manager, asked him to dinner just as though he had a deposit account. (The bank manager invited the deposit accounts to dinner, the current accounts to tea; and there was nothing for those with overdrafts. The bank dealt firmly with the townspeople, living and dead.) Gorman took fright. There were no more notices up to say "Back at 12" and the medicines got delivered. Gorman went even farther: he employed a new assistant—a country boy who was proposing to start up on his own and who had excellent connections in the eastern part of the country.

Still, Tom was nervous. He was afraid of open spaces. He knew the main drawback of open spaces was that you couldn't whisper something at one side without being immediately overheard at the other. He had no particular desire to get married, but if his career required him to get married, he wished he could marry a girl instead of a whole community. For a city man there is always something frightening in the thought that you can't have a quiet domestic quarrel that doesn't involve fifty or sixty hot-tempered people, all licensed to carry firearms. At the same time, he realized that the echoing quality of the open spaces induces a sort of deafness in the inhabitants. Whatever Hilda might have heard about himself and Maudie, she didn't seem to hold it against him, and she agreed, though in a nervous way, to marry him.

Then he had to see her father. He came with his account books all ready to show that he was concealing nothing. Mr. Doherty was in his element, looking more than ever like a pirate chief, and he discussed the Republicans for a full hour while Tom sat clutching his account books on his knee in a fever of anxiety.

"Now, about this little business of ours," Mr. Doherty said benignly at last.

"I brought the books," squeaked Tom, leaning forward and blushing.

"Never mind about the books," said Mr. Doherty, letting his lids sink sleepily over his eyes. "Are they good books or bad books? That's all I want to know."

"They're bloody awful books," Tom said candidly, without apparently disturbing the other man's equanimity.

"What would be the reason for that?" he asked, joining his fingers and staring at the ceiling.

Tom just held himself back from saying that it was because the natives were all savages.

"I suppose because I'm a stranger," he stammered.

Suddenly, Mr. Doherty shot out a finger and glared at him. "Are you capable of asserting yourself?" he snorted.

"I don't know," Tom said despairingly, waving his hands. "I only know that I can work as hard as the next. I'm not clever or pushing or anything like that."

"Never mind that," thundered Mr. Doherty. "Are you capable of being master in your own house? For if you're not, have nothing to do with my daughter. You think she's quiet. She is quiet. You think she's affectionate and obedient. She is affectionate and obedient. And believe me, Tom Looney, within a month—what am I saying?—within a week of your marrying her, that girl will contradict you flat. If you ask me how I know, I can tell you. I married her mother." By this time he was towering over Tom with upraised hand, and Tom was staring desperately up at him. Suddenly his tone changed and he shook Tom by the hand. "I'm delighted," he said. "Delighted. I think ye'll get on."

III

After that, everything went grand. As a commercial traveller for sheep-dip and cattle medicines, Mr. Doherty was out on his own. He canvassed his prospective son-in-law's business as if Tom were standing for Parliament. Tom began to realize that it wasn't his mother at all; it was himself. All his life he had conducted himself *pianissimo,* and even now to hear himself rendered like this on the brass gave him a headache, but it worked like magic. Dorgan saw that he was overlooking the smartest young businessman in town, and asked Tom's opinion of a new hotel that Tom might be able to buy an interest in. And with Hilda's money to back him, there was no reason why he shouldn't. He was in.

Then, one day, a messenger came from the hospital to say that Hilda had been admitted there with her pelvis and right shoulder broken. The damned horses again! Tom got so faint he had to send out for a glass of whisky to keep himself going. Michael Doherty came in later with fresh news. He affected a bluff heartiness which only concealed his anxiety, and assured Tom that, whatever happened, he would not lack for friends. Tom knew he meant that there was a good chance that Hilda would not walk again.

He was not an unfeeling man but, like most people with an

aim in life, he tended to take a subjective view of things, and however sorry he was for Hilda, he was sorrier still for himself. Ever since he had come to town, luck had been against him. He had done everything a young businessman could do; grown a moustache, gone to church, attended funerals, even indulged in horses and love-making, and everywhere, in every way, he was thwarted. He knew that Hilda would not walk again, not because of anything wrong with her pelvis but because there was a destiny that would break a hundred pelvises to get one swipe at him.

He was all a man in such a situation should be, but Hilda was very difficult. As if things weren't hard enough for him, each day he called she told him that he shouldn't do it, that she would never walk again and wouldn't dream of marrying him. She could not be satisfied with the damage she had done to herself, and insisted that the doctors were fooling them both. "As if we didn't know!" she said bitterly, and Tom shrugged his shoulders despairingly. As if he didn't know!

Maudie was full of sympathy for him. Even Kitty was touched. She wanted Maudie to go to the shop with her and inquire for Hilda, but this was too much for Maudie, who thought it would look forward.

"For goodness' sake, Maudie," Kitty said impatiently, "don't always be running away for fear of what people will think of you. They'll only think worse."

"Oh, Kitty, how could they think worse?" asked Maudie.

"They'll think you're not inquiring out of spite, and that you're glad of what happened."

"I don't believe it, Kitty," Maudie said aghast. "People could never be so bad."

"You'll see how bad people can be," Kitty replied darkly. "You should never be afraid of doing the big, bold thing."

But, whatever people might think, Maudie didn't feel big and bold enough for that. Finally it was almost by accident that they met Tom one evening as he came home from the hospital. He came towards them, walking very fast, as his way was, and without noticing them.

"For goodness' sake, look who's coming!" Kitty exclaimed.

"Now you can ask him about Hilda without anyone's saying anything."

"Oh, I couldn't, Kitty; I couldn't do that at all," Maudie said in alarm.

"Very well, I will," Kitty said scornfully, and she stood and spoke to Tom, who started out of his day-dream and grabbed at his hat.

"How's Hilda today, Mr. Looney?" she asked sympathetically.

"Poorly, miss," he replied politely, clearly not knowing her from the sky over her. "Hullo, Maudie," he added, and turned to Kitty again with his strained and anxious air. "Afraid she'll never be all right again. Dreadful, isn't it?"

"It is dreadful," said Maudie with tears in her eyes.

"That's the way," he muttered sadly. "Awful to see her lying there and not knowing will she ever get up again."

"Yes, and worse for you than for her," said Kitty. "You'd nearly prefer it to be yourself."

"That's true, you would," he said with a look of surprise, realizing that in some ways he was better equipped by his life of frustration for such a final disaster than Hilda was, and that he would probably endure it with more resignation. "You're becoming a great stranger, Maudie."

"I haven't the time," she said with her head bowed and her eyes turned up to him. "I'd like to drop in and inquire how she is though."

"Any time," he said; "delighted," and was off again with a sweep of his hat, a most gentlemanly fellow, as even Kitty admitted.

All that evening Maudie was in high spirits. It was mainly the feeling that Tom could no longer believe her silence was malicious—or so she persuaded herself. It was also the prospective pleasure of dropping into the shop.

Tom really did welcome her visits. He found that he needed someone sympathetic to talk to. He even found that he needed someone gentle to make love to. It wasn't much, just a few kisses and regrets, but they made life easier. He was beginning to discover, as every man does sooner or later, that one woman is not enough. You need one for stability and another for sympathy.

Maudie wasn't quite sure if she was justified in extending her sympathy as far as that, so she coaxed Kitty to come to the shop with her.

"Ah, I'm too old a hand to play gooseberry," said Kitty.

"You know it's nothing like that," Maudie said in a hurt tone. "It's only to keep his mind off his troubles."

"There are better ways of keeping a man's mind off his troubles," said Kitty, but she was obliged.

It was very pleasant in the evenings when the three of them chatted behind in the dispensary, chats interrupted every few minutes by a new customer, and the gossip that followed him. And always there was the perpetually renewed subject of Tom's career. On this Kitty had surprisingly strong views.

"You made an awful mistake, coming to this town," she said. "A man should never go from a big place to a small one. If you had gone to Cork or Limerick, you'd have a different story."

"But they're full," he protested. "You have no idea. There are two chemists' shops in every street."

"That makes no difference at all," she said flatly. "You should never be put off a job or a place because it seems to be full. The fuller the better, if you have the ability."

"Ah, if you have!" he said with a mournful shrug, remembering his mother's warning.

"If you haven't, you can always work," she said. "For every ten people in one job, there's nine that can't work and one that can. Going to a small place is like trying to get into clothes you've grown out of."

"You think I should look for bigger chances?" Tom asked, scratching his head. The problem had never been put to him like that before.

"Of course you should. That's how people get on."

"I suppose that's true," he said doubtfully, looking despairingly at the wall. "People are narrow-minded here. Now, in Asragh they mix a lot more—even with Protestants."

"You're lost here," said Kitty. "Go to Cork! Go to Dublin! Those are the places for you."

It all became plain to Maudie, seeing it put like that, and she realized that the source of Tom's troubles from the start was that he was too big a man for the town, and that if only he could start again in some new place, there might be a chance of his having an aim in life that didn't exclude her.

Maudie was too innocent to be aware that already there was talk; her visits to the shop had been noticed, and though Tom went as before to the hospital, there was a certain coolness between himself and the Dohertys. It had only needed that to revive all the local mistrust of city men and their inherently unstable character. On the other hand, those who had admired Tom's adaptability were wondering whether he hadn't a fresh card up his sleeve to surprise them with.

He surprised them, all right. One morning, it leaked out from Phelan's, the solicitors, that his shop had been sold entire to Gorman's assistant and that Tom and Kitty were in Dublin, getting married. He had discovered that even two women are not enough; a man needs one for stability, one for sympathy, and a third for inspiration. By that time Hilda was walking again.

A foolish man not to know when he was well off. But city fellows are like that—clever enough, but lacking in tenacity.

THE SHEPHERDS

FATHER WHELAN, the parish priest, called on his curate, Father Devine, one evening in autumn. Father Whelan was a tall, stout man with a broad chest, a head that didn't detach itself too clearly from the rest of his body, bushes of wild hair in his ears, and the rosy, innocent, good-natured face of a pious old countrywoman who made a living by selling eggs.

Devine was pale and worn-looking, with a gentle, dreamy face which had the soft gleam of an old piano keyboard, and he wore pince-nez perched on his unhappy, insignificant little nose. He and Whelan got on very well, considering—considering, that is to say, that Devine, who didn't know when he was well off, had fathered a dramatic society and an annual festival on Whelan, who had to put in an attendance at both; and that whenever the curate's name was mentioned, the parish priest, a charitable old man who never said an unkind word about anybody, tapped his forehead and said poor Devine's poor father was just the same. "A national teacher—sure, I knew him well, poor man!"

What Devine said about Whelan in that crucified drawl of his consisted mostly of the old man's words, with just the faintest inflection which isolated and underlined their fatuity. "I know some of the clergy are very opposed to books, but I like a book myself. I'm very fond of Zane Grey. Even poetry I like. Some of the poems you see on advertisements are very clever." And then Devine, who didn't often laugh, broke into a thin little cackle at the thought of Whelan representing the intellect and majesty of the Church. Devine was clever; he was lonely; he had a few good original water-colours and a bookcase full of works that were a constant source of wonder to Whelan. The old man stood in front of them now, his hat in his hands, lifting his warty old nose, while his eyes held a blank, hopeless, charitable look.

"Nothing there in your line, I'm afraid," said Devine with his maddeningly respectful, deprecating air, as if he put the parish priest's tastes on a level with his own.

" 'Tisn't that," said Whelan in a hollow faraway voice, "but I see you have a lot of foreign books. I suppose you know the languages well."

"Well enough to read," Devine said wearily, his handsome head on one side. "Why?"

"That foreign boat at the jetties," Whelan said without looking round. "What is it? French or German? There's terrible scandal about it."

"Is that so?" drawled Devine, his dark eyebrows going up his narrow, slanting forehead. "I didn't hear."

"Terrible," Whelan said mournfully, turning on him the full battery of his round, rosy old face and shining spectacles. "There's girls on it every night. I told Sullivan I'd go round tonight and give them the hunt. It occurred to me we might want someone to speak the language."

"I'm afraid my French would hardly rise to that," Devine said dryly, but he made no other objection, for, except for his old-womanly fits of virtue, Whelan was all right as parish priests go. Devine had had sad experience of how they could go. He put on his faded old coat and clamped his battered hat down over his pince-nez, and the two priests went down the Main Street to the post-office corner. It was deserted but for two out-of-works supporting either side of the door like ornaments, and a few others hanging hypnotized over the bridge while they studied the foaming waters of the weir. Devine had taken up carpentry himself in order to lure them into the technical classes, but it hadn't worked too well.

"The dear knows," he said thoughtfully, "you'd hardly wonder where those girls would go."

"Ah," said the parish priest, holding his head as though it were a flowerpot that might fall and break, "what do they want to go anywhere for? They're mad on pleasure. That girl Nora Fitzpatrick is one of them, and her mother at home dying."

"That might be her reason," said Devine, who visited the Fitzpatricks and knew what their home was like, with six children, and a mother dying of cancer.

"Ah, the girl's place is at home," said Whelan without rancour.

They went down past the Technical School to the quays, these, too, deserted but for a coal boat and the big foreign grain boat, rising high and dark above the edge of the quay on a full tide. The town was historically reputed to have been a great place—well, about a hundred years ago—and had masses of grey stone warehouses, all staring with sightless eyes across the river. Two men who had been standing against the wall, looking up at the grain boat, came to join them. One was a tall, gaunt man with a long, sour, melancholy face which looked particularly hideous because it sported a youthful pink and white complexion and looked exactly like the face of an old hag, heavily made-up. He wore a wig and carried a rolled-up umbrella behind his back. His name was Sullivan; he was the manager of a shop in town, and was forever in and out of the church. Devine hated him. The other, Joe Sheridan, was a small, fat, Jewish-looking man with dark skin and an excitable manner. Devine didn't dislike him so much. He was merely the inevitable local windbag, who got drunk on his own self-importance. As the four men met, Devine looked up and saw two young foreign faces, propped on their hands, peering at them over the edge of the boat.

"Well, boys?" asked Whelan.

"There's two aboard at present, father," Sullivan said in a shrill scolding voice. "Nora Fitzpatrick and Phillie O'Malley."

"Well, you'd better go aboard and tell them come off," Whelan said tranquilly.

"I wonder what our legal position is, father?" Sheridan asked, scowling. "I mean, have we any sort of *locus standi?*"

"Oh, in the event of your being stabbed, I think they could be tried," Devine replied with bland malice. "Of course, I don't know if your wife and children could claim compensation."

The malice was lost on Whelan, who laid one hairy paw on Devine's shoulder and the other on Sheridan's to calm the fears of both. He exuded a feeling of pious confidence. It was the eggs all over again. God would look after His hens.

"Never mind about the legal position," he said paternally. "I'll be answerable for that."

"That's good enough for me, father," Sheridan said, and, pulling his hat down over his eyes and joining his hands behind his back, he strode up the gangway, with the air of a detective in a bad American film, while Sullivan, clutching his umbrella against the small of his back, followed him, head in air. A lovely pair, Devine thought. They went up to the two sailors.

"Two girls," Sullivan said in his shrill, scolding voice. "We're looking for the two girls that came aboard a half an hour ago."

Neither of the sailors stirred. One of them turned his eyes lazily and looked Sullivan up and down.

"Not this boat," he said impudently. "The other one. There's always girls on that."

Then Sheridan, who had glanced downstairs through an open doorway, began to beckon.

"Phillie O'Malley!" he shouted in a raucous voice. "Father

Whelan and Father Devine are out here. Come on! They want to talk to you."

"Tell her if she doesn't come I'll go and bring her," the parish priest called anxiously.

"He says if you don't he'll come and bring you," repeated Sheridan.

Nothing happened for a moment or two. Then a tall girl with a consumptive face emerged on deck with a handkerchief pressed to her eyes. Devine couldn't help feeling sick at the sight of her wretched finery, her cheap hat and bead necklace. He was angry and ashamed and a cold fury of sarcasm rose in him. The Good Shepherd indeed!

"Come on, lads," the parish priest said encouragingly. "What about the second one?"

Sheridan, flushed with triumph, was about to disappear down the companionway when one of the sailors gave him a heave which threw him to the edge of the ship. Then the sailor stood nonchalantly in the doorway, blocking the way. Whelan's face grew red with anger and he only waited for the girl to leave the gangway before going up himself. Devine paused to whisper a word to her.

"Get off home as quick as you can, Phillie," he said, "and don't upset yourself."

At the tenderness in his voice she took the handkerchief from her face and began to weep in earnest. Then Devine went up after the others. It was a ridiculous scene with the fat old priest, his head in the air, trembling with senile anger and astonishment.

"Get out of the way at once!" he said.

"Don't be a fool, man!" Devine said with quiet ferocity. "They're not accustomed to being spoken to like that. If you got a knife in your ribs, it would be your own fault. We want to talk to the captain." And then, bending forward with his eyebrows raised in a humble, deprecating manner, he asked: "I wonder if you'd be good enough to tell the captain we'd like to see him."

The sailor who was blocking their way looked at him for a moment and then nodded in the direction of the upper deck. Taking his parish priest's arm and telling Sullivan and Sheridan to stay behind, Devine went up the ship. When they had gone a little way the second sailor passed them out, knocked at a door, and said something Devine did not catch. Then, with a scowl, he held open the door for them. The captain was a middle-aged man with a heavily lined, sallow face, close-cropped black hair, and a black moustache. There was something Mediterranean about his air.

"Bonsoir, messieurs," he said in a loud, businesslike tone which did not conceal a certain nervousness.

"Bonsoir, monsieur le capitaine," Devine said with the same plaintive, ingratiating air as he bowed and raised his battered old hat. *"Est-ce que nous vous dérangeons?"*

"Mais, pas du tout; entrez, je vous prie," the captain said heartily, clearly relieved by Devine's amiability. *"Vous parlez français alors?"*

"Un peu, monsieur le capitaine," Devine said deprecatingly. *"Vous savez, ici en Irlande on n'a pas souvent l'occasion."*

"Ah, well," the captain said cheerfully, "I speak English too, so we will understand one another. Won't you sit down?"

"I wish my French were anything like as good as your English," Devine said as he sat.

"One travels a good deal," the captain replied with a flattered air. "You'll have a drink? Some brandy, eh?"

"I'd be delighted, of course," Devine said regretfully, "but I'm afraid we have a favour to ask you first."

"A favour?" the captain said enthusiastically. "Certainly, certainly. Anything you like. Have a cigar?"

"Never smoke them," Whelan said in a dull stubborn voice, looking first at the cigar-case and then looking away; and, to mask his rudeness, Devine, who never smoked cigars, took one and lit it.

"I'd better explain who we are," he said, sitting back, his head on one side, his long, delicate hands hanging over the arms of the chair. "This is Father Whelan, the parish priest. My name is Devine; I'm the curate."

"And mine," the captain said proudly, "is Platon Demarrais. I bet you never before heard of a fellow called Platon?"

"A relation of the philosopher, I presume," said Devine.

"The very man! And I have two brothers, Zenon and Plotin."

"What an intellectual family!"

"Pagans, of course," the captain explained complacently. "Greeks. My father was a school-teacher. He called us that to annoy the priest. He was anticlerical."

"That's not confined to school-teachers in France," Devine said dryly. "My father was a school-teacher, but he never got round to calling me Aristotle. Which might be as well," he added with a chuckle. "At any rate, there's a girl called Fitzpatrick on the ship, with some sailor, I suppose. She's one of Father Whelan's parishioners, and we'd be very grateful to you if you'd have her put off."

"Speak for yourself, father," said Whelan, raising his stubborn old peasant head and quelling fraternization with a glance. "I wouldn't be grateful to any man for doing what 'tis only his duty to do."

"Then, perhaps you'd better explain your errand yourself, Father Whelan," Devine said with an abnegation not far removed from waspishness.

"I think so, father," Whelan said stubbornly. "That girl, Captain Whatever-your-name-is," he went on slowly, "has no business to be on your ship at all. It is no place for a young unmarried girl to be at this hour of night."

"I don't understand," the captain said uneasily, with a sideway glance at Devine. "Is she a relative of yours?"

"No, sir," Whelan said emphatically. "She's nothing whatever to me."

"Then I don't see what you want her for," said the captain.

"That's as I'd expect, sir," Whelan said stolidly, studying his nails.

"Oh, for Heaven's sake!" exclaimed Devine, exasperated by the old man's boorishness. "You see, captain," he said patiently, bending forward with his worried air, his head tilted back as though he feared his pince-nez might fall off, "this girl is one of Father Whelan's parishioners. She's not a very good girl—not that I mean there's much harm in her," he added hastily, catching a note of unction in his own tone which embarrassed him, "but she's a bit wild. It's Father Whelan's duty to keep her as far as he can from temptation. He is the shepherd, and she is one of his stray sheep," he added with a faint smile at his own eloquence.

The captain bent forward and touched him lightly on the knee.

"You're a funny race," he said with interest. "I've travelled the whole world and met with Englishmen everywhere, and I will never understand you. Never!"

"We're not English, man," Whelan said with the first trace of interest he had so far displayed. "Don't you know what country you're in? This is Ireland."

"Same thing," said the captain.

"It is not the same thing," said Whelan.

"Surely, captain," Devine protested gently with his head cocked, sizing up his man, "we admit some distinction?"

"Distinction?" the captain said. "Pooh!"

"At the Battle of the Boyne you fought for us," Devine said persuasively. "We fought for you at Fontenoy and Ramillies.

> *When on Ramillies bloody field*
> *The baffled French were forced to yield,*
> *The victor Saxon backward reeled*
> *Before the shock of Clare's Dragoons."*

He recited the lines with the same apologetic smile he had worn when speaking of sheep and shepherds, as though to excuse his momentary lapse into literature, but the captain waved him aside impatiently.

"Your beard!" he said with a groan and a shrug. "I know all that. You call yourselves Irish, and the others call themselves Scotch, but you are all English. There is no difference. It is always the same; always women, always hypocrisy; always the plaster saint. Who is this girl? The *curé's* daughter?"

"The *curé's* daughter?" Devine exclaimed in surprise.

"Whose daughter?" asked Whelan with his mouth hanging.

"Yours, I gather," Devine said dryly.

"Well, well, well!" the old man said blushing. "What sort of upbringing do they have? Does he even know we can't get married?"

"I should say he takes it for granted," replied Devine over his shoulder, more dryly even than before. *"Elle n'est pas sa fille,"* he added with amusement to the captain.

"C'est sûr?"

"C'est certain."

"Sa maîtresse alors?"

"Ni cela non plus," Devine replied evenly with only the faintest of smiles on the worn shell of his face.

"Ah, bon, bon, bon!" the captain exclaimed excitedly, springing from his seat and striding about the cabin, scowling and waving his arms. *"Bon. C'est bon. Vous vous moquez de moi, monsieur le curé. Comprenez donc, c'est seulement par politesse que j'ai voulu faire croire que c'était sa fille. On voit bien que le vieux est jaloux. Est-ce que je n'ai pas vu les flics qui surveillent mon bateau toute la semaine? Mais croyez-moi, monsieur, je me fiche de lui et de ses agents."*

"He seems to be very excited," Whelan said with distaste. "What is he saying?"

"I'm trying to persuade him that she isn't your mistress," Devine couldn't refrain from saying with quiet malice.

"My what?"

"Your mistress; the woman you live with. He says you're jealous and that you've had detectives watching his ship for a week."

The blush which had risen to the old man's face began to spread to his neck and ears, and when he spoke, his voice quavered with emotion.

"Well, well, well!" he said. "We'd better go home, Devine. 'Tis no good talking to that man. He's not right in the head."

"He probably thinks the same of us," Devine said as he rose. *"Venez manger demain soir et je vous expliquerai tout,"* he added to the captain.

"Je vous remercie, monsieur," the captain replied with a shrug, *"mais je n'ai pas besoin d'explications. Il n'y a rien d'inattendu, mais vous en faites toute une histoire."* He clapped his hand jovially on Devine's shoulder and almost embraced him. *"Naturellement je vous rends la fille, parce que vous la demandez, mais comprenez bien que je le fais à cause de vous, et non pas à cause de monsieur et de ses agents."* He drew himself up to his full height and glared at the parish priest, who stood in a dumb stupor.

"Oh, quant à moi," Devine said with weary humour, *"vous feriez mieux en l'emmenant où vous allez. Et moi-même aussi."*

"Quoi?" shouted the captain in desperation, clutching his forehead. *"Vous l'aimez aussi?"*

"No, no, no, no," Devine said good-humouredly, patting him on the arm. "It's all too complicated. I wouldn't try to understand it if I were you."

"What's he saying now?" asked Whelan with sour suspicion.

"Oh, he seems to think she's my mistress as well," Devine replied pleasantly. "He thinks we're sharing her, so far as I can see."

"Come on, come on!" said Whelan despairingly, making for the gangway. "My goodness, even I never thought they were as bad as that. And we sending missions to the blacks!"

Meanwhile, the captain had rushed aft and shouted down the stairway. The second girl appeared, small, plump, and weeping too, and the captain, quite moved, slapped her encouragingly on the shoulder and said something in a gruff voice which Devine suspected must be in the nature of advice to choose younger lovers for the future. Then the captain went up bristling to Sullivan, who stood by the gangway, leaning on his folded umbrella, and with fluttering hands and imperious nods ordered him off the vessel.

"Allez-vous-en!" he said curtly. *"Allez, allez, allez!"*

Sullivan and Sheridan went first. Dusk had crept suddenly along the quays and lay heaped there the colour of blown sand. Over the bright river-mouth, shining under a bank of dark cloud, a star twinkled. "The star that bids the shepherd fold," Devine thought with sad humour. He felt hopeless and lost, as though he were returning to the prison-house of his youth. The parish priest preceded him down the gangway with his old woman's dull face sunk in his broad chest. At the foot he stopped and gazed back at the captain, who was scowling fiercely at him over the ship's side.

"Anyway," he said heavily, "thanks be to the Almighty God, your accursed race is withering off the face of the earth."

Devine, with a bitter smile, raised his battered old hat and pulled the skirts of his coat about him as he stepped on the gangway.

"Vous viendrez demain, monsieur le capitaine?" he asked in his most ingratiating tone.

"Avec plaisir. A demain, monsieur le berger," replied the captain with a knowing look.

THE OLD FAITH

IT WAS a great day when, on the occasion of the Pattern at Kilmulpeter, Mass was said in the ruined cathedral and the old Bishop, Dr. Gallogly, preached. It was Father Devine, who was a bit of an antiquarian, who looked up the details of the life of St. Mulpeter for him. There were a lot of these, mostly contradictory and all queer. It seemed that, like most of the saints of that remote period, St. Mulpeter had put to sea on a flagstone and floated ashore in Cornwall. There, the seven harpers of the King had just been put to death through the curses of the Druids and the machinations of the King's bad wife. St. Mulpeter miraculously brought them all back to life, and, through the great mercy of God, they were permitted to sing a song about the Queen's behaviour, which resulted in St. Mulpeter's turning her into a pillar-stone and converting the King to the one true faith.

The Bishop had once been Professor of Dogmatic Theology in a seminary; a subject that came quite naturally to him, for he was a man who would have dogmatized in any station of life. He was a tall, powerfully built, handsome old man with a face that was both long and broad, with high cheekbones that gave the lower half of his face an air of unnatural immobility but drew attention to the fine blue, anxious eyes that moved slowly and never far. He was a quiet man who generally spoke in a low voice, but with the emphasizing effect of a pile-driver.

For a dogmatic theologian, he showed great restraint on reading Father Devine's digest of the saint's life. He raised his brows a few times and then read it again with an air of resignation. "I suppose that's what you'd call allegorical, father," he said gravely.

He was a man who rarely showed signs of emotion. He seemed to be quite unaffected by the scene in the ruined cathedral, though it deeply impressed Father Devine, with the crowds of country people kneeling on the wet grass among the tottering crosses and headstones, the wild countryside framed in the mullioned windows, and the big, deeply moulded clouds drifting overhead. The Bishop disposed neatly of the patron by saying that though we couldn't all go to sea on flagstones, a feat that required great faith in anyone who attempted it, we could all have the family Rosary at night.

After Mass, Father Devine was showing the Bishop and some of the other clergy round the ruins, pointing out features of archæological interest, when a couple of men who had been hiding in the remains of a twelfth-century chapel bolted. One of them stood on a low wall, looking down on the little group of priests with a scared expression. At once the Bishop raised his umbrella and pointed it accusingly at him.

"Father Devine," he said in a commanding tone, "see what that fellow has."

"I have nothing, Your Eminence," wailed the man on the wall.

"You have a bottle behind your back," said the Bishop grimly. "What's in that?"

"Nothing, Your Eminence, only a drop of water from the Holy Well."

"Give it here to me till I see," ordered the Bishop, and when Father Devine passed him the bottle he removed the cork and sniffed.

"Hah!" he said with great satisfaction. "I'd like to see the Holy Well that came out of. Is it any use my preaching about poteen year in year out when ye never pay any attention to me?"

" 'Tis a cold, windy quarter, Your Eminence," said the man, "and I have the rheumatics bad."

"I'd sooner have rheumatics than cirrhosis," said the Bishop.

"Bring it with you, father," he added to Devine, and stalked on with his umbrella pressed against his spine.

The same night they all had dinner in the palace: Father Whelan, a dim-witted, good-natured old parish priest; his fiery Republican curate, Father Fogarty, who was responsible for the Mass in the ruined cathedral as he was for most other manifestations of life in that wild part, and Canon Lanigan. The Bishop and the Canon never got on, partly because the Canon was an obvious choice for the Bishop's job and he and his supporters were giving it out that the Bishop was getting old and needed a coadjutor, but mainly because he gave himself so many airs. He was tall and thin, with a punchinello chin and a long nose, and let on to be an authority on Church history and on food and wine. That last was enough to damn anyone in the Bishop's eyes, for he maintained almost *ex cathedra* that the best food and wine in the world were to be had on the restaurant car from Holyhead to Euston. The moment Lanigan got on to his favourite topic and mentioned Châteauneuf-du-Pape, the Bishop turned to Father Devine.

"Talking about drink, father," he said with his anxious glare, "what happened the bottle of poteen you took off that fellow?"

"I suppose it's in the hall," said Father Devine. "I need hardly say I wasn't indulging in it."

"You could indulge in worse," said the Bishop with a side-glance at the Canon. "There was many a good man raised on it. Nellie," he added, going so far as to turn his head a few inches, "bring in that bottle of poteen, wherever it is. . . . You can have it with your tea," he added graciously to the Canon. "Or is it coffee you want?"

"Oh, tea, tea," sighed the Canon, offering it up. He had a good notion what the Bishop's coffee was like.

When Nellie brought in the poteen, the Bishop took out the cork and sniffed it again with his worried look.

"I hope 'tis all right," he said in his expressionless voice. "A pity we didn't find out who made it. When they can't get the rye, they make it out of turnips or any old thing."

"You seem to know a lot about it, my Lord," said Devine with his waspish air.

"Why wouldn't I?" said the Bishop. "Didn't I make it myself? My poor father—God rest him!—had a still of his own. But I didn't taste it in something like sixty years."

He poured them out a stiff glass each and drank off his own in a gulp, without the least change of expression. Then he looked at the others anxiously to see how they responded. Lanigan made a wry face; as a member of the Food and Wine Society he probably felt it was expected of him. Father Fogarty drank it as if it were altar wine, but he was a nationalist and only did it on principle. Father Devine disgraced himself; spluttered, choked, and then went petulantly off to the bathroom.

Meanwhile the Bishop, who had decided that it wasn't bad, was treating his guests to another round, which they seemed to feel it might be disrespectful to refuse. Father Devine did refuse, and with a crucified air that the Bishop didn't like. The Bishop, who, like all bishops, knew everything and had one of the most venomously gossipy tongues in the diocese, was convinced that he was a model of Christian charity and had spoken seriously to Father Devine about his sharpness.

"Was it on an island you made this stuff?" the Canon asked blandly.

"No," replied the Bishop, who always managed to miss the point of any remark that bordered on subtlety. "A mountain."

"Rather desolate, I fancy," Lanigan said dreamily.

"It had to be if you didn't want the police coming down on top of you," said the Bishop. "They'd have fifty men out at a time, searching the mountains."

"And bagpipes," said the Canon, bursting into an old woman's cackle as he thought of the hilly road from Beaune to Dijon with the vineyards at each side. "It seems to go with bagpipes."

"There were no bagpipes," the Bishop said contemptuously. "As a matter of fact," he continued with quiet satisfaction, "it was very nice up there on a summer's night, with the still in a hollow on top of the mountain, and the men sitting round the edges, talking and telling stories. Very queer stories some of them were," he added with an old man's complacent chuckle.

"Ah," the Canon said deprecatingly, "the people were half-savage in those days."

"They were not," said the Bishop mildly, but from his tone Father Devine knew he was very vexed. "They were more refined altogether."

"Would you say so, my Lord?" asked Father Fogarty, who, as a good nationalist, was convinced that the people were rushing to perdition and that the only hope for the nation was to send them all back to whitewashed cabins fifty miles from a town.

"Ah, a nicer class of people every way," put in Father Whelan mournfully. "You wouldn't find the same nature at all in them nowadays."

"They had a lot of queer customs all the same, father," said the Bishop. "They'd always put the first glass behind a rock. Would that have something to do with the fairies?" he asked of Father Devine.

"Well, at any rate," the Canon said warmly, "you can't deny that the people today are more enlightened."

"I deny it *in toto,*" the Bishop retorted promptly. "There's no comparison. The people were more intelligent altogether, better balanced and better spoken. What would you say, Father Whelan?"

"Oh, in every way, my Lord," said Father Whelan, taking out his pipe.

"And the superstitions, my Lord?" the Canon hissed superciliously. "The ghosts and the fairies and the spells?"

"They might have good reason," said the Bishop with a flash of his blue eyes.

"By Gor, you're right, my Lord," Father Fogarty said in a loud voice, and then, realizing the attention he had attracted, he blushed and stopped short.

"There are more things in heaven and earth, Horatio, than are dreamt of in our philosophy," added the Bishop with a complacent smile.

"Omar Khayyám," whispered Father Whelan to Father Fogarty. "He's a fellow you'd want to read. He said some very good things."

"That's a useful quotation," said the Canon, seeing he was getting the worst of it. "I must remember that the next time I'm preaching against fortune-tellers."

"I wouldn't bother," the Bishop said curtly. "There's no analogy. There was a parish priest in our place one time," he added reflectively. "A man called Muldoon. Father Whelan might remember him."

"Con Muldoon," defined Father Whelan. "I do, well. His nephew, Peter was on the Chinese Mission."

"He was a well-meaning man, but very coarse, I thought," said the Bishop.

"That was his mother's side of the family," explained Whelan. "His mother was a Dempsey. The Dempseys were a rough lot."

"Was she one of the Dempseys of Clasheen?" said the Bishop eagerly. "I never knew that. Anyway, Muldoon was always preaching against superstition, and he had his knife in one poor old fellow up the Glen called Johnnie Ryan."

"Johnnie the Fairies," said Father Whelan with a nod. "I knew him."

"I knew him well," said the Bishop. "He was their Living Man."

"Their what?" asked Father Devine in astonishment.

"Their Living Man," repeated the Bishop. "They had to take him with them wherever they were going, or they had no power. That was the way I heard it anyway. I remember him well playing the Fairy Music on his whistle."

"You wouldn't remember how it went?" Father Fogarty asked eagerly.

"I was never much good at remembering music," said the Bishop, to the eternal regret of Father Devine, who felt he would cheerfully have given five years of his life to hear the Bishop of Moyle whistle the Fairy Music. "Anyway, I was only a child. Of course, there might be something in that. The mountain over our house, you'd often see queer lights on it that they used to say were a fairy funeral. They had some story of a man from our place that saw one on the mountain one night, and the fairies let down the coffin and ran away. He opened the coffin, and inside it there was a fine-looking girl, and when he bent over her she woke up. They said she was from the Tuam direction; a changeling or something. I never checked the truth of it."

"From Galway, I believe, my Lord," said Father Whelan respectfully.

"Was it Galway?" said the Bishop.

"I dare say, if a man had enough poteen in, he could even believe that," said the Canon indignantly.

"Still, Canon," said Father Fogarty, "strange things do happen."

"Why then, indeed, they do," said Father Whelan.

"Was this something that happened yourself, father?" the Bishop asked kindly, seeing the young man straining at the leash.

"It was, my Lord," said Fogarty. "When I was a kid going to school. I got fever very bad, and the doctor gave me up. The mother, God rest her, was in a terrible state. Then my aunt came to stay with us. She was a real old countrywoman. I remember them to this day arguing downstairs in the kitchen, the mother saying we must be resigned to the will of God, and my aunt telling her not to be a fool; that everyone knew there were ways."

"Well! Well! Well!" Father Whelan said, shaking his head.

"Then my aunt came up with the scissors," Father Fogarty continued with suppressed excitement. "First she cut off a bit of the tail of my shirt; then she cut a bit of hair from behind my ear, and the third time a bit of a fingernail, and threw them all into the fire, muttering something to herself, like an old witch."

"My! My! My!" exclaimed Father Whelan.

"And you got better?" said the Bishop, with a quelling glance at the Canon.

"I did, my Lord," said Father Fogarty. "But that wasn't the strangest part of it." He leaned across the table, scowling, and dropped his eager, boyish voice to a whisper. "I got better, but her two sons, my first cousins, two of the finest-looking lads you ever laid eyes on, died inside a year." Then he sat back, took out a cigar, and scowled again. "Now," he asked, "wasn't that extraordinary? I say, wasn't it extraordinary?"

"Ah, whatever was waiting to get you," Father Whelan said philosophically, emptying his pipe on his plate, "I suppose it had to get something. More or less the same thing happened to an old aunt of mine. The cock used to sleep in the house, on a perch over the door—you know, the old-fashioned way. One night the old woman had occasion to go out, and when she went to the door, the cock crowed three times and then dropped dead at her feet. Whatever was waiting for her, of course," he added with a sigh.

"Well! Well! Well!" said the Canon. "I'm astonished at you, Father Whelan. Absolutely astonished! I can't imagine how you can repeat these old wives' tales."

"I don't see what there is to be astonished about, Canon," said the Bishop. "It wasn't anything worse than what happened to Father Muldoon."

"That was a bad business," muttered Father Whelan, shaking his head.

"What was it, exactly?" asked Father Devine.

"I told you he was always denouncing old Johnnie," said the Bishop. "One day, he went up the Glen to see him; they had words, and he struck the old man. Within a month he got a breaking-out on his knee."

"He lost the leg after," Father Whelan said, stuffing his pipe again.

"I suppose next you'll say it was the fairies' revenge," said the Canon, throwing discretion to the winds. It was too much for him; a man who knew Church history, had lived in France, and knew the best vintages backwards.

"That was what Father Muldoon thought," said the Bishop grimly.

"More fool he," the Canon said hotly.

"That's as may be, Canon," the Bishop went on sternly. "He went to the doctor, but treatment did him no good, so he went back up the valley to ask Johnnie what he ought to do. 'I had nothing to do with that, father,' said Johnnie, 'and the curing of it isn't in my hands.' 'Then who was it?' asks Muldoon. 'The Queen of the Fairies,' said Johnnie, 'and you might as well tell the doctor to take that leg off you while he's at it, for the Queen's wound is the wound that never heals.' No more it did," added the Bishop. "The poor man ended his days on a peg leg."

"He did, he did," muttered Father Whelan mournfully, and there was a long pause. It was clear that the Canon was routed, and soon afterwards they all got up to go. It seemed that Father Fogarty had left his car outside the seminary, and the Bishop, in a benevolent mood, offered to take them across the field by the footpath.

"I'll take them," said Father Devine.

"The little walk will do me good," said the Bishop.

He, the Canon, and Father Fogarty went first. Father Devine followed with Father Whelan, who went sideways down the steps with the skirts of his coat held up.

"As a matter of fact," the Bishop was saying ahead of them, "we're lucky to be able to walk so well. Bad poteen would deprive you of the use of your legs. I used to see them at home, talking quite nicely one minute and dropping off the chairs like bags of meal the next. You'd have to take them home on a door. The head might be quite clear, but the legs would be like gateposts."

"Father Devine," whispered Father Whelan girlishly, stopping in his tracks.

"Yes, what is it?" asked Father Devine gently.

"What his Lordship said," whispered Father Whelan guiltily. "That's the way I feel. Like gateposts."

And before the young priest could do anything, he put out one of the gateposts, which didn't seem to alight properly on its base, the other leaned slowly towards it, and he fell in an ungraceful parody of a ballet dancer's final curtsy.

"Oh, my! My! My!" he exclaimed. Even in his liquor he was melancholy and gentle.

The other three turned slowly round. To Father Devine they looked like sleepwalkers.

"Hah!" said the Bishop with quiet satisfaction. "That's the very thing I mean. We'll have to mind ourselves."

And away the three of them went, very slowly, as though they owed no responsibility whatever towards the fallen guest. Paddy, the Bishop's "boy," who was obviously expecting something of the sort, immediately appeared and, with the aid of Father Devine, put the old man on a bench and carried him back to the palace. Then, still carrying the bench between them, they set out after the others. They were just in time to see the collapse of the Canon, but in spite of it the other two went on. Father Fogarty had begun to chuckle hysterically. They could hear him across the field, and it seemed to Father Devine that he was already rehearsing the lovely story he would tell about "the night I got drunk with the Bishop."

Devine and Paddy left the Canon where he had fallen, and where he looked like being safe for a long time to come, and followed the other two. They had gone wildly astray, turning in a semicircle round the field till they were at the foot of the hill before a high fence round the plantation. The Bishop never hesitated, but immediately began to climb the wall.

"I must be gone wrong, father," he said anxiously. "I don't know what happened me tonight. I can usually do this easy enough. We'll go over the wall and up the wood."

"I can't," shouted Father Fogarty in a paroxysm of chuckles.

"Nonsense, man!" the Bishop said sternly, holding on to a bush and looking down at him from the top of the wall. "Why can't you?"

"The fairies have me," roared Father Fogarty.

"Pull yourself together, father," the Bishop said sternly. "You don't want to be making an exhibition of yourself."

Next moment Father Fogarty was lying flat at the foot of the wall, roaring with laughter. Father Devine shouted to the Bishop, but he slid obstinately down at the other side of the wall. "The ould divil!" Paddy exclaimed admiringly. "That's more than we'll be able to do at his age, father."

A few minutes later they found him flat under a tree in the starlight, quite powerless, but full of wisdom, resignation, and peace. They lifted him on a bench, where he reclined like the effigy on a tomb, his hands crossed meekly on his breast, and carried him back to bed.

"Since that evening," Father Devine used to say in the waspish way the Bishop so much disliked, "I feel there's nothing I don't know about fairies. I also have some idea about the sort of man who wrote the life of St. Mulpeter of Moyle."

THE MIRACLE

VANITY, according to the Bishop, was the Canon's great weakness, and there might be some truth in that. He was a tall, good-looking man, with a big chin, and a manner of deceptive humility. He deplored the fact that so many of the young priests came of poor homes where good manners weren't taught, and looked back regretfully to the old days when, according to him, every Irish priest read his Virgil. He went in a lot for being an authority on food and wine, and ground and brewed his own coffee. He refused to live in the ramshackle old presbytery which had served generations of priests, and had built for himself a residence that was second only to the Bishop's palace and that was furnished with considerably more taste and expense. His first innovation in the parish had been to alter the dues which, all over the Christian world, are paid at Christmas and Easter and have them paid four times a year instead. He said that this was because poor people couldn't afford large sums twice a year, and that it was easier for them to pay their dues like that; but in fact it was because he thought the dues that had been fixed were far too low to correspond in any way with the dignity of his office. When he was building his house he had them collected five times during the year, and, as well as that, threw in a few raffles and public subscriptions. He disliked getting into debt. And there he ate his delicate meals with the right wines, brewed coffee and drank green chartreuse, and occasionally dipped into ecclesiastical history. He liked to read about days when the clergy were really well off.

It was distasteful to the Canon the way the lower classes were creeping into the Church and gaining high office in it, but it was a real heartbreak that its functions and privileges were being usurped by new men and methods, and that miracles were now being performed out of bottles and syringes. He thought that a very undignified way of performing miracles himself, and it was a real bewilderment of spirit to him when some new drug was invented to make the medicine men more indispensable than they were at present. He would have liked surgeons to remain tradesmen and barbers as they were in the good old days, and, though he would have been astonished to hear it himself, was as jealous as a prima donna at the interference of Bobby Healy, the doctor, with his flock. He would have liked to be able to do it all himself, and sometimes thought regretfully that it was a peculiar dispensation of Providence that when the Church was most menaced, it couldn't draw upon some of its old grace and perform occasional miracles. The Canon knew he would have performed a miracle with a real air. He had the figure for it.

There was certainly some truth in the Bishop's criticism. The Canon hated competition, he liked young Dr. Devaney, who affected to believe that medicine was all hocus-pocus (which was what the Canon believed himself), and took a grave view of Bobby Healy, which caused Bobby's practice to go down quite a bit. When the Canon visited a dying man he took care to ask: "Who have you?" If he was told "Dr. Devaney," he said: "A good young man," but if it was "Dr. Healy" he merely nodded and looked grave, and everyone understood that Bobby had killed the unfortunate patient as usual. Whenever the two men met, the Canon was courteous and condescending, Bobby was respectful and obliging, and nobody could ever have told from the doctor's face whether or not he knew what was going on. But there was very little which Bobby didn't know. There is a certain sort of guile that goes deeper than any cleric's: the peasant's guile. Dr. Healy had that.

But there was one person in his parish whom the Canon disliked even more than he disliked the doctor. That was a man called Bill Enright. Nominally, Bill was a farmer and breeder of greyhounds; really, he was the last of a family of bandits who had terrorized the countryside for generations. He was a tall, gaunt man with fair hair and a tiny, gold moustache; perfectly rosy skin, like a baby's, and a pair of bright blue eyes which seemed to expand into a wide unwinking, animal glare. His cheekbones were so high that they gave the impression of cutting his skin. They also gave his eyes an Oriental slant, and, with its low, sharp-sloping forehead, his whole face seemed to point out-ward to the sharp tip of his nose and then retreat again in a pair of high teeth, very sharp and very white, a drooping lower lip, and a small, weak, feminine chin.

Now, Bill, as he would be the first to tell you, was not a bad man. He was a traditionalist who did as his father and grand-father had done before him. He had gone to Mass and the Sacra-ments and even paid his dues four times a year, which was not traditional, and been prepared to treat the Canon as a bandit of similar dignity to himself. But the Canon had merely been in-censed at the offer of parity with Bill and set out to demonstrate that the last of the Enrights was a common ruffian who should be sent to jail. Bill was notoriously living in sin with his house-keeper, Nellie Mahony from Doonamon, and the Canon ordered her to leave the house. When he failed in this he went to her brothers and demanded that they should drag her home, but her brothers had had too much experience of the Enrights to try such a risky experiment with them, and Nellie remained on, while Bill, declaring loudly that there was nothing in religion, ceased going to Mass. People agreed that it wasn't altogether Bill's fault, and that the Canon could not brook another authority than his own—a hasty man!

To Bobby Healy, on the other hand, Bill Enright was bound by the strongest tie that could bind an Enright, for the doctor had once cured a greyhound for him, the mother of King Kong. Four or five times a year he was summoned to treat Bill for an overdose of whisky; Bill owed him as much money as it was fitting to owe to a friend, and all Bill's friends knew that when they were in trouble themselves, it would be better for them to avoid further trouble by having Dr. Healy as well. Whatever the Canon might think, Bill was a man it paid to stand in well with.

One spring day Bobby got one of his usual summonses to the presence. Bill lived in a fine Georgian house a mile outside the town. It had once belonged to the Rowes, but Bill had got them out of it by the simple expedient of making their lives a hell for them. The avenue was overgrown, and the house with its fine Ionic portico looked dirty and dilapidated. Two dogs got up and barked at him in a neighbourly way. They hated it when Bill was sick, and they knew Bobby had the knack of putting him on his feet again.

Nellie Mahony opened the door. She was a small, fat country girl with a rosy complexion and a mass of jet-black hair that shone almost as brilliantly as her eyes. The doctor, who was some-times seized with these fits of amiable idiocy, took her by the waist, and she gave a shriek of laughter that broke off suddenly.

"Wisha, Dr. Healy," she said complainingly, "oughtn't you to be ashamed, and the state we're in!"

"How's that, Nellie?" he asked anxiously. "Isn't it the usual thing?"

"The usual thing?" she shrieked. She had a trick of snatching up and repeating someone's final words in a brilliant tone, a full octave higher, like a fiddle repeating a phrase from the double-bass. Then with dramatic abruptness she let her voice drop to a whisper and dabbed her eyes with her apron. "He's dying, doctor," she said.

"For God's sake!" whispered the doctor. Life had rubbed down his principles considerably, and the fact that Bill was suspected of a share in at least one murder didn't prejudice him in the least. "What happened him? I saw him in town on Monday and he never looked better."

"Never looked better?" echoed the fiddles, while Nellie's beautiful black eyes filled with a tragic emotion that was not far removed from joy. "And then didn't he go out on the Tuesday morning on me, in the pouring rain, with three men and two dogs, and not come back till the Friday night, with the result" (this was a boss phrase of Nellie's, always followed by a dramatic pause and a change of key) "that he caught a chill up through him and never left the bed since."

"What are you saying to Bobby Healy?" screeched a man's

voice from upstairs. It was nearly as high-pitched as Nellie's, but with a wild nervous tremolo in it.

"What am I saying to Bobby Healy?" she echoed mechanically. "I'm saying nothing at all to him."

"Well, don't be keeping him down there, after I waiting all day for him."

"There's nothing wrong with his lungs anyway," the doctor said professionally as he went up the stairs. They were bare and damp. It was a lifelong grievance of Bill Enright's that the Rowes had been mean enough to take the furniture to England with them.

He was sitting up in an iron bed, and the grey afternoon light and the white pillows threw up the brilliance of his colouring, already heightened with a touch of fever.

"What was she telling you?" he asked in his high-pitched voice—the sort of keen and unsentimental voice you'd attribute in fantasy to some cunning and swift-footed beast of prey, like a fox.

"What was I telling him?" Nellie echoed boldly, feeling the doctor's authority behind her. "I was telling him you went out with three men and two dogs and never came back to me till Friday night."

"Ah, Bill," said the doctor reproachfully, "how often did I tell you to stick to women and cats? What ails you?"

"I'm bloody bad, doctor," whinnied Bill.

"You look it," said Bobby candidly. "That's all right, Nellie," he added by way of dismissal.

"And make a lot of noise downstairs," said Bill after her.

Bobby gave his patient a thorough examination. So far as he could see there was nothing wrong with him but a chill, though he realized from the way Bill's mad blue eyes followed him that the man was in a panic. He wondered whether, as he sometimes did, he shouldn't put him in a worse one. It was unprofessional, but it was the only treatment that ever worked, and with most of his men patients he was compelled to choose a moment, before it was too late and hadn't yet passed from fiction to fact, when the threat of heart-disease or cirrhosis might reduce their drinking to some reasonable proportion. Then the inspiration came to him like heaven opening to poor sinners, and he sat for several moments in silence, working it out. Threats would be lost on Bill Enright. What Bill needed was a miracle, and miracles aren't things to be lightly undertaken. Properly performed, a miracle might do as much good to the doctor as to Bill.

"Well, Bobby?" asked Bill, on edge with nerves.

"How long is it since you were at Confession, Bill?" the doctor asked gravely.

Bill's rosy face turned the colour of wax, and the doctor, a kindly man, felt almost ashamed of himself.

"Is that the way it is, doctor?" Bill asked in a shrill, expressionless voice.

"I put it too strongly, Bill," said the doctor, already relenting. "Maybe I should have a second opinion."

"Your opinion is good enough for me, Bobby," said Bill wildly, pouring coals of fire on Bobby as he sat up in bed and pulled the clothes about him. "Take a fag and light one for me. What the hell difference does it make? I lived my life and bred the best greyhound bitches in Europe."

"And I hope you'll live to breed a good many more," said the doctor. "Will I go for the Canon?"

"The Half-Gent?" snorted Bill indignantly. "You will not."

"He has an unfortunate manner," sighed the doctor. "But I could bring you someone else."

"Ah, what the hell do I want with any of them?" asked Bill. "Aren't they all the same? Money! Money! That's all that's a trouble to them."

"Ah, I wouldn't say that, Bill," the doctor said thoughtfully as he paced the room, his wrinkled old face as grey as his homespun suit. "I hope you won't think me intruding," he added anxiously. "I'm talking as a friend."

"I know you mean it well, Bobby."

"But you see, Bill," the doctor went on, screwing up his left cheek as though it hurt him, "the feeling I have is that you need a different sort of priest altogether. Of course, I'm not saying a word against the Canon, but, after all, he's only a secular. You never had a chat with a Jesuit, I suppose?"

The doctor asked it with an innocent air, as if he didn't know that the one thing a secular priest dreads after Old Nick himself is a Jesuit, and that a Jesuit was particularly hateful to the Canon, who considered that as much intellect and authority as could ever be needed by his flock was centered in himself.

"Never," said Bill.

"They're a very cultured order," said the doctor.

"What the hell do I want with a Jesuit?" Bill cried in protest. "A drop of drink and a bit of skirt—what harm is there in that?"

"Oh, none in the world, man," agreed Bobby cunningly. " 'Tisn't as if you were ever a bad-living man."

"I wasn't," said Bill with unexpected self-pity. "I was a good friend to anyone I liked."

"And you know the Canon would take it as a personal compliment if anything happened you—I'm speaking as a friend."

"You are, Bobby," said Bill, his voice hardening under the injustice of it. "You're speaking as a Christian. Anything to thwart a fellow like that! I could leave the Jesuits a few pounds for Masses, Bobby," he added with growing enthusiasm. "That's what would really break Lanigan's heart. Money is all he cares about."

"Ah, I wouldn't say that, Bill," Bobby said with a trace of alarm. His was a delicate undertaking, and Bill was altogether too apt a pupil for his taste.

"No," said Bill with conviction, "but that's what you mean. All right, Bobby. You're right as usual. Bring whoever you like and I'll let him talk. Talk never broke anyone's bones, Bobby."

The doctor went downstairs and found Nellie waiting for him with an anxious air.

"I'm running over to Aharna for a priest, Nellie," he whispered. "You might get things ready while I'm away."

"And is that the way it is?" she asked, growing pale.

"Ah, we'll hope for the best," he said, again feeling ashamed.

In a very thoughtful frame of mind he drove off to Aharna, where an ancient Bishop called McGinty, whose name was remembered in clerical circles only with sorrow, had permitted the Jesuits to establish a house. There he had a friend called Father Finnegan, a stocky, middle-aged man with a tight mouth and little clumps of white hair in his ears. It is not to be supposed that

Bobby told him all that was in his mind, or that Father Finnegan thought he did, but there is very little a Jesuit doesn't know, and Father Finnegan knew that this was an occasion.

As they drove up the avenue, Nellie rushed out to meet them.

"What is it, Nellie?" the doctor asked anxiously. He couldn't help dreading that at the last moment Bill would play a trick on him and die of shock.

"He's gone mad, doctor," she replied reproachfully, as though she hadn't thought a professional man would do a thing like that to her.

"When did he go mad?" Bobby asked doubtfully.

"When he seen me putting up the altar. Now he's after barricading the door and says he'll shoot the first one that tries to get in."

"That's quite all right, my dear young lady," said Father Finnegan soothingly. "Sick people often go on like that."

"Has he a gun, Nellie?" Bobby asked cautiously.

"Did you ever know him without one?" retorted Nellie.

The doctor, who was of a rather timid disposition, admired his friend's coolness as they mounted the stair. While Bobby knocked, Father Finnegan stood beside the door, his hands behind his back and his head bowed in meditation.

"Who's there?" Bill cried shrilly.

" 'Tis only me, Bill," the doctor replied soothingly. "Can I come in?"

"I'm too sick," shouted Bill. "I'm not seeing anyone."

"One moment, doctor," Father Finnegan said calmly, putting his shoulder to the door. The barricade gave way and they went in. One glance was enough to show Bobby that Bill had had time to get panic-stricken. He hadn't a gun, but this was the only thing that was lacking to remind Bobby of Two-Gun Joe's last stand. He was sitting well up, supported on his elbows, his head craned forward, his bright blue eyes flashing unseeingly from the priest to Bobby and from Bobby to the improvised altar. Bobby was sadly afraid that Bill was going to disappoint him. You might as well have tried to convert something in the zoo.

"I'm Father Finnegan, Mr. Enright," the Jesuit said, going up to him with his hand stretched out.

"I didn't send for you," snapped Bill.

"I appreciate that, Mr. Enright," said the priest. "But any friend of Dr. Healy is a friend of mine. Won't you shake hands?"

"I don't mind," whinnied Bill, letting him partake slightly of a limp paw but without looking at him. "But I warn you I'm not a religious sort of bloke. I never went in for that at all. Anyone that thinks I'm not a hard nut to crack is in for a surprise."

"If I went in for cracking nuts, I'd say the same," said Father Finnegan gamely. "You look well able to protect yourself."

Bill gave a harsh snort indicative of how much could be said on that score if the occasion were more propitious; his eyes continued to wander unseeingly like a mirror in a child's hand, but Bobby felt the priest had struck the right note. He closed the door softly behind him and went down to the drawing-room. The six windows opened on three landscapes. The lowing of distant cows pleased his ear. Then he swore and threw open the door to the hall. Nellie was sitting comfortably on the stairs with her ear cocked. He beckoned her down.

"What is it, doctor?" she asked in surprise.

"Get us a light. And don't forget the priest will want his supper."

"You don't think I was listening?" she asked indignantly.

"No," Bobby said dryly. "You looked as if you were joining in the devotions."

"Joining in the devotions?" she cried. "I'm up since six, waiting hand and foot on him, with the result that I dropped down in a dead weakness on the stairs. Would you believe that now?"

"I would not," said Bobby.

"You would not?" she repeated incredulously. "Jesus!" she added after a moment. "I'll bring you the lamp," she said in a defeated tone.

Nearly an hour passed before there was any sound upstairs. Then Father Finnegan came down, rubbing his hands briskly and complaining of the cold. Bobby found the lamp lit in the bedroom and the patient lying with one arm under his head.

"How are you feeling now, Bill?" the doctor asked.

"Fine, Bobby," said Bill. "I'm feeling fine. You were right about the priest, Bobby. I was a fool to bother my head about the

Canon. He's not educated at all, Bobby, not compared with that man."

"I thought you'd like him," said Bobby.

"I like a fellow to know his job, Bobby," said Bill in the tone of one expert appraising another. "There's nothing like the bit of education. I wish I met him sooner." The wild blue eyes came to rest hauntingly on the doctor's face. "I feel the better of it already, Bobby. What sign would that be?"

"I dare say 'tis the excitement," said Bobby, giving nothing away. "I'll have another look at you."

"What's that she's frying, Bobby? Sausages and bacon?"

"It smells like it."

"There's nothing I'm so fond of," Bill said wistfully. "Would it make me worse, Bobby? My stomach feels as if it was sand-papered."

"I don't suppose so. But tea is all you can have with it."

"Hah!" crowed Bill. " 'Tis all I'm ever going to have if I live to be as old as Methuselah. But I'm not complaining, Bobby. I'm a man of my word. Oh, God, yes."

"Go on!" said Bobby. "Did you take the pledge?"

"Christ, Bobby," said the patient, giving a wild heave in the bed, "I took the whole bloody ship, masts and anchor. . . . God forgive me for swearing!" he added piously. "He made me promise to marry the Screech," he said with a look which challenged the doctor to laugh if he dared.

"Ah, well, you might do worse, Bill," said the doctor.

"How sure he is I'll have him!" bawled Nellie cheerfully, showing her moony face at the door.

"You see the way it is, Bobby," said Bill without rancour. "That's what I have to put up with."

"Excuse me a minute, Nellie," said the doctor. "I'm having a look at Bill. . . . You had a trying day of it," he added, sitting on the bed and taking Bill's wrist. Then he took his temperature, and flashed the torch into his eyes and down his throat while Bill looked at him with a hypnotized glare.

"Begor, Bill, I wouldn't say but you're right," the doctor said approvingly. "I'd almost say you were a shade better."

"But that's what I'm saying, man!" cried Bill, beginning to do physical exercises for him. "Look at that, Bobby! I couldn't do that before. I call it a blooming miracle."

"When you've seen as much as I have, you won't have so much belief in miracles," said the doctor. "Take a couple of these tablets anyway, and I'll have another look at you in the morning."

It was almost too easy. The most up-to-date treatments were wasted on Bobby's patients. What they all secretly desired was to be rubbed with three pebbles from a Holy Well. Sometimes it left him depressed.

"Well, on the whole, Dr. Healy," Father Finnegan said as they drove off, "that was a very satisfactory evening."

"It was," Bobby said guardedly. He had no intention of telling his friend how satisfactory it was from his point of view.

"People do make extraordinary rallies after the Sacraments," went on Father Finnegan, and Bobby saw it wasn't even necessary to tell him. Educated men can understand one another without embarrassing admissions. His own conscience was quite easy. A little religion wouldn't do Bill the least bit of harm. The Jesuit's conscience, he felt, wasn't troubling him either. Even without a miracle Bill's conversion would have opened up the Canon's parish to the order. With a miracle, they'd have every old woman, male and female, for miles around, calling them in.

"They do," Bobby said wonderingly. "I often noticed it."

"And I'm afraid, Dr. Healy, that the Canon won't like it," added the Jesuit.

"He won't," said the doctor as though the idea had only just occurred to himself. "I'm afraid he won't like it at all."

He was an honest man who gave credit where credit was due, and he knew it wasn't only the money—a couple of hundred a year at the least—that would upset the Canon. It was the thought that under his own very nose a miracle had been worked on one of his own parishioners by one of the hated Jesuits. Clerics are almost as cruel as small boys. The Canon wouldn't be allowed to forget the Jesuit miracle the longest day he lived.

But for the future he'd let Bobby alone.

THE FRYING-PAN

FATHER FOGARTY's only real friends in Kilmulpeter were the Whittons. Whitton was the teacher there. He had been to the seminary and college with Fogarty, and, like him, intended to be a priest, but when the time came for him to take the vow of celibacy, he had contracted scruples of conscience and married the principal one. Fogarty, who had known her too, had to admit that she wasn't without justification, and now, in this lonely place where chance had thrown them together again, she formed the real centre of what little social life he had. With Tom Whitton he had a quiet friendship compounded of exchanges of opinion about books or wireless talks. He had the impression that Whitton didn't really like him and considered him a man who would have been better out of the Church. When they went to the races together, Fogarty felt that Whitton disapproved of having to put on bets for him and thought that priests should not bet at all. Like other outsiders, he knew perfectly what priests should be, without the necessity for having to be that way himself. He was sometimes savage in the things he said about the parish priest, old Father Whelan. On the other hand, he had a pleasant sense of humour and Fogarty enjoyed retailing his cracks against the cloth. Men as intelligent as Whitton were rare in country schools, and soon, too, he would grow stupid and wild for lack of educated society.

One evening Father Fogarty invited them to dinner to see some films he had taken at the races. Films were his latest hobby. Before this it had been fishing and shooting. Like all bachelors, he had a mania for adding to his possessions, and his lumber-room was piled high with every possible sort of junk from chest-developers to field-glasses, and his library cluttered with works on everything from Irish history to Freudian psychology. He passed from craze to craze, each the key to the universe.

He sprang up at the knock, and found Una at the door, all in furs, her shoulders about her ears, her big, bony, masculine face blue with cold but screwed up in an amiable monkey-grin. Tom, a handsome man, was tall and self-conscious. He had greying hair, brown eyes, a prominent jaw, and was quiet-spoken in a way that concealed passion. He and Una disagreed a lot about the way the children should be brought up. He thought she spoiled them.

"Come in, let ye, come in!" cried Fogarty hospitably, showing the way into his warm study with its roaring turf fire, deep leather chairs, and the Raphael print above the mantelpiece; a real bachelor's room. "God above!" he exclaimed, holding Una's hand a moment longer than was necessary. "You're perished! What'll you have to drink, Una?"

"Whi-hi-hi—" stammered Una excitedly, her eyes beginning to pop. "I can't say the bloody word."

"Call it malt, girl," said the priest.

"That's enough! That's enough!" she cried laughingly, snatching the glass from him. "You'll send me home on my ear, and then I'll hear about it from this fellow."

"Whisky, Tom?"

"Whisky, Jerry," Whitton said quietly with a quick concilia-tory glance. He kept his head very stiff and used his eyes a lot instead.

Meanwhile Una, unabashably inquisitive, was making the tour of the room with the glass in her hand, to see if there was any-thing new in it. There usually was.

"Is this new, father?" she asked, halting before a pleasant eighteenth-century print.

"Ten bob," the priest said promptly. "Wasn't it a bargain?"

"I couldn't say. What is it?"

"The old courthouse in town."

"Go on!" said Una.

Whitton came and studied the print closely. "That place is gone these fifty years and I never saw a picture of it," he said. "This is a bargain all right."

"I'd say so," Fogarty said with quiet pride.

"And what's the sheet for?" Una asked, poking at a tablecloth pinned between the windows.

"That's not a sheet, woman!" Fogarty exclaimed. "For God's sake, don't be displaying your ignorance!"

"Oh, I know," she cried girlishly. "For the pictures! I'd forgotten about them. That's grand!"

Then Bella, a coarse, good-looking country girl, announced dinner, and the curate, with a self-conscious, boyish swagger, led them into the dining-room and opened the door of the sideboard. The dining-room was even more ponderous than the sitting-room. Everything in it was large, heavy, and dark.

"And now, what'll ye drink?" he asked over his shoulder, studying his array of bottles. "There's some damn good Burgundy—'pon my soul, 'tis great!"

"How much did it cost?" Whitton asked with poker-faced humour. "The only way I have of identifying wines is by the price."

"Eight bob a bottle," Fogarty replied at once.

"That's a very good price," said Whitton with a nod. "We'll have some of that."

"You can take a couple of bottles home with you," said the curate, who, in the warmth of his heart, was always wanting to give his treasures away. "The last two dozen he had—wasn't I lucky?"

"You have the appetite of a canon on the income of a curate," Whitton said in the same tone of grave humour, but Fogarty caught the scarcely perceptible note of criticism in it. He did not allow this to upset him.

"Please God, we won't always be curates," he said sunnily.

"Bella looks after you well," said Una when the meal was nearly over. The compliment was deserved so far as it went, though it was a man's meal rather than a woman's.

"Doesn't she, though?" Fogarty exclaimed with pleasure. "Isn't she damn good for a country girl?"

"How does she get on with Stasia?" asked Una—Stasia was Father Whelan's old housekeeper, and an affliction to the community.

"They don't talk. Stasia says she's an immoral woman."

"And is she?" Una asked hopefully.

"If she isn't, she's wasting her own time and my whisky," said Fogarty. "She entertains Paddy Coakley in the kitchen every Saturday night. I told her I wouldn't keep her unless she got a boy. And wasn't I right? One Stasia is enough for any parish. Father Whelan tells me I'm going too far."

"And did you tell him to mind his own business?" Whitton asked with a penetrating look.

"I did, to be sure," said Fogarty, who had done nothing of the sort.

"Ignorant, interfering old fool!" Whitton said quietly, the ferocity of his sentiments belied by the mildness of his manner.

"That's only because you'd like to do the interfering yourself," said Una good-humouredly. She frequently had to act as peacemaker between the parish priest and her husband.

"And a robber," Tom Whitton added to the curate, ignoring her. "He's been collecting for new seats for the church for the last ten years. I'd like to know where that's going."

"He had a collection for repairing my roof," said the curate, "and 'tis leaking still. He must be worth twenty thousand."

"Now, that's not fair, father," Una said flatly. "You know yourself there's no harm in Father Whelan. It's just that he's certain he's going to die in the workhouse. It's like Bella and her boy. He has nothing more serious to worry about, and he worries about that."

Fogarty knew there was a certain amount of truth in what Una said, and that the old man's miserliness was more symbolic than real, and at the same time he felt in her words criticism of a different kind from her husband's. Though Una wasn't aware of it she was implying that the priest's office made him an object of pity rather than blame. She was sorry for old Whelan, and, by implication, for him.

"Still, Tom is right, Una," he said with sudden earnestness. "It's not a question of what harm Father Whelan intends, but what harm he does. Scandal is scandal, whether you give it deliberately or through absent-mindedness."

Tom grunted, to show his approval, but he said no more on the subject, as though he refused to enter into an argument with his wife about subjects she knew nothing of. They returned to the study for coffee, and Fogarty produced the film projector. At once the censoriousness of Tom Whitton's manner dropped away, and he behaved like a pleasant and intelligent boy of seventeen. Una, sitting by the fire with her legs crossed, watched them with amusement. Whenever they came to the priest's house, the same sort of thing happened. Once it had been a microscope, and the pair of them had amused themselves with it for hours. Now they were kidding themselves that their real interest in the cinema was educational. She knew that within a month the cinema, like the microscope, would be lying in the lumber-room with the rest of the junk.

Fogarty switched off the light and showed some films he had taken at the last race meeting. They were very patchy, mostly out of focus, and had to be interpreted by a running commentary, which was always a shot or two behind.

"I suppose ye wouldn't know who that is?" he said as the film showed Una, eating a sandwich and talking excitedly and demonstratively to a couple of wild-looking country boys.

"It looks like someone from the County Club," her husband said dryly.

"But wasn't it good?" Fogarty asked innocently as he switched on the lights again. "Now, wasn't it very interesting?" He was exactly like a small boy who had performed a conjuring trick.

"Marvellous, father," Una said with a sly and affectionate grin.

He blushed and turned to pour them out more whisky. He saw that she had noticed the pictures of herself. At the same time, he saw she was pleased. When he had driven them home, she held his hand and said they had had the best evening for years—a piece of flattery so gross and uncalled-for that it made her husband more tongue-tied than ever.

"Thursday, Jerry?" he said with a quick glance.

"Thursday, Tom," said the priest.

The room looked terribly desolate after her; the crumpled

cushions, the glasses, the screen and the film projector, everything had become frighteningly inert, while outside his window the desolate countryside had taken on even more of its supernatural animation; bogs, hills, and fields, full of ghosts and shadows. He sat by the fire, wondering what his own life might have been like with a girl like that, all furs and scent and laughter, and two bawling, irrepressible brats upstairs. When he tiptoed up to his bedroom he remembered that there would never be children there to wake, and it seemed to him that with all the things he bought to fill his home, he was merely trying desperately to stuff the yawning holes in his own big, empty heart.

On Thursday, when he went to their house, Ita and Brendan, though already in bed, were refusing to sleep till he said good-night to them. While he was taking off his coat the two of them rushed to the banisters and screamed: "We want Father Fogey." When he went upstairs they were sitting bolt-upright in their cots, a little fat, fair-haired rowdy boy and a solemn baby girl.

"Father," Brendan began at once, "will I be your altar boy when I grow up?"

"You will to be sure, son," replied Fogarty.

"Ladies first! Ladies first!" the baby shrieked in a frenzy of rage. "Father, will I be your altar boy?"

"Go on!" Brendan said scornfully. "Little girls can't be altar boys, sure they can't, father?"

"I can," shrieked Ita, who in her excitement exactly resembled her mother. "Can't I, father?"

"We might be able to get a dispensation for you," said the curate. "In a pair of trousers, you'd do fine."

He was in a wistful frame of mind when he came downstairs again. Children would always be a worse temptation to him than women. Children were the devil! The house was gay and spot-less. They had no fine mahogany suite like his, but Una managed to make the few coloured odds and ends they had seem deliberate. There wasn't a cigarette end in the ashtrays; the cushions had not been sat on. Tom, standing before the fireplace (not to disturb the cushions, thought Fogarty), looked as if someone had held his head under the tap, and was very self-consciously wearing a new brown tie. With his greying hair plastered flat, he looked schoolboyish, sulky, and resentful, as though he were meditating ways of restoring his authority over a mutinous household. The thought crossed Fogarty's mind that he and Una had probably quarrelled about the tie. It went altogether too well with his suit.

"We want Father Fogey!" the children began to chant monotonously from the bedroom.

"Shut up!" shouted Tom.

"We want Father Fogey," the chant went on, but with a groan in it somewhere.

"Well, you're not going to get him. Go to sleep!"

The chant stopped. This was clearly serious.

"You don't mind if I drop down to a meeting tonight, Jerry?" Tom asked in his quiet, anxious way. "I won't be more than half an hour."

"Not at all, Tom," said Fogarty heartily. "Sure, I'll drive you."

"No, thanks," Whitton said with a smile of gratitude. "It won't take me ten minutes to get there."

It was clear that a lot of trouble had gone to the making of supper, but out of sheer perversity Tom let on not to recognize any of the dishes. When they had drunk their coffee, he rose and glanced at his watch.

"I won't be long," he said.

"Tom, you're not going to that meeting?" Una asked appealingly.

"I tell you I have to," he replied with unnecessary emphasis.

"I met Mick Mahoney this afternoon, and he said they didn't need you."

"Mick Mahoney knows nothing about it."

"I told him to tell the others you wouldn't be coming, that Father Fogarty would be here," she went on desperately, fighting for the success of her evening.

"Then you had no business to do it," her husband retorted angrily, and even Fogarty saw that she had gone the worst way about it, by speaking to members of his committee behind his back. He began to feel uncomfortable. "If they come to some damn fool decision while I'm away, it'll be my responsibility."

"If you're late, you'd better knock," she sang out gaily to cover up his bad manners. "Will we go into the sitting-room, father?" she asked over-eagerly. "I'll be with you in two minutes. There are fags on the mantelpiece, and you know where to find the whi-hi-hi—blast that word!"

Fogarty lit a cigarette and sat down. He felt exceedingly uncomfortable. Whitton was an uncouth and irritable bastard, and always had been so. He heard Una upstairs, and then someone turned on the tap in the bathroom. "Bloody brute!" he thought indignantly. There had been no need for him to insult her before a guest. Why the hell couldn't he have finished his quarrelling while they were alone? The tap stopped and he waited, listening, but Una didn't come. He was a warm-hearted man and could not bear the thought of her alone and miserable upstairs. He went softly up the stairs and stood on the landing. "Una!" he called softly, afraid of waking the children. There was a light in the bedroom; the door was ajar and he pushed it in. She was sitting at the end of the bed and grinned at him dolefully.

"Sorry for the whine, father," she said, making a brave attempt to smile. And then, with the street-urchin's humour which he found so attractive: "Can I have a loan of your shoulder, please?"

"What the blazes ails Tom?" he asked, sitting beside her.

"He—he's jealous," she stammered, and began to weep again with her head on his chest. He put his arm about her and patted her awkwardly.

"Jealous?" he asked incredulously, turning over in his mind the half-dozen men whom Una could meet at the best of times. "Who the blazes is he jealous of?"

"You!"

"Me?" Fogarty exclaimed indignantly, and grew red, thinking of how he had given himself away with his pictures. "He must be mad! I never gave him any cause for jealousy."

"Oh, I know he's completely unreasonable," she stammered. "He always was."

"But you didn't say anything to him, did you?" Fogarty asked anxiously.

"About what?" she asked in surprise, looking up at him and blinking back her tears.

"About me?" Fogarty mumbled in embarrassment.

"Oh, he doesn't know about that," Una replied frantically. "I never mentioned that to him at all. Besides, he doesn't care that much about me."

And Fogarty realized that in the simplest way in the world he had been brought to admit to a married woman that he loved her and she to imply that she felt the same about him, without a word being said on either side. Obviously, these things happened more innocently than he had ever thought possible. He became more embarrassed than ever.

"But what is he jealous of so?" he added truculently.

"He's jealous of you because you're a priest. Surely, you saw that?"

"I certainly didn't. It never crossed my mind."

Yet at the same time he wondered if this might not be the reason for the censoriousness he sometimes felt in Whitton against his harmless bets and his bottles of wine.

"But he's hardly ever out of your house, and he's always borrowing your books, and talking theology and Church history to you. He has shelves of them here—look!" And she pointed at a plain wooden bookcase, filled with solid-looking works. "In my b-b-bedroom! That's why he really hates Father Whelan. Don't you see, Jerry," she said, calling him for the first time by his Christian name, "you have all the things he wants."

"I have?" repeated Fogarty in astonishment. "What things?"

"Oh, how do I know?" she replied with a shrug, relegating these to the same position as Whelan's bank-balance and his own gadgets, as things that meant nothing to her. "Respect and responsibility and freedom from the worries of a family, I suppose."

"He's welcome to them," Fogarty said with wry humour. "What's that the advertisements say?—owner having no further use for same."

"Oh, I know," she said with another shrug, and he saw that from the beginning she had realized how he felt about her and been sorry for him. He was sure that there was some contradiction here which he should be able to express to himself, between her almost inordinate piety and her light-hearted acceptance of his adoration for her—something that was exclusively feminine, but which he could not isolate with her there beside him, willing him to make love to her, offering herself to his kiss.

"It's a change to be kissed by someone who cares for you," she said after a moment.

"Ah, now, Una, that's not true," he protested gravely, the priest in him getting the upper hand of the lover who had still a considerable amount to learn. "You only fancy that."

"I don't, Jerry," she replied with conviction. "It's always been the same, from the first month of our marriage—always! I was a fool to marry him at all."

"Even so," Fogarty said manfully, doing his duty by his friend with a sort of schoolboy gravity, "You know he's still fond of you. That's only his way."

"It isn't, Jerry," she went on obstinately. "He wanted to be a priest and I stopped him."

"But you didn't."

"That's how he looks at it. I tempted him."

"And damn glad he was to fall!"

"But he did fall, Jerry, and that's what he can never forgive. In his heart he despises me and despises himself for not being able to do without me."

"But why should he despise himself? That's what I don't understand."

"Because I'm only a woman, and he wants to be independent of me and every other woman as well. He has to teach to keep a home for me, and he doesn't want to teach. He wants to say Mass and hear confessions, and be God Almighty for seven days of the week."

Fogarty couldn't grasp it, but he realized that there was something in what she said, and that Whitton was really a lonely, frustrated man who felt he was forever excluded from the only things which interested him.

"I don't understand it," he said angrily. "It doesn't sound natural to me."

"It doesn't sound natural to you because you have it, Jerry," she said. "I used to think Tom wasn't normal, either, but now I'm beginning to think there are more spoiled priests in the world than ever went into seminaries. You see, Jerry," she went on in a rush, growing very red, "I'm a constant reproach to him. He thinks he's a terrible blackguard because he wants to make love to me once a month. . . . I can talk like this to you because you're a priest."

"You can, to be sure," said Fogarty with more conviction than he felt.

"And even when he does make love to me," she went on, too full of her grievance even to notice the anguish she caused him, "he manages to make me feel that I'm doing all the love-making."

"And why shouldn't you?" asked Fogarty gallantly, concealing the way his heart turned over in him.

"Because it's a sin!" she cried tempestuously.

"Who said it's a sin?"

"He makes it a sin. He's like a bear with a sore head for days after. Don't you see, Jerry," she cried, springing excitedly to her feet and shaking her head at him, "it's never anything but adultery with him, and he goes away and curses himself because he hasn't the strength to resist it."

"Adultery?" repeated Fogarty, the familiar word knocking at his conscience as if it were Tom Whitton himself at the door.

"Whatever you call it," Una rushed on. "It's always adultery, adultery, adultery, and I'm always a bad woman, and he always wants to show God that it wasn't him but me, and I'm sick and tired of it. I want a man to make me feel like a respectable married woman for once in my life. You see, I feel quite respectable with you, although I know I shouldn't." She looked in the mirror of the dressing-table and her face fell. "Oh, Lord!" she sighed. "I don't look it. . . . I'll be down in two minutes now, Jerry," she said eagerly, thrusting out her lips to him, her old, brilliant, excitable self.

"You're grand," he muttered.

As she went into the bathroom, she turned in another excess of emotion and threw her arms about him. As he kissed her, she pressed herself close to him till his head swam. There was a mawkish, girlish grin on her face. "Darling!" she said in an agony of passion, and it was as if their loneliness enveloped them like a cloud.

As he went downstairs, he was very thoughtful. He heard Tom's key in the lock and looked at himself in the mirror over the fireplace. He heard Tom's step in the hall, and it sounded in his ears as it had never sounded before, like that of a man carrying a burden too great for him. He realized that he had never before seen Whitton as he really was, a man at war with his animal nature, longing for some high, solitary existence of the intellect and imagination. And he knew that the three of them, Tom, Una, and himself, would die as they had lived, their desires unsatisfied.

VANITY

THERE are a lot of things old bishops have to put up with besides old age, loneliness, and lack of domestic comforts, and the worst of these is coadjutors. To be God Almighty—the just and moral Governor of the universe—for years and years, and then have an assistant God Almighty tagged on you to see that your justice and morality are of the proper kind, is a more than human ordeal. The Bishop of Moyle, the Most Reverend Dr. Gallogly, called his coadjutor the Stump, the Spy, or the Boy, according to the way he felt about him. Mostly the Boy. The Boy had nasty supercilious ways that the Bishop detested. He let on to know a lot about French history, gave himself out for an authority on food and wine, jeered at Dr. Gallogly's coffee—the best bottled coffee on the market—and mocked at Dr. Gallogly's statement that the best food and wine in the world were to be had on the train from Holyhead to Euston. It must be admitted that the Bishop was vulnerable to that sort of criticism. As a one-time Professor of Dogmatic Theology he tended to turn everything into a dogma.

What was worse than that, the coadjutor was a bit of a snob, and what was worst of all, he had the illusion that at eighty-six the Bishop was past his prime, whereas the Bishop knew well that he had never been brighter in his wits. Just to show Lanigan, he would suddenly order round the car, drive a couple of hundred miles to Dublin, stay at the best hotel, interview three Ministers and ask them all about their Departments, and then come home and tell Lanigan nothing. Lanigan let on to be amused at this as just another example of the old Bishop's irresponsibility, but, being an inquisitive man himself, the Bishop knew he was mad at not knowing what went on, and only pretended not to care out of vanity. Vanity—the besetting sin of people in religion, according to Dr. Gallogly—was Lanigan's as well, and at heart the Bishop knew he was wild.

Whenever the notion of going to Dublin struck the Bishop, he always made inquiries about people from Moyle who might be staying there, so that he could call. He knew they liked that; it was a thing they could brag about, and afterwards they came back and said what a wonderful old man he was—another thorn in Lanigan's flesh.

One morning before he set out, he discovered that one of his curates was in a nursing home in Dublin for a major operation.

"Father O'Brien?" he exclaimed in astonishment. "What's he doing with an operation. Sure, he's only—what is he, father?"

"Forty-five, my Lord."

"Forty-five! And having operations! Sure, there's no sense in that. Remind me to go and see Father O'Brien, Paddy," he added to his chauffeur.

Even the Bishop's best friend wouldn't have pretended that this was pure kindness, though he had plenty of that. It was mainly wonder at himself, having reached the age of eighty-six without a surgeon's ever sticking a knife in him, while a whole generation of priests was growing up that couldn't even reach forty-five without an operation of some sort. Motor-cars! It couldn't be anything else only motor-cars.

And every step he climbed up to the first-floor room of the nursing home, the Bishop vacillated between good nature and complacency; good nature in being able to do a good turn for a lonesome young priest, far from his friends and family, and a furious complacency that it wasn't the young fellow of forty-five who was coming to visit the old man, but the fine, upstanding old man of eighty-six who was coming to visit the young fellow. And the two emotions mingled in the triumphant smile with which he opened the young priest's door and trumpeted joyously "Father O'Brien, do you want me to suspend you? Wouldn't you get up out of that and attend to your duties?" That would get back to Lanigan as well.

What at home might have been an ordeal for the curate became, because of the unfamiliar surroundings and the Bishop's excitement, a most enjoyable occasion for both. The Bishop was no fool, but because he was behaving rather foolishly, he talked with more freedom than he would otherwise have permitted himself about the Moyle clergy and their families. A bishop has to know everything, and he realized that you could never know a man unless you knew his family. You could never explain the extraordinary behaviour of a man like Lanigan unless you knew about his brother, the parish priest, who not only had died young of a particularly wishy-washy disease that would never have killed anyone else but had suffered for two years before he died from scruples. Scruples!

"Nerves!" said the Bishop. "All that family were neurotic. You'll see, he'll go just the same way."

He returned to his hotel, saying to Paddy, his "man": "That'll show them, Paddy," and Paddy grinned because he knew well whom the Bishop was referring to. There is nobody who resents a coadjutor more than a Bishop's man. The lounge of the hotel was crowded and several people were waiting for the lift, but by this time the Bishop's complacency was contemptuous of every obstacle. "Ah, I can't be bothered waiting for that machine," he said, loud enough to be overheard by everyone; and went up the stairs "like a hare," as Paddy put it, though this was really comparison gone mad.

He negotiated the main stair successfully, but when he came to a flight of six steps leading disconcertingly from one level to another, he slipped. He had only six steps to fall, but he knew they might as well have been twenty. He was dished. He didn't move; he knew it wasn't safe. "Pride goeth before a fall," he thought. "I should have waited for that blooming old lift."

"I think I'm hurt," he said to the waiter who rushed to his aid. "Don't tell anyone. Get something to lift me in on and call Dr. Jameson."

It was agony being transferred to the stretcher and from the stretcher to the bed, but pain was the least of the Bishop's troubles, and the tears in his blue eyes were as much humiliation as anything else. After an irreproachable life of eighty-six years he was suddenly, because of what he now called "a mad vagary," no longer his own master, and as much subject to stretcher-bearers, doctors, and nurses as any poor curate. Lanigan's opportunity had come. No longer would they talk of him in Moyle as a wonderful old man. The shock of it was almost enough to make him lose his reason.

"Am I bad?" he asked the doctor bleakly.

"It looks as if you've broken your shoulder and leg," said the doctor, a brisk, moon-faced young man. "We'll have to get you to hospital and see if there's anything else."

"Am I going to die?" asked the Bishop almost hopefully. If he were really going to die, there would be no further problem.

"You must be pretty tough to have reached your age," said the doctor, who was privately convinced that the Bishop wouldn't leave the hospital outside a box.

"Ah, I'm tough enough," said the Bishop. "Couldn't you do whatever you have to do here?"

"I could not," said the doctor in alarm.

"Why couldn't you?" asked the Bishop angrily. He hated to be contradicted in that positive way—it is one of the drawbacks of having been Almighty God.

"Because I have to get an X-ray at once."

"Couldn't you get it here? I'm a busy man. I haven't the time for going to hospital."

"But you have to go to hospital."

"If you were in my position, you'd see why I don't want to go to hospital," the Bishop said earnestly. "People think when a man has authority that he can do as he likes. He can't. He always has people after him, trying to make out he's not fit to look after himself. They want to treat you as if you were a child. If this gets round, it's going to be very awkward for me."

"But an accident can happen to anybody," protested the doctor.

"An accident can happen to a young man," the Bishop said, wincing. "What happens to an old man isn't supposed to be an accident. You'd think, the way they go on, that we did it out of spite. The manager here is an old friend of mine. I can trust him to keep his mind to himself."

"You're asking for impossibilities," the doctor said. "You needn't be worried about the nursing home. You'll be as comfortable there as you are here."

"I don't give a rap about comfort," said the Bishop with an indignant flash of his blue eyes. "But if I go into a nursing home, 'twill be all round Moyle by tomorrow."

"It'll be all round Moyle anyway."

"It will not be all round Moyle, if I can prevent it."

"But people will have to know."

"Why will they have to know?" the Bishop asked fiercely. It was bad enough to be enduring that pain and worse to be enduring complete helplessness, without being contradicted into the bargain. "What business is it of anyone's?" Then, as his mind began again to play with the possibilities, his voice grew milder. "Supposing I do go to hospital, can't I go under a false name?"

"But you'd have to tell the nuns," said the doctor aghast.

"I would *not* tell the nuns," the Bishop said with renewed irascibility. "You don't know what you're talking about I know more about nuns than you do, and I wouldn't tell a nun anything."

"But they'd have to know you were a clergyman."

"I tell you you don't know what you're talking about, man. A clergyman in this country has no privacy. The first thing they'd want to know was what diocese I was from, and then there would be a nun or a nurse with a brother a priest in the same diocese. As a matter of fact, there's a curate there from my own diocese. There's too much curiosity about priests in this country."

"Let me give you something to ease that pain before you talk any more," said the doctor, seeing that the Bishop was on the point of collapse.

"I'm not going to be taking any drugs from you till I know where I stand," said the Bishop. "What sort of woman is the Reverend Mother in that place?"

"She's a nice, friendly woman."

"Never mind how friendly she is. Where is she from?"

"I never asked her."

"And isn't it a great wonder you wouldn't find out?" said the Bishop, who knew that if only he knew her father or her brother, he could guess how reliable she was. "Is she young or old?"

"Oldish."

"Ask her to come here and talk to me."

"Do you know, my Lord, you're a very obstinate old man?" said the doctor.

"Ah, if you had my responsibilities, you'd be the same," grunted the Bishop without rancour. He liked to be told he was obstinate. It showed that he was a man who knew his own mind. "Bring her here to me and I'll talk to her myself."

Ten minutes later the doctor returned with the nun. She was an oldish, soft-mannered, gigglesome woman who almost smothered the Bishop with her solicitude. He let her moan on, knowing it was only part of her stock in trade, and waited till the doctor left the room before putting his hand on hers.

"The doctor is a very bright young man, mother," he said earnestly, "but he's not easy to talk to. 'Tisn't often you'll find a layman that can understand the difficulties of people in religion."

"Sure, how could he?" she asked.

"And the reason is," he said solemnly, "that every calling has its own graces and temptations. Now, the great temptation of religious people is vanity."

"I wonder, my Lord," she said coyly, as if she had noticed a few others.

"You needn't," replied the Bishop in the tone he used for proclaiming the merits of the Holyhead train. "That is what makes it so hard for people in religion to be growing old. You're a young woman yet," he went on with brazen flattery, "so you wouldn't know."

"Oh, indeed, I'm afraid, so far as that goes, I'm older than you give me credit for," she said, growing alarmingly girlish.

"Why then, indeed, you are not," said the Bishop confidently, knowing that he had won her ear. "But your own turn will come. You'll see the young people pushing you to make way for them, watching you and criticizing you; waiting for you to make a slip."

"Ah, indeed, my Lord, I've seen it already."

"I can see you're an understanding woman," said the Bishop solemnly. "Now, mother, this is a thing I could not say to a lay person, but I can say it to you. I have a coadjutor, and we do not get on. I know this won't go any further. That young man takes too much on himself. He thinks I'm not fit to look after myself. If he knows I had an accident, it will give him a hold over me. He will say I am not fit to be taking decisions on my own. I do not like to be criticizing, but there is nothing he is not vain enough to think."

"My Lord," she said in alarm, "I don't think you know what you're asking."

"Mother," he said compellingly, "there is nothing an intelligent woman cannot do, if she puts her mind to it."

"My Lord," she said, "there is nothing an inquisitive woman can't find out if she puts her mind to it."

However, she gave her word to do her best. There had been, she admitted, certain private patients whose identity had had to be concealed for reasons of policy, and some distinguished patients whose delirium tremens had to be disguised as something else. She would do what she could. That evening the Bishop was comfortably settled in a room corridors away from the rest of the nursing home, with two old nuns to look after him. The old nuns had long ceased to be active; one of them was crippled with rheumatics and the other slightly gone in the head, but they rejoiced in their responsibility, exulted in the fact that at last they had been found indispensable, revenged themselves on those who had slighted their age and infirmity by a scornful silence, and guarded the Bishop with something approaching ferocity.

The Bishop was in great pain, but even the pain didn't hinder his feeling of complacency. He had arranged everything. The curate was in the same nursing home, and was probably lying awake marvelling at the Bishop's sturdy health, while all the time the Bishop was lying near him, as helpless as himself, but content in the feeling that what Father O'Brien didn't know wouldn't harm him. The essence of authority consists in keeping your secrets.

But after the first day or two even the Bishop became aware of the atmosphere of mystery in which Reverend Mother had wrapped him. She was the only other nun permitted to visit him. The nurses weren't allowed into his room at all. But the trouble with the Bishop's gallant old watch-dogs was that they had lost their teeth. They were easy game for the younger nuns and the nurses, because Sister Martha's bad head and Sister Dympna's bad legs meant that when they left his room there was no guarantee that they would ever get back. On the third day the door suddenly opened and a middle-aged, scraggy-looking nurse came in and looked at him in apparent astonishment.

"I'm sorry," she said, giving him a crooked smile. "Are you Mr. Murphy?"

"No," said the Bishop with a glare. "I'm Mr. Dempsey."

"You wouldn't be one of the Dempseys from Limerick?" she asked. "The motor people?"

"No," he replied brazenly. "My family came from Kanturk."

"We had a nurse one time from Kanturk," she said, screwing up her eyes. "Lucey, her name was. You wouldn't know her?"

"She must be from another part of Kanturk," said the Bishop.

"I dare say," she said, realizing that she had met her match. "From the other side of the post office. What happened you anyway?"

"A fall I got off my bicycle," said the Bishop.

An inquisitive man himself, the Bishop deeply resented inquisitiveness, and he had never met inquisitiveness to match that of the nurse. For a while after she left the room he was boiling with rage and decided that it was almost a matter for a pastoral letter. But as he thought of it, he realized that there was something about the nurse's air which he resented even more. The

woman had been familiar with him. She had shown him no
proper respect. As he thought of it his anger vanished and gave
place to a feeling of his own guile. He realized now that Reverend Mother had really succeeded in baffling her staff, and that
they thought he was probably a rich businessman or politician
whose illness had to be concealed from his enemies. It impressed
him that even as such he had been treated with such little ceremony. As a young priest he had noticed how conversation
changed when he entered a room. Now, in his old age, he was
getting the real thing—the tone people adopted among themselves. The religious life was too sheltered. As a result he never
reported the visit of the nurse and even waited impatiently for
her to come back.

In her place there came a young and good-looking girl who
didn't even pretend to have strayed into his room by accident.
She looked at him with a guilty air, and then her small, keen
eyes started to wander, looking for a clue.

"They say you were in America; were you?" she asked.

"What makes them think that?" asked the Bishop.

"I don't know. I suppose because you don't seem to have any
family here."

"Well, I'll tell you the truth, girl," the Bishop said slyly, "I
haven't a family. I was never what you'd call a marrying man."

"Why would you?" she asked with a shrug. "I suppose you
can get them without."

For a moment the Bishop was so stunned that he almost gave
himself away. He looked at the young nurse again, but her pretty
face still remained vague and sweet and innocent.

"Isn't that a shocking thing for a girl like you to say?" he asked
indignantly.

"What's shocking about it?" she asked ingenuously. "I suppose you're not going to pretend you did without them?"

It left the Bishop very thoughtful. There were apparently lots
of things that had escaped him even in his eighty-six years. "Too
sheltered," he muttered to himself again. "Too blooming sheltered. We don't know the half that's going on. We might as well
have blinkers." What surprised him most was that he was be-

coming almost attached to his anonymity, and grew quite hopeful when he heard a woman's step outside his door that it might be another of the nurses coming to pump him. When the first nurse returned to test a new theory of his identity and told him a dirty story, he wasn't even shocked. It had never occurred to him before that women knew dirty stories. "We live and learn," he thought.

Reverend Mother arranged his departure as she had arranged his arrival. The two old nuns knelt for his blessing, and had a little bawl because they would again be regarded as old and useless. One of them guarded the landing and another the hall while Paddy took down the bags. They passed the door of the curate's room. He was still there, poor fellow, though beginning to come round.

"I suppose you'll go straight to the hotel?" said the doctor.

"I will not," replied the Bishop. "I want to know what's going on in Moyle. That coadjutor of mine only waits till my back is turned."

"I can tell you now you're a very lucky man," said the doctor. "I thought you were for the long road. I have a patient of twenty-two that the same thing happened to, and he'll never walk again."

"Poor fellow! Poor fellow!" said the Bishop perfunctorily. "I suppose a lot of it is having the stamina."

He was bitterly disappointed on reaching Moyle to discover that everyone knew of his accident, but surprised at the warmth of his welcome. Crowds gathered and knelt for his blessing in the street, and the second day, when he called at Cronin's Hotel, he was cheered as he emerged. It puzzled him a lot. As a dogmatic theologian he never enthused himself, and he didn't understand other people's enthusing. It wouldn't have occurred to him that in a small town even the presence of two bishops was nearly as good a tonic as a boxing match.

"What the blazes ails them?" he asked Jerry Cronin.

"Ah, well, people were very upset when they heard of the accident," said Jerry in surprise.

"And I suppose they knew all about it within twenty-four hours?" said the Bishop indignantly.

"Oh, sooner than that, my Lord, sooner than that," said Jerry with a shocked air.

"Nuns! Nuns! Nuns!" muttered the Bishop. "You can never trust nuns."

DARCY IN THE LAND
OF YOUTH

I

ONE of the few things Mick Darcy remembered of what the monks in the North Monastery had taught him was the story of Oisin, an old chap who fell in love with a fairy queen called Niamh and went to live with her in the Land of Youth. Then, one day when he was a bit homesick, he got leave from her to come back and have a look at Ireland, only she warned him he wasn't to get off his horse. When he got back, he found his pals all dead and the whole country under the rule of St. Patrick, and, seeing a poor labourer trying to lift a heavy stone that was too big for him but that would have been nothing at all to fellows of his own generation, Oisin bent down to give him a hand. While he was doing it, the saddle-girth broke and Oisin was thrown to the ground, an old, tired, spiritless man with nothing better to do than get converted and be thinking of how much better things used to be in his day. Mick had never thought much of it as a story. It had always struck him that Oisin was a bit of a mug, not to know when he was well off.

But the old legends all have powerful morals though you never realize it till one of them gives you a wallop over the head. During the war, when he was out of a job, Mick went to England as a clerk in a war factory, and the first few weeks he spent there were the most miserable of his life. He found the English as queer as they were always supposed to be; people with a great welcome for themselves and very little for anyone else.

Then there were the air-raids, which the English pretended not to notice. In the middle of the night Mick would be awakened by the wail of a siren, and the thump of faraway guns like all the windowpanes of heaven rattling: the thud of artillery, getting louder, accompanied a faint buzz like a cat's purring that seemed to rise out of a corner of the room and mount the walls to the ceiling, where it hung, breathing in steady spurts, exactly like a cat. Pretending not to notice things like that struck Mick as too much of a good thing. He would rise and dress himself and sit lonesome by the gas fire, wondering what on earth had induced him to leave his little home in Cork, his girl, Ina, and his pal, Chris—his world.

The daytime was no better. The works were a couple of miles outside the town, and he shared an office with a woman called Penrose and a Jew called Isaacs. Penrose called him "Mr. Darcy," and when he asked her to call him "Mick" she wouldn't. The men all called him "Darcy," which sounded like an insult. Isaacs was the only one who called him "Mick," but it soon became plain that he only wanted to convert Mick from being what he called "a fellow traveller," whatever the hell that was.

"I'm after travelling too much," Mick said bitterly.

He wasn't a discontented man, but he could not like England or the English. On his afternoons off, he took long, lonesome country walks, but there was no proper country either, only red-brick farms and cottages with crumpled oak frames and high red-tiled roofs; big, smooth, sick-looking fields divided by low, neat hedges which made them look as though they all called one another by their surnames; handsome-looking pubs that were never open when you wanted them, with painted signs and non-sensical names like "The Star and Garter" or "The Shoulder of Mutton." Then he would go back to his lodgings and write long, cynical, mournful letters home to Chris and Ina, and all at once he and Chris would be strolling down the hill to Cork city in the evening light, and every old house and bush stood out in his imagination as if spotlit, and everyone who passed hailed them and called him Mick. It was so vivid that when his old landlady came in to draw the black-out, his heart would suddenly turn over.

But one day in the office he got chatting with a girl called Janet who had something to do with personnel. She was a tall, thin, fair-haired girl with a quick-witted laughing air. She listened to him with her head forward and her eyebrows raised. There was nothing in the least alarming about Janet, and she didn't seem to want to convert him to anything, unless it was books, which she seemed to be very well up in, so he asked her politely to have supper with him, and she agreed eagerly and even called him Mick without being asked. She seemed to know as if by instinct that this was what he wanted.

It was a great ease to him; he now had someone to argue with, and he was no longer scared of the country or the people. Besides, he had begun to master his job, and that always gave him a feeling of self-confidence. He had a quiet conviction of his own importance and hated servility of any sort. One day a group of them, including Janet, had broken off work for a chat when the boss's brisk step was heard, and they all scattered—even Janet hastily said: "Good-bye." But Mick just gazed out the window, his hands still in his pockets, and when the boss came in, brisk and lantern-jawed, Mick looked at him over his shoulder and gave him a greeting. The boss only grinned. "Settling in, Darcy?" he asked. "Just getting the hang of things," Darcy replied modestly. Next day the boss sent for him, but it was only to ask his advice about a scheme of office organization. Mick gave his opinions in a forthright way. That was another of his little weaknesses; he liked to hear himself talk. Judging by the way the boss questioned him, he had no great objection.

But country and people still continued to give him shocks. One evening, for instance, he had supper in the flat which Janet shared with a girl called Fanny, who was an analyst in one of the factories. Fanny was a good-looking, dark-haired girl with a tendency to moodiness. She asked how Mick was getting on with Mrs. Penrose.

"Oh," Mick said with a laugh, sitting back with his hands in his trousers pockets, "she still calls me Mister Darcy."

"I suppose that's only because she expects to be calling you something else before long," said Fanny.

"Oh, no, Fanny," said Janet. "You wouldn't know Penrose now. She's a changed woman. With her husband in Egypt, Peter posted to Yorkshire, and no one to play with but George, she's started to complain of people who can't appreciate the simple things of life. Any day now she'll start talking about primroses."

"Penrose?" Mick exclaimed with gentle incredulity, throwing himself back farther in his chair. "I never thought she was that sort. Are you sure, Janet? I'd have thought she was an iceberg."

"An iceberg?" Janet said gleefully, rubbing her hands. "Oh, boy! A blooming fireship!"

"You're not serious?" murmured Mick, looking doubtfully at the two girls and wondering what fresh abysses might remain beneath the smooth surface of English convention.

Going home that night through the pitch-dark streets, he no longer felt a complete stranger. He had made friends with two of the nicest girls a man could wish for—fine broad-minded girls you could talk to as you'd talk to a man. He had to step in the roadway to make room for a couple of other girls, flicking their torches on and off before them; schoolgirls, to judge by their voices. "Of course, he's married," one of them said as they passed, and then went off into a rippling scale of laughter that sounded almost unearthly in the sinister silence and darkness.

A bit too broad-minded, thought Mick, coming to himself. Freedom was all very well, but you could easily have too much of that too.

II

But the shock about Penrose was nothing to the shocks that came on top of it. In the spring evenings Janet and he cycled off into the near-by villages and towns for their drinks. Sometimes Fanny came too, but she didn't seem very keen on it. It was as though she felt herself in the way, but at the same time she saw them go off with such a reproachful air that she made Janet feel bad.

One Sunday evening they went to church together. It seemed to surprise Janet that Mick insisted on going to Mass every Sun-

day morning, and she wanted him to see what a Protestant service was like. Her own religion was a bit mixed. Her father had
been a Baptist lay preacher; her mother a Methodist; but Janet
herself had fallen in love with a parson at the age of eleven and
become church for a while till she joined the Socialist Party and
decided that church was too conservative. Most of the time she
did not seem to Mick to have any religion at all, for she said that
you were just buried and rotted and that was all anyone knew.
That seemed the general view. There were any amount of religions, but nobody seemed to believe anything.

It was against Mick's principles, but Janet was so eager that
he went. It was in a little town ten miles from where they lived,
with a brown Italian fountain in the market-place and the old
houses edging out the grey church with its balustraded parapet
and its blue clock-face shining in the sun. Inside there was a
young sailor playing the organ while another turned over for
him. The parson rang the bell himself. Only three women, one of
whom was the organist, turned up.

The service, to Mick's mind, was an awful sell. The parson
turned his back on them and read prayers at the east window; the
organist played a hymn, which the three people in church took
up, and then the parson read more prayers. There was no religion
in it that Mick could see, but Janet joined in the hymns and
seemed to get all worked up.

"Pity about Fanny," she said when they were drinking their
beer in the inn yard later. "We could be very comfortable in the
flat only for her. Haven't you a friend who'd take her off our
hands?"

"Only in Ireland," said Mick.

"Perhaps he'd come," said Janet. "Tell him you've a nice girl
for him. She really is nice, Mick."

"Oh, I know," said Mick in surprise. "But hasn't she a fellow
already?"

"Getting a fellow for Fanny is the great problem of my life,"
Janet said ruefully. "I'll never be afraid of a jealous husband
after her. The sight of her johns with the seat up is enough to
depress her for a week."

"I wonder if she'd have him," Mick said thoughtfully, thinking

how very nice it would be to have a friend as well as a girl. Janet
was excellent company, and a good woman to learn from, but
there were times when Mick would have been glad of someone
from home with whom he could sit in judgment on the country
of his exile.

"If he's anything like you, she'd jump at him," said Janet.

"Oh, there's no resemblance," chuckled Mick, who had never
before been buttered up like this and loved it. "Chris is a holy
terror."

"A terror is about what Fanny needs," Janet said grimly.

It was only as the weeks went on that he realized that she
wasn't exaggerating. Fanny always received him politely, but he
had the feeling that one of these days she wouldn't receive him at
all. She didn't intend to be rude, but she watched his plate as
Janet filled it, and he saw she begrudged him even the food he
ate. Janet did her best to shake her out of it by bringing her with
them.

"Oh, come on, Fanny!" she said one evening with a weary air.
"I only want to show Mick the Plough in Alton."

"Well, who'd know it better?" Fanny asked sepulchrally.

"There's no need to be difficult," Janet replied with a flash of
temper.

"Well, it's not my fault if I'm inhibited, is it?" Fanny asked
with a cowed air.

"I didn't say you were inhibited," Janet replied in a ringing
tone. "I said you were difficult."

"Same thing from your point of view, isn't it?" Fanny asked.
"Oh, I suppose I was born that way. You'd better let me alone."

All the way out, Janet was silent and Mick saw she was in a
flaming temper, though he failed to understand what it was all
about. It was distressing about Fanny, no doubt, but things were
pleasanter without her. The evening was fine and the sun in
wreath and veil, with the fields a bright blue-green. The narrow
road wound between bulging walls of flint, laced with brick, and
rows of old cottages with flower-beds in front that leaned this
way and that as if they were taking life easy. It wasn't like Ireland, but still it wasn't bad. He was getting used to it as he was
to being called Darcy. At the same time the people sometimes

left him as mystified as ever. He didn't know what Fanny meant about being inhibited, or why she seemed to think it wrong. She spoke of it as if it was some sort of infectious disease.

"We'll have to get Chris for Fanny all right," he said. "It's extraordinary, though. An exceptional girl like that, you'd think she'd have fellows falling over her."

"I don't think Fanny will ever get a man," Janet replied in the shrill, scolding voice she used when upset. "I've thrown dozens of them in her way, but she won't even make an effort. I believe she's one of those quite attractive women who go through life without ever knowing what it's about. She's just a raging mass of inhibitions."

There it was again—prohibitions, exhibitions, inhibitions! He wished to God Janet would use simple words. He knew what exhibitions were from one old man in the factory who went to jail because of them. You would assume that inhibitions meant the opposite, but if so, what were the girls grousing about?

"Couldn't we do something about them?" he asked helpfully, not wishing to display his ignorance.

"Yes, darling," she replied with a mocking air. "You can take her away to hell and give her a good roll in the hay."

Mick was so staggered that he didn't reply. Even then it took a long time for Janet's words to sink in. By this time he was used to English dirty jokes, but he knew that this was something different. No doubt Janet was joking about the roll in the hay—though he wasn't altogether sure that she was joking about that either and didn't half hope that he might take her at her word—but she was not joking about Fanny. She really meant that all that was wrong with Fanny was that she was still a virgin, and that this was a complaint she did not suffer from herself.

The smugness horrified him as much as the savagery with which it was uttered. Put in a certain way, it might be understandable, and even forgivable. Girls of Janet's kind were known at home as "damaged goods," but he had never permitted the expression to pass. He had a strong sense of justice and always tended to take the side of the underdog. Some girls had not the same strength of character as others; some were subjected to greater temptation than others; he had never met any, but he was quite sure that if he had he would have risen to the occasion. But to have a girl like that stand up and treat her own weakness as strength and another girl's strength as weakness was altogether too much for him to take. It was like asking him to stand on his head.

Having got rid of her spite, Janet began to brighten. "This is wonderful," she sighed with tranquil pleasure as they floated downhill towards Alton and the Plough, a pleasant little inn, standing at the bridge, half-timbered above and stone below, with a big yard to one side where a dozen cars were parked, and at the other a long garden with rustic seats overlooking the river. Mick didn't feel it was so very wonderful. He felt as lonely as he had done in his first weeks there. While Janet sat outside, he went to the bar for beer and stood there for a few minutes unnoticed. There was a little crowd at the bar; a bald fat man in an overcoat, with a pipe, a good-looking young man with a fancy waistcoat, and a local with a face like a turnip. The landlord, a man of about fifty, had a long, haggard face with horn-rimmed glasses, and his wife, apparently twenty years younger, was a good-looking young woman with bangs and a Lancashire accent. They were discussing a death in the village.

"I'm not against religion," the local spluttered excitedly. "I'm chapel myself, but I never tried to force me views on people. All them months poor Harry was paralysed, his wife and daughter never so much as wet his lips. That idn't right, is it? That idn't religion?"

"No, Bill," the landlord said, shaking his head. "Going too far, I call that."

"Everyone is entitled to his views, but them weren't old Harry's views, were they?"

"No, Bill," sighed the landlord's wife, "they weren't."

"I'm for freedom," Bill said, tapping his chest. "The night before he died, I come in here and got a quart of old and mild, didn't I, Joe?"

"Mild, wadn't it, Bill?" the publican asked anxiously, resettling his glasses.

"No, Joe, old and mild was always Harry's drink."

"That's right, Joe," the landlady expostulated. "Don't you re-member?"

"Funny," said her husband. "I could have swore it was mild."

"And I said to Millie and Sue, 'All right,' I said. 'You got other things to do. I'll sit up with old Harry.' Then I took out the bottle. His poor eyes lit up. Couldn't move, couldn't speak, but I shall never forget the way he looked at that bottle. I had to hold his mouth open"—Bill threw back his head and pulled one side of his mouth awry in illustration—"and let it trickle down. No. If that's religion give me beer!"

"Wonder where old Harry is now?" the fat man said, remov-ing his pipe reverently. "It's a mystery, Joe, i'nt it?"

"Shocking," the landlord said, shaking his head.

"We don't know, do we, Charles?" the landlady said sadly.

"Nobody knows," Bill bawled scornfully as he took up his pint again. "How could they? Parson pretends to know, but he don't know any more than you and me. Shove you in the ground and let the worms get you—that's all anybody knows."

It depressed Mick even more, for he felt that in some way Janet's views and those of the people in the pub were of the same kind and only the same sort of conduct could be expected from them. Neither had any proper religion and so they could not know right from wrong.

"Isn't it lovely here?" Janet sang out when he brought the drinks.

"Oh, grand," said Mick without much enthusiasm.

"We must come and spend a few days here some time. It's wonderful in the early morning. . . . You don't think I was too bitchy about Fanny, do you, Mick?"

"Oh, it's not that," he said, seeing that she had noticed his de-pression. "I wasn't thinking of Fanny particularly. It's the whole set-up here that seems so queer to me."

"Does it?" she asked with interest.

"Well, naturally—fellows and girls from the works going off on week-ends together, as if they were going to a dance."

He looked at her with mild concern as though he hoped she

might enlighten him about a matter of general interest. But she didn't respond.

"Having seen the works, can you wonder?" she asked, and took a long drink of her beer.

"But when they get tired of one another, they go off with someone else," he protested. "Or back to the fellow they started with. Like Hilda in the packing shed. She's knocking round with Dorman, and when her husband comes back she'll drop him. At least, she says she will."

"Isn't that how it usually ends?" she asked politely, raising her brows and speaking in a superior tone that left him with nothing to say. This time she really succeeded in scandalizing him.

"Oh, come, come, Janet!" he said scornfully. "You can't take that line with me. You're not going to pretend there's nothing more than that in it?"

"Well, I suppose, like everything else, it's just what you make of it," she replied with a sophisticated shrug.

"But that's not making anything at all of it," he said, beginning to grow heated. "If it's no more than a roll in the hay, as you call it, there's nothing in it for anybody."

"And what do you think it should be?" she asked with a politeness that seemed to be the equivalent of his heat. He realized that he was not keeping to the level of a general discussion. He could distinctly hear how common his accent had become, but excitement and a deep-seated feeling of injury carried him away.

"But look here, Janet," he protested, sitting back stubbornly with his hands in his trousers pockets, "learning to live with somebody isn't a thing you can pick up in a week-end. It's a blooming job for life. You wouldn't take up a job somewhere in the middle, expecting to like it, and intending to drop it in a few months' time if you didn't, would you?"

"Oh, Mick," she groaned in mock distress, "don't tell me you have inhibitions too!"

"Oh, you can call them what you like," retorted Mick, growing commoner as he was dragged down from the heights of abstract discussion to the expression of his own wounded feelings. "I saw the fellows who have no inhibitions, as you call them, and they didn't seem to me to have very much else either. If that's all you want from a man, you won't have far to go."

By this time Janet had realized that she was dealing with feelings rather than with general ideas and was puzzled. After a moment's thought she began to seek for a point of reconciliation.

"But after all, Mick, you've had affairs yourself, haven't you?" she asked reasonably.

Now, of all questions, this was the one Mick dreaded most, because, owing to a lack of suitable opportunities, for which he was in no way to blame, he had not. For the matter of that, so far as he knew, nobody of his acquaintance had either. He knew that in the matter of experience, at least, Janet was his superior, and, coming from a country where men's superiority—affairs or no affairs—was unchallenged, he hesitated to admit that, so far as experience went, Fanny and he were in the one boat. He was not untruthful, and he had plenty of moral courage. There was no difficulty in imagining himself settling deeper down onto his bench and saying firmly and quietly: "No, Janet, I have not," but he did not say it.

"Well, naturally, I'm not an angel," he said in as modest a tone as he could command and with a shrug intended to suggest that it meant nothing in particular to him.

"Of course not, Mick," Janet replied with all the enthusiasm of a liberal mind discovering common ground with an opponent. "But then there's no argument."

"No argument, maybe," he said coldly, "but there are distinctions to be made."

"What distinctions?"

"Between playing the fool and making love," he replied with a weary air as though he could barely be bothered explaining such matters to a girl as inexperienced as she. From imaginary distinctions he went on to out-and-out prevarication. "If I went out with Penrose, for instance, that would be one thing. Going out with you is something entirely different."

"But why?" she asked as though this struck her as a doubtful compliment.

"Well, I don't like Penrose," he said mildly, hoping that he sounded more convincing than he felt. "I'm not even vaguely interested in Penrose. I am interested in you. See the difference?"

"Not altogether," Janet replied in her clear, unsentimental way. "You don't mean that if two people are in love with one another, they should have affairs with somebody else, do you?"

"Of course I don't," snorted Mick, disgusted by this horrid example of English literal-mindedness. "I don't see what they want having affairs at all for."

"Oh, so that's what it is!" she said with a nod.

"That's what it is," Mick said feebly, realizing the cat was out of the bag at last. "Love is a serious business. It's a matter of responsibilities. If I make a friend, I don't begin by thinking what use I can make of him. If I meet a girl I like, I'm not going to begin calculating how cheap I can get her. I don't want anything cheap," he added with passion. "I'm not going to rush into anything till I know the girl well enough to try and make a decent job of it. Is that plain?"

"Remarkably plain," Janet replied icily. "You mean you're not that sort of man. Let me buy you a drink."

"No, thanks."

"Then I think we'd better be getting back," she said, rising and looking like the wrath of God.

Mick, crushed and humiliated, followed her at a slouch, his hands still in his trousers pockets. It wasn't good enough. At home a girl would have gone on with the argument till one of them fell unconscious, and in argument Mick had real staying power, so he felt she was taking an unfair advantage. Of course, he saw that she had some reason. However you looked at it, she had more or less told him that she expected him to be her lover, and he had more or less told her to go to hell, and he had a suspicion that this was an entirely new experience for Janet. She might well feel mortified.

But the worst of it was that, thinking it over, he realized that even then he had not been quite honest. He had not told her he already had a girl at home. He believed all he had said, but he did not believe it quite so strongly as all that; not so as not to make exceptions. Given time, he might quite easily have made an exception of Janet. She was the sort of girl people made an exception of. It was the shock that had made him express himself so violently; the shock of realizing that a girl he cared for had lived with other men. He had reacted that way almost in protest against them.

But the real shock had been the discovery that he minded so much what she was.

III

They never resumed the discussion openly, on the same terms, and it seemed as though Janet had forgiven him, but only just. The argument was always there beneath the surface, ready to break out again. It flared up whenever she mentioned Fanny—"I suppose one day she'll meet an Irishman, and they can discuss one another's inhibitions." Or when she mentioned other men she had known, like Bill, with whom she had spent a holiday in Dorset, or an American called Tom with whom she had gone to the Plough in Alton, she seemed to be contrasting the joyous past with the dreary present, and she became cold and insolent.

Mick gave as good as he got. He had a dirty tongue, and he had considerable more ammunition than she. The canteen was always full of gossip about who was living with whom, or who had stopped living with whom, or whose wife or husband had returned and found him or her living with someone else, and he passed it on with a quizzical air. The first time she said "Good!" in a ringing voice. After that, she contented herself with a shrug, and Mick suggested ingenuously that perhaps it took all those religions to deal with so much fornication. "One religion would be more than enough for Ireland," she retorted, and Mick grinned and admitted himself beaten.

But, all the same, he could not help feeling that it wasn't nice. He remembered what Fanny had said about nobody's knowing the Plough better, and Janet about how nice it was in the early morning. Really, really, it wasn't nice! It seemed to show a complete lack of sensibility in her to think of bringing him to a place where she had stayed with somebody else, and made him suspicious of every other place she brought him. He had never been able to share her enthusiasm for old villages of red-brick cottages, all coloured like geraniums, grouped about a grey church tower,

but he lost even the desire to share it when he found himself
wondering what connection it had with Bill or Tom.

At the same time, he could not do without her. They met every
evening after work, went off together on Saturday afternoons,
and she even came to Mass with him on Sunday mornings. Nor
was there any feeling that she was critical of it. She followed the
service with great devotion. As a result, before he returned home
on his first leave, everything seemed to have changed between
them. She no longer criticized Fanny's virginity and ceased altogether to refer to Bill and Tom. Indeed, from her conversation
it would have been hard to detect that she had ever known such
men, much less been intimate with them. Mick wondered whether
it wasn't possible for a woman to be immoral and yet remain innocent at heart and decided regretfully that it wasn't likely. But
no wife or sweetheart could have shown more devotion than she
in the last week before his return, and when they went to the
station and walked arm-in-arm to the end of the long, draughty
platform to say good-bye, she was stiff with unspoken misery. She
seemed to feel it was her duty to show no sign of emotion.

"You will come back, Mick, won't you?" she asked in a clear
voice.

"Why?" Mick asked banteringly. "Do you think you can keep
off Americans for a fortnight?"

Then she spat out a word that showed only too clearly her
intimacy with Americans and others. It startled Mick. The English had strong ideas about when you could joke and when you
couldn't, and she seemed to think this was no time for joking. To
his surprise, he found she was trembling all over.

At any other time he would have argued with her, but already
in spirit he was half-way home. There, beyond the end of the line,
was Cork, and with it home and meat and butter and nights of
tranquil sleep. When he leaned out of the window to wave good-
bye, she was standing like a statue, looking curiously desolate.
Her image faded quickly, for the train was crowded with Irish
service-men and women, clerks and labourers, who gradually
sorted themselves out into north and south, country and town,
and within five minutes, Mick, in a fug of steam heat and tobacco

smoke, was playing cards with a group of men from the South Side who were calling him by his Christian name. Janet was already farther away than any train could leave her.

It was the following evening when he reached home. He had told no one of his coming and arrived in an atmosphere of sensation. He went upstairs to his own little whitewashed room with the picture of the Sacred Heart over his bed and lost himself in the study of his shelf of books. Then he shaved and, without waiting for more than a cup of tea, set off down the road to Ina's. Ina was the youngest of a large family, and his arrival there created a sensation too. Elsie, the eldest, a fat, jolly girl, just home from work, shouted with laughter at him.

"He smelt the sausages."

"You can keep your old sausages," Mick said scornfully. "I'm taking Ina out to supper."

"You're what?" shouted Elsie. "You have high notions like the goats in Kerry."

"But I have to make my little brothers' supper, honey," Ina said laughingly as she smoothed his hair. She was a slight, dark, radiant girl with a fund of energy.

"Tell them make it themselves," Mick said scornfully.

"Tell them, you!" cried Elsie. "Someone ought to have told them years ago, the caubogues! They're thirty, and they have no more intention of marrying than flying. Have you e'er an old job for us over there? I'm damned for the want of a man."

Ina rushed upstairs to change. Her two brothers came in, expressed astonishment at Mick's appearance, satisfaction at his promotion, incredulity at his view that the English weren't beaten, and began hammering together on the table with their knives and forks.

"Supper up! Supper up!" shouted the elder, casting his eyes on the ceiling. "We can't wait all night. Where the hell is Ina?"

"Coming out to dinner with me," replied Mick with a sniff, feeling that for the first time in his life he was uttering a curtain line.

They called for Chris, an undersized lad with a pale face like a fist and a voice like melted butter. He expressed pleasure at seeing them, but gave no other signs of it. It was part of Chris's line never to be impressed by anything. In a drawling voice he commented on priests, women, and politicians, and there was little left of any of them when he had done. He had always regarded Mick as a bit of a softy because of his fondness for Ina. For himself, he would never keep a girl for more than a month because it gave them ideas.

"What do you want going to town for supper for?" he drawled incredulously, as though this were only another indication that Mick was a bit soft in the head. "Can't ye have it at home?"

"You didn't change much anyway," said Mick with a snort of delight. "Hurry up!"

He insisted on their walking so as not to miss the view of the city he had been dreaming of for months; the shadowy perspective of winding road between flowering trees, and the spires, river, and bridges far below in evening light. His heart was overflowing. Several times they were stopped by neighbours who wanted to know how things were in the outside world. Because of the censorship, their ideas were very vague.

"Oh, all right," Mick replied modestly.

"Ye're having it bad."

"A bit noisy at times, but you get used to it," he said lightly.

"I dare say, I dare say."

There was pity rather than belief in their voices, but Mick didn't mind. It was good to be back where people cared whether you were having it bad or not. But in his heart Mick felt you didn't get used to it, that you never could, and that all of it, even Janet, was slightly unreal. He had a suspicion that he would not return. He had had enough of it.

Next morning, while he was lying in bed in his little attic, he received a letter from Janet. It must have been written while he was still on the train. She said that trying to face things without him was like trying to get used to an amputated limb; she kept on making movements before realizing that it wasn't there. He dropped the letter at that point without trying to finish it. He couldn't help feeling that it sounded unreal too.

Mick revisited all his old haunts. "You should see Fair Hill," his father said with enthusiasm. " 'Tis unknown the size that place is growing." He went to Fair Hill, to the Lough, to Glanmire, seeing them with new eyes and wishing he had someone like Janet to show them off to. But he began to realize that without a job, without money, it would not be very easy to stay on. His parents encouraged him to stay, but he felt he must spend another six months abroad and earn a little more money. Instead, he started to coax Chris into coming back with him. He knew now that his position in the factory would ensure a welcome for anyone he brought in. Besides, he grew tired of Ina's brothers telling him how the Germans would win the war, and one evening was surprised to hear himself reply in Chris's cynical drawl: "They will and what else?" Ina's brothers were surprised as well. They hadn't expected Mick to turn his coat in that way.

"You get the feeling that people here never talk of anything only religion and politics," he said one evening to Chris as they went for their walk up the Western Road.

"Ah, how bad it is!" Chris said mockingly. "Damn glad you were to get back to it. You can get a night's sleep here anyway."

"You can," Mick said in the same tone. "There's no one to stop you."

Chris looked at him in surprise, uncertain whether or not Mick meant what he seemed to mean. Mick was developing out of his knowledge entirely.

"Go on!" he said with a cautious grin. "Are they as good-natured as that?"

"Better come and see," Mick said sedately. "I have the very girl for you."

"You don't say so!" Chris exclaimed with the smile of a child who has ceased to believe in Santa Claus but likes to hear about it just the same.

"Fine-looking girl with a good job and a flat of her own," Mick went on with a smile. "What more do you want?"

Chris suddenly beamed.

"I wouldn't let Ina hear me talking like that if I was you," he said. "Some of them quiet-looking girls are a terrible hand with a hatchet."

At that moment it struck Mick with cruel force how little Ina had to reproach him with. They were passing the college, and pairs of clerks and servant girls were strolling by, whistling and calling to one another. There was hardly another man in Ireland who would have behaved as he had done. He remembered Janet at the station with her desolate air, and her letter, which he had not answered. Perhaps, after all, she meant it. Suddenly everything seemed to turn upside down in him. He was back in the bar in Alton, listening to the little crowd discussing the dead customer, and carrying out the drinks to Janet on the rustic seat. It was no longer this that seemed unreal, but the Western Road and the clerks and the servant girls. They were like a dream from which he had wakened so suddenly that he had not even realized that he was awake. And he had waked up beside a girl like Janet and had not even realized that she was real.

He was so filled with consternation that he almost told Chris about her. But he knew that Chris would no more understand him than he had understood himself. Chris would talk sagaciously about "damaged goods" as if there were only one way in which a woman could be damaged. He knew that no one would understand, for already he was thinking in a different language. Suddenly he remembered the story of Oisin that the monks had told him, and it began to have meaning for him. He wondered wildly if he would ever get back or if, like Oisin in the story, he would suddenly collapse and spend the rest of his days walking up and down the Western Road with people as old and feeble as himself, and never again see Niamh or the Land of Youth. You never knew what powerful morals the old legends had till they came home to you. On the other hand, their heroes hadn't the advantages of the telephone.

"I have to go back to town, Chris," he said, turning in his tracks. "I've just remembered I have a telephone call to put through."

"Good enough," Chris said knowingly. "I suppose you might as well tell her I'm coming too."

IV

When Chris and himself got in, the alert was still on and the station was in pitch-darkness. Outside, against the clear summer sky, shadowy figures moved with pools of light at their feet, and searchlights flickered like lightning over the battlements of the castle. For Chris, it had all the novelty it had once had for Mick, and he groaned. Mick gripped his arm and steered him confidently.

"This is nothing," he said cheerfully. "Probably only a scouting plane. Wait till they start dropping a few wagons of high explosive and you'll be able to talk."

It was sheer delight to Mick to hear himself speak in that light-hearted way of high explosives. He seemed to have become forceful and cool all at once. It had something to do with Chris's being there, as though it gave occupation to all his protective instincts. But there was something else as well. It was almost as though he were arriving home.

There was no raid, so he brought Chris round to meet the girls, and Chris groaned again at the channel of star-shaped traffic signals that twinkled between the black cliffs of houses whose bases opened mysteriously to reveal pale stencilled signs or caverns of smoky light.

Janet opened the door, gave one hasty, incredulous glance at Chris, and then hurled herself at Mick's neck. Chris opened his eyes with a start—he later admitted to Mick that he had never before seen a doll so quick off the mark. But Mick was beyond caring for appearances. While Chris and Fanny were in the throes of starting a conversation, he followed Janet into the kitchen, where she was recklessly tossing a week's rations into the pan. She was hot and excited and used two dirty words in quick succession, but he didn't mind these either. He leaned against the kitchen wall with his hands in his trousers pockets and smiled at her.

"I'm afraid you'll find I've left my principles behind me this time," he said with amusement.

"Oh, good!" she said—not as enthusiastically as he might have expected, but he put that down to the confusion caused by his unexpected arrival.

"What do you think of Chris?"

"A bit quiet, isn't he?" she asked doubtfully.

"Scared," replied Mick with a sniff of amusement. "He'll soon get over that. Should we go off somewhere for the week-end?"

"Next week-end?" she asked aghast.

"Or the one after. I don't mind."

"You're in a hurry, aren't you?"

"So would you be if you'd spent a fortnight in Cork."

"All of us?"

"The more the merrier. Let's go somewhere really good," he went on enthusiastically. "Take the bikes and make a proper tour of it. I'd like Chris to see a bit of the country."

It certainly made a difference, having Chris there. And a fortnight later the four of them set off on bicycles out of town. It was a perfect day of early summer. Landscape and houses gradually changed; old brick and flint giving place to houses of small yellow tile, tinted with golden moss, and walls of narrow tile-like stone with deep bands of mortar that made them seem as though woven. Out of the woven pull-overs rose gables with coifs of tile, like nuns' heads. It all came over Mick in a rush; the presence of his friend and of his girl and a country that he had learned to understand. While they sat on a bench outside a country public-house, he brought out the beer and smiled with quiet pride.

"Good?" he asked Chris with a slight lift of his brows.

"The beer isn't up to much, if that's what you mean," replied Chris, who still specialized in not being impressed.

In the late evening they reached their destination, having cycled through miles of suburb with gardens in flower, and dismounted in the cobbled yard of an inn where Queen Elizabeth was supposed to have stayed and Shakespeare's company performed; the walls of the narrow, twisting stairs were dark with old prints, and the windows deep embrasures that overlooked the yard. The dining-room had great oak beams and supports. At either end there was an oak dresser full of willow-ware, with silver sauce-boats hanging from the shelves and brass pitchers on top.

"You'd want to mind your head in this hole," Chris said with an aggrieved air.

"But this place is four hundred years old, man," protested Mick.

"Begor, in that time you'd think they'd make enough to re-build it," said Chris.

He was still acting in character, but Mick was just the least bit disappointed in him. He hit it off with Fanny, who had been thrown into such a panic that she was prepared to hit it off with anyone, but he seemed to have lost a lot of his dash. Mick wasn't quite sure yet but that he would take fright before Fanny. He would certainly do so if he knew what a blessed innocent she was. Whenever Mick looked at her, her dark, sullen face broke into a wistful smile that made him think of a Christian martyr's first glimpse of the lion. No doubt he would lead her to paradise, but the way was messy and uncomfortable.

After supper Janet showed them the town and finally led them to a very nice old pub which was on no street at all but was approached by a system of alleyways. The little barroom was full, and Janet and he were crowded into the yard, where they sat on a bench in the starlight. Beyond the clutter of old tiled roofs a square battlemented tower rose against the sky. Mick was perfectly happy.

"You're certain Fanny will be all right with Chris?" Janet asked anxiously.

"Oh, certain," replied Mick with a slight feeling of alarm lest his troops had opened negotiations behind his back. "Why? Did she say anything?"

"No," said Janet in a bustle of motherly solicitude, "but she's in a flat spin. I've told her everything, but she's afraid she'll get it mixed up, and if anyone could that girl will. He does understand, doesn't he?"

"Oh, perfectly," said Mick with a confidence he did not feel, but his troops were already sufficiently out of hand. If Janet started to give orders they would undoubtedly cut and run.

When they returned to the hotel and the boys retired to their room, the troops were even more depressed.

"A fellow doesn't know how well off he is," said Chris mournfully.

He said it by way of a joke, but Mick knew it was something more. Chris was even more out of his element than he had been. All his life he had practised not being impressed by anything, but in this new country there was far too much not to be impressed about.

"Why?" Mick asked from his own bed. "Would you sooner be up the Western Road?"

"Don't talk to me about the Western Road!" groaned Chris. "I think I'll never see it."

He didn't sound in the least dashing, and Mick only hoped he wouldn't break down and beg Fanny to let him off. It would be a sad end to the picture he had built up of Chris as the romantic Irishman.

Then the handle of their door turned softly and Janet tiptoed in in her bathing-wrap, her usual competent self, as though arriving in men's bedrooms at that hour of night was second nature to her. "Ready, Chris?" she whispered. Chris was a lad of great principle and Mick couldn't help admiring his manliness. With a face like death on him he went out, and Janet closed the door cautiously behind him. Mick listened to make sure he didn't hide in the toilet. Then Janet switched off the light, drew back the black-out, and, shivering slightly, opened the window on the darkened inn yard. They could hear the Klaxons from the street, while the stuffy room filled with the smells and rustlings of a summer night.

V

In the middle of the night Mick woke up and wondered where he was. When he recollected, it was with a feeling of profound satisfaction. It was as if he had laid down a heavy burden he had been carrying all his life, and in the laying down had realized that the burden was quite unnecessary. For the pleasantest part of it was that there was nothing particular about the whole business and that it left him the same man he had always been.

With a clearness of sight which seemed to be part of it, he realized that all the charm of the old town had only been a put-up job of Janet's because she had been there already with someone else. He should have known it when she took them to the pub. That, too, was her reason for suggesting this pleasant old inn. She had stayed there with someone else. It was probably the American and possibly the same bed. Women had no interest in scenery or architecture unless they had been made love to in them. And, Mick thought with amusement, that showed very good sense on their part. If he ever returned with another woman, he would also bring her here, because he had been happy here. Happiness, that was the secret the English had and the Irish lacked.

It was only then that he realized that what had wakened him was Janet's weeping. She was crying quietly beside him. At first it filled him with alarm. In his innocence he might quite easily have made a mess of it without even knowing. It was monstrous, keeping men in ignorance up to his age. He listened till he could bear it no longer.

"What is it, Jan?" he asked in concern.

"Oh, nothing," she replied, dabbing her nose viciously with her handkerchief. "Go to sleep."

"But how can I and you like that?" he asked plaintively. "Was it anything I did?"

"No, of course not, Mick."

"Because I'm sorry if it was."

"Oh, it's not that, it's not that," she replied, shaking her head miserably. "I'm just a fool, that's all."

The wretchedness of her tone made him forget his own doubts and think of her worries. Being a man of the world was all right, but Mick would always be more at home with other people's troubles. He put his arm about her and she sighed and threw a bare leg over him. It embarrassed him for a moment, but then he remembered that now he was a man of the world.

"Tell me," he whispered gently.

"Oh, it's what you said that night at the Plough," she sobbed.

"The Plough?" he echoed in surprise.

"The Plough at Alton."

Mick found it impossible to remember what he had said at the Plough, but he was used to the peculiar way women remembered things which some man had said and forgotten, and which he would have been glad if they had forgotten too.

"Remind me of it," he said.

"Oh, when you said love was a matter of responsibilities."

"Oh, yes, yes," he said. "I remember now." But he didn't. What he remembered mostly was that she had told him about the other men, and he had argued with her. "But you shouldn't take that too seriously, Jan."

"Oh, what else could I do but take it seriously?" she asked fiercely. "I was mad with you, but I knew you were right. I knew that was the way I'd always felt myself, only I blinded myself. Just as you said; taking up love like a casual job you could drop whenever you pleased. I'm well paid for my own bloody folly."

She began to sob again. Mick found it very difficult to readjust his mind to the new situation. One arm about her and the other supporting his head, he looked out the window and thought about it.

"Oh, of course, that's perfectly true, Janet," he agreed, "but, on the other hand, you can take it to the fair. You have to consider the other side of the question. Take people who're brought up to look at the physical facts of love as inhuman and disgusting. Think of the damage they do to themselves by living like that in superstitions. It would be better for them to believe in fairies or ghosts if they must believe in some sort of nonsense."

"Yes, but if I had a daughter, I'd prefer to bring her up like that than in the way I was brought up, Mick. At least she wouldn't fool with serious things, and that's what I've done. I made fun of Fanny because she didn't sleep around like the rest of us, but if Fanny falls for Chris, the joke will be on me."

Mick was silent again for a while. The conversation was headed in a direction he had not foreseen, and he could not yet see the end of it.

"You don't mean you didn't want to come?" he asked in astonishment.

"Oh, it's not that," she cried, beating her forehead with her fist. "Don't you see that I wanted to prove to myself that I could be a decent girl for you, and that I wasn't just one of the factory janes who'll sleep with anything? I wanted to give you something worth while, and I have nothing to give you."

"Oh, I wouldn't say that," Mick said in embarrassment. He was feeling terribly uncomfortable. Life was like that. At one moment you were on top of the world, and the next you were on the point of tears. At the same time it was hard to sacrifice his new-found freedom from inhibitions, all in a moment, as you might say. Here he had lain, rejoicing at being at last a man of the world, and now he was being asked to sacrifice it all and be an ordinary decent fellow again. That was the worst of dealing with the English, for the Irish, who had to be serious whether they liked it or not, only wanted to be frivolous, while the one thing in the world that the English seemed to demand was the chance of showing themselves serious. But the man of the world was too new a development in Mick to stand up to a crisis.

"Because you don't have to do it unless you like," he added gently. "We could always be married."

That threw her into positive convulsions, because if she agreed to this, she would never have the opportunity of showing him what she was really like, and it took him a long time to persuade her that he had never really thought her anything but a serious-minded girl—at least, for most of the time. Then she gave a deep sigh and fell asleep in the most awkward manner on his chest. Outside, the dawn was painting the old roofs and walls in the stiff artless colours of a child's paint-box. He felt a little lonely. He would have liked to remain a man of the world for just a little longer, to have had just one more such awakening to assure him that he had got rid of his inhibitions, but clearly it was not to be. He fell asleep himself soon after, and was only wakened by Chris, who seemed to have got over his ordeal well.

Chris was furious when Mick told him, and Mick himself realized that as a man of the world he had been a complete washout. Besides, Chris felt that now Fanny would expect him to marry her as well. She had already given indications of it.

Later, he became more reconciled to the idea, and when last heard of was looking for a house. Which seems to show that marriage comes more natural to us.

THE SENTRY

FATHER MACENERNEY was finding it hard to keep Sister Margaret quiet. The woman was lonesome, but he was lonesome himself. He liked his little parish outside the big military camp near Salisbury; he liked the country and the people, and he liked his little garden (even if it was raided twice a week by the soldiers), but he suffered from the lack of friends. Apart from his housekeeper and a couple of private soldiers in the camp, the only Irish people he had to talk to were the three nuns in the convent, and that was why he went there so frequently for his supper and to say his office in the convent garden.

But even here his peace was being threatened by Sister Margaret's obstreperousness. The trouble was, of course, that before the war fathers, mothers, sisters, and brothers, as well as innumerable aunts and cousins, had looked into the convent or spent a few days at the inn, and, every week, long, juicy letters had arrived from home, telling the nuns by what political intrigue Paddy Dunphy had had himself appointed warble-fly inspector for the Benlicky area, but now it was years since anyone from Ireland had called and the letters from home were censored at both sides of the channel by inquisitive girls with a taste for scandal until a sort of creeping paralysis had descended on every form of intimacy. Sister Margaret was the worst hit, because a girl from her own town was in the Dublin censorship, and, according to Sister Margaret, she was a scandalmonger of the most objectionable kind. He had a job keeping her contented.

"Oh, Father Michael," she sighed one evening as they were

walking round the garden, "I'm afraid I made a great mistake. A terrible mistake! I don't know how it is, but the English seem to me to have no nature."

"Ah, now, I wouldn't say that," protested Father Michael in his deep, sombre voice. "They have their little ways, and we have ours, and if we both knew more about one another we'd like one another better."

Then, to illustrate what he meant, he told her the story of old Father Dan Murphy, a Tipperary priest who had spent his life on the mission, and the Bishop. The Bishop was a decent, honourable little man, but quite unable to understand the ways of his Irish priests. One evening old Father Dan had called on Father Michael to tell him he would have to go home. The old man was terribly shaken. He had just received a letter from the Bishop, a terrible letter, a letter so bad that he couldn't even show it. It wasn't so much what the Bishop had said as the way he put it! And when Father Michael had pressed him the old man had whispered that the Bishop had begun his letter: "Dear Murphy."

"Oh!" cried Sister Margaret, clapping her hand to her mouth. "He didn't, Father Michael?"

So, seeing that she didn't understand the situation any more than Father Dan had done, Father Michael explained that this was how an Englishman would address anyone except a particular friend. It was a convention; nothing more.

"Oh, I wouldn't say that at all," Sister Margaret exclaimed indignantly. " 'Dear Murphy'? Oh, I'm surprised at you, Father Michael! What way is that to write to a priest? How can they expect people to have respect for religion when they show no respect for it themselves? Oh, that's the English all out! Listen, I have it every day of my life from them. I don't know how anyone can stand them."

Sister Margaret was his best friend in the community; he knew the other nuns relied on him to handle her, and it was a genuine worry to him to see her getting into this unreasonable state.

"Oh, come! Come!" he said reproachfully. "How well Sister Teresa and Sister Bonaventura get on with them!"

"I suppose I shouldn't say it," she replied in a low, brooding voice, "but, God forgive me, I can't help it. I'm afraid Sister Teresa and Sister Bonaventura are not *genuine.*"

"Now, you're not being fair," he said gravely.

"Oh, now, it's no good you talking," she cried, waving her hand petulantly. "They're not genuine, and you know they're not genuine. They're lickspittles. They give in to the English nuns in everything. Oh, they have no independence! You wouldn't believe it."

"We all have to give in to things for the sake of charity," he said.

"I don't call that charity at all, father," she replied obstinately. "I call that moral cowardice. Why should the English have it all their own way? Even in religion they go on as if they owned the earth. They tell me I'm disloyal and a pro-German, and I say to them: 'What did you ever do to make me anything else?' Then they pretend that we were savages, and they came over and civilized us! Did you ever in all your life hear such impudence? People that couldn't even keep their religion when they had it, and now they have to send for us to teach it to them again."

"Well, of course, that's all true enough," he said, "but we must remember what they're going through."

"And what did we have to go through?" she asked shortly. "Oh, now, father, it's all very well to be talking, but I don't see why we should have to make all the sacrifices. Why don't they think of all the terrible things they did to us? And all because we were true to our religion when they weren't! I'm after sending home for an Irish history, father, and, mark my words, the next time one of them begins picking at me, I'll give her her answer. The impudence!"

Suddenly Father Michael stopped and frowned.

"What is it, father?" she asked anxiously.

"I just got a queer feeling," he muttered. "I was wondering was there someone at my onions."

The sudden sensation was quite genuine, though it might have happened in a normal way, for his onions were the greatest anxiety of Father Michael's life. He could grow them when the convent gardener failed, but, unlike the convent gardener, he grew them where they were a constant temptation to the soldiers at the other side of his wall.

"They only wait till they get me out of their sight," he said, and then got on one knee and laid his ear to the earth. As a country boy he knew what a conductor of sound the earth is.

"I was right," he shouted triumphantly as he sprang to his feet and made for his bicycle. "If I catch them at it they'll leave me alone for the future. I'll give you a ring, sister."

A moment later, doubled over the handle-bars, he was pedalling down the hill towards his house. As he passed the camp gate he noticed that there was no sentry on duty, and it didn't take him long to see why. With a whoop of rage he threw his bicycle down by the gate and rushed across the garden. The sentry, a small man with fair hair, blue eyes, and a worried expression, dropped the handful of onions he was holding. His rifle was standing beside the wall.

"Aha!" shouted Father Michael. "So you're the man I was waiting for! You're the fellow that was stealing my onions!" He caught the sentry by the arm and twisted it viciously behind his back. "Now you can come up to the camp with me and explain yourself."

"I'm going, I'm going," the sentry cried in alarm, trying to wrench himself free.

"Oh, yes, you're going all right," Father Michael said grimly, urging him forward with his knee.

"Here!" the sentry cried in alarm. "You let me go! I haven't done anything, have I?"

"You haven't done anything?" echoed the priest, giving his wrist another spin. "You weren't stealing my onions!"

"Don't twist my wrist!" screamed the sentry, swinging round on him. "Try to behave like a civilized human being. I didn't take your onions. I don't even know what you're talking about."

"You dirty little English liar!" shouted Father Michael, beside himself with rage. He dropped the man's wrist and pointed at the onions. "Hadn't you them there, in your hand, when I came in? Didn't I see them with you, God blast you!"

"Oh, those things?" exclaimed the sentry, as though he had

suddenly seen a great light. "Some kids dropped them and I picked them up."

"You picked them up," echoed Father Michael savagely, drawing back his fist and making the sentry duck. "You didn't even know they were onions!"

"I didn't have much time to look, did I?" the sentry asked hysterically. "I seen some kids in your bleeding garden, pulling the bleeding things. I told them get out and they defied me. Then I chased them and they dropped these. What do you mean, twisting my bleeding wrist like that? I was only trying to do you a good turn. I've a good mind to give you in charge."

The impudence of the fellow was too much for the priest, who couldn't have thought up a yarn like that to save his life. He never had liked liars.

"You what?" he shouted incredulously, tearing off his coat. "You'd give me in charge? I'd take ten little sprats like you and break you across my knee. Bloody little English thief! Take off your tunic!"

"I can't," the sentry said in alarm.

"Why not?"

"I'm on duty."

"On duty! You're afraid."

"I'm not afraid."

"Then take off your tunic and fight like a man." He gave the sentry a punch that sent him staggering against the wall. "Now will you fight, you dirty little English coward?"

"You know I can't fight you," panted the sentry, putting up his hands to protect himself. "If I wasn't on duty I'd soon show you whether I'm a coward or not. You're the coward, not me, you Irish bully! You know I'm on duty. You know I'm not allowed to protect myself. You're mighty cocky, just because you're in a privileged position, you mean, bullying bastard!"

Something in the sentry's tone halted the priest. He was almost hysterical. Father Michael couldn't hit him in that state.

"Get out of this so, God blast you!" he said furiously.

The sentry gave him a murderous look, then took up his rifle and walked back up the road to the camp gate. Father Michael stood and stared after him. He was furious. He wanted a fight, and if only the sentry had hit back he would certainly have smashed him up. All the MacEnerneys were like that. His father was the quietest man in County Clare, but if you gave him occasion he'd fight in a bag, tied up.

He went in but found himself too upset to settle down. He sat in his big chair and found himself trembling all over with frustrated violence. "I'm too soft," he thought despairingly. "Too soft. It was my one opportunity and I didn't take advantage of it. Now they'll all know that they can do what they like with me. I might as well give up trying to garden. I might as well go back to Ireland. This is no country for anyone." At last he went to the telephone and rang up Sister Margaret. Her voice, when she answered, was trembling with eagerness.

"Oh, father," she cried, "did you catch them?"

"Yes," he replied in an expressionless voice. "One of the sentries."

"And what did you do?"

"Gave him a clout," he replied in the same tone.

"Oh," she cried, "if 'twas me I'd have killed him!"

"I would, only he wouldn't fight," Father Michael said gloomily. "If I'm shot from behind a hedge one of these days, you'll know who did it."

"Oh, isn't that the English all out?" she said in disgust. "They have so much old talk about their bravery, and then when anyone stands up to them, they won't fight."

"That's right," he said, meaning it was wrong. He realized that for once he and Sister Margaret were thinking alike, and that the woman wasn't normal. Suddenly his conduct appeared to him in its true light. He had behaved disgracefully. After all his talk of charity, he had insulted another man about his nationality, had hit him when he couldn't hit back, and, only for that, might have done him a serious injury—all for a handful of onions worth about sixpence! There was nice behaviour for a priest! There was good example for non-Catholics! He wondered what the Bishop would say to that.

He sat back again in his chair, plunged in dejection. His atrocious temper had betrayed him again. One of these days it would land him in really serious trouble, he knew. And there were no amends he could make. He couldn't even go up to the camp, find the man, and apologize. He faithfully promised himself to do so if ever he saw him again. That eased his mind a little, and after saying Mass next morning he didn't feel quite so bad. The run across the downs in the early morning always gave him pleasure, the little red-brick village below in the hollow with the white spire rising out of black trees which resembled a stagnant pool, and the pale chalk-green of the hills with the barrows of old Celts showing on their polished surface. They, poor devils, had had trouble with the English too! He was nearly in good humour again when Elsie, the maid, told him that an officer from the camp wished to see him. His guilty conscience started up again like an aching tooth. What the hell was it now?

The officer was a tall, good-looking young man about his own age. He had a long, dark face with an obstinate jaw that stuck out like some advertisement for a shaving-soap, and a pleasant, jerky, conciliatory manner.

"Good morning, padre," he said in a harsh voice. "My name is Howe. I called about your garden. I believe our chaps have been giving you some trouble."

By this time Father Michael would cheerfully have made him a present of the garden.

"Ah," he said with a smile, "wasn't it my own fault for putting temptation in their way?"

"Well, it's very nice of you to take it like that," Howe said in a tone of mild surprise, "but the C.O. is rather indignant. He suggested barbed wire."

"Electrified?" Father Michael asked ironically.

"No," Howe said. "Ordinary barbed wire. Pretty effective, you know."

"Useless," Father Michael said promptly. "Don't worry any more about it. You'll have a drop of Irish? And ice in it. Go on, you will!"

"A bit early for me, I'm afraid," Howe said, glancing at his watch.

"Coffee, so," said the priest authoritatively. "No one leaves this house without some nourishment."

He shouted to Elsie for coffee and handed Howe a cigarette. Howe knocked it briskly on the chair and lit it.

"Now," he said in a businesslike tone, "this chap you caught last night—how much damage had he done?"

The question threw Father Michael more than ever on his guard. He wondered how the captain knew.

"Which chap was this?" he asked noncommittally.

"The chap you beat up."

"That I beat up?" echoed Father Michael wonderingly. "Who said I beat him up?"

"He did," Howe replied laconically. "He expected you to report him, so he decided to give himself up. You seem to have scared him pretty badly," he added with a laugh.

However much Father Michael might have scared the sentry, the sentry had now scared him worse. It seemed the thing was anything but over, and if he wasn't careful, he might soon find himself involved as a witness against the sentry. It was like the English to expect people to report them! They took everything literally, even to a fit of bad temper.

"But why did he expect me to report him?" he asked in bewilderment. "When do you say this happened? Last night?"

"So I'm informed," Howe said shortly. "Do you do it regularly? . . . I mean Collins, the man you caught stealing onions last evening," he went on, raising his voice as though he thought Father Michael might be slightly deaf, or stupid, or both.

"Oh, was that his name?" the priest asked watchfully. "Of course, I couldn't be sure he stole them. There were onions stolen all right, but that's a different thing."

"But I understand you caught him at it," Howe said with a frown.

"Oh, no," replied Father Michael gravely. "I didn't actually catch him at anything. I admit I charged him with it, but he denied it at once. At once!" he repeated earnestly as though this were an important point in the sentry's favour. "It seems, according to what he told me, that he saw some children in my garden and chased them away, and, as they were running, they dropped the onions I found. Those could be kids from the village, of course."

"First I've heard of anybody from the village," Howe said in astonishment. "Did you see any kids around, padre?"

"No," Father Michael admitted with some hesitation. "I didn't, but that wouldn't mean they weren't there."

"I'll have to ask him about that," said Howe. "It's a point in his favour. Afraid it won't make much difference though. Naturally, what we're really concerned with is that he deserted his post. He could be shot for that, of course."

"Deserted his post?" repeated Father Michael in consternation. This was worse than anything he had ever imagined. The wretched man might lose his life and for no reason but his own evil temper. He felt he was being well punished for it. "How did he desert his post?" he faltered.

"Well, you caught him in your garden," Howe replied brusquely. "You see, padre, in that time the whole camp could have been surprised and taken."

In his distress, Father Michael nearly asked him not to talk nonsense. As if a military camp in the heart of England was going to be surprised while the sentry nipped into the next garden for a few onions! But that was the English all out. They had to reduce everything to the most literal terms.

"Oh, hold on now!" he said, raising a commanding hand. "I think there must be a mistake. I never said I caught him in the garden."

"No," Howe snapped irritably. "He said that. Didn't you?"

"No," said Father Michael stubbornly, feeling that casuistry was no longer any use. "I did not. Are you quite sure that man is right in his head?"

Fortunately, at this moment Elsie appeared with the coffee and Father Michael was able to watch her and the coffee-pot instead of Howe, who, he knew, was studying him closely. If he looked as he felt, he thought, he should be worth studying.

"Thanks," Howe said, sitting back with his coffee-cup in his hand, and then went on remorselessly: "Am I to understand that you beat this chap up across the garden wall?"

"Listen, my friend," Father Michael said desperately, "I tell you that fellow is never right in the head. He must be a hopeless neurotic. They get like that, you know. He'd never talk that way if he had any experience of being beaten up. I give you my word of honour it's the wildest exaggeration. I don't often raise my fist to a man, but when I do I leave evidence of it."

"I believe that," Howe said with a cheeky grin.

"I admit I did threaten to knock this fellow's head off," continued Father Michael, "but that was only when I thought he'd taken my onions." In his excitement he drew closer to Howe till he was standing over him, a big, bulky figure of a man, and suddenly he felt the tears in his eyes. "Between ourselves," he said emotionally, "I behaved badly. I don't mind admitting that to you. He threatened to give me in charge."

"The little bastard!" said Howe incredulously.

"And he'd have been justified," the priest said earnestly. "I had no right whatever to acuse him without a scrap of evidence. I behaved shockingly."

"I shouldn't let it worry me too much," Howe said cheerfully.

"I can't help it," said Father Michael brokenly. "I'm sorry to say the language I used was shocking. As a matter of fact, I'd made up my mind to apologize to the man."

He stopped and returned to his chair. He was surprised to notice that he was almost weeping.

"This is one of the strangest cases I've ever dealt with," Howe said. "I wonder if we're not talking at cross purposes. This fellow you mean was tall and dark with a small moustache, isn't that right?"

For one moment Father Michael felt a rush of relief at the thought that after all it might be merely a case of mistaken identity. To mix it up a bit more was the first thought that came to his mind. He didn't see the trap until it was too late.

"That's right," he said.

"Listen, padre," Howe said, leaning forward in his chair while his long jaw suddenly shot up like a rat-trap, "why are you telling me all these lies?"

"Lies?" shouted Father Michael, flushing.

"Lies, of course," said Howe without rancour. "Damned lies, transparent lies! You've been trying to fool me for the last ten minutes, and you very nearly succeeded."

"Ah, how could I remember?" Father Michael said wearily. "I don't attach all that importance to a few onions."

"I'd like to know what importance you attach to the rigmarole you've just told me," snorted Howe. "I presume you're trying to shield Collins, but I'm blessed if I see why."

Father Michael didn't reply. If Howe had been Irish, he wouldn't have asked such a silly question, and as he wasn't Irish, he wouldn't understand the answer. The MacEnerneys had all been like that. Father Michael's father, the most truthful, God-fearing man in County Clare, had been threatened with a prosecution for perjury committed in the interest of a neighbour.

"Anyway," Howe said sarcastically, "what really happened was that you came home, found your garden robbed, said 'Good night' to the sentry, and asked him who did it. He said it was some kids from the village. Then you probably had a talk about the beautiful, beautiful moonlight. Now that's done, what about coming up to the mess some night for dinner?"

"I'd love it," Father Michael said boyishly. "I'm destroyed here for someone to talk to."

"Come on Thursday. And don't expect too much in the way of grub. Our mess is a form of psychological conditioning for modern warfare. But we'll give you lots of onions. Hope you don't recognize them."

And he went off, laughing his harsh but merry laugh. Father Michael laughed too, but he didn't laugh long. It struck him that the English had very peculiar ideas of humour. The interview with Howe had been anything but a joke. He had accused the sentry of lying, but his own attempts at concealing the truth had been even more unsuccessful than Collins's. It did not look well from a priest. He rang up the convent and asked for Sister Margaret. She was his principal confidante.

"Remember the sentry last night?" he asked expressionlessly.

"Yes, father," she said nervously. "What about him?"

"He's after being arrested."

"Oh!" she said, and then, after a long pause: "For what, father?"

"Stealing my onions and being absent from duty. I had an officer here, making inquiries. It seems he might be shot."

"Oh!" she gasped. "Isn't that awful?"

" 'Tis bad."

"Oh!" she cried. "Isn't that the English all out? The rich can do what they like, but a poor man can be shot for stealing a few onions! I suppose it never crossed their minds that he might be hungry. What did you say?"

"Nothing."

"You did right. I'd have told them a pack of lies."

"I did," said Father Michael.

"Oh!" she cried. "I don't believe for an instant that 'tis a sin, father. I don't care what anybody says. I'm sure 'tis an act of charity."

"That's what I thought too," he said, "but it didn't go down too well. I liked the officer, though. I'll be seeing him again and I might be able to get round him. The English are very good like that, when they know you."

"I'll start a novena at once," she said firmly.

FATHER AND SON

DURING the holidays Min wrote to say that she'd like to see the children again before they grew out of her knowledge. She suggested coming for the week-end and asked Dan to find her a room in some public-house. Min was Dan's first wife, and as he read the letter he was full of foreboding. It was as though he was being haunted by the ghost of his first marriage. Mildred waited till the children had left the room before she said anything.

"Something wrong?" she asked sympathetically.

"Only Min wanting to come for the week-end to see the children," he replied expressionlessly.

"Well, there's nothing wrong with that, is there?"

"Only that it may prove a little awkward," he said in the same tone. "She wants us to get her a room."

"Why on earth doesn't she stay here?" Mildred asked in surprise. "There's heaps of room."

"Oh, have a heart!" said Dan impatiently.

"You think it might be too embarrassing for her?" Mildred asked in a puzzled tone.

"I wasn't thinking of her," he replied coldly. "I was thinking about myself."

"Well, in that case I'll simply take Flurry to Helen's for the week-end and you can have the house to yourselves," she went on reasonably.

"Oh, for Heaven's sake!" he snapped, exasperated at her denseness.

"Really, duckie," she sighed in that maddening, superficial way of hers, "you're awfully hard to please."

There were times when Dan felt Mildred's silliness like a judgment. Flurry (short for Florence, a great name among men of the McCarthy family) was their own child. As well as Flurry they had Min's children, Bawn and Tim. Mildred had been an excellent stepmother. Girls, even small girls, soon get to know whether they have the right accent and the right frock, and as Mildred knew everything about accents and frocks, she and Bawn got on fine. Boys are different; they don't mind about frocks. Tim was older than Bawn; he stole, he told lies, and to show his contempt for Mildred, he used to hack his way through the house, putting on the commonest Cockney accent he could pick up. Mildred had been very good with him too, affecting nothing, explaining everything, and then boxing his ears hard when he defied her. But it had been no good. One day he'd kicked her savagely. Mildred, a girl of great spirit and resource, had kicked him back, but Dan had decided that the time had come for Tim to go to boarding-school. Mildred and he had had words about that, because she disapproved of boarding-schools.

"You make an awful fuss about nothing," she'd said. "Oh, boy, it's nothing to the kick I gave him! He'll be sore for weeks."

At the same time Dan knew she was as conventional as they

made them—it went with the accent and the frocks, and he wouldn't have changed it for anything—and, though they got on so much better than most husbands and wives, he knew she still had a guilty feeling that he was Min's husband, not hers; the father of Bawn and Tim, not of Flurry.

"Let's put it the other way round," he said with masculine reasonableness. "Suppose you'd been the married one, and your first attempt came to see you and the children, how would you like my going off with Flurry and letting you alone with him?"

This reversal of roles was one of his favourite devices, intended to produce an objective and critical estimate of any position, and it nearly always maddened her, but this time she only smiled.

"Some day you'll wake up and find yourself walking on the ceiling, Daniel, and then we'll see how you like it."

"But isn't it true?"

"All right. Then I can go to Helen's with an easy mind."

"Damn!"

"What have I said wrong now, duckie?"

But he didn't try to explain. There was something ludicrous in the very idea of her being concerned about letting him alone with Min, but he knew she wouldn't understand it; that she couldn't realize that nothing in the world was so over as a marriage that was over.

It wasn't until she was actually getting on the bus with Flurry that it began to dawn on her how uncomfortable he was.

"I'm rather sorry now I said I'd go," she said.

"It's a bit late in the day to change your mind," he said, rubbing it in for what it was worth.

"Dan, promise not to let it upset you too much. I know I'm a silly bitch, but you knew that yourself when you married me."

He made a suitably gloomy reply and set off down the road to meet Min's train. He knew it was all going to be very unpleasant. That he couldn't imagine the form the unpleasantness would take only made it more alarming.

In fact, it wasn't unpleasant at all. Min came out of the carriage laughing and holding out her arms as though they had met only yesterday. She was older and fatter, and perhaps had a shade too much make-up, but she was as lively and unselfconscious as ever. Within five minutes they were chattering like the old cronies they were. They had a drink at the bar outside the station and went home on the bus. As they reached the house Min goggled and pretended she was going to run away.

"Is this yours?" she asked breathlessly. "My goodness, I feel like the new maid."

Bawn came running up the path and Min gave her a great hug.

"Child of grace!" she cried. "Where did you get the looks from? Not from your father!"

Then Tim appeared, a bit red and a fraction of a second off the beat and Dan could have murdered him. For a boy of his age he had a heavy, sullen, angry face. He warmed up when he saw his mother.

"Hullo, Mum," he said in a voice he tried to make deeper than it was.

"Oh, Tim," she cried, "you've grown such a great big man!"

Dan and she got the supper. She was all lit up, and it wasn't only being with the children and himself, though that had something to do with it. It was also the novelty of the arrangement, the unfamiliarity of the house. She poked her nose everywhere, commenting loudly on the taste and convenience of it all, and Dan suddenly felt frightfully guilty about having put her to sleep in the spare room. It was extraordinary. It would never have occurred to him that she should sleep anywhere else, but now, with the children and herself all there together, it seemed uncouth, as though he were trying to emphasize a gap that was already only too plain. It wasn't that he wanted anything more to do with her—he knew that this was all over and done with years before; it was just that he could not erect artificial barriers between himself and a woman who at any moment could let drop a remark that brought back all their past life together; the little estate house, her efforts at gardening and his at carpentry, and their worries over Bawn and Tim.

While they were at supper the telephone rang and Dan answered it. It was a long-distance call, and he felt sure it must be Mildred ringing up from Helen's to know how he was getting on. Instead it turned out to be some man who wanted to speak to Min, and he found himself as sore as hell against Mildred for having left him in that position, without having even the decency to ring up. It would serve her right if he did piece her out. Then he grinned, amused at his own touchiness.

Min returned, red and laughing, obviously pleased to have been rung up and embarrassed at having to explain it.

"A friend of mine giving me a tip for the big race tomorrow," she said modestly.

"Oh, still on the horses?" Dan said, raising his brows. The horses had been one of the things they had disagreed about.

He felt a fool when he went to her room to show her how the electric fire worked. She did one of her schoolgirl acts, joining her hands behind her back and raising herself on her toes with her eyebrows ingenuously lifted and her eyes sparkling with malice. Min had none of his inhibitions, and was getting enormous fun out of his embarrassment. At last she made him laugh too and he threw a towel at her head.

"Ah, do go on!" she said mockingly. "Mildred's made a proper toff of you."

Then they sat by the bedroom fire till late in the night, drinking tea and discussing the children.

"Of course, Bawn is lovely," she said thoughtfully. "Anybody would get on with Bawn."

"Ah, Tim is all right too," he said defensively. "It's just that he's so moody."

"I fancy there are times when Tim hates the whole lot of us," she said without changing her tone. "He's more sensitive than Bawn, really."

"Don't let me disillusion you, my dear," he said, and kissed her good-night.

He found himself very wakeful. He was all churned up inside, going over his own conduct and Min's conduct and growing so heated that he felt like going downstairs and having it all out with her again. Then he wondered whether she wasn't feeling the same. He fancied he could hear crying. Crying in a sleeping house had always been a horror to him. He could hear it even when there was nothing to hear but the sound of the wind; it was

like no one you knew crying about nothing you could understand: it was like the whole world crying in its sleep. Once in a
boarding-house he had got up and poked round till at last he
had found himself in the bedroom of a drunken old woman who
had told him her troubles about her daughter-in-law. The faces
you saw in the street or round the house never told you anything;
it was only those faces you rarely saw that told the truth, and
the truth was something that no one ever knew. He rose and
went out on the landing. Either the crying had stopped or, as
usual when he was excited, he had been imagining it. He went
downstairs and listened at Min's door until he assured himself
that she was asleep. Then he went back to bed.

Next morning Bawn beckoned him into the kitchen.

"Daddy, I wish you'd talk to Tim," she said in her forthright
way.

"Why? What's Tim been up to?" he asked without interest.

"He won't even make an effort to be nice to Mummy," she
said angrily. "He just sits there the whole time with his book and
his disapproving air, as if Mum was the Penitent Thief or the
Prodigal Son or something."

"It's probably only strangeness, you know," said Dan.

"You can call it strangeness. I call it plain snobbery. Mum isn't
grand enough for him. And you know she cares more about that
little twerp's big toe than she does for my whole body."

Dan reflected on the remarkable understanding girls had of
their mothers and wondered whether this wasn't the reason that
their mothers appreciated them so little.

"If I catch him at it I'll soon knock the snobbery out of him,"
he said. "Where is Mum?"

"Probably in your room, dolling herself up," Bawn replied
with a guilty air. "You can't even see yourself in that old bathroom mirror." It was perfectly plain to Dan that Bawn and Min
had been having a heavenly time in the bedroom with Mildred's
frocks. "Did she tell you her friend had bought a new house?"
she added, changing the subject hastily.

"Which friend is that?" Dan asked guardedly.

"The lady who rang her up last night."

"No, I didn't know," said Dan, amused at Min's sudden access

of modesty, but relieved that there were limits to Bawn's understanding of her.

Bawn hadn't missed much about Tim though. At lunch he was
sulky, silent, superior, scowling at them all from under heavy
brows.

"We rise at seven," he told Min when she asked him about his
life in school. "We retire at nine thirty."

"And when do you go to bed?" Dan asked, but Tim only
looked at him in a puzzled way.

"Nine thirty," he said. "I told you."

Bawn was handling it all magnificently, exactly as Mildred
might have done. A high-spirited, lower-class Irish girl in a
snobbish English school, she had a rough time, but made it all
sound so entertaining that Dan and Min both laughed. The
laughter seemed to irritate Tim.

"It's entirely your own fault if they treat you that way," he
said suddenly in his deepest voice.

"How is it her fault, Tim?" Dan asked, trying to keep his own
voice from growing rancorous.

"She behaves exactly like the Stuarts," said Tim, pushing away
his plate. "She treats the other girls as the Stuarts treated their
parliaments and then she's surprised because they don't like her."

"I'd sooner be Charles II than your old Cromwell anyway,"
Bawn said hotly.

"I wasn't defending Cromwell," Tim said coldly, giving her
an angry look.

"And how do you manage, may we ask?" Dan asked.

Tim looked at his father like an owl. "I model my conduct entirely on Queen Elizabeth," he said.

"Yes," spluttered Bawn, "and if Queen Elizabeth had the girls
in our school to deal with, she mightn't be such a model either."

That evening they went to the pictures and had tea when they
got home. After one restless night Dan was yawning his head
off and went straight to bed. This was a bad mistake, as he discovered when he tried to sleep. He put on the light again and
started to read. Then he thought he heard a noise downstairs
and opened the bedroom door quietly. This time there could
be no mistake. Someone was crying. He no longer felt any sense

of guilt about going to Min's room. If Mildred had been there he would have acted just the same. All he wanted was to take that stubborn, stupid woman in his arms and console her for what she'd done to him and the children. He went quickly down the stairs.

"Asleep, Min?" he asked, pushing in the door softly.

There was no reply, and he could hear her breathing quite evenly. She seemed to be asleep. And suddenly panic, real panic, swept over him. He went hastily back upstairs and switched the light on in Tim's room.

"Well, Tim?" he said in a voice he tried to make natural.

Tim started up with a brave show of astonishment. His eyes were red.

"Hullo, Daddy. What time is it?"

"It's early yet," Dan said, sitting on the side of his bed. "You didn't hear anything?"

"No, Daddy."

"My imagination, I suppose."

"It might be the pictures," Tim suggested sagaciously. "Pictures keep me awake too."

"No, it's not the pictures with me. It's Mum."

"Mum?" Tim asked, sitting up and reaching for Dan's hand, a purely instinctive gesture. "How, Dad?"

"Don't you find it upsetting, after all the years?"

"I suppose so," Tim said in a low voice, and Dan saw the sudden flash of fresh tears.

He hadn't realized what he was going to say, but from the moment he saw the tears he knew he must say everything, good and bad, sentimental and sordid; that Tim and he were in the same state of mind and Tim was going under. That was something even Mildred wouldn't understand. Dan was a cautious, secretive man. He knew more harm was done by people trying to say what they meant than ever was done by deception. He had told nobody the full story of his married life. Now he began at the beginning and went through to the end, not seeking his words nor evading them when they came to him, trying to be fair to Min but not trying too hard. It wasn't fairness that Tim wanted from him but a sense of the human reality, even if it hurt. He sat there, his hands about his knees, his eyes fixed on Dan's face as though to catch some shade of meaning that might evade him, and Dan remembered that he had sat in the same way years before when listening to a bedtime story. This was *Treasure Island,* grown up.

"That's how it is," Dan ended. "I was fond of her once, and I'm fond of her still, but we've been apart too long. We haven't enough things to talk about the way you and I can talk. The real reason I wasn't sleeping is that I behaved like a pig. I never went to her room to say good-night as I should have done."

"Why not, Daddy?" Tim asked tensely.

"I suppose I was modelling my conduct on Queen Elizabeth," Dan replied, and Tim gave a feeble grin. "For all I knew, she was lying awake, brooding over it. I knew it might be years before I could make up for it, or that one of us might die before I ever got the chance. That's how it happens. You pass a room and wonder if it's worth your while going in to say good-morning, and day after day you pass it again and feel there's nothing you wouldn't give for the chance of a talk with someone who isn't there any more. So I went to see if she was asleep."

"And was she?"

"Yes. I'll make it up to her tomorrow. Good night, old man."

"Good night, Daddy," said Tim. "And don't worry about Mum," he added, turning his head to follow Dan out the door. "She knows you're fond of her all right."

Dan noticed there was a slight emphasis on the "you." Half an hour later he heard Tim's door open and shut. This was something he hadn't been expecting, but he decided it was better to let it alone. Anyway, it was now Min's turn for a sleepless spell.

Next morning Tim was round the house, bold as brass, quarrelling with Bawn, and humming what he took to be a very dirty song about lavatories that he knew she hated.

"You must have said something to Tim," Bawn said after Min and he had gone off to Mass together. She was jealous. Dan could scarcely blame her, considering how she had worked.

"That was only strangeness," he said. "You'd be the same with me if you didn't see me for so long."

"I'm glad I can see you, Daddy," she said languishingly while she cuddled up to him. She had no one else to flirt with yet, so she took it out on him.

The week-end was a real success, and it was agreed that the children should spend part of the Christmas holidays with Min. When she left they were both crying.

Then, on Tuesday evening, as they sat in the front room, feeling that the bottom had dropped out of their world, Tim suddenly started up and charged out the hall.

"That's Mildred," he called back, and before Dan had even risen heard him shouting: "Hullo, Mildred! Welcome home! Hullo, Flurry, old scout! You sit down and I'll get the tea, Mildred."

"Don't attempt it," Bawn said, storming out after him. "You'll only make a mess of that kitchen again."

"Please, Bawn," Mildred said, laughing, "put Flurry to bed for me and let Tim make the tea. Poor Flurry's exhausted. He's longing for bed. Aren't you, pet?"

"I am not," screamed Flurry, beginning to dance with fury, but Dan saw that Mildred only wanted to get him alone. She was all lit up about something, and though he was glad enough to see her, he suspected that she only wanted to make fun of him.

"Had a lovely time?" she asked, giggling.

Dan put on a despondent air. He remembered that she hadn't rung up, and waited for the opportunity of reminding her.

"Lovely," he said in a dull voice. "And you seem to have enjoyed yourself quite a bit. May we ask who the man was?"

"Tim," she gasped, taking his hands and squeezing them. "What on earth have you done to Tim? Do you know he kissed me?"

JEROME

JEROME KIELY was a Corkman who worked in our place in England; a nice chap as Corkmen go, but cautious about everything from his friends to his food, and most cautious of all about what he took to be his own recklessness. Jerome seemed to think his one great fault was his resemblance to Galloping Hogan, the Irish Rapparee.

Now, Jerome was a good-looking young fellow, and he wasn't long there before he started walking out with one of the factory girls called Hilda Kenyon. The factory hands in the main were a rough lot, but Hilda was a really superior type of girl. She was small and slight, and she went through life apparently following some ghostly figure which preceded her at a distance of about twenty feet. If you broke into her reverie she smiled and shrieked with the rest of them, but mostly she seemed to be thinking about the ghost and wondering where he wanted her to go next. She was a terriffic worker and a secret reader, who went to concerts and plays on the side.

Now, having a girl of his own was a great step forward in Jerome's life, but for that very reason it worried him a lot. He knew of old that most of the world's troubles were caused by women, and it was no satisfaction to him that Hilda didn't look as if she would ever be much trouble to anyone. Knowing his weakness, the other Irish chaps played on it, and pulled Jerome's leg for all they were worth. This was the easiest thing in the world, for all you needed was to pretend that you thought Jerome

was being reckless for him to start showing you how smart he
was: a part that didn't come natural to him and made him give
away more than he knew.

"Ah, Chrisht, what a fool I am!" he said with a boyish guffaw.
(Jerome was one of the most pious chaps in the factory and at
the same time a terrible man to swear.) "Is it the best hand in
the works?"

"Ahadie, Jerome, so you looked up her production chart!"

"And why the hell wouldn't I?" Jerome asked unblushingly.
"Is it a pig in a poke you want me to buy?"

At the same time Jerome couldn't help feeling that people
would never go on talking like that about his recklessness unless
he really was that way, so as there was another Irish lad walking
out a girl in the factory, Jerome chummed up with him, just for
protection.

Flurry Donoghue, his new friend, was a Kerryman. He was a
good-looking young fellow too, with an easy, slouching gait and
a manner of the most disarming charm. Flurry went with girls
the way he drank or smoked, on the principle that anything went,
but before Jerome had stopped calling Hilda "miss" he was wor-
rying about what his people in the Ballinlough Road would
think of her. The factory hands were a rough lot; there was no
denying that, and though Hilda was a girl of high principle, she
said things that could be misinterpreted. "When a girl has a
flirtation while her husband is away, she should drop it when she
knows he's coming home," or "They should have made sure the
children were in bed," were the height of morality where she
worked, but he hoped to God she wouldn't say them in front of
his mother and sister.

By this time Hilda, a serious-minded girl, was also beginning
to wonder what she'd think of the Ballinlough Road. Jerome
was a nice fellow and well informed and all the rest of it, but
still he wasn't English, and you never knew with foreigners, did
you? Hilda was afraid she could never be content with people
who didn't go in for cleanliness and classical music. It was she
who suggested that the two of them should go away together
for the holidays. This was a regular custom among the locals
who were keeping company, and Hilda thought it might serve to

indicate whether they were suited, but to Jerome's cautious mind
it suggested nothing but impropriety and trouble.

"Ah, what trouble, man?" Flurry said, laughing at him with a
great mouthful of teeth. "The divil a bit of harm is in it. Go
away with the girl and enjoy yourself."

"Still, Flurry," Jerome said steadily, doing the man of the
world on him, "a thing like that could be misunderstood."

"You try any tricks on Hilda, and you'll damn soon see they
won't be misunderstood," replied Flurry, though it was beginning to dawn on his optimistic mind that tricks and Jerome were
a combination he would never see.

"Ah, Chrisht, man, I'd be in dread, going off by myself with
a girl," said Jerome with boyish candour. "I suppose yourself and
Rosie would never come with us?"

"Ah, I don't see why we wouldn't," said Flurry, who was game
for anything at any time. "Sure, we might as well be there as
anywhere else. I'll ask her anyway."

The result was that the four of them went off to the seaside
together and stayed in the same lodging-house. The boys had
one room, the girls another, and the girls bought the food and
did the cooking. Or, rather, Hilda did the cooking, for Rosie,
a thin, lively spitfire of a blonde, lacked the necessary concentration.

Jerome found it all very instructive and managed to collect a
lot of valuable information which would occupy his mind for
months to come, but Flurry had the time of his life. He was the
sort of man who could not go to a fun-fair without making the
round of every side-show, and there wasn't a peep-show or slot-
machine in the town that he hadn't tried his luck on. Jerome died
a thousand deaths, seeing the way he went on.

"Chrisht," he said, "I never saw a man to get through the
money the way you do."

"Ah, 'twill be after us," Flurry replied with a wide grin.

To add to Jerome's troubles, Rosie made fun of his attempts
at instructive conversation and did her best to embarrass him.

"Jerome," she would cry, stopping at some stationer's window
and picking out a scandalous postcard, "what does this mean?
It's beyond me."

"Chrisht, 'tis beyond me too, girl," Jerome would say, gazing at it gravely.

"And well it might be," Flurry would say delightedly.

"Listen, you Irish lout, I was asking Jerome. He's an educated man, but you don't even read the daily papers. Don't know where Yugoslavia is."

"Well, let Hilda here explain it to you, some time we're not round."

"Oh, I couldn't, Flurry," Hilda would cry with a demure laugh.

"Hilda is only a simple working-girl like me," Rosie would add with great dignity. "It's not our fault if we're not well up like Jerome."

It would take an hour for the meaning of a scene like that to dawn on Jerome, and by that time he would be in a state of mental collapse.

"Chrisht, Hilda, I don't know how the bloody man stands that girl. She'd drive me into the asylum. And what did she mean about Yugoslavia? What has that to do with it?"

"Oh, but she's very clever, Jerome," Hilda would say. In her quiet, anxious way she had a profound admiration for what she took to be Rosie's social graces.

One day the two girls went off to the hairdresser's together, and the boys were left to walk along the promenade by themselves. It was a summer evening, and the light off the water gave brilliance to the shabby gimcrack town. They suddenly came upon a little booth which they had failed to notice before. The announcement outside it said that the proprietor was phrenologist to all the crowned heads of Europe.

"I declare to my God!" exclaimed Flurry, standing back to study it. "And to think we nearly missed him!"

"But you're not going in?" Jerome asked in alarm, realizing that it was liable to lead to fresh expense. "Sure, that's only a bloody racket, man. You don't believe in that, surely?"

"Ah, what the hell!" chuckled Flurry, jingling the coins in his pocket. "What is it only a couple of bob?"

"I wouldn't be too sure of that."

"And, sure, can't we ask?" cried Flurry with a lordly wave of his arm. "What harm did a civil question ever do anyone?"

And in he strode with Jerome behind. Inside, there was a display of coloured charts, showing the anatomy of the skull, and a pedestal with the head of a good-looking man mapped out in areas like a globe in school. The owner was a plump, crushed-looking man with a round face, brown eyes, and a drooping brown moustache. His clothes didn't suggest that there had been many crowned heads among his recent callers.

"Good afternoon, gentlemen," he said in a quiet insinuating voice that instantly made Jerome suspicious. "Can I help you?"

" 'Tis this old pate of mine," said Flurry, indicating it with an infectious grin. "I have it a long time, and I'm beginning to think 'tis nearly wore out. How much do you charge?"

"Half a crown, gentlemen," said the phrenologist in a doubtful tone as though he were wondering whether he shouldn't reduce his prices. But haggling was beneath Flurry.

"Ah, 'twould be a queer thing if a man's own head wasn't worth that to him," he said, taking a seat. "Don't be too hard on me now. I come from a backward sort of place."

"What do you call backward?" asked the phrenologist, who obviously thought that Flurry was a great card. "Where do you think I come from?"

"Ah, go to hell!" Flurry crowed delightedly, sticking out his front teeth at him. "You don't mean it? What part do you come from?"

"Cork. My family did, at least. They left when I was only two or three."

"Cork?" said Flurry. "Where better could you come from? Ye're in every bloody racket. There's another crooked Cork whoor there, and he has the heart broke in me."

But Jerome was really interested now. This was real information.

"What part of Cork were they from?" he asked, screwing up his face.

"Don't ask me," said the phrenologist. "I was too young to know. But my old mother often talked of it."

"What did you say the name was?" Jerome asked unblushingly.

"Creedy."

"Creedy? That's an old Cork name all right. I used to know a family of Creedys on the College Road. Auctioneers, I think they were. You wouldn't be one of them?"

"I shouldn't say so," the phrenologist replied. "We'd have been among the auctioned rather than the auctioneers."

But Flurry could see that Jerome wouldn't be long without trying to find out. It is very important to a Corkman to know who a fellow Corkman's father was. Meanwhile Creedy went on with the study of Flurry's head, and Jerome leaned against the wall in a way that was intended to show his lack of interest and his general incredulity. He was a pious lad, and this sort of thing didn't seem very different from spiritualism. Besides, it cost a lot of money. The phrenologist made vague references to Flurry's work with machinery, and his love of music, and hoped he was telling him something.

"Ah, I'm afraid there's nothing inside," said Flurry without rancour. "Try your luck with this fellow here. He has the brains of the party."

"That's exactly what I'd like to do," said Mr. Creedy, looking hard at Jerome, who instantly made ready to go.

"Ah, you can leave me out of it," he said.

"May I ask why?" asked Mr. Creedy politely.

"Ah, that sort of thing isn't in my line at all," replied Jerome. "I wouldn't be bothered with it."

"What did I tell you?" Flurry said admiringly. "Another Corkman!"

"As a Corkman, he should recognize a bargain when he sees one," said Mr. Creedy. "I'll make him a fair offer. I'll do him, and if I don't tell him something interesting, he needn't pay. That's fair, isn't it?"

"But when I tell you I don't believe in it, man?" said Jerome, turning on him from the door. "I'd as soon believe in one of them fortune-telling machines on the promenade."

"That's all the more reason you needn't be afraid of risking your money," said Mr. Creedy quietly.

"Ah, come on, Jerome!" cried Flurry, who felt he was being deprived of something good in the way of entertainment. "I'll pay for the two of us."

"Oh, begod, you'll do nothing of the kind," said Jerome, who saw how he had been trapped again. "I'll pay for myself. But mind," he added in a warning tone, "I'll keep you to your bargain."

"You needn't worry about that," Mr. Creedy said soothingly as he sat down, still very upset. "I'm not after your halfcrown. You have a very interesting head and I wanted a look at it, that's all. . . . A very interesting head," he added a few moments later, and he stood back and looked at Jerome between the eyes. "Though I wouldn't be the owner of it for a good deal of money. Now, why," he added, pointing a forefinger at Jerome, "did you say you didn't believe in phrenology?"

"Because I don't, man," shouted Jerome, staring steadily back at him.

"You do," replied Mr. Creedy quietly, nodding his head firmly as though he were bowing. "You do, my friend. There is no use in denying it. You believe in it, but you didn't want to part with your halfcrown. That's all."

"How do you make that out?" Jerome asked.

"You're too cautious," replied Mr. Creedy gravely. "I can feel it here," he added, pressing a protuberance over Jerome's left ear. "I've been in this business a long time, and I never saw anything to equal it. It's a phenomenon," he said excitedly. "A phenomenon, that's what it is. You notice it?" he asked Flurry who began to run his hand lightly over his own head. Then Mr. Creedy stood back again and contemplated Jerome as if he were posing for a picture. "Very secretive too, aren't you?" he asked.

"I wouldn't say that," replied Jerome with a worried air. "I mind my own business, if that's what you mean."

"No, my friend," Mr. Creedy replied gravely, pointing his forefinger at Jerome again, "that is not what I mean at all. Now, take it easy. I'm not speaking personally. I'd like to help you if I could. I like to help all my clients. Haven't made much of a success of your life so far, have you?" he added.

"I'd hardly be here if I had," replied Jerome, refusing to be impressed, and showing that he knew how Mr. Creedy came by his occasional lucky guesses.

"It doesn't follow, my friend. It doesn't follow at all. I've had bigger people than you in here, you know. And you don't feel yourself very popular with your mates? They make a lot of fun of you, don't they?"

"I don't give a damn what they say about me," Jerome said indignantly.

"Oh, yes you do," Mr. Creedy said, standing back and almost throwing his forefinger in Jerome's face. "Don't kid yourself. You care a great deal, as a matter of fact—more than your mate here does. You'd like to be popular, but you're so cautious and secretive you don't give people the chance. It's not that you're not clever, mind," he said, walking about in his excitement and giving Jerome a penetrating glance over his shoulder. "No, it's not that you're not clever. See that, don't you?" he added triumphantly to Flurry, pointing out some other peculiarity of Jerome's skull. "That's intellect, all right."

"Begor, Jerome, he has you taped," Flurry said admiringly.

"But your intellect isn't developed," Mr. Creedy went on eagerly, moulding the situation with his hand like a conductor in an orchestra. "Every time it makes an independent move, up comes the other side and knocks it flat again. The result is, you feel yourself inferior to other people, which you're not really—not by any means—and hence put on an air of bumptiousness and pretending to understand things you do not understand at all. Am I telling you something?" he added with a gleeful look.

"You are not," said Flurry. "You're reading him like a book."

"Go on anyway," said Jerome, impressed in spite of himself.

"You don't drink?" asked Mr. Creedy.

"If you had a father like mine, you wouldn't either," replied Jerome.

"Oh, yes, I should, my friend," Mr. Creedy replied warmly. "I'd never let my old man distort my natural development in that way. . . . As a matter of fact," he added with a chuckle, putting his two hands on his knees and bending almost double, "the old bastard drank like a fish." Then he laughed so much he had to rub his fingers in his eyes. "You should let yourself go more," he added earnestly. "I'm serious now. Don't always be taking heed of the morrow. The morrow won't pay any heed to you. Have a drink and put a bob or two on a horse, and you'll be surprised how different people will feel about you. Sublimity is all you lack, old man. Sublimity, ideality, and optimism. Now have I told you something?"

"You're after telling me a lot," Jerome replied darkly. "Whether there's any truth in it or not is another thing entirely."

"Oh, yes," Mr. Creedy said confidently, "there's plenty of truth in it. Sorry I had to be so critical, though. I have to tell what I see. Never mind about the money."

"Oh, begor, I don't see why you wouldn't be paid for your work the same as the rest of us," Jerome said generously.

"I'm glad you feel like that about it," said Mr. Creedy. "It's the sign of an open mind. I try to be as helpful as I can. Any time you think I can be of use, just drop in."

And away went the two young men in the evening light towards the glittering pier. Jerome had a worried look. Things like that worried Jerome a lot.

"Do you know, I wouldn't be surprised if that fellow had a police record at home," he said.

"Ah, what makes you think that, man?" Flurry asked in surprise.

"I don't know," Jerome replied, nodding sagaciously. " 'Tis a sort of feeling I had. There's something about that fellow. You don't believe all that blooming stuff he talks, do you?"

"Ah, to be sure I don't," said Flurry who was impressed by everything but never for long, and was already beginning to look round for fresh entertainment. "I suppose the poor devil is only swinging the lead like the rest of us."

"You wouldn't bring Rosie along to him, for instance?" asked Jerome.

"What in God's name would I bring Rosie to him for?" Flurry asked, so astonished that he stopped dead.

"Ah," Jerome said lightly, "if you were thinking of marrying a girl, it struck me that you might like to find out something about her first."

"I am not thinking of marrying her, then," said Flurry. "And when I want to find out something about her, 'tisn't her bumps I'll be feeling," he added with a merry laugh.

Flurry had obviously dismissed the whole thing from his mind.

But Jerome never dismissed anything in that way. The phrenologist had made a real impression on him. There was something slightly uncanny about it. It had never occurred to Jerome before, but it was true that he was on the cautious side, and it would be a serious matter if his caution were hindering the development of his intellect. He knew he had a good one, but it never seemed to get him anywhere. And it was also true that he would have liked to be as popular as Flurry if only he knew how, and if only it didn't involve spending quite so much money. He decided that, whatever happened, he would have a few bob on a horse whenever he found someone who could give him a good one.

But he continued to think about Mr. Creedy, and each time he felt a little shudder. The thing was uncanny, however you looked at it. He wondered, with the knowledge that the man must have, that he couldn't do better for himself. With that knowledge, Jerome felt he would take a big house on the South Mall and not open his gob under ten pounds. He'd have nobody only rich men coming to him, and he would give them the works. "You're destroying yourself, Mr. Murphy," he would say shortly. But there was probably something unlucky about it. Money got that way probably didn't prosper.

Next day, when he and Hilda were walking, he deliberately led her past the booth and then stood outside it, pretending to be surprised.

"This is where Flurry and myself went yesterday," he said. "Come in and see what he makes of you."

"Oh, Jerome!" she said reproachfully. "It's so silly!"

"Ah, sure, of course it is," replied Jerome with an unconvincing imitation of Flurry at a fun-fair. " 'Tis only passing the time."

"But it's such a wicked waste of money," Hilda protested, feeling that here at last was the foreign blood breaking out in Jerome and the justification of her workmates' warnings against Irishmen.

"Ah, what's half a crown, girl?" he said, and to avoid a scene, she followed him in.

Mr. Creedy did not seem surprised to see them, and was so cheerful and easy in his manner that he soon dispelled Hilda's alarm. He cracked his little jokes with her as he told her the usual things about machinery and music, and she became properly impressed and interested.

"Yes," she said, "I am very fond of music. Good music. Not that popular stuff. I don't know what people see in that, do you?"

"No," he agreed. "And I should say, judging by what I see, that you're very clean about the house?"

"I try to be," said Hilda, though she had some vague notion that he must be in league with the devil.

"And you're an excellent cook. Am I telling you something?"

"Not bad," she replied modestly. "I'm very good at savouries. But it's not so easy these days, what with the shortages and all that, is it?"

"No," he said, and then he stepped back and looked at her closely. "Now, I'm going to ask you something. Have you ever thought of taking up nursing?"

"As a matter of fact, I have," she replied, now really impressed. "There was a woman up our road, a trained nurse, that I admired ever so much. I never forgot one night when she bandaged up one of the kids that got himself spiked on a railing. But there isn't the money in nursing, is there?"

"I wouldn't say that where you were concerned," he replied gravely. "You'd make a very successful nurse. You'd be successful at any career for which you were really suited."

Jerome was becoming impatient with all this. He hadn't come there to be told that Hilda would make a successful nurse. He didn't want her to be a nurse at all, because he didn't think it a nice occupation for a girl.

"Well," Mr. Creedy said at last, "that's the lot, and I hope I've told you something."

"Oh, yes, very interesting, it was," Hilda said, relieved that nothing had been revealed that she wouldn't like Jerome to hear.

"But it didn't satisfy your friend," Mr. Creedy said slyly.

"Didn't it, Jerome?" she asked in genuine surprise.

"Ah, well, 'twas entertaining," Jerome admitted grudgingly.

"But not in your line," said Mr. Creedy.

"Ah," Jerome said in embarrassment, "there was nothing much you could get hold of."

"Oh, I don't know, Jerome," Hilda said, feeling that Jerome

was being quite ungentlemanly. "It was all quite true, you know. You know yourself about the music, and I simply don't know how this gentleman guessed about the nursing."

"You expected me to tell you whether she'd make a success of you," Mr. Creedy said to Jerome with a grin.

"Ah, I expected something more to the point," said Jerome. . "Sure, there's nothing in that."

"Well, let me tell you, my friend, if she can make a success of you, she can make a success of anything," Mr. Creedy said, coming up to Jerome with his forefinger outstretched. "Didn't I tell you yesterday what was wrong with you? Didn't I warn you against being so cautious and close? And what do you do? Go home and tell this young lady what I said? No. You plan to find out things about her instead. When you came in that door I knew what you wanted. Maybe you don't believe me, but my heart sank. 'He didn't listen to me,' I said. 'He's come here to take an unfair advantage of his young lady. He is not the man I took him for.' You don't know me, my friend. Perhaps I know the things you want to know, but if I do, I don't tell. No, there are things nobody can tell. This young lady can rise to an occasion, and you have to do the same. Try it, my friend! Take a chance! Find out for yourself by Nature's great method of trial and error."

I doubt myself if Jerome ever took the advice. Trial and error is too slow for a Corkman. But he did take the tip about Hilda, and her sublimity, ideality, and optimism were equal to the occasion. She'll find them useful in dealing with Jerome.

UNAPPROVED ROUTE

BETWEEN men and women, as between neighbouring states, there are approved roads which visitors must take. Others they take at their peril, no matter how high-minded their intentions may be.

When I lived in England I became friendly with another Irishman named Frankie Daly. Frankie was the sort of man men like. He was scrupulous, but not so as to irritate people who might have scruples of a different kind. Exacting with himself, he was tolerant of others. The good qualities he had—conscientiousness, loyalty, and generosity—were not those he demanded of his friends, and, as a result, they made great efforts to show them where he was concerned. Even Mick Flynn, who lived by borrowing, made a hullabaloo about paying back a pound he owed to Frankie.

Frankie and I were also friendly with two schoolmistresses who had a little cottage in School Lane, and they frequently joined us in the pub for a drink. Rosalind and Kate could have been sisters, they had so little in common. Kate was a born spinster, lean, plain, and mournful, and with the kindest heart in the world. She was very left-wing and tended to blame capitalism for most of her troubles. Rosalind was a good-looking girl with a fat and rather sullen face, who was always up and down with some man, usually—according to Kate, at any rate—of the shadiest kind. Women with a man on their hands usually vote Tory—they dislike being interrupted—and Rosalind was a Conservative. Cooking being a form of activity associated with love-making, she was also an excellent cook, while Kate, who adored food, not only couldn't cook herself but was driven into hysterics of fastidiousness by the mere sight of cooking fat. She felt about grease as she felt about men, and I sometimes had a suspicion that she identified the two. I often wondered how she could face the liquidation of capitalists and all the blood and mess it would involve.

One day another fellow countryman of Frankie and myself turned up on a temporary job. He was a shambling, good-natured, high-spirited man, given to funny stories and inexplicable fits of morose anger. Lodgings were scarce and hotels expensive, so the girls offered him a room in the cottage. He settled down so well with them that inside a week or so he and Rosalind were lovers. She simply could not be kept away from men.

Kate then devoted herself entirely to the task of hating Jim Hourigan, and being as rude to him as she dared with Rosalind there. Having a lover of Rosalind's in the cottage was like having endless greasy frying-pans to dodge; she couldn't move without seeing a masculine singlet or a pair of socks. Kate derived enormous pleasure from her own griefs, and she told us with gloomy humour that it had been bad enough before, lying awake and wondering what Rosalind was up to, but this had been nothing to lying awake and knowing what she was up to. She couldn't kick up a row with Rosalind, who had an unpredictable and violent temper where men were concerned. Kate rationalized this to herself by saying that Rosalind, being a girl of exceptional intelligence, knew they were all wasters but was too proud to admit it. She told us that Rosalind never had had any taste, that all the men she knew had exploited her, that Jim Hourigan was only another of them, and that the only consolation was that she was there herself, ready to pick up the pieces when the inevitable disillusionment came. Frankie and I only laughed at Kate's groans. We didn't know what sort Jim Hourigan was, and we didn't really care much.

When his job ended, he returned to Ireland after making many promises of bringing the girls for a long summer holiday there, and of returning himself at the first opportunity. Kate was very cheerful because she was quite convinced that he didn't mean a word of it—she had the lowest view of his character and motives —and was delighted to have Rosalind and the cottage to herself again. Rosalind, too, was cheerful because, never before having had anything to do with an Irishman, she took all his promises for gospel, had everything ready for her holiday in the summer, and was certain that Hourigan would then ask her to marry him. She wrote him long, animated letters, cleverly recalling our little town and the characters he had met there, and quoting Kate's doleful predictions about the weather, the European situation, and the cost of living.

There was an alarming lack of response to her letters; finally they did produce a wet spark of a picture postcard saying how much Hourigan looked forward to coming back, which might have encouraged a more persevering correspondent but merely infuriated Rosalind. She wasn't accustomed to having her brilliant letters treated with such lack of ceremony and told him so, but this didn't produce even a spark. Kate began to put on weight, though how she did was a miracle, because Rosalind was so upset that she refused to cook, and Kate had not only to eat sausages—which she loathed—but even to clean the disgusting frying-pan herself.

But that wasn't the end of Kate's troubles. Imprudent as usual, Rosalind was having a baby. Now, in the natural way of things, a nice baby without any messy father to get in the way would have been Kate's idea of bliss, but bliss of that sort is not contemplated in English provincial towns. To begin with, Rosalind would lose her job; women teachers cannot have babies without marriage lines; the thing is unknown. Besides, the landlady would be bound to ask them to leave; this was also part of the drill, and even if the landlady had been a considerate woman, which she wasn't, she would still have found it difficult to overlook such conduct. They would have to try and hush things up and put the baby out to nurse.

This was where Rosalind became completely unmanageable. She said she wanted to keep her baby, and she didn't mind who knew. Just the same, she stopped coming to the public-house with the rest of us, and Kate, gloomier than ever, came alone. She was depressed by her failure to make Rosalind see reason. It would only be for a couple of years, and then they could make some arrangement, like pretending to adopt the baby.

"That wouldn't be so very good, Kate," Frankie said when she mentioned it to him.

"Well, what else can she do, Frankie? Go out as a char-woman?"

"Those are questions that answer themselves, Kate," he said stubbornly. "A baby put out to nurse is a question that never answers itself."

Next evening, without saying anything to Kate or me, he called at the cottage and found Rosalind sitting alone over the fire.

"Coming down to the pub, Rosa?" he asked cheerfully.

"No, Frankie, thanks," she said, without looking up.

"Why not? You know it's not the same without you."

She covered her face with her hands. Frankie sat awkwardly with his legs stretched out, sucking his pipe.

"Kate tells me you don't want to part with the child."

"It seems I'm not likely to be asked."

"All the same, I think you're right and Kate is wrong," he said gravely.

"That's easily said, Frankie," she replied. "It isn't so easy for Kate, with her job to mind."

"If that's how you feel about it, wouldn't it be better for you to marry?"

"The man who got me would get a treasure," she said savagely. "Whistled after in the street!"

"That's a matter for him," said Frankie. "Plenty of men would be very glad to marry you. You mustn't let a thing like this make you undervalue yourself."

"Ah, talk sense, Frankie!" she said wearily. "Who'd marry me in the middle of all this scandal?"

"I would, to begin with—if you hadn't anyone you liked bet-ter."

"You?" she asked incredulously.

"And consider myself very much honoured," Frankie added steadily.

"Are you serious, Frankie?" she asked, almost angrily.

"Of course I'm serious."

"And face all the humiliation of it?"

"There isn't any humiliation," he said flatly. "That's where you're mistaken. There's no humiliation where there hasn't been any offence. The offence is in deceiving others, not in being deceived ourselves."

"Oh, I can't, Frankie, I can't," she said desperately. "I've made a fool of myself over this waster, and I can't let another man shoulder my burdens."

"There's no particular burden either," he said. "You mustn't think I'm asking you only because you're in a fix. I'd have asked you anyway when this thing was all over and you could make up your own mind. I'm only asking now in case it might make the immediate future a bit easier."

"Why didn't you ask me before?"

"Maybe because I felt I hadn't much to offer you," Frankie said with a shy smile.

"My God," she said, rising. "I'd have married you like a shot."

She sat on his knee and hugged him despairingly. He was a clumsy lover. He talked in an apologetic, worried tone about his job, his home, and his family; how much he earned and where they could live. She didn't listen. She thought of what it would mean to her to start life again, free of this nightmare. Then she took him by the shoulders and looked into his eyes with the air of a sleepwalker.

"I'll do it," she said. "God help me, Frankie, I hate it, but I'll do it for the kid's sake. All I can say is that I'll make it up to you. You needn't be afraid of that. I'll make it up to you all right."

Kate, whose low view of life had led her to take a low view of its Creator, almost got converted because of it. She had always liked Frankie, but her experience of people she liked had been that they only got her into fresh trouble, and that it was better, if you could manage it, to have nothing to do with anybody. She wasn't the only one who admired Frankie's behaviour. It dawned on others of us that he had done exactly what we would have done ourselves except for what people might think. Actually, as we discovered, "people," meaning the neighbours with one or two exceptions, liked Rosalind and were pleased to see her escape the machine of social ignominy reserved for women with more feeling than calculation in them.

Frankie and Rosalind were married quietly and went to live in a little cottage some miles outside the town, a rather lonely cottage with low beams, high chimneys, and breakneck staircases, but it had a big garden, which Rosalind enjoyed. She kept on her job; she knew the other teachers knew, but now it only amused her. It was wonderful to have Frankie there as a prop. Up to this, all the men she had lived with had taken advantage of her, and she had accepted it in a cynical, good-humoured way as part of the price you had to pay for being too fond of them. She believed, as Kate did, that men were like that, but she was lacking in any desire to reform them.

Under Frankie's care she grew round as a tub, stupid, and quite remarkably beautiful, while Kate managed to look as like the anxious father of her unborn child as a girl could look. But the change in Frankie was even more remarkable. He had always kept a youthful freshness, but now he suddenly began to look like a boy of seventeen. It might have been something to do with Rosalind's cooking—Kate, who had begun to feel the lack of it, visited them every day—but he rang her up regularly at the school to see that she was all right, raced for his bus to get home early in the evenings, and took her for her evening walk to the pub. He was full of banter and tricks, and Rosalind looked on with the affectionate calm of a woman watching the man she loves make a fool of himself. And it really was pleasant those summer evenings outside the public-house, watching that late flowering of emotion, the bachelor crust of caution breaking up, the little shoots of sentiment beginning to peer out.

Their happiness was lyrical. It was only at odd times that Rosalind remembered her griefs, and usually it was in the early morning when she was waked by the heaving of the child within her, listened to the birds outside their window, and felt deserted even with Frankie beside her. Not to wake him, she sniffled quietly into her handkerchief, her back turned on him and her body shaken with suppressed sobs. When he woke, she still tried to keep away from him.

"What ails you now didn't ail you before?" he would ask humorously.

"What you've got in me."

"What's that?"

"I told you—a daisy!"

"No, that was what I told you," he said, and slapped her bottom affectionately.

Then she bawled without restraint and beat her stomach.

"Why can't it be yours?" she cried despairingly.

"One thing at a time," said Frankie.

He believed her; that was his mistake. He really thought when he heard her lonely weeping that it was merely the ambiguity of her position that caused it, and not the humiliation of being rejected and hounded into marriage with someone else by a tramp like Hourigan. Frankie was a decent man; he didn't realize that in circumstances like those no woman can ever be happy, even with the best man in the world—even with the man she loves. Love, in fact, has nothing to do with it. To ignore that is to ignore a woman's vanity, the mainspring of her character.

Her time came in the middle of the night, and Frankie returned from the nursing home in the early morning in a stupor of misery and astonishment; misery at the mere possibility that her life might be in danger, astonishment that anyone's life could possibly mean so much to him. He lit the fire, but then found that he couldn't bear the little cottage without her; it, too, seemed in a stupor of misery, wondering when she would come back, put on that house-coat, boil that kettle, and wash those dishes. He wanted to make himself breakfast, but could not bring himself to touch the things that were properly hers and that stood waiting for her with the infinite patience of inanimate things. He swore at himself when he realized that he was identifying his grief with that of a common teakettle. He had some breakfast in a café, and then went off walking through the countryside, merely halting for a drink while he rang up the nursing home. It was evening before everything was over and Rosalind and the child—a son—safe, and then he took a car straight there.

She was still stupefied with drugs when he was admitted, but she clung to him passionately.

"Don't look!" she said fiercely. "Not till the next time."

"I thought he was yours," Frankie said with a grin, and smiled down at the little morsel in the cot. "Cripes!" he added savagely. "Wouldn't you think they could get them out without clawing them?"

"Did you hear the children playing on the doorstep?" she asked happily.

"No," Frankie said in surprise. "What were they playing?"

"*Hamlet,* I think," she said, closing her eyes, and, seeing how her thoughts drifted in and out of the drug, he tiptoed out. In sheer relief he knocked back three whiskies in quick succession, but failed to get drunk. Then he tried for some of the old gang to sit and drink with, but, by one of those coincidences that always occur at moments like that, we were all out. It was just that he didn't want to go home. When he did get out of the bus and crossed the common towards the cottage, he saw a man's figure step out of the shadow of the trees beside it and knew at once who it was. His heart sank.

"Frankie!" Jim Hourigan said imploringly, "I'd like a word with you."

Frankie halted. He had a sudden feeling of foreboding.

"You'd better come inside," he said in a troubled voice.

He went ahead into the sitting-room and switched on the light and the electric fire, which stood in the big open hearth. Then he turned and faced Hourigan, who was standing by the door. The man looked half-distracted, his eyes were wild, his hair was in disorder.

"What is it?" Frankie asked curtly.

"Frankie," Hourigan muttered, "I want a word with Rosalind."

"Rosalind is in hospital."

"I know, I know," Hourigan said, flapping his hands like an old man. "She said she was going there. But I wanted to see you first, to get your permission. It's only to explain to her, Frankie— that's all."

Frankie concealed his surprise at Hourigan's statement that Rosalind had told him anything.

"I don't think she's in a state for seeing anybody, you know," he said in a level tone. "The boy was born only a couple of hours ago."

"Christ!" Hourigan said, beating the table with his fist and shaking his head as though tossing water from his eyes. "That's all that was missing. I came late for the fair as usual. My first child is born and I'm not even there. All right, Frankie, all right," he added in a crushed tone, "I see 'tis no good. But tell her all the same. Tell her I never knew a thing about it till I got her letter. That God might strike me dead this minute if the idea ever crossed my mind!"

Frankie looked at him in surprise. There was no mistaking the man's abject misery.

"What letter was this?" he asked.

"The letter she sent me before she went in," Hourigan hurried on, too distraught to notice the bewilderment in Frankie's voice. "You don't think I'd have treated her like that if I knew? You can think what you like of me, Frankie, and it won't be anything worse than I think of myself, but not that, Frankie, not that! I wouldn't do it to a woman I picked up in the street, and I loved that girl, Frankie. I declare to God I did." He began to wave his arms wildly again, looking round the little sitting-room without seeing anything. "It's just that I'm no damn good at writing letters. The least thing puts me off. I'd be saying to myself I'd be there before the letter. I said the same thing to her on a card, Frankie, but then the mother died, and I was in a terrible state— oh, the usual things! I know 'tis no excuse, and I'm not making excuses, but that's the way I am. If I had any idea, I'd have been over to her by the first boat. You must tell her that, Frankie. She must know it herself."

"When did you get this letter?" asked Frankie.

"Oh, only yesterday, Frankie," exclaimed Hourigan, entirely missing the import of Frankie's question. "I swear to God I didn't waste an hour. I'm travelling all night. I couldn't sleep and I couldn't eat. It was all that damn letter. It nearly drove me out of my mind. Did you see it, Frankie?"

"No," said Frankie.

"Well, you'd better. Mind, I don't blame her a bit, but it's not true, it's not true!"

He took the letter from his wallet and passed it to Frankie. Frankie sat down and put on his glasses. Hourigan bent over the back of the armchair, reading it again in a mutter.

"Dear Jim Hourigan," Frankie read silently, "By this time to-morrow I'll be in a hospital, having your child. This will probably be more satisfaction to you than it is to me and my husband. I am sure you will be disappointed to know that I have a husband, but in this life we can't expect everything."

"Now, that's what I mean, Frankie," Hourigan said desperately, jabbing at the lines with his forefinger. "That's not fair and she knows it's not fair. She knows I'm not as mean as that, whatever faults I have."

"I wouldn't worry too much about that," Frankie said heavily, realizing that Hourigan and he were not reading the same letter. It was almost as though they were not concerned with the same woman. This was a woman whom Frankie had never seen. He went on reading.

"If the child takes after you, it might be better for more than Frank and myself that it shouldn't live. My only hope is that it may learn something from my husband. If ever a good man can make up to a child for the disaster of a bad father, your child will have every chance. So far as I can, I'll see that he gets it, and will never know any more of you than he knows now." It was signed in full: "Rosalind Daly."

Hourigan sighed. "You explain to her, Frankie," he said despairingly. "I couldn't."

"I think it would be better if you explained it yourself," Frankie said, folding up the letter and giving it back.

"You think she'll see me?" Hourigan asked doubtfully.

"I think she'd better see you," Frankie said in a dead voice.

"Only for ten minutes, Frankie; you can tell her that. Once I explain to her, I'll go away, and I give you my word that neither of you will ever see me here again."

"I'll talk to her myself in the morning," Frankie said. "You'd better ring me up at the office some time after twelve."

Hourigan shambled away across the common, babbling poetic blessings on Frankie's head and feeling almost elated. How Frankie felt he never said. Perhaps if Hourigan had known how he felt, he might have left that night without seeing Rosalind. He wasn't a bad chap, Jim Hourigan, though not exactly perceptive, even as regards the mother of his child.

But Rosalind had perception enough for them both. When Frankie called next morning, the effect of the drug had worn off, and she knew from the moment he entered that something serious had happened. He was as gentle as ever, but he had withdrawn into himself, the old Frankie of the days before his marriage, hurt but self-sufficient. She grabbed his hands feverishly.

"Is anything wrong at home, Frankie?"

"Nothing," he replied in embarrassment. "Just a visitor, that's all."

"A visitor? Who?"

"I think you know," he said gently.

"What brought that bastard?" she hissed.

"Apparently, a letter from you."

Suddenly she began to weep, the core of her hysteria touched.

"I didn't tell you, because I didn't want to upset you," she sobbed. "I just wanted him to know how I despised him."

"He seems to have got the idea," Frankie said dryly. "Now he wants to see you, to explain."

"Damn his explanations!" she cried hysterically. "I know what you think—that I sent that letter without telling you so as to bring him here. How could I know there was enough manliness in him to make him even do that? Can't you imagine how I felt, Frankie?"

"You know," he said paternally, "I think you'd better have a word with him and make up your mind about exactly what you did feel."

"Oh, Christ!" she said. "I tell you I only meant to hurt him. I never meant to hurt you, and that's all I've succeeded in doing."

"I'd rather you didn't let your feelings run away with you again and hurt yourself and the child," Frankie said in a gentler tone.

"But how can I avoid hurting myself when I'm hurting you?" she asked wildly. "Do you think this is how I intended to pay you back for what you did for me? Very well; if he's there, send him up and I'll tell him. I'll tell him in front of you. I'll tell you both exactly how I feel. Will that satisfy you?"

"He'll call this afternoon," Frankie said firmly. "You'd better see him alone. You'd better let him see the child alone. And remember," he added apologetically, "whatever you decide on I agree to beforehand. I may have behaved selfishly before. I don't want to do it again."

He smiled awkwardly and innocently, still bewildered by the disaster which had overtaken him, and Rosalind held her hands to her temples in a frenzy. She had never realized before how hurt he could be, had probably not even known that she might hurt him.

"I suppose you think I'm going to let you divorce me so that I can go back to Ireland with that waster? I'd sooner throw myself and the child into a pond. Oh, very well, I'll settle it, I'll settle it. Oh, God!" she said between her teeth. "What sort of fool am I?"

And as he went down the stairs, Frankie knew that he was seeing her for the last time as his wife, and that when they met again, she would be merely the mother of Jim Hourigan's child, and realized with a touch of bitterness that there are certain forms of magnanimity which are all very well between men but are misplaced in dealing with women, not because they cannot admire them but because they seem to them irrelevant to their own function in life. When he saw Hourigan again, he knew that the change had already taken place. Though nothing had been decided, Jim Hourigan was almost professionally protective of Frankie's interests and feelings. That was where the iron in Frankie came out. He made it plain that his interests were not in question.

There were plenty—Kate among them—to say that he had behaved absurdly; that with a little more firmness on his part the crisis would never have arisen; that Rosalind was in no condition to make the decision he had forced on her and needed only gentle direction to go on as she had been going; that, in fact, he might have spared her a great deal of unhappiness by refusing to see Jim Hourigan in the first place.

As for unhappiness, nothing I have heard suggests that Rosalind is unhappy with Jim Hourigan. It is a grave mistake to believe that that sort of thing leads to unhappiness. Frankie's conduct certainly does, but is that not because to people like him happiness is merely an incidental, something added which, taken away, leaves them no poorer than before?

LONELY ROCK

I

In England during the war I had a great friend called Jack Courtenay who was assistant manager in one of the local factories. His job was sufficiently important to secure his exemption from military service. His family was originally from Cork, but he had come to work in England when he was about eighteen and married an English girl called Sylvia, a school-teacher. Sylvia was tall, thin, fair, and vivacious, and they got on very well together. They had two small boys, of seven and nine. Jack was big-built, handsome, and solemn-looking, with a gravity which in public enabled him to escape from the usual English suspicion of Irish temperament and in private to get away with a schoolboy mania for practical joking. I have known him invite someone he liked to his office to discuss an entirely imaginary report from the police, accusing the unfortunate man of bigamy and deserting a large family. He could carry on a joke like that for a long time without a shadow of a smile, and end up by promising his victim to try and persuade the police that it was all a case of mistaken identity.

He was an athlete, with an athlete's good nature when he was well and an athlete's hysteria when he wasn't. A toothache or a cold in the head could drive him stark, staring mad. Then he retired to bed (except when he could create more inconvenience by not doing so) and conducted guerrilla warfare against the whole household, particularly the children, who were diverting the attention which should have come to himself. His face, normally expressionless, could convey indescribable agonies on such occasions, and even I felt that Sylvia went too far with her air of indifference and boredom. "Do stop that shouting!" or "Why don't you see the dentist?" were remarks that caused me almost as much pain as they caused her husband.

Fortunately, his ailments were neither serious nor protracted, and Sylvia didn't seem to mind so much about his other weakness, which was girls. He had a really good eye for a girl and a corresponding vanity about the ravages he could create in them, so he was forever involved with some absolutely stunning blonde. At Christmas I was either dispatching or receiving presents that Sylvia wasn't supposed to know about. These flirtations (they were nothing more serious) never went too far. The man was a born philanderer. Because I was fresh from Ireland and disliked his schoolboy jokes, he regarded me as a puritan and gave me friendly lectures with a view to broadening my mind and helping me to enjoy life. Sylvia's mind he had apparently broadened already.

"Did you know that Jack's got a new girl, Phil?" she asked, while he beamed proudly on both of us. "Such a relief after the last! Didn't he show you the last one's photo? Oh, my dear, the commonest-looking piece."

"Now, now, who's jealous?" Jack would say severely, wagging his finger at her.

"Really, Jack," she would reply with bland insolence, "I'd have to have a very poor opinion of myself to be jealous of that. Didn't you say she was something in Woolworth's?"

To complete the picture of an entirely emancipated household, I was supposed to be in love with her and to indulge in all sorts of escapades behind his back. We did our best to keep up the game, but I am afraid she found me rather heavy going.

There was a third adult in the house; this was Jack's mother, whom Sylvia, with characteristic generosity, had invited to live with them. At the same time I don't think she had had any idea what she was letting herself in for. It was rather like inviting a phase of history. Mrs. Courtenay was a big, bossy, cheerful woman and an excellent housekeeper, so Jack and Sylvia had at least the advantage of being able to get away together whenever they liked. The children were fond of her and she spoiled them, but at the same time her heart was not in them. They had grown up outside her scope and atmosphere. Her heart was all the time in the little house in Douglas Street in Cork, with the long garden and the apple trees, the old cronies who dropped in for a cup of tea and a game of cards, and the convent where she went to Mass and to visit the lifelong friend whom Sylvia persisted in calling Sister Mary Misery. Sister Mary Misery was always in some trouble and always inviting the prayers of her friends. Mrs. Courtenay's nostalgia was almost entirely analogical, and the precise degree of pleasure she received from anything was conditioned by its resemblance to something or somebody in Cork. Her field of analogy was exceedingly wide, as when she admired a photograph of St. Paul's because it reminded her of the Dominican Church in Cork.

Jack stood in great awe of his mother, and this was something Sylvia found it difficult to understand. He did not, for instance, like drinking spirits before her, and if he had to entertain while she was there, he drank sherry. When at ten o'clock sharp the old woman rose and said: "Wisha, do you know, I think I'll go to my old doss; good night to ye," he relaxed and started on the whisky.

There was hardly a day, wet or fine, well or ill, but Mrs. Courtenay was up for morning Mass. This was practically her whole social existence, as her only company, apart from me, was Father Whelan, the parish priest; a nice, simple poor man, but from Waterford—"not at all the same thing," as Sylvia observed. For a Waterford man he did his best. He lent her the papers from home; sometimes newspapers, but mostly religious papers: "simple papers for simple people," he explained to Sylvia, just to show that he wasn't taken in.

But if he implied that Mrs. Courtenay was simple, he was wrong.

"Wisha, hasn't Father Tom a beautiful face, Phil?" she would exclaim with childish pleasure as she held out the photograph of some mountainous sky-pilot. "You'd never again want to hear another Passion sermon after Father Tom. Poor Father Whelan does his best, but of course he hasn't the intellect."

"How could he?" Sylvia would say gravely. "We must remember he's from Waterford."

Mrs. Courtenay never knew when Sylvia was pulling her leg.

"Why then, indeed, Sylvia," she said, giving a reproving look over her spectacles, "some very nice people came from Waterford."

Though Mrs. Courtenay couldn't discuss it with Sylvia, who might have thought her prejudiced, she let me know how shocked she was by the character of the English, who seemed from the age of fifteen on to do nothing but fall in and out of love. Mrs. Courtenay had heard of love; she was still very much in love with her own husband, who had been dead for years, but this was a serious matter and had nothing whatever in common with those addle-pated affairs you read of in the newspapers. Fortunately, she never knew the worst, owing to her lack of familiarity with the details. Once an old schoolmistress friend of Sylvia's with a son the one age with Jack tried to start a little chat with her about the dangers young men had to endure, but broke down under the concentrated fire of Mrs. Courtenay's innocence.

"Willie's going to London worries me a lot," she said darkly.

"Why, then, indeed, ma'am, I wouldn't blame you," said Mrs. Courtenay. "The one time I was there, the traffic nearly took the sight out of my eyes."

"And it's not the traffic only, is it, Mrs. Courtenay?" asked the schoolmistress, a bit taken aback. "I mean, we send them out into the world healthy, and we want them to come back to us healthy."

"Ah, indeed," said Mrs. Courtenay triumphantly, "wasn't it only the other day I was saying the same thing to you, Sylvia? Whatever he gets to eat in London, Jack's digestion is never the same."

Not to wrong her, I must admit that she wasn't entirely ignorant of the subject, for she mentioned it herself to me (very confidentially while Sylvia was out of the room) in connection with a really nice sodality man from the Watercourse Road who got it through leaning against the side of a ship.

Sylvia simply did not know what to make of her mother-in-law's ingenuousness, which occasionally bordered on imbecility, but she was a sufficiently good housekeeper herself to realize that the old woman had plenty of intelligence, and she respected the will-power that kept her going, cheerful and uncomplaining, through the trials of loneliness and old age.

"We're very busy these days," she would sigh after Mrs. Courtenay had gone to bed, and she was enjoying what her husband called "the first pussful." "We're doing another novena for Sister Mary Misery's sciatica. The last one misfired, but we'll wear Him down yet! Really, she talks as if God were a Corkman!"

"Well," said Jack, "some very nice people came from Cork."

"But it's fantastic, Jack! It's simply fantastic!" Sylvia cried, slamming her palm on the arm-rest of her chair. "She's upstairs now, talking to God as she talked to us. She feels she will wear Him down, exactly as she says."

"She probably will," said I.

"I shouldn't be in the least surprised," Sylvia added viciously. "She's worn me down."

II

Naturally, Jack and Sylvia both told me of the absolutely stunning brunette he had met in Manchester, driving a Ministry car. Then, for some reason, the flow of confidences dried up. I guessed that something had gone wrong with the romance, but knew better than to ask questions. I knew that Jack would tell me in his own good time. He did too, one grey winter evening when we had walked for miles up the hills and taken refuge from the wind in a little bar-parlour where a big fire was roaring. When he brought in the pints, he told me in a slightly superior way with a smile that didn't seem quite genuine that he was having trouble about Margaret.

"Serious?" I asked.

"Well, she's had a baby," he said with a shrug.

He expected me to be shocked, and I was, but not for his reasons. It was clear that he was badly shaken, did not know how his philandering could have gone so far or had such consequences, and was blaming the drink or something equally irrelevant.

"That's rotten luck," I said.

"That's the worst of it," he said. "It's not luck."

"Oh!" I said. I was beginning to realize vaguely the mess in which he had landed himself. "You mean she—?"

"Yes," he cut in. "She wanted it. Now she wants to keep it, and her family won't let her, so she's left home."

"Oh," I said again. "That is rotten."

"It's not very pleasant," he said, unconsciously trying to reassert himself in his old part as a man of the world by lowering the key of the conversation.

"Does Sylvia know?"

"Good Lord, no," he exclaimed with a frown, and this time it was he who was shocked. "There's no point in upsetting her."

"She'll be a damn sight more upset if she hears of it from someone else," I said.

"Yes," he replied after a moment. "I see your point."

I don't know whether he did or not. He had the sort of sensitiveness which leads men into the most preposterous situations in the desire not to give pain to people they love. It never minimizes the pain in the long run, of course, or so it seemed to me. I had no experience of that sort of situation and was all for giving the pain at once and getting it over. I should even have been prepared to break the news to Sylvia myself, just to be sure she had someone substantial to bawl on. Nowadays I wouldn't rush into it so eagerly.

Instead, Sylvia talked to me about it, in her official tone. It was a couple of months later. She had managed to get rid of her mother-in-law for half an hour, and we were drinking cocktails.

"Did you know Jack's got himself into a scrape with the brunette, Phil?" she said lightly, crossing her legs and smoothing her skirt. "Has he told you?"

I could have shaken her. There was no need to do the stiff upper lip on me, and at any rate I couldn't reply to it. I like a bit more intimacy myself.

"He has," I said uncomfortably. "How are things going?"

"Baby's ill, and she's had to chuck her job. Jack is really quite worried."

"I don't wonder," I said. "What's he going to do?"

"What can he do?" she exclaimed with a shrug and a mow. "He should look after the girl. I've told him I'll divorce him."

I hardly knew what to say to this. Sweet reasonableness may be all very well, but usually it bears no relation to the human facts.

"Is that what you want to do?"

"Well, my feelings don't count for much in this."

"That's scarcely how Jack looks at it," I said.

"So he says," she muttered with a shrug.

"Oh, don't be silly, Sylvia!" I said.

She looked at me for a moment as though she might throw something at me, and I almost wished she would.

"Oh, well," she said at last, "if that's how he feels he should bring her here. You can't even imagine what girls in her position have to go through. It'll simply drive her to suicide, and then he will have something to worry about. I do wish you'd speak to him, Phil."

"What's his objection?"

"Mother doesn't know we drink," she said maliciously. "Anyhow, as if it would ever cross her mind that he was responsible! She probably thinks it's something you catch from leaning against a tree."

"I'll talk to him," I said. I had a feeling that between them they would be bound to make a mess of it.

"Tell him Granny need never know," she said. "He doesn't even have to pretend he knows the girl. She can be a friend of mine. And at a time like this, who's going to inquire about her husband? We can kill him off in the most horrible manner. She just loves tragedies."

This was more difficult than it sounded. Jack didn't want to talk at all, and when he talked he was in a bad humour. I had had to take him out to the local pub, and we talked in low voices between the family parties and the dart-players. Jack's masculine complacency revolted as much at taking advice from me as at taking help from Sylvia. He listened in a peculiar way he had, frowning with one side of his face, as if with half his mind he was considering your motion while with the other he ruled it out of order.

"I'm afraid it's impossible," he said stiffly.

"Well, what are you going to do?"

"Sylvia said she'd divorce me," he replied in a sulky voice that showed it would be a long time before he forgave Sylvia for her high-minded offer.

"Is that what you want?"

"But, my dear fellow, it's not a matter of what I want," he said scoffingly.

"You mean you won't accept Sylvia's kindness, is that it?"

"I won't go on my knees to anybody, for anything."

"Do you want her to go on her knees to you?"

"Oh," he replied ungraciously, "if that's how she feels—"

"You wouldn't like me to get a note from her?" I asked. (I knew it was mean, but I couldn't resist it.)

III

That was how Margaret came to be invited to the Courtenays'. I promised to look in, the evening she came. It was wet, and the narrow sloping High Street with its rattling inn-signs looked the last word in misery. As I turned up the avenue to the Courtenays', the wind was rising. In the distance it had blown a great gap through the cloud, and the brilliant sky had every tint of metal from blue steel at the top to bronze below. Mrs. Courtenay opened the door to me.

"They're not back from the station yet," she said cheerfully. "Would you have a cup of tea?"

"No," I said. "All I want is to get warm."

"I suppose they'll be having it when they come in," she said. "The train must be late."

Just then the taxi drove up, and Sylvia came in with Margaret, a short, slight girl with a rather long, fine-featured face; the sort of face that seems to have been slightly shrunken to give its fea-

tures a certain precision and delicacy. Jack came in, carrying the
baby's basket, and set it on a chair in the hall. His mother went
straight to it, as though she could see nothing else.

"Isn't he lovely, God bless him?" she said, showing her gums
while her whole face lit up.

"I'd better get him settled down," Margaret said nervously with
a quick, bright smile.

"Yes," Sylvia said. "Margaret and I will take him up. Will you
pour her a drink first, Jack?"

"Certainly," said Jack, beginning to beam. "Nothing I like so
much. Whisky, Mrs. Harding?"

"Oh, whisky—Mr. Courtenay," she replied with her sudden,
brilliant laugh.

"Won't you call me Jack?" he asked with a mock-languishing
air. I think he was almost enjoying the mystification, which had
something in common with his own practical jokes.

While the girls went upstairs with the baby, Mrs. Courtenay
sat before the fire, her hands joined in her lap. Her eyes had a
faraway look.

"God help us!" she sighed. "Isn't she young to be a widow?"

At ten Mrs. Courtenay drew the shawl about her shoulders,
said as usual "I'll go to my old doss," and went upstairs. Some
time later we were interrupted by a sickly little whine. Margaret
jumped up with an apologetic smile.

"That's Teddy," she said. "I shan't be a minute."

"I shouldn't trouble, dear," Sylvia said in her bland, insolent
way, and we heard a door open softly. "I rather thought Granny
would come to the rescue," she explained.

"He'll be afraid of a stranger," Margaret said tensely, and we
all listened again. We heard the old woman's voice, soft and almost continuous, and the crying ceased abruptly. Apparently
Teddy didn't consider Mrs. Courtenay a stranger. I noticed as if
for the first time the billows of wind break over the house.

Next morning, when Teddy had been settled in the garden in
his pram, Mrs. Courtenay said: "I think I'll take him for a little
walk. They get very tired of the one place." She apparently knew
things about babies that weren't in any textbook, and uttered
them in a tone of quiet authority which made textbooks an im-

pertinence. She didn't appear again until lunch-time, having taken him to the park—"they're very fond of trees." His father's death in an air-crash in the Middle East had proved a safe introduction to the other women, and Mrs. Courtenay, who usually complained of the stand-offishness of the English, returned in high good humour, full of gossip—the untold numbers blinded, drowned, and burned to death, and the wrecked lives of young women who became too intimate with foreigners. The Poles, in particular, were a great disappointment to her—such a grand Catholic nation, but so unreliable.

That evening, when we heard the shriek from the bedroom, there was no question about who was to deal with it. "Don't upset yourselves," Mrs. Courtenay said modestly, pulled the shawl firmly about her, and went upstairs. Margaret, a very modern young woman, had Teddy's day worked out to a time-table, stipulating when he should be fed, lifted, and loved, but it had taken that baby no time to discover that Mrs. Courtenay read nothing but holy books and believed that babies should be fed, lifted, and loved when it suited themselves. Margaret frowned and shook herself in her frock.

"I'm sure it's bad for him, Sylvia," she said.

"Oh, dreadful," Sylvia sighed with her heartless air as she threw one long leg over the arm of the chair. "But Granny is thriving on it. Haven't you noticed?"

A curious situation was developing in the house, which I watched with fascination. Sylvia, who had very little use for sentiment, was quite attracted by Margaret. "She really is charming, Phil," she told me in her bland way. "Really, Jack has remarkably good taste." Margaret, a much more dependent type, after hesitating for a week, developed quite a crush on Sylvia. It was Jack who was odd man out. Their friendship was a puzzle to him, and what they said and thought about him when they were together was more than he could imagine, but judging by the frown that frequently drew down one side of his face, he felt it couldn't be very nice.

Sylvia was older, shrewder, more practical, and Margaret's guilelessness took her breath away. Margaret's experience of love had been very limited; she had fluttered round with some highly

inappropriate characters, and from them drew vast generaliza-
tions, mostly derogatory, which included all races and men. Jack
had been the first real man in her life, and she had grabbed at the
chance of having his child. Now she envisaged nothing but a
future dedicated to the memory of a couple of week-ends with
him and to the upbringing of his child. Sylvia in her cool way
tried to make her see things more realistically.

"Really, Phil," she told me, "she is the sweetest girl, but, oh,
dear, she's such an impossible romantic. What she really needs is
a husband to knock some of the romance out of her."

I had a shrewd idea that she regarded me as a likely candidate
for the honours of knocking the romance out of Margaret, but I
felt the situation was already complicated enough. At the same
time, it struck me as ironic that the world should be full of men
who would be glad of a decent wife, while a girl like Margaret,
whom any man could be proud of, made a fool of herself over a
married man.

IV

One Saturday afternoon I went up early, just after lunch, for
my walk with Jack. He wasn't ready, so I sat in the front room
with Sylvia, Margaret, and Mrs. Courtenay. I had the impression
that there were feelings, at least on the old lady's part, and I was
right. It had taken Teddy a week to discover that she had a bedroom of her own, and when he did, he took full advantage of it.
She had now become his devoted slave, and when we met, I had
to be careful that she didn't suspect me of treating him with in-
sufficient respect. Two old women on the road had made a mortal
enemy of her because of that. And it wasn't only strangers. Margaret too came in for criticism.

The criticism this afternoon had been provoked first by Margaret's inhuman refusal to feed him half an hour before his feed-
ing time, and secondly by the pointed way the two younger
women went on with their talk instead of joining her in keeping
him company. In Margaret this was only assumed. She was inclined to resent the total occupation of her baby by Mrs. Courtenay, but this was qualified by Teddy's antics and quite suddenly
she would smile and then a quick frown would follow the smile.

Sylvia was quite genuinely uninterested. She had the capacity for surrounding herself in her own good manners.

The old woman could, of course, have monopolized me, but it gave her more satisfaction to throw me to the girls and make their monstrous inhumanity obvious even to themselves.

"Wisha, go on, Phil," she said with her sweet, distraught smile. "You'll want to be talking. He'll be getting his dinner soon anyway. The poor child is famished."

Most of this went over my head, and I joined the girls gladly enough, while Mrs. Courtenay, playing quietly with Teddy, suffered in silence. Just then the door opened quietly behind her and Jack came in. She started and looked up.

"Ah, here's Daddy now!" she said triumphantly. "Daddy will play with us."

"Daddy will do nothing of the sort," retorted Jack with remarkable presence of mind. "Daddy wants somebody to play with him. Ready, Phil?"

But even this didn't relax the tension in the room. Margaret looked dumbfoundered. She looked at Jack and grinned; then frowned and looked at me. Sylvia raised her shoulders. Meanwhile her mother-in-law, apparently quite unaware of the effect she had created, was making Teddy sit up and show off his tricks. Sylvia followed us to the door.

"Does she suspect anything?" she asked anxiously with one hand on the jamb.

"Oh, not at all," Jack said with a shocked expression that almost caused one side of his face to fold up. "That's only her way of speaking."

"Hm," grunted Sylvia. "Curious way of speaking."

"Not really, Sylvia," I said. "If she suspected anything, that's the last thing in the world she'd have said."

"Like leaning against a ship?" Sylvia said. "I dare say you're right."

But she wasn't sure. Jack walked down the avenue without speaking, and I knew he was shaken too.

"Awkward situation," he said between his teeth.

Since Margaret's arrival he had become what for him was almost forthcoming. It was mainly the need for someone to confide

in. He couldn't any longer confide in Margaret or Sylvia because
of their friendship.

"I don't think it meant what Sylvia imagined," I said as we set
off briskly up the hill. We both liked the hilly country behind
the town, the strong thrust of the landscape that made walking
like a bird's flight on a stormy day.

"I dare say not, but still, it's awkward—two women in a
house!"

"I suppose so."

"You know what I mean?"

I thought I did, and I liked his delicacy. Being a chap who
never cared to hurt people's feelings, he probably left both girls
very much alone. Having had so much to do with them both, and
being the sort who is accustomed to having a lot to do with
women, he probably found this a strain. They must have found it
so likewise, because their behaviour had grown decidedly ob-
streperous. One evening I had watched them, with their arms
about one another's waists, guying him, and realized that behind
it there was an element of hysteria. The situation was becoming
impossible.

We had come out on the common, with the little red houses to
one side, and the uplands sweeping away from them.

"Last night Sylvia woke me when the alert went, to keep Margaret company," he went on in a tone in which pain, bewilderment, and amusement were about equally blended. It was as
though he were fastidiously holding up something small, frail,
and not quite clean for your inspection. "She said she'd go if I
didn't. I'd have preferred her to go, but then she got quite cross.
She said: 'Margaret won't like it, and you've shown her little
enough consideration since she came.'"

"Rather tactless of Sylvia," I said.

"I know," he added with a bewildered air. "And it's so unlike
her. She said I didn't understand women."

"And did you go?"

"I had to."

I could fill in the gaps in his narrative and appreciate his embarrassment. Obviously, before he went to Margaret's room, he

had to go to his mother's to explain Sylvia's anxiety for her old
school friend, and having done everything a man could do to
spare the feelings of three women, had probably returned to bed
with the feeling that they were all laughing at him. And though
he told it lightly, I had the feeling that it was loneliness which
made him tell it at all, and that he would never again be quite
comfortable with either Sylvia or Margaret. "Now your days of
philandering are over," was running through my head. I wasn't
sure that he would be quite such a pleasant friend.

Margaret remained for some months until the baby was quite
well and she had both got a job and found a home where Teddy
would be looked after. She was full of gaiety and courage, but I
had the feeling that her way was not an easy one either. Even
without the aid of a husband, the romance had been knocked out
of her. It was marked by the transference of her allegiance from
Jack to Sylvia. And Sylvia was lonesome too. She kept pressing
me to come to the house when Jack was away. She corresponded
with Margaret and went to stay with her when she was in town.
They were linked by something which excluded Jack. To each
of them her moment of sacrifice had come, and each had risen to
it, but nobody can live on that plane forever, and now there
stretched before them the commonplace of life with no prospect
that ever again would it call on them in the same way. Never
again would Sylvia and Jack be able to joke about his philandering, and the house seemed the gloomier for it, as though it had
lost a safety valve.

Mrs. Courtenay too was lonely after Teddy, though with her
usual stoicism she made light of it. "Wisha, you get very used to
them, Phil," she said to me as she pulled her shawl about her.
Now she felt that she had no proper introduction when she went
to the park, was jealous of the mothers and grandmothers who
met there, and decided that the English were as queer and stand-
offish as she had always supposed them to be. For weeks she slept
badly and talked with resignation of "being in the way" and
"going to her long home." She never asked about Teddy, always
about his mother, and when Margaret, who seemed suddenly to
have got over her dislike of the old woman, sent her a photo of

the child, she put it away in a drawer and did not refer to it again.

One evening, while Sylvia was in the kitchen, she startled me by a sudden question.

"You never hear about Mrs. Harding?" she asked.

"I believe she's all right," I said. "Sylvia could tell you. She hears from her regularly."

"They don't tell me," she said resignedly, folding her arms and looking broodingly into the fire—it was one of her fictions that no one ever told her anything. "Wisha, Phil," she added with a smile, "you don't think she noticed me calling Jack his daddy?"

She turned a searching look on me. It was one of those occasions when whatever you say is bound to be wrong.

"Who's that, Mrs. Courtenay?"

"Sylvia. She didn't notice?"

"I wouldn't say so. Why?"

"It worries me," she replied, looking into the fire again. "It could make mischief."

"I doubt it," I said. "I don't think Sylvia noticed anything."

"I hope not. I made a novena that she wouldn't. She's a nice, simple poor girl."

"She's one in a thousand," I said.

"Why then, indeed, Phil, there aren't many like her," she agreed humbly. "I could have bitten my tongue out when I said it. But, of course, I knew from the first minute I saw him in the hall. Didn't you?"

"Know what?" I stammered, wondering if I looked as red as I felt.

"That Jack was his daddy," she said in a low voice. "Sure you must."

"Oh, yes," I said. "He mentioned it."

"He didn't say anything to me," she said, but without reproach. You could see she knew that Jack would have good reason for not telling her. "I suppose he thought I'd tell Sylvia, but of course I wouldn't dream of making mischief. And the two of them such great friends too—wisha, isn't life queer, Phil?"

In the kitchen Sylvia suddenly began to sing "Lili Marlene." It was then the real poignancy of the situation struck me. I had seen it only as the tragedy of Jack and Sylvia and Margaret, but what was their loneliness to that of the old woman, to whom tragedy presented itself as in a foreign tongue? Now I realized why she did not care to look at the photograph of Margaret's son.

"It might be God's will her poor husband was killed," Mrs. Courtenay said. "God help us, I can never get the poor boy out of my head. I pray for him night and morning. 'Twould be such a shock to him if he ever found out. And the baby so lovely and all —oh, the dead image of Jack at his age!"

Sylvia accompanied me to the door as usual. Now when we kissed good-night it wasn't such an act on her part; not because she cared any more for me but because she was already seeking for support in the world outside. The bubble in which she lived was broken. I was tempted to tell her about her mother-in-law, but something held me back. Women like their own mystifications, which give them a feeling of power; they dislike other people's, which they always describe as slyness. Besides, it would have seemed like a betrayal. I had shifted my allegiance.

A NOTE ON THE TYPE

This book is set in GRANJON, *a type named in compliment to Robert Granjon, type-cutter and printer—Antwerp, Lyon, Rome, Paris—active from 1523 to 1590. The boldest and most original designer of his time, he was one of the first to practice the trade of type-founder apart from that of printer.*

This type face was designed by George W. Jones, who based his drawings on a type used by Claude Garamond (1510–61) in his beautiful French books, and it more closely resembles Garamond's own than do any of the various modern types that bear his name.

The book was composed, printed, and bound by Kingsport Press, Inc., Kingsport, Tennessee.